THE CREPE MYRTLE

Charles B. Packard

authorHOUSE®

AuthorHouse™
1663 Liberty Drive
Bloomington, IN 47403
www.authorhouse.com
Phone: 1-800-839-8640

This book is a work of fiction. People, places, events, and situations are the product of the author's imagination, except all Packard and Foster names are real people who were, or are, alive. Any resemblance to actual persons, living or dead, or historical events, is purely coincidental.

© 2009 Charles B. Packard. All rights reserved.

No part of this book may be reproduced, stored in a retrieval system, or transmitted by any means without the written permission of the author.

First published by AuthorHouse 11/11/2009

ISBN: 978-1-4389-8476-6 (e)
ISBN: 978-1-4389-8474-2 (sc)
ISBN: 978-1-4389-8475-9 (hc)

Printed in the United States of America
Bloomington, Indiana

This book is printed on acid-free paper.

myrtle (murt'l) n. [....<L myrtus <Gr myrtos, myrtle, prob. < akin to Ar murr, myrrh]
1. any of a genus (Myrtus) of plants of the myrtle family, with evergreen leaves, white or pinkish flowers, and dark, fragrant berries
2. any of various other plants, as the periwinkle and the California Laurel

> ....from Webster's New World College Dictionary (Fourth Edition) Copyright 2005 by Wiley Publishing, Inc., Cleveland, Ohio.

Author's Note: The flowers of the crepe myrtle—whether white or pink—are like so many tiny blossoms, not unlike what one might create from wrinkled crepe paper....

My son, hear the instruction of thy Father,
and forsake not the law of thy mother.
Proverbs 1:8

Charles Bowman Packard
2008

Dedication

This book is dedicated to and in memory of Mary Elizabeth Holden, a most gracious lady, teacher, and friend who had often urged one of her high school students to become a writer and in the process, inspired this story. . . .

Foreword

This is a story of our family, a story I began working on more than 35 years ago (not all that long a period of time, when you consider this story spans almost 500 years—from the early 1500s to the present). Actually, it is a story of our two families—the Packard family and the Foster family. The one family came from England and, among other notables, produced an old seafaring salt, Captain Charles Howard Packard. The other family, quite likely also hailing from *"merrie olde"* England, gave us not only a splendid assortment of characters but also spun off a hearty bunch of pioneers who helped settle a frontier territory—The Republic of Texas!

But I'm getting way ahead of our story. . . .

In the early stages of writing this I created a very simple story outline, one which would serve my purposes of merely passing along all the stories I had heard, as well as those I had a part in during our growing up years. Growing up in the country in Central Texas in the 1940s presented me with countless tales and legends told and retold by family members during our many get-togethers. And for whatever reason, these have wondrously endured in my memory.

All along it has been my intention to include all of these tales—tall or otherwise. You see, true to our Texas roots, a number of these "tall tales" and legends, though unquestionably very interesting and venturesome in nature, nevertheless seemed a bit farfetched to me. But include them I would, if for no other reason than to lend a bit of color and spice to some of our stories concerning our early Texas ancestors.

And, then a curious thing happened. After years of digging into our families' pasts and seeking to establish links to those long-ago times, I was contacted by two separate and very distant cousins who brought our pasts into unbelievable focus and depth. I had been somewhat pleased with my efforts in tracing the Packard family back to New England in the very early 1800s, and the Fosters back to Mississippi and Tennessee in the late 1800s. These distant relatives—considerably more expert at family research and genealogy than I—were themselves at the time wrapping up their own family stories and were merely seeking to fill in our family gaps in their own story lines of documented family histories. To this very day, what they each shared with me continues to amaze and astound me.

Alan Packard of Olathe, Kansas provided me with research data and genealogical records which traced our Packard family back to England in the late 1500s. Within a few months, I would receive similar family history from one Ralph Cowgill concerning our Foster ancestors. Married to a descendant of Randolph Foster, one of John Foster, Sr.'s sons, this distant cousin forwarded to me copies of the family records tracing our Foster ancestors back to South Carolina in the early 1700s. Needless to say, this treasure of family history resulted in a great deal of editing and rewriting of our family story—starting all over, so to speak.

And much to my surprise, I quickly learned that a lot of our "tall tales" were not so tall, after all. Many of them proved to be quite true. Some years later, I came across one of Mark Twain's witticisms—as told through one of his characters—which simply stated:

> "Truth is stranger than fiction, but it is because fiction is obliged to stick to possibilities; truth isn't." ("Pudd'nhead Wilson's New Calendar," The Tragedy of Pudd'nhead Wilson, Mark Twain, 1897.)

Not a small amount of effort has gone into the preparation of this story—and not just by me, but by many others, as well. I have gleaned a lot of this material from books of history (Elizabethan England, Colonial America to 1763, Colonial South Carolina, and Gone to Texas) as well as from professional researchers.

Most assuredly, many long, enjoyable hours were spent poring over letters, birth and death certificates, land deeds, and other such archival data provided by Mrs. Nina Fuller, a professional genealogy researcher from Belton, Texas. Her efforts helped establish the accuracy and framework of our Texas history. In fact, Mrs. Fuller first presented the possibility that our family may have descended from one of the Fosters who helped settle Texas in 1822. Whereas her research tentatively identified Moses Foster as our link to this treasured bit of Texas heritage, subsequent research revealed that it was actually John Foster, Sr. through whom our legacy was established. And our descent is from a son, John Foster, Jr. who also was an early Texas settler.

I have gathered up all this history and reconstructed what I believe could well have occurred within their lives in Elizabethan England in the late 1500s and early 1600s, Colonial South Carolina in the 1700s, New England in the mid-1600s to mid-1800s, and, of course, Texas and Louisiana in the 1800s.

The Packard and Foster names mentioned in this story are true ancestors; they were real people, established by family historians long before I started our family story. Also, I have attempted to follow, in chronological order, the lives and adventures of these ancestors. In so doing, you will find I have necessarily alternated between these families as the story progresses.

And lastly, and quite possibly the most crucial point I wish to make concerning this, our family story: while the early stories are, of necessity, imaginative creations based on all these factual data, I trust that you, too, will come to realize that it is *not* the names, dates, and places which drive this story but rather the very people themselves—who lived out their existence in these extraordinary times and experienced hardships, dangers, and circumstances which we cannot begin to grasp nor fully understand—they provide the very heartbeat of this story.

As you journey through our story you may very well question some of the events and tales, just as I did; and it's quite possible that not all of the stories happened the way I have written them. . . .but if not—well, just maybe they should have. . . .

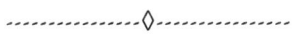

Earlier, I had serious misgivings regarding our Great-grandfather Charles Howard Packard's being a ship captain—not only a Mississippi riverboat captain but possibly on international freighters, as well. That story, I came to learn, was verifiably true.

And then the tale of the great-great something or other cowboy relative who "froze to death on horseback," I really rolled my eyes on that one until I learned that the same tale had been passed down from a separate line of the Foster ancestry; so with that in mind, I included this legendary tale, in what I believe to be a very credible possibility.

A few other tales of passing interest which I have included concern some likely encounters that very easily could have occurred: one, involving Mark Twain and our steamboat captain, the same Charles Howard Packard, meeting on the Mississippi River. Another involves our Foster ancestors meeting and actually serving with Moses Austin and Stephen F. Austin in settling Texas and crossing paths with Davy Crockett on his way to the Alamo; and historical evidence of both Packard and Foster ancestors fighting against the British in the American Revolutionary War.

All of the known historical data has been blended into these stories which have endured through the years. I have placed endnotes so you can examine the evidence that I have gathered.

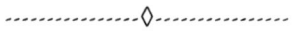

One little side note: in my reference to our Great-grandfather Charles Howard Packard forming an acquaintance with Mark Twain, some Packard cousins still living in the Deep South related to me how their parents had on occasion heard this grandfather of theirs complain about a character in one of Mark Twain's stories. It seems that this story had a character named "Jake Packard" and that earlier Mark Twain told Charles Howard Packard he was going to name a character after him in a story he was writing. But this Packard ancestor apparently wasn't impressed and expressed his disapproval in a few well-chosen words, seeing as how "Jake Packard" was a would-be thief and a person of "questionable character"! This cousin, Frank (Sonny) Packard, Jr., said his father, Frank, Sr., and other Packard siblings often heard this grandfather voice his displeasure about the Mark Twain character—seems Captain Charles Howard Packard was a very strict and forthright old salt and cared not in the least to have a ficticious scoundrel bear his name!

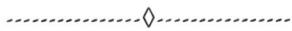

Writing our family story has been very gratifying, yet, at times, equally frustrating. Frustrating because, if for no other reason than to honor a long-ago request from a greatly admired English teacher, I've found myself compelled to start over until everything . . .well, until it just felt right.

In some strange fashion, this has often felt like an assignment from her—one in which effort absolutely had to match the accuracy of that which has been written. To do less would dishonor a most honorable lady. . .you see, Mary Elizabeth Holden held to impossibly high standards in her teaching profession.

Then, there was the matter of honoring those about whom this story is written. Though some of you had yet to grace this story with your presence when first I started, many who had and whose lives filled those pages throughout the early 1900s, have gently passed into wonderfully bittersweet memories. . . . For those who are gone, but far from forgotten, it is my hope to honor them with these remembrances of their lives.

Places, like people, tend to pass away. Things that once were can vanish overnight. Homes, buildings, even communities can slowly pass into little more than distant memories. The farm community of Oenaville, at least the one near which we grew up, is gone. The three homes, the pump house and office, and even the oil-storage tanks—all were gone.

But here and there I found traces that spoke of those long ago times. Traces that reminded me that once we were there. And once we all shared in those wonderful years gone by.

Prologue

Thursday, March 11, 1989

The phone call woke me on the first ring. Even as I reached half awake to answer, I already knew who was calling and what the call was about. We had anticipated this very moment for several months; nevertheless, it was not a thing for which you can ever be fully prepared.

Wayne's subdued voice confirmed all that I had sensed: Mom was near death. The doctors had just moments earlier reached Wayne at his home to advise that Mom had slipped deeper into her coma; they did not expect her to live through the night and suggested we gather our family as soon as possible. As I hung up the phone, I glanced at my clock and was vaguely aware that it was somewhere near 3:00 a.m. . . . March 11, 1989 would be a surprisingly warm day. . . .

Wayne had already made arrangements for a chapel service in Dallas the following Monday afternoon. I told him I would try to leave Saturday afternoon—Sunday morning at the latest—and drive straight through.

Bob left Baylor University that Thursday afternoon to stand vigil alongside her bed. I.B. and Debbie would catch an early morning flight on Friday out of Hartford as would my daughter, Lynda, and grandson, Brennen, from Kansas City. We would all be gathering to pay our last respects—hopefully in time to be with Ruby in her last moments. All, that is, except Inez. I knew she would not be there; I knew she *could not* be there. The relationship between those two was very special. Sis often told Mom she would do everything possible for her except be there at her funeral.

Sunday, March 14, 1989

Just before leaving Indianapolis early Sunday morning I called Wayne one last time, just to check on Mom's condition—still no change. Throughout that weekend, Mom had clung to life to the complete astonishment of her doctors. And though we knew Mom's time was very short, we were all somehow aware how typical of our Mother—in this, her last apparent act of defiance—to just show us all that she would go when *she* was damn well ready.

Most all of you shared time with her and perhaps even came to know her—for that, I am grateful. Ruby was quite a character.

This time the drive down to Dallas was anything but boring. My thoughts for much of the trip were of Mom and our family. Once again, I began feeling guilt stirring in me for not having made more progress on this story of our family. But for whatever the reasons, I had just been unable to put everything into a proper narrative. I knew the things I wanted to tell you; what wasn't real clear, was where to begin.

For the time being, at least, as remembered moments passed in and out of my thoughts, I realized that getting to Dallas was about all I could manage. The story would have to wait awhile longer.

---------------◊---------------

The last time I had been to Dallas to see Mom was Thanksgiving, 1987, about a year and a half earlier. The kids and I had driven to Texas to spend the holiday with Mom, Wayne, Kathy, and their kids. We were looking forward to our visit, and on the drive down I had this sense that this was promising to be one of our best Thanksgivings ever. I hoped so. . . .

Thanksgiving morning brought the usual pleasures—steaming cups of coffee, the Dallas Sports section, and the stirrings of the younger Packard Clan. The fire in the fireplace added a fragrant warmth to what was already present.

Mom was in her wheelchair at the table enjoying her late morning breakfast which Kathy had prepared for her. The rest of us were in various stages of "getting ready" for Thanksgiving dinner. The aromas from the kitchen were all that Thanksgiving should be and more. Over the years, Mom had taught Kathy well the secrets of her cornbread dressing—we were anticipating another memorable feast. And, hopefully, by the time the pumpkin and pecan pies were being wiped out, so too, would be the Thanksgiving Day opponents of our Cowboys!

Wayne, Clay, and I were watching the pre-game show in the TV room, while Kelly was with Kara and Katie as they were in the family room playing the piano. Mom had moved her wheelchair in front of the large glass wi[ndow] looking out over the patio; she enjoyed watching Sam, the family's golden L[ab], frolicking with her rubber ball. Occasionally, both the ball and the dog wound up in the pool much to Mom's enjoyment.

Since her most recent paralyzing stroke, Mom had lost most all her zest and vitality; she just wasn't quite the same anymore. At times, she looked so forlorn and sad. . . .

Kara had just started playing "Silent Night," when Matt called out: "Dad, Uncle Chuck, come here, quick!" We found Matt standing near his grandmother who was still gazing, somewhat trance-like, out the window—only she was singing! In a soft, barely audible whisper Mom was singing the words to "Silent Night;" and we stood around her, transfixed by the emotions of that moment. Mom wasn't even aware of our presence; it was as though she were back in some long-ago time, caught up in a special memory known only to her. We looked at one another and smiled; it would be a moment we would cherish.

The next day I drove down to Temple, intending to say hello to some of my friends and to take Matt and Clay out to Oenaville for a visit. I showed them the site where our old Temple High School used to be—where now sat the town offices, fire station, and other such civic "improvements." I drove them out to old Woodson Field, where I, and thousands before and after me, had worn Temple's Blue and White for Friday night battles on the gridiron.

I'm sure Matt and Clay knew this visit was for me. . . . The fence was sagging and rusted with age. Weeds choked the walkways and bleachers, and graffiti marred the once-thriving concession buildings. The fieldhouse was literally falling apart; they didn't even bother locking the doors anymore. The words were badly faded, but above the doorway you could still read the legend, "The Fightin' Temple Wildcats." There was a haunting stillness about the place. Memories were still very strong, and I stood there taking it all in as I thought back to the time. . . .

"Dad, c'mon, let's get going!" Clay brought me out of my reverie, and I managed a rather strained smile as I realized this was not a special place to them. They hadn't sweated out push-ups and grass drills at 7:00 a.m. back

…t two-a-day workouts. I wondered if they realized what …

…he cemetery to visit Dad's grave. I cleaned it up a bit, …ases that flanked the headstone and pulled a few weeds that the ……s had missed. Mom's side was still thankfully incomplete: "RUBY INEZ – BORN December 16, 1904   DIED

Matt and Clay asked about their grandfather, so we stood there for a time as I shared a few special stories about him. "My Dad's a telephone lineman—a troubleshooter—bless his heart."—maybe someday I will tell them about this childhood phrase.

We headed on out the farm-to-market road toward Oenaville, observing as I drove, how very much the countryside had changed since back in the late 1940s. The road was smoothly paved, for one thing; and for another, they had efficiently straightened out the curves and sharp turns. Most of the farmhouses were now gone, as well. It seemed such a totally different place. . . . I liked the old curves and turns a lot better—even the old gravel road.

Oenaville had changed even more. Cumbee Allen's general store was gone; so, too, were Mr. Ewing's tiny store and Post Office, as well as Mr. Roy's blacksmith shop down near the creek. Only Jesse and Dick Roy's service station remained. Most of the houses were gone, too.

I pointed out the large vacant field—now overrun with weeds and a few saplings growing there and about—where once had stood Oenaville Grade School. I wondered if Matt and Clay realized how big that school used to seem to us as kids. Across the road and up a small side road sat the little Baptist church where so much of our family life had been centered. From the outside, it still looked the same. In fact, other than fresh coats of paint, it still looked exactly the same. We went inside, and for the briefest of moments, it felt as though I had somehow stepped back in time about 40 years. The piano sat in its customary place; and the attendance board was where it had always hung, right there on the wall behind the pulpit. I walked to the very back row of pews and showed Matt and Clay where I used to sit—me, Garlon, Charlie, Jr., and the others. And, I had them sit beside me so I could point out exactly where their grandfather used to sit—up with the other deacons. I told them that when we boys would become a bit too boisterous, Dad and the other deacons would glare at us, letting us know that it was past time to quieten down and sit still!

And we did, too. . . .

I walked back into the small classroom wing which had been added by our church at about the time Garlon and I had been about 8 years old—an addition which still held four very small classrooms for Sunday School. I had just walked into the little room where Mrs. Lancaster used to conduct our Bible Sword Drills when I heard Matt call out: "Uncle Chuck, come look at this! Is this our Uncle Bob?" I hurried into the back room where Matt and Clay stood facing a large framed roster of names. Incredibly, I read down the list of names, still not fully believing what hung on the wall before us. . . .

This Oenaville Community Service Roll was a listing of all the young men from this Central Texas community who had served during World War II. This Service Roll had probably been placed there around 1944-1945 and still hung as a memorial to those who had fought and to some who had died for their country. As Matt had discovered, there was the name Robert Packard; Inez's husband, Charles Walters; and so many other names I recognized, as well: Davis, Lancaster, Ewing, Sevier, Belk—more than 50 names of servicemen from the Oenaville community. Some names were in gold letters; they would eternally remain young and would never come home to discover the gravel roads paved nor the curves and turns straightened out. . . .

We drove a few miles out of Oenaville to the pump station where my childhood home had been, among all our farming neighbors. Back then, there had been three company houses—homes of the Porters, the McDonalds, and ours. Our homes sat about 300 yards from the pump-house station, where these Atlantic Oil Company employees had worked. There had been a pump house with power generators, a very small office, and just off to the side of these buildings had stood two large round oil-storage tanks and a bit farther still, a small farm pond.

Now, as we pulled up the gravel road that passed in front of this company acreage, I could see that much had changed here, as well. Two small buildings stood where the pump-house station had been; everything else was gone—houses, oil-storage tanks—everything, including the smell of crude oil, which I still love—that was gone, too.

All was gone but the crepe myrtle bush and now it was larger, several times larger than it had been back in the 1940s. Mom had planted this flowering bush alongside our front porch shortly after we moved to Oenaville in 1942 when I was about 3 years old. In spite of the ravages of time and Texas weather, it had somehow survived and now stood like a lonely sentry to mark what once had been. The crepe myrtle was all that remained of what we had once called home. Home, with so many warm, wonderful memories. . .(my sense of things proved to be true; this would be one of the best Thanksgivings ever). . . .

Monday, March 15, 1989

I crossed into Texas early Monday morning and called Wayne from a truck stop; Mom was still alive. (The doctors would later say that incredibly, Mom's survival for that length of time absolutely defied medical reason; with all her complications, they could not see how she survived this long.) Perhaps, they just did not know Ruby. . . .

Now, I began to hope against hope that I, too, would reach her bedside as had the other family members. I arrived in Dallas just before noon and again called Wayne to see how Mom was doing. I got the answering machine. A mild panic set in as I realized they were probably all at the hospital—and I wasn't even sure at which one. In all the rush, I had failed to ask Wayne where Mom was hospitalized.

I called several area hospitals before one hospital's Patient Information confirmed that "yes, they had a patient by the name of Ruby Inez Packard," and "no, they could not give out any more information than that."

A quick address check and help from a service station's wall city map had me on the way in about 15 minutes. I pulled up in the visitor parking lot and went inside the hospital for room information at exactly 12:00 noon.

I hurried up to Mom's room. Standing around her bed were Wayne, I.B., and Debbie; there were two nurses, and behind them stood my daughter, Lynda, holding Brennen. And I saw Mom; she was lying very still but her eyes were open. I didn't care whether anyone saw the tears; I had made it.

I hugged all the family, especially my daughter and little grandson, and approached the bed. I managed to choke off a cry of disbelief as I stood looking down at Mom...Mom? This couldn't be our Mother, not this pathetic little figure lying so helplessly before us.

Wayne had already warned me how gaunt and frail Mom had become, as the last couple of strokes had taken their toll. But I wasn't prepared for this—not by any stretch of the imagination. She was just barely alive. Wayne said she could no longer speak and sometimes wondered if she heard and if so, did she comprehend?

I very gently leaned over to hug her, all the while careful not to squeeze too tightly, yet, knowing this could well be my last time. I just wanted to hold on for all those times when I was too young and stupid and hugging your mother just was not something a boy did. We take so long in growing up.... I whispered the things I had thought about during my drive to Dallas—things that had slowly crept into my awareness about Mom and our family. Not that the things I had to say would be all that terribly important to Mom even if she could hear them, but it was something which was very important that I say.

We stayed near Mom the next few days, visiting her and sharing remembrances as we recalled her earlier, more robust years. At one point during our visits, a nurse had remarked to a few of our family how incredibly close we all seemed to be, especially considering how far apart we lived from one another. I suppose, like most families, we share a closeness that is much more than merely living near one another; it is more of an inner bond. It was just there.

That last day before we all returned to our homes, we were standing around Mom's bed, sharing some lighthearted moments. From time to time, one of us would say something to Mom, not really sure if she heard us; and if she did, not sure if she comprehended what was said. The nurse had asked Mom if she would like some juice or some water. But there had been no response. There was a momentary silence and with a mischievous grin Lynda spoke out: "Mommaw, I'll bet I know what you'd like—a cold beer!" Mom's only reply was a very hearty, exuberant grunt—we all laughed spontaneously, not only at the relevance of what Lynda had said, but at the realization that Mom heard and understood—just as we understood that she truly would have enjoyed one last cold beer!

The drive back to Indiana was gratifying in so many ways; a lot of bridges had been crossed. And while painful, Mother's condition had pulled us all back together once again in very special ways. All was as well as could be expected, even knowing her time was drawing to a close.

This time my thoughts of Mom and our family seemed much more alive—more focused. I found myself storing away bits and pieces of family history. . .doing mental cataloging for our story. . . . Right then I wished that someone else were driving so I could jot down the conversations and the recently shared remembrances while they were still fresh in my mind. I wished that somehow you could hook up your memories to a machine and just record all that which was stored away. Then you would never need worry that you might forget something or someone.

I couldn't help noticing, as Mom lay in her hospital bed, how much like Grandma Foster she looked. My maternal grandmother had died at 92 years of age in 1968. She, too, had become a very gaunt and frail little woman, as time had taken its toll and life ebbed from her. But Grandma Foster had not always been like that—nor had Grandmother Packard—nor so many others, whom I remembered as they, too, had grown old and, one by one, passed into our memories—and in those reflectively quiet, peaceful moments, as I drove back to Indiana, I was caught up in mental images of those whose times had passed and wondered, in curious ways, what my grandparents were like when they were kids. . .and all the others, what were they like and how had they lived and where? I remembered the stories of how the Fosters had come to Texas but from where I really didn't know. And the Packards, it seemed, had come over from England. But when? And what were they like, so long ago?. . . *so very, very long ago.* . . .

CHAPTER 1

ELIZABETHAN ENGLAND

Timeline: 1558-1608

By 1558 England, under its new monarch, Queen Elizabeth I, was no longer deemed in the Middle Ages nor functioning under the old "lord and vassal" feudal system of land control so common throughout medieval Europe. The defeat of Richard III by Henry Tudor in 1485 ended, for all practical purposes, the former circumstance while a developing and changing society in the late 1500s brought about the slow demise of the latter. While undoubtedly there remained throughout England some regions which clung to this medieval practice of feudalism, an ever-growing number of titled landholders had adapted to a more practical method of control over their lands. Referred to as "the gentle class," these landholders initiated the practice of charging monthly rents from the commoners and laborers who toiled in their fields and farmlands. And on some occasions, this was supplemented by payment of produce, grain, and even livestock—an even older practice. Such were the changes taking place in 16th Century England. (Elizabethan England, William W. Lace, 2006.)

The families living during these times of England's changing history also found themselves confronted with a number of other significant, life-changing circumstances:

- *In 1585 the first colonial settlement in the New Land had been established at Roanoke Island, in what would become North Carolina; this settlement ended quite mysteriously in 1587 and was found abandoned in 1590.*

- *From 1586-1598 poor harvests imperiled the very livelihood of England's landholders and those supported by these "families" of the gentle class.*

- In 1603, and barely 40 years removed from the previous devastating attack, another deadly plague swept throughout most of England's major towns and some nearby villages; and in this same year King James I came to the throne following the death of Queen Elizabeth I.

- The years 1605-1606 brought forth two new charter companies, The London Company and The Plymouth Company, both established solely for the purpose of exploring and colonizing the New Land, Virginia, which covered most all the coastal lands.

- In 1607 the first permanent English settlement was founded at Jamestown, Virginia.

- In 1608 Captain John Smith was given governorship over this Jamestown settlement.

But one circumstance over which the English subjects eventually exercised some manner of control was in their quest for freedom of religion. Throughout this period of England's history and woven, like coarse threads of evil, were the ongoing hostilities and religious wars between the Roman Catholic Church and The Church of England. Upon the rather harsh excommunication of Queen Elizabeth I by Pope Pius V on February 25, 1570, international tensions grew ever more strained. And closer to home, The Church of England was further embattled by a contentious society which had grown increasingly resentful of having a state-controlled religion imposed upon their way of life. As head of The Church of England, the King ruled as its sole authority, and, on occasions, sometimes quite brutally.

Of all these troubling circumstances, freedom of religion was by far one of the most compelling factors that led many to seek their hopes and fortunes in the New Land. Great numbers left their homes in England as they journeyed to this New Land. For the most part, these were the younger, more venturesome souls seeking after a hoped-for better life. (Elizabethan England, William W. Lace, 2006.)

But there were those, like Squire George Packard, who chose to stay the course and tend to all that which he had begun.

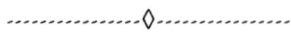

Chapter 2

Squire George Packard

Timeline: 1578-1638

George Packard found the carriage ride into the village of Stonham-Aspal quite pleasant as was the conversation with his liveryman, "olde" Jedediah Moore. This day was a most uplifting spring day and by mid-morning the village was fairly abustle in its affairs.

A warm fragrance from the baking shoppe's ovens filled the streets, mingling its aroma with those of the street vendor's food carts, as well as those from the Boar's Head Tavern, as its noontime fare was being prepared in the kitchens. As a matter of fact, this very tavern was where Squire Packard and many of his companions would soon gather in a welcomed respite from their many duties. These were, for the most part, special occasions for sharing in pleasant fellowship and partaking of a hearty feast to warm one's innards, as well as one's spirits. The good squire looked forward to these visits, and with all things considered, he found, that indeed, life was good. . .the year was 1608.

"Heare now, Jedediah," Squire Packard spoke, "whyn't thee partake of this most faire morn to share a mug of ale with thy goode fellows, whilst in the village?"

"Prithee, sire," Jedediah responded, "indeed that wouldst grant thy humble servant great pleasure. But I beseech thee, sire, to consider the disrepair of thy harnesses and bridles, and a wheel rim, as well."

George Packard asked, "Am I to understand that these be of a troubling nature?"

"Indeed they be, sire. Only this morn, as I harnessed thy carriage didst I take notice of these conditions. I feare I must needs seek the blacksmythe and with great haste, to work his craft this fine morn, ere we return to thy manor."

"Well spoken, Jedediah. See thee to that task, and thence take leave of thy labours to rest thy bones. I shan't be but til mid-afternoon at the tavern; when thy tasks be compleat, see that thou bringeth my carriage at that appointed tyme. That is, Jedidiah, if yon smithy hath worked his skill."

With a wink, and curt nod toward Jedediah, George Packard stepped down from his carriage onto the cobblestoned street and strode briskly toward the Boar's Head Tavern. As Jedediah pulled away toward the nearby blacksmythe shoppe, George heard his name called: "Good day to thee, George," Squire Henry Smythe cried out, "and what, pray tell, doth the menu board boast of this day?"

Both men turned their attention toward the large board propped against the tavern wall, as George recited: "It doth appear the offering this day be roast leg of beefe, venison, and, let us see—yes, I doth find also baked partridge hens and pheasants, as well."

"Best there be blood pudding!—and my nose doth, if not mistaken, detect the most delectable odour of roast suckling pig turning upon a spit within," a third voice rang out.

Turning towards the newcomer, George Packard replied: "And well ye might, Horace, well ye might; tis the same pleasant aroma I now be sensing as we speake."

All laughed heartily, as the portly, and jovial Squire Horace Venable joined his companions. Still caught up in a spirit of merriment and goode cheer, the three squires entered the festive warmth of the tavern.

Greeting them warmly, the tavern's host led them toward their usual table neare the crackling fireplace. There they found the fourth member of their party, Ezekiah Moresby, beaming with a glow upon his countenance, no doubt from the tankard of browne ale hoisted in glee towards his friends.

"Tis late ye be," Squire Moresby chuckled lustily, "for I daresay I have started the festivities afore ye."

The tavern maids descended upon their table, filling their empty hands with tankards of the same browne ale being quaffed joyously by Ezekiah Moresby.

A momentary silence settled about them, as each squire drank heartily from his tankard, and, sighing loudly with contentment, each proceeded to wipe the specks of foam from his lips with the back of his coat sleeves.

Conversation drifted pleasantly amongst them, as first one topic, then another, paraded itself around the table. This was an occasion cherished by each member, as they managed, at times, to take leave of their respective manors, for just such light-hearted moments.

"Pray tell, George," Squire Smythe inquired, "how much longer shall olde Jedediah have care of thy livery and carriage matters? Wouldst thee not be better suited in vesting this in the hands of a younger lad, one possessed of a sturdier back and a livelier mind?" George pondered on this for several moments, and with great forethought, spoke his response: "In due course, I wouldst agree, Henry. But as long as my faithful servant doth choose to remain thusly—and he hast only within the last fortnight expressed that very desire—then these tasks shall remain upon his capable shoulders. Thee must know that his companionship doth bring me great pleasure. And ye'll not find here and about a livelier mind than what abideth in Olde Jedediah."

A few around the table nodded their approval, and after George had sliced a goodly portion from his partridge hen's breast, speared it with his knife and thrust it into his mouth, he soon spoke once more. "And doest not thee agree, good gentlemen, that when we plante our field crops, we tend them most faithfully in cultivating, watering, and weeding, lest they wither and perish? And in the matters of the human being, doth not the same hold true?" Henry now nodded his agreement.

"No," George continued, "I'll not be quicke in retiring Jedediah to a manor cottage, not whilst his desire is to remain in the harness. Idling a busy soul can ofttimes only lead to its early demise."

Silence prevailed amongst the gathered, as each occupied himself with plates of baked fowl and roasted game, as well as great slabs of the roasted pig. The tavern maids proceeded to refill the tankards, and the feasting took on a life of its own.

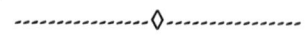

Many of George Packard's labourers tended their own homesteads upon the good squire's landholdings, while certain others, along with the servants and handmaidens, lived in his manor home near the village of Stonham-Aspal, Suffolk, England. All were considered part of his extended family, which was customary in the early traditions of England.

In this rural setting northeast of London, the settlements like that at Stonham-Aspal were ofttimes sparse and not quite so populated as the southern and central regions of England. In many ways this was, indeed, a blessing, as sicknesses and diseases seldom reached into these outlying areas—certainly not in such epidemic proportions as ravaged other regions. But this remoteness presented a unique problem to just such rural villages as that of Stonham-Aspal—and that was in the matter of communications. Major news events sometimes were delayed for weeks, or even months, before finally reaching the inhabitants in these outlying areas. When the last plague had struck London in 1603, it was two fortnights before word of this calamitous event reached Stonham-Aspal's villagefolk. Word travelled most often by wandering minstrels and troubadours, and, unfortunately, as "olde" news by the time it was received.

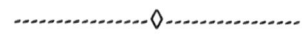

At this time in her history, England's main product of commerce was wool; and in its rural populations agriculture gave the thrust to its economy. With his herds, farmlands and fields, Squire Packard and all the inhabitants, both of his manor and those tenants living on his lands, endured and prospered with a self-sufficiency that was vital to their existence.

Over the next few years, life continued at a rather pleasant pace, and good fortune held sway at George Packard's manor. With but few exceptions, he found that in keeping practice of the Golden Rule that which he displayed to others was returned manyfold. His kind and steady hand of stewardship over his lands, as well as that of his people, brought him abundant returns in crop yields and livestock and deep loyalty from those who labored for him. Blessings often found their way to his doorsteps, and none were more well received than when his good wife, Mary Wyther, delivered, but a mere fortnight previous, a boy whom they named Samuel. The village midwife had attended Mary through her hours of labor and applied her care and gentle touch to both mother and child. George was, quite naturally, left to fend for himself, and he well knew his place in such moments.

And on occasions like these, concerns for the new baby were understandably mixed, not only for the infant's well-being, but also that which hovered for sometime—the cold, chillingly-practical matter of survival. Oftentimes, newborns did not survive the first few days as infections and other such common perils exacted a heavy toll—that was just the way life was.

But thus far, infant Samuel had appeared in good health and thrived reasonably well. With a measure of good fortune, and by Grace of the Almighty, George understood that this young child just might survive these first critical months of his young life. One could hope. After all, these were better times and quite unlike the more perilous times in the late 1500s; those were sometimes treacherous years—had it not been with considerable concern regarding his own existence at birth? Forsooth, and his very own parents had beseeched the Almighty for those many days on end, had they not, in the matter of his most tenuous survival? Those long past days, such being their worth back in 1578 at his time of coming forth, had been fraught with peril. Indeed, they were treacherous years. But after all—this was 1612!

And survive he did, for by his thirteenth year in 1625, young Samuel had grown into a fine, strapping young lad, one who unfailingly took up his yoke of responsibility on his family's manor. Those chores and tasks given him—not only by his father, but by the good squire's overseer—were set upon by Samuel with a zeal and energy which, at times, astounded even the most brawny and industrious of his father's laborers—a tribute to his parentage.

By his birthright, Samuel could well have laid eventual claim to his inheritance of his father's holdings, as this, too, was customary in 17th Century England. But early on, Samuel already had a calling for more than just life as usual. And so the decision was jointly made that Samuel, like most other young English gentlemen on their thirteenth year, would enter into an apprenticeship for the purpose of acquiring valuable skills in some worthy trade—not to mention testing by fire his ascent into adulthood. This was of even greater importance as much to Samuel's benefit as anything else.

Samuel departed from the Packard manor at Stonham-Aspal and journeyed to Wymondham, Norfolk, England, whereupon he served apprenticeship under a master craftsman in the building trade; he studied and practiced the art of wood craftsmanship and various such skills relating to construction of houses and general framing of larger buildings. He was a gifted apprentice and learned the skills well—skills that, although unbeknownst to him at the time, would one day serve him and his future family quite well.

Well into his apprenticeship and having proved himself a most apt and capable student of his craft, Samuel's skills and knowledge impressed not only his master craftsman but many as well throughout the village of Wymondham. As his reputation as a skilled craftsman grew, so, too, did the number of those who sought after his services in the building of their homes. He had progressed well past the status of journeyman in his trade field and helped construct many houses and buildings in the growing community of Wymondham.

By his twenty-first birthday, in the year 1633, Samuel Packard was successfully and, quite profitably, pursuing his trade and adding well to his growing reputation. All in good time, and like his father before him, Samuel found life to be very rewarding. A lot of life's blessings were coming to Samuel—a lot, indeed—for such was the hope and promises of the eternal optimism of youth. And one of these blessings, eventually would be a young lady of Wymondham, by the name of Elizabeth Stream, who would come into his life, giving even more meaning and contentment to his comfortable existence. Their meeting had occurred some months previous at the village church; and under the watchful eyes of both their minister and Elizabeth's family, their courtship and affections for each other followed a most natural progression of Godly passions. One's observance of their behavior could not but discern how proper and above reproach was their demeanor. They were young and obviously quite taken with one another. Their betrothal merely followed a most natural sequence of their circumstances; and after a rather lengthy engagement, they were wed at Wymondham in 1635. Their wedded bliss blossomed further with the arrival of their first child, Mary, in 1637.

As he cradled his new infant Mary—whom he had named after his very own mother—Samuel beamed with the pleasante emotions of a new father. Gazing with fondness upon his wife, Elizabeth, who was still recovering from the recent exhaustions of her labours, Samuel spoke softly: "Rest ye well, deare Elizabeth, for thee hath given me a most faire and lovely child. And knowest thou that once thee and little Mary have sufficient strength, perhaps in a yeare or so, thence shall we embark upon the venture we have prayed about."

In a soft voice, and little more than a whisper, Elizabeth replied: "If that be thy desires, Samuel, then I and baby Mary shall gladly accompany thee, for I doth feel that thee knowest best in such matters."

"Twas a blessing to me," Samuel responded, "when first my gaze fell upon thee at thy church, deare wife. For thou art a devoted wife and companion; and now, too," Samuel beamed as his eyes rested upon the infant within his arms, "thou hast become a parent!"

Samuel paced slowly about the room, as he looked first upon his wife, Elizabeth, and thence upon his childe. In that moment, Samuel felt warming emotions flooding upon him, emotions that he knew had ne'er before visited his being.

As much to himself as to his beloved wife, Samuel spoke softly: "And tis a vow I doth make to thee, and thy infant daughter—that all of the talents and skills which the goode Lord hath blessed me with shall be employed most faithfully in our new land. Forasmuch as I hath prospered our family here in Wymondham, so also shall we prosper there. And if, perchance, the goode Lord doth choose to bless us with more babes, then those blessings shall but add to our prosperity." Smiling, Samuel added: "Tis just that those children shall not be English borne."

The continuing religious turmoil in England was ample reason for many to seek a new home with the new opportunities it afforded to establish a more embraceable church doctrine. And many families fled to the New Lands for that reason alone; for them that promise was well worth whatever risks awaited in a faraway continent. For others, the added allure of property ownership and starting one's life over in a new beginning, was an attraction that was quite irresistible. The reports that spoke of beautiful new lands and an abundance of game and freedom from pestilence and disease swayed many. This combination offered a bright promise that easily swayed Samuel Packard, as well. He and his family would leave England for this New Land.

In June 1638 Samuel, Elizabeth, and their infant Mary Packard made their way to the small port of Ipswich, England to board the ship lying at anchor in Gravesend Harbor. Making their way aboard the *Diligent*, they joined with the other English families with whom they would very soon set sail for a new port—a New Port, in a New Land. . .and a New Life. . . .

---------------◊---------------

Chapter 3

The Packards of New England

Timeline: August 1638-June 1832

This New Land was a magnificent land with verdant woods and forests plentiful with game and skies abounding with numberless flights of wild turkeys, geese, and pheasants. Countless flocks of wild fowl, such as the pigeon, would at times literally darken the very heavens. Streams and rivers teemed with almost every type of freshwater fish imaginable; and the nearby Atlantic Ocean held limitless quantities of shellfish and saltwater fish. Food was abundant.

A majestic and glorious wilderness, this green jewel would one day become the United States. The natives who thrived there held it in sacred trust. Someone once claimed that its forests were at one time so expansive that had a squirrel started on the Atlantic Coast and traveled all the way to the Mississippi River, it need never touch the land—maybe even beyond.

This was what the explorers and colonists discovered when first they set foot upon its shores. These brave people hailed from Spain, Portugal, France, England, and other adventurous European nations. For the most part, they found easily accessible coastlines with natural inlets and harbors that facilitated their many excursions and explorations.

The first settlement in this New Land was made in 1565 by the Spaniards at St. Augustine in a region that would one day become Florida. These early explorers, like the ones who eventually established more permanent English settlements in the early 1600s, would likewise come to realize the vastness and abundance of this land. Throughout the Atlantic colonies, they, too found ample supplies of wild game and fowl for food, forests teeming with trees and timbers for building cabins, and beautiful settings for their colonies.

Perhaps, the only things lacking in this New Land were sicknesses, pestilence, and diseases...and the colonists brought those with them.

Sickness and disease were not the only issues the settlers had to face in this New Land. Starvation exacted a deadly toll as did attacks from Indian tribes. Perhaps, every bit as deadly was the lingering presence of the Little Ice Age. Lasting from the late 1500s through the middle 1700s, the Little Ice Age visited some of the worst winter conditions imaginable upon these hardy adventurers. Winter storms brought devastating blasts of ice and snow oftentimes decimating many of the settlements and sparing none. The extremely harsh circumstances confronting these brave settlers were the most inhospitable one could possibly imagine. Looking back upon these perilous times, one could be excused for questioning how anybody could realistically have survived such ordeals.... (Colonial America, Oscar Theodore Barck, Jr., 1968.)

The *HMS Diligent* arrived in Boston Harbor on August 10, 1638. The voyage across the Atlantic had taken some two months; over 60 long, harsh days of this perilous journey had not gone without tragedy. A few of the passengers aboard ship lost their lives at sea. In this regard the *HMS Diligent* had actually fared quite well; during the voyages of many ships, it was reported that sometimes as many as a third of the passengers were lost at sea. The hardships these hardy souls confronted were many: raging storms, angry seas that too often swept unsuspecting novices off ship decks, sickness and disease. Some of those aboard who left England were weak and infirm with much less than the necessary stamina and strength required for such demanding and tortuous a journey. And sometimes it was just bad luck.

Fortunately, Samuel, Elizabeth, and little Mary Packard were among those who survived the arduous voyage and eventually settled at Hingham, Plymouth, Massachusetts. In due course, Samuel fulfilled his vow to Elizabeth as he diligently and industriously plied his trade; by the year 1644 Samuel Packard had built or had helped in building scores of houses and lodgings amongst the colony. His reputation grew considerably, as did his and Elizabeth's family. Over the ensuing 13 years, they were blessed with the births of 11 more brothers and sisters for their first child, Mary.

In 1654 the family resettled in Weymouth, where Samuel Packard served until 1664 as Selectman for the Towne Council. Here in Weymouth two more children were born to the Packard family.

Over the next several years, Samuel would serve the towne of Bridgewater as Constable, along with other important positions. By the time of his passing on November 7, 1684, this colonist from England had not only served his communities in many key positions of responsibility, but he had helped contribute to their growing populations with 14 of his own offspring. Most all of Samuel and Elizabeth's children would survive these perilous early years and spread their influence throughout the Massachusetts and New England colonies. Their children would marry and start their own families; and, the Packard generations would thrive. . . . Zaccheus Packard, the eighth of Samuel's 14 children, was born April 20, 1651. He and his wife, Sarah Howard, raised nine children; and all of these children survived to start families; of these, their seventh child, also named Zaccheus after his father, was born September 4, 1693.

Of significance, this Zaccheus would also grow up in Plymouth, Massachusetts and on October 21, 1725, marry John Alden's granddaughter, Mercy Alden. *(John Alden was one of the 149 passengers and crew aboard the double-deck, three-mast Mayflower who left Plymouth, England and landed at Provincetown Harbor on November 21, 1620. Their voyage over had taken 65 days. Only one death had occurred at sea, but the passenger count was balanced by the birth of a boy during this trip. On December 25 these Mayflower adventurers crossed the bay to the Plymouth location. They had spent over a month on the Cape Cod Point, surviving increasingly harsh wintry weather and scant food supplies.)* (Colonial America, Oscar Theodore Barck, Jr., 1968.)

Zacchaeus and Mercy produced six children; the fifth, Simeon Packard, was born at Plymouth, Massachusetts on May 30, 1736. Simeon Packard and Mary Perkins were married on July 6, 1761, and they had 12 children. Their first child, also named Simeon, served in George Washington's Continental Army and died in service on October 22, 1782. Their seventh child was Barnabas Packard born on November 28, 1772. Barnabas and two brothers, Alden Packard and Benjamin Packard, grew up and relocated to Maine.

In addition to the youthful second-generation Simeon Packard who died October 22, 1782, during the Revolutionary War, a number of Samuel and Elizabeth Packard's descendants served bravely throughout the colonists' fight with England. They fought from Maine to Virginia. And in their quest for independence, some of them died.

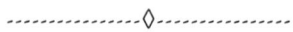

Barnabas and Emelitiah Packard were married on October 2, 1794. All three of their children were born in Sidney, Maine. For several years Reverend Barnabas Packard traveled widely throughout Maine as a journeyman pastor, serving many churches. According to the History of Winthrop, Massachusetts Reverend Barnabas Packard disappeared during the War of 1812 between the Americans and the British. The good Reverend turned up sometime later—probably freed from captivity during this conflict—and lived out his life in Maine. He died April 3, 1856, at the age of 84—a long and interesting life.

Ebenezer Packard, the oldest son of Reverend Barnabas Packard, was born in Sidney, Maine on July 3, 1796. Sidney was a small settlement hard by the Kennebec River and just seven or so miles north of the village of Augusta.

Most of the settlement folks engaged in fishing, harvesting timber, and fur trapping for their livelihood. The Kennebec was abundant with fish; and whether for profit or pleasure, most all the inhabitants at one time or the other wet their lines in this cold, crystal blue river and often returned home with supper. Fishing was a favorite pastime of the good Reverend and at times he would make his way to the river's banks, accompanied by a son or two, once they were of trustworthy age and temperament. Many happy moments were shared by Barnabas and his sons along the banks of this beautiful waterway in southern Maine.

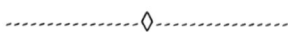

Ebenezer or Eb, as his childhood friends shortnamed him, especially took to adventure on the Kennebec. As he grew older and more daring,

Eb and his mates would ride canoes or small skiffs downstream to Augusta, and then pole their way back to Sidney. Skill and much effort were required, as they worked their way back against the current, staying out of the mainstream, along the banks. Most times they portaged their canoe even though poling was the greater challenge to these lads.

One day they came upon an old dugout—probably lost, or abandoned sometime ago by Indians—and rode it all the way downstream past Augusta and just beyond Hallowell. The boys never once gave thought to rassling this cumbersome "log" back home as it was quite heavy. This day they made a pledge to each other that someday they would ride it "all the way to the ocean;" they pulled it back a ways from the bank, covered it completely with dead branches and leaves, and hid it cleverly in the undergrowth of a ravine. Then, they walked back the mile or so to Augusta. Tired and hungry from the efforts of this adventure, they stopped at a shoppe in Augusta for some tea cakes and hot cider, having barely amongst themselves the coins to purchase this feast. Being thus refreshed, they easily hiked back the seven miles to Sidney—all in all, a great afternoon of sporting fun among friends.

----------◊----------

One adventure some years later proved a bit more harrowing. One crisp, glorious day in May 1808, a few short months to his twelfth birthday, Eb and a friend, Michael, were scouring the woods for black walnuts and berries when they spotted a moose just a short way back in the forest. "Let's work a bit closer," Eb suggested, "and give'er a bit of a run." They did not mean to cause harm to her, just have a bit of sport at her expense. A chase was good to stir up the blood.

As they ambled a little closer, the cow started a slow gait deeper into the woods, and the boys picked up their own pace trying to narrow the gap. Coming up on a slight rise as they made the crest, they saw that the cow was starting a slow turn; and her massive head was now turned hard left. As she swung her body in the looping turn, that's when the two boys realized it was not just they and the moose in the action. Off to their left, just below the rise, stood her calf! "She's got a young'un," Eb shouted. "Let's give'er a go this way," he motioned over toward his right, away from the direction the cow was turning. They scrambled through the fairly dense woods, now striving mightily to lengthen the gap between them and the moose. By now the cow had made her turn and was crashing and stomping furiously in full pursuit of this threat to her young. Hooves, legs, and feet were fairly flying.

The chase was on! Weaving and dodging through the trees and saplings—the moose didn't dodge the saplings, as she simply stomped over them—the two boys were losing ground, as they could tell from the snortin' sounds of the cow looming closer. They had to find safety, and they'd best find it quick. The tundra and undergrowth beneath their feet hampered their flight—but not by much!

At that moment Eb spotted what appeared to be a deep ravine just ahead, one ringed with fairly thick growth of trees and some underbrush. "Up here," Eb yelled, and motioned to Michael to swing off to the right. They closed the distance and both threw themselves between several large trees and into the brush at the edge of the ravine. For a moment they became airborne and tumbled head over heels down into the deep ravine, gathering dirt, brush, leaves and all sorts of debris on their descent. They rolled to a stop at the bottom, and with the dust starting to settle around them, they glanced up to the rim of the ravine for any sign of the lumbering beast. At first they didn't. . . .

The moose stood gazing down at them, stoically unmoved by the recent, violent chase, looking for all the world like some combatant considering the fate of her vanquished foe. She towered over the underbrush through which the boys had recently launched themselves; and she instinctively knew not to negotiate the deep ravine nor leave her calf unprotected any longer. With a snort of defiance, she once more swung her massive head, and, with a lumbersome jerk, turned back towards her calf. The threat was over.

For a moment the boys gazed upward, with mouths wide open, wonderment filling their every sense. Slowly, their gaze swung toward each other, as the full impact of what had just transpired flooded over them. And then it hit them; they didn't just laugh, they guffawed! With loud, boisterous gales of shouts and yells, as much in joyous relief as in glee, they leaped at each other in boyish exuberance, grabbing and pounding one another as they rolled and tumbled once more in the ravine, laughing, over and over, with indescribable joy! Finally, they fell back, exhausted once again from these recent exertions and noisily expelled their heavy breathing in gasps of pure delight.

"What an adventure! What an incredible, heart-pounding, hell of adventure we just had," whispered Eb, as much to himself as to anyone else.

"Of a truth, of a truth," repeated Michael.

And then they both sensed there was nothing more that needed to be spoken—and grew silent. For a moment they lingered there, each deep in his own personal thoughts. Someday, Eb thought, I'll grow old—old like Great-grandfather Simeon—he was really old. And if I have a rocking chair and grandchildren, like him, well, maybe I'll sit rocking in front of my own fireplace and have all the tykes around...and I'll tell'em about the moose.

But first Ebenezer had to have children in order to have grandchildren—and before that, a wife. He took this step when, as a young man almost 36, he married Hannah Cromwell of New Brunswick, Canada on June 19, 1832. They were wed at Hallowell, Maine by his father, Reverend Barnabas Packard. As he rode to the church in Hallowell, he remembered back to his childhood days when he and a few friends traveled in that dugout canoe down the Kennebec; and they had hidden it somewhere near the river. They had also pledged to one another that someday they would ride it "all the way to th' ocean." Maybe, he thought, someday we will.

If they could ever find it....

Chapter 4

The Fosters of Colonial South Carolina

Timeline: 1724-1781

Settlements in the Carolina colony were slow in forming, much slower than the colonies in New England and elsewhere along the Atlantic seaboard. By the mid-1600s these were much more advanced in their development than was the Carolina charter. Even though Carolina was part of the charter granted for the colonization of "Virginia" in 1606, very little progress had been made.

The expressed wishes of King Charles I in 1629 for the Province of Carolina— or Land of Charles—to be colonized, also went for naught. Aside from the occasional settlers wandering in from time to time, some from Virginia, the West Indies, and a few from the New York colonies, no meaningful efforts on the part of England to settle the Carolina region were made.

Some of the reasons for this apparent lack of interest were the political squabbles between the colony proprietors, the governors, and grant-holders from the major colonies. Also, there was unmistakable evidence of greed as shown by many proprietors, greed which soured many would-be investment partnerships and development opportunities. Other reasons were simply geographical; much of Carolina particularly the northern area, had harbors and inlets that posed challenging, if not dangerous hindrance to ships of trade; and the southern obstacle: the overland routes were deemed too difficult to negotiate. Trade would suffer, or so it was thought. And for these reasons, many charters were simply allowed to expire. All this, in spite of reports from a few earlier explorations and expeditions that told of glorious lands that were "most abundantly fruitful," giving crop yields twice that of Virginia colonies. These reports were particularly favorable toward the "southern Carolina," which was seen as most pleasant. By 1680 as few as 3,000 settlers lived in all of the Carolina colony.

Meanwhile, as trade with some of the New England colonies, as well as with the West Indies, grew, so too did the region of "South" Carolina. And England, especially, sent ships of trade more frequently. South Carolina was becoming prosperous. The reasons were obvious: South Carolina had a booming agriculture, as most of her settlers had proven quite skilled at farming and cultivating the land. Crops of sugarcane, rice, and tobacco were produced; they exported furs, meats, and forest timber of many varieties. And they grew indigo; this dye from plants of the pea family became a major crop and important to the growth of the region of South Carolina. These goods, while abundant in South Carolina, were not widely available in many other colonies.

In November 1682 quite a number of sailing vessels, ships of trade, were present in the harbor of "Olde Charles Towne." Trade with the other colonies, the West Indies, and especially with England, had grown substantially, leading to greater immigration from the colonies of New York, New England, and Virginia, and also Barbados, the West Indies, and increasingly, from France and England. By 1700 the population of South Carolina exceeded 6,000; Charles Town itself, more than 3,000 strong, was more populous than all of "North" Carolina. Immigrants continued toward South Carolina, and some came from New Jersey.

----------------◊----------------

The colony of New Jersey was chartered in June 1664. Practically from its inception, problems abounded throughout the late 17^h Century. Many of its controversies—much like those of South Carolina—resulted from confusion and disorder between the new settlers, the established residents, and the proprietors of the colony. Mostly these disputes were over jurisdiction and land titles. The colony slowly prospered. Yet, the scarcity of good, tillable land became ever more a problem for those settlers coming in, seeking new homesites.

The settlement at Salem, New Jersey was no exception. Though it offered much in the way of industry and commerce, primarily owing to its location along the Salem River at Salem Cove, it nevertheless suffered some in matters such as agriculture and livestock. For many of its inhabitants who sought after better and larger acreage, there was a fortunate set of circumstances: a few of the proprietors of these larger northern colonies were also involved with or part *of the proprietorship of South Carolina; and they passed along the encouraging good news of successful farmlands and available acreage in Charles Town. For some future settlers, it would offer an irresistible opportunity.* (Colonial South Carolina—A History, Robert M. Weir, 1983 and In Colonial New England, Deborah Kent, 2000.)

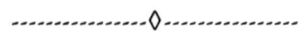

William James Foster was born at Salem, New Jersey in 1724. Mary Hill was also born there on July 11, 1727. They became good childhood friends; and as they grew older, the friendship blossomed into deeper bonds of trust. Their affection for each other eventually led to a marriage at Salem, New Jersey in the year 1750. They had waited until William Foster had finally built them a small log and clapboard two–room cabin; he had cleared the small acreage over the previous year, trying to establish a homestead for himself and Mary. Their place was just outside Salem, closer to the settlement at Pointers. Those first few years they had good crops and a few cattle. Winters were quite harsh, but they managed. With hardwork, they just managed.

Twin boys were born to them in 1752; but during the very cold winter of 1752-1753, one infant passed away. It brought a deep sadness to their lives and deep heartache to Mary. She grieved over her lost child and asked William if it would be possible to move someplace warmer and away from the sad memories which lingered so oppressively about them. Even though little James had survived, the loss cut deeply. Reluctantly, but fully aware of his wife's grief, William made some inquiries of the colony's proprietor about relocating to the settlement of Charles Town in South Carolina.

After some months of discussions and inquiries made to the new colonial government in South Carolina, William was informed that arrangements had been made. They would first need settle their affairs in Salem, and by the spring they should be on their way. Passage was arranged on a trade vessel bound for Charles Town, and on May 14, 1753, they set sail. For Mary, the day brought much joy. Hopefully, the days of heartache and loss would fade away, much like the waters left in their wake. William James Foster, Mary Hill Foster, and little James were on their way to a new home, and, in particular, a new life in South Carolina.

Their ship arrived in Charles Town on May 30, 1753, following a few days anchorage at the Virginia colony settlement near Portsmouth, to offload supplies and to board a few more passengers bound for Charles Town. It rained steadily as their ship entered Charles Town Harbor; a warm rain with a fragrance wafting from the forested shores filled them with a sense of clean freshness that was much needed after the two weeks at sea.

William secured lodging for them at an inn, and the next few days were spent somewhat leisurely. Business with the Privy Council was explored in the matter of land acreage and establishment of their new homestead. The opportunities were many. Arrangements proceeded reasonably well, and within a fortnight William James and his family had moved their belongings to a small settlement just inland from Charles Town; and with help from a few neighbors, they started work on a new cabin. His plan called for a large one-room log cabin laid out in such a manner that would lend itself to future room additions. He planned wisely, and the cabin was completed in only four days. A calming sense of permanence now enveloped William James and Mary Foster.

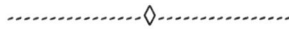

The years passed pleasantly enough for the Foster family; they were industrious and not given to slovenly ways. Hardwork was not a stranger to their home; in fact, they welcomed it. By the summer of 1756 they had added two more rooms to their home, cleared several acres for crops, and added a few head of livestock.

Once again, happiness filled their days and a gratifying sense of accomplishment prevailed. And by late September Mary was filled with an even greater sense of accomplish-ment; she knew she was again with child.

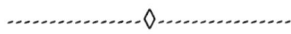

John Foster was born on May 25, 1757. He was a healthy infant and would remain so in the days to come. Mary smiled contentedly as she nursed little John Foster; mother and child rocked easily in the fine oak rocking chair that William James had made some months earlier. They had both displayed quite a bit of optimism during this approaching birth. Aided considerably, that is, by their daily prayers for a strong, healthy baby—and that it was. At last, Mary Hill Foster had the child she had so greatly longed for.

Two more sons were born into this Foster family, and by spring 1761 William James Foster had, of necessity, added yet another room to their home. The house, as well as the family, was definitely growing.

All four of the Foster boys would grow into robust, able-bodied young men. This would be a good thing, and of significant benefit to Charles Town. Problems with England and her Parliament were growing more ominous; serious conflicts loomed on the horizon. The Foster sons would one day prove of critical need.

By 1763, following the end of the French and Indian War, a relative peace settled upon the colonies, and South Carolina, in particular, returned once more to her prosperous ways—more or less considering the political unease.

With increasing numbers of British soldiers in the colonies, relations had grown a bit strained; and new taxation, such as in the Plantation Act of 1764, only made things worse. Increasingly, Parliament was adding new tax laws and imposing tariff duties on a number of basic items imported to the American colonies. These were being forced upon them with oppressive arrogance and high-handedness. Tensions came to a head following confrontations with some customs officials in Boston; and in October 1768 British troops were called in to quell the uprisings among the Americans.

Over the ensuing years, disputes within their own colonial structure, as well as with royalist government leaders had stretched relations to the breaking point. The resentment by the colonists to the British indifference to their situation finally reached a point of no turning back in 1773.

The Boston Tea Party put the British and the American colonists squarely on the path toward armed conflict. The American Revolution was imminent. (In Colonial New England, Deborah Kent, 2000.)

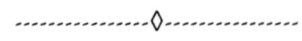

William James and Mary Hill Foster had no wish for hostilities with the English crown; trade with England and several other countries, as well, had been of considerable benefit to the Fosters and to Charles Town and all its merchants and populace. But they and their sons knew full well that conditions were incompatible with the industrious and independent nature of the American colonists who had made their own way, with their own hands. With their own sweat and blood and personal sacrifices they had carved out their own part of this land and, in the process, the whole of the American colonies. They had fought to build all this for their own family and for the several other families, as well; they would not in the least hesitate to fight to protect what was theirs. It was not in their nature not to fight.

The Foster boys were mature young men; James Foster was 21; John Foster was 16; and the young William and Thomas were at the age of manhood. They had often heard their parents speak of life in New Jersey and how they had made the decision to resettle in South Carolina. As young boys, they had helped in building new rooms to their home and in farming and cultivating the land. They had helped herd their cattle. They would help fight.

Some of the British militant action was intended to intimidate and force into submission the various American colonies—more or less, to divide and conquer—but had exactly the opposite effect. The tyrannical attitude of the British forces united the Americans into a determined, committed cause. Rather than meekly retreat into submissiveness, the colonists rose up in anger, strengthened in their aim to redress the wrongs that had been visited upon them. They were in a very foul mood.

The British had grievously misjudged the disposition of the Americans.

Word reached Charles Town of the battles at Lexington and Concord in Massachusetts in May 1775. In quick response, Charles Town's Council of Safety sent out ships to capture arms and munitions from other ships offshore.

Munitions captured by the British at Fort Charlotte on the Savannah River were just as quickly regained by a militia group of a few hundred men. The Foster brothers, James and John, assisted in this action by the Charles Town militia, and some loyalists were arrested in the skirmish and jailed.

After a number of encounters in which both sides counted casualties, Governor Campbell removed his loyalist offices from Charles Town on September 15, 1775. Attempting to blockade some of the harbor channels, a colonial ship was fired upon by a British warship. War in South Carolina had begun in earnest and would rapidly accelerate.

John Foster and his brothers had become more involved in colonial action, moving arms and munitions for various militia units around Charles Town. With William and Thomas helping move supplies to units along the Cooper River, James and John Foster assisted in mounting the cannons for defending the town; they covered all of the approaches into Charles Town.

On June 28, 1776, the British planned to move three of their ships to attack the fort on Sullivan's Island. This maneuver across a narrow and shallow channel led to all three running aground—they were sitting ducks. The cannons the Fosters helped to position for defense proceeded to pound the British warships. The British troops suffered four times the casualties sustained by the colonists, losing a couple of ships in the battle, as well; many munitions were captured by the militia. The first battle of Charles Town resulted in an American victory.

The Declaration of Independence was read to the citizenry of Charles Town on August 5, 1776. The cheering throngs included the Foster families, as patriotic fever swept throughout the region. By the following day the armies and militia throughout the harbor area, with its several forts, and troop emplacements in the surrounding countryside, had heard the United States of America's Declaration of Independence.

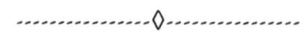

As the war dragged on, there was little, if any, military action in South Carolina over the next couple of years; even so, the British Army was gaining in numbers and military might. Savannah fell to the British in 1779. On May 12, 1780, the once, valiant Charles Town Army was forced to surrender. Word went out that some British, as well as their loyalist Tories, had committed unpardonable atrocities in the slaughter of unarmed prisoners. Over the next several months, many of the Charles Town populace fled into the back country to escape what they feared would be vicious retaliations on the part of loyalist troops. In 1781 John Foster and his young family were among them, afraid that their property and their lives were in mortal danger.

◊

During the unsettled times from 1773 to 1778 the community at Charles Town witnessed a number of drastic changes—and not a small amount of turmoil. The same was true for the Foster family. In spite of troubles all about, they managed to carry on with normal family activities—at least as normal as possible, considering the war, or threat of war that raged around them.

John Foster and Rachel Gibson were married near Charles Town in the fall of 1775. Their first child, Gideon Gibson Foster, named after his mother's father, was born a year later in the fall of 1776, some five years before the entire Foster family—brothers, mother, and children—fled from South Carolina. The atrocities committed by some of the loyalist militia, under protection of the British, were a life-threatening risk the Foster family chose not to be confronted with.

In the spring of 1781 they headed west, out of harm's way. To where, they weren't sure. . . .

◊

Chapter 5

The "Ole Three Hundred"

Timeline: 1782-1824

Leaving Charles Town, the Foster and Gibson families fled northwest, seeking a haven of safety. Wherever that would be almost had to be better than what was behind them; with a certainty, they had been made aware that the Tories or loyalists had targeted their possessions and their families—targeted with a vengeance.

The Gibson party consisted of Gideon Gibson, Mary Gibson, their nine children, and their spouses and children.

The Foster group had John, his wife, Rachel, his mother, Mary Foster, and their son, Gideon. Also, with them were John Sr.'s older brother, James, his sister, Nancy, and the younger brothers, William and Thomas, along with all their families. Altogether, the two parties consisted of more than 35 hearty souls leaving South Carolina in search of new homes.

These parties crossed into the western reaches of the northern part of Carolina four weeks later, and by the middle of summer arrived at the south fork of the Holston River, two days journey from the settlement of Boatyard. Purchasing two large flatboats, they worked their way downriver, reaching the Tennessee River on July 18, 1781. The Foster-Gibson party had now been gone from Charles Town more than two months. And more dangers lay ahead....

The Fosters and Gibsons learned that hostile bands of Cherokees, armed with weapons supplied by the British, had been attacking river traffic in recent weeks. John and Gideon moved away from the women and children so they could talk privately. "Gideon, I reckon as how we oughta' take care in how we load air barges, ya' know?"

Gideon replied, "Yep, I s'pects yore right, John, ya got enny thoughts on thet?"

"Let's set up both with th' crates 'n barrels 'n enny heavy bundles towards th' outside 'n make pockets fer pertection o' th' wimmen 'n little'uns on th' inside. What'cha think o' that?"

"Thet sounds right smart t' me, John, 'n mebbe we could pack some smaller stuff up top, so's we would have sum pertected slots t' shoot from, ya' know?"

After several minutes of planning and working out more details, they started dividing up the arms and munitions they had brought with them from Charles Town. All told, they had 14 muskets, 7 new long rifles, 3 mortars, and a sizable quantity of gunpowder and ball ammunitions. John picked up the flintlock pistols and turning to Gideon, said, "Lets give these t' sum o' th' wimmen' 'n th' older boys...ya' know, jest in case." Gideon knew full well what he meant; neither man would want the womenfolk or children taken alive by savage Indians.

The first skirmish with hostiles occurred two days into the trip along the Tennessee; a small war party fired upon their floating forts causing no serious damage. A barrel of drinking water was hit, along with some other provisions. One of the Gibson men sustained a flesh wound to his leg after being struck by a musketball. The women cleaned and dressed all the wounds as best they could, and both men soon recovered. John's younger brother, William, had an arrow removed from his shoulder, causing a bit of blood loss. William had a rough time for several days, having come down with a fever from infection in his wounds. Using provision cases for support, and with only one good arm, William was soon able to fire his musket well enough. Several weeks later William and his musket would be sorely needed.

After a few more days downriver, the Foster-Gibson party poled ashore near the juncture with the Hiwassee River and took on supplies and provisions at the small settlement's trading post. Finding little in the way of medical supplies, they would have to make do.

The Fosters and Gibsons camped near the trading post a couple of days, resting from the recent attack. Gideon approached John, calling some of the older boys and the other men to a campfire. "Wa'l, I jest larned a coupla' river travelers' whut wuz on th' Tennessee River a day er so ago got attack'd by th' Injuns; one wuz kilt, sev'ral injured. We best be well stocked up with gunpowder 'n rations, ya' know? No way o' tellin' what we may come 'cross." Late August of 1781 found the Foster-Gibson party crossing into the region of west Florida that would one day become the Alabama Territory.

-----------◊-----------

John Foster paced along the front of the barge, feeling the heat and humidity that hung above the river. Sure is peaceful 'n quiet, John thought to himself; mebbe too quiet. The hair on his neck started to rise. He had just turned to shout something to Gideon when several musket shots shattered the stillness. Both barges were taking heavy fire from their attackers along the east riverbank. John yelled to no one in particular: "There's a lot o' musket fire comin' at us; everyone stay low." A few of the Foster and Gibson men cried out as they were struck by musket balls but fortunately none of the wounds proved very serious. "Gideon," John again shouted, "git yer barge closer t' us, 'n let's see iffen we kin cons'n'trate air fire!"

A sudden thought struck John. "Gideon! Load up yer mortar with a good charge o'powder, 'n pack in some nails 'n shrapnel. Hurry! 'N aim o'er thet way, towards th' poplars!" John yelled at his men to load their mortars in the same way. The women and some of the children kept busy reloading and ramming the balls and waddings down the musket barrels. The older boys had quenched most of the fires, as these were now just smoldering and smoking up the barges. John told his crew to aim their mortars a bit left of where Gideon's was aimed.

Both mortars erupted with a blast of flame and smoke, and almost immediately the trees and underbrush along the riverbank rippled and shredded as the shrapnel and nails tore into and through them. Simultaneously, there were screams and cries coming from the underbrush; they had hit their enemies pretty good.

John yelled to Gideon again, "Load up a'gin, this time with one o' air mortar bombs, 'n aim 'bout th' same as b'fore." His team did the same. The Fosters and Gibsons had about half a dozen of the explosive mortar bombs which were already loaded with jagged bits of steel and other types of shrapnel.

"Gideon! Whils't they'r a bit rattled, pole yer barge o'er towards th' right, so's we kin get a bit o' distance a'fore we set off th' bomb blast." The men on the barges continued firing their muskets toward the smoke bursts coming from the attackers' muskets. The barrage of fire from the Fosters 'n Gibsons was apparently taking its toll as the fire from shore seemed to be tapering off. The women and children were now reloading the muskets with rapid skill, allowing a steady and deadly fire towards their enemies.

"All right, men, let's give 'em a good partin' shot with th' bombs. Light 'em up!" The mortars again erupted in smoke and flames as the mortar bombs whistled toward the tree line....

The blasts were timed near perfectly—boom! boom! ... boom! as the bombs exploded some 15 or 20 feet above the underbrush. Simultaneously, screams and cries rang out from the underbrush as the mortar bursts hit the attackers with devastating effectiveness. The cries of pain and anguish told the Fosters and Gibsons they had inflicted heavy casualties among the attackers. With only a parting shot or two, the attackers had had enough. The fighting ended almost as suddenly as it had begun....

The settlers then counted their own casualties, and they were numerous. Almost half of the two family groups had suffered wounds, some quite serious. While there were many flesh wounds to limbs as well as a few chest and stomach injuries, a couple proved fatal. One of the Gibson lads—Gideon's 13-year old grandson—had suffered a mortal head wound. By night fall, he had succumbed. One of the Foster granddaughters had likewise taken an arrow into her side, and though it initially appeared less than life-threatening, internal hemorrhaging and infection took their deadly toll; she died two days later. Reaching a fairly cleared area, with no sign of hostiles, the families stopped to bury their dead—a time of deep sorrow with them that lingered for many days.

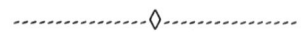

By early September 1781 the Foster-Gibson settlers had been through several colonial territories (both Carolinas, Tennessee, and part of Alabama) and had yet to locate lands suitable for their homestead needs. Only a few settlements were discovered, and even fewer protective forts.

Upon reaching the waters of the Ohio River sometime later, the decision was jointly made to continue downriver to the Mississippi and head on down to Natchez, near the West Florida territory. (During this time the region described as West Florida consisted, wholly or in part of the future states of Alabama, Mississippi, Georgia, and parts of Tennessee.) This journey was accomplished with little incident over the next several weeks, and the surviving members of the original Foster-Gibson group reached Natchez on October 28, 1781. After more than six months of difficult travel, they had reached an area that showed much promise for their respective families. It would again be pleasant to put down roots.

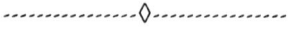

John Foster, Sr. built his homestead near a creek just north of Natchez and along the well-traveled road which would one day be called The Natchez Trace (The Natchez Trace was actually an old trail or path which had once been a route through the woods and forests used by wild game and the Indian tribes which hunted them.) The Trace had existed for many, many years before explorers and travelers began using it in ever-increasing numbers. In time, sections were cleared and covered wagons began traversing its some 400-mile length as they headed towards Natchez, Mississippi. It was here they would cross the mighty river as they continued their westward journey. Mary Hill Foster settled in comfortably on the plantation her son named Old Oaklands that was situated on St. Catherine's Creek outside Natchez. John's two younger brothers, William and Thomas, settled there, also. Late that summer of 1782, John Foster and his wife, Rachel, brought another son into the family; the little boy was named John Foster, Jr. after his father.

From 1782 to 1797 John Foster's leadership and political skills manifested themselves in ways that benefited his family, his Natchez community, and the new government under President George Washington.

Land was acquired which greatly expanded the holdings of John Foster, Sr. and his extended family. He soon helped with the survey and plot for a townsite to be situated on his property. This town was to be named Washington in honor of the new nation's president; he also helped found a school and a college, established as Jefferson College in 1803.

John had been appointed to an official position by the Spanish Governor for West Florida and served variously as a representative between the United States and Spain regarding political matters in this region. Following the death of his wife, Rachel Gibson Foster, in 1795, John Foster, Sr. remarried on October 26, 1797. John and his new bride, the young widow, Mary Smith Kelsey, would eventually raise seven more Foster children. (In addition to his older sons, Gideon Foster and John Foster, Jr., John and Rachel produced Sara Foster, Randolph Foster, Isaac G. Foster, and Moses Foster.)

From 1776 to 1810 John Foster, Sr. had fathered a total of 13 children. Many of these would figure prominently in helping settle and establish a new territory in this new, growing nation. The territory would become Texas.

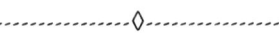

Randolph Foster was born March 12, 1790, the fourth child of John and Rachel Foster. Randolph was also born of adventure; he enjoyed nothing more than hunting wild game and exploring the woods and forests in the surrounding territories—territories that would become the states of Mississippi, Arkansas, Louisiana, and Texas. He was at home in the wild. For months at a time, his travels took him through these regions where he set up camps for hunting, exploring, and generally scouting out the land. Some of these excursions found him returning often to areas of south Texas, and in particular what would be Fort Bend County.

In 1821 Randolph Foster learned that Moses Austin, a native son of Connecticut, had recently obtained permission from the Spanish Governor at San Antonio to settle 300 families in this province. This proposal had been presented the day after Christmas in 1820 and included provisions to establish a town at the mouth of the Colorado River.

Confident in his success at having his proposal accepted by the Spanish Governor, Moses Austin began his return trip to his home in Missouri. Unfortunately, harsh wintry weather impeded his progress, and before too long he grew weakened and fell quite ill. He eventually reached home but never recovered. Moses Austin died in June 1821.

On his deathbed he asked that word of this venture be passed along to his son, Stephen Austin, in hopes that the settlement of Texas might yet be completed.

Stephen F. Austin, later called the "Father of Texas," was born in Virginia in 1793. In 1800, at the age of seven, he moved with his father to Missouri and eventually entered his family's business and served 5 years in the Missouri legislature.

After the Panic of 1819, which wiped out his family's finances, he moved down to New Orleans in December 1820 and hoped to somehow revive the family fortune.

In June 1821 he first learned that his father's proposal for the settlement of Texas had been approved by the authorities of Monterrey, Mexico. Having already decided to assist his father, Stephen headed toward Texas. At that time the news reached him that his father had passed away but that the newly independent Mexican government would probably allow him to assume this responsibility. Stephen F. Austin crossed the Sabine River into Texas on July 16, 1821. He was possessed of a new ambition. (Gone to Texas, Randolph B. Campbell, 2003.)

At about this same time Randolph Foster, on one of his exploratory trips through the Louisiana Territory, learned of the soon-to-form Texas colony. Heading on to Texas, he fell in with Stephen F. Austin; and they proceeded to the provincial capitol at San Antonio.

Because of his many previous hunting and scouting trips into Texas—especially the vast area being proposed for this new settlement—Randolph Foster proved a valuable help to Austin in all the planning and surveying stages.

The Crepe Myrtle

With Governor Martinez's request for a comprehensive and detailed plan for land distribution, this team of venturesome authorities set about mapping out the lands of the Brazos and Colorado Rivers and spent considerable time in the exploration and study of the lands south of San Antonio and east toward the Brazos River.

The plans were to provide each family with over 1,300 acres for their homesteads; 320 acres would be along the river with another 640 adjoining acres for grazing of livestock. With additional acreage for family members, the new settlers would acquire not only sizable holdings of fertile lands for grazing and farming but also lands of remarkable low cost. Elsewhere in the United States land sold for around $1.25 per acre; this was the prevailing rate after 1820. Austin's proposal to Governor Martinez was that he, Austin, would receive a mere 12½ cents per acre from the Texas settlers.

Lands in other areas in 1,000 acre quantities cost the new settlers more than $1,200; Texas land would cost one-tenth that amount or about $125. This bargain proved irresistible to many.

Stephen Austin enlisted the aid of a friend back in Louisiana to help promote his planned colony of 300 families; the response was overwhelming. Cheap land was now available, and they applied in droves.

Randolph Foster surveyed the lands which would soon comprise the John Foster grant there in Fort Bend County. "Early in 1822, John Foster and Isaac Foster joined Randolph Foster in Texas. On July 14, 1824, John Foster received title to 2½ <u>sitios</u> and 3 <u>labors</u> of land (11,601 acres)—the largest single grant in present-day Fort Bend County." (John Foster (1757-1837) and Randolph Foster (1790-1878), Gordon Leigh Briscoe of the Foster Family Association, 2003.)

The considerable reputations and skills of John Foster, Sr. and his sons and all their families had made all this possible; Stephen F. Austin knew it would require settlers of this stripe to make this colony successful.

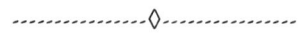

Chapter 6

Charles Howard Packard, Stowaway

Timeline: September, 1832-April, 1853

Hallowell was a quiet, peaceful village on the Kennebec River. The folks were industrious, reserved, and strong in their faith and their worship—a very nice place to raise a family.

In mid-November of 1832 Hannah informed Ebenezer that she was with their first child and expressed that she would be most pleased if they could birth in her parents' home. Even though this would require a considerable distance of travel for his pregnant wife, Ebenezer knew he would be wise to comply with Hannah's wishes. He made arrangements to have neighbors look after their homesite, and, not wishing to risk hazardous winter travel for his wife and unborn child, departed Hallowell, Maine late in November. They spent the winter and spring at his in-laws home near Frederickton, New Brunswick. As spring yielded to summer, Hannah fairly bulged with child.

With her mother attending during her labor, Hannah gave birth on July 25, 1833, to their firstborn son and named him, Charles Howard Packard.

On September 10, 1837, the 4 year old Charles had a baby brother, Theodore Packard. In short order, Mary Reynolds Packard was born October 8, 1839, and Ebenezer Packard, named for his father, was born April 3, 1843.

----------------◊----------------

Charles Howard was near on to 10 years old, and as his father before him, spent most of his spare time on the river. Ebenezer had told Charles Howard of many of the adventures he, Ebenezer, and his friends had shared on those very waters on and around the Kennebec. And, true to his protective, fatherly nature, cautioned Charles that he should not embark upon certain of those "risky" adventures until he was a bit older. As he, Ebenezer, had done in his childhood days; naturally, these warnings had about as much effect as spittin' in the wind. Charles Howard understood fully the warnings and concerns he received from his father; he was only too well aware of some unfortunate drownings that had occurred in recent years in the waters of the Kennebec.

But Charles also understood his own skills and knowledge of the river; his own father had often remarked—in jest, perhaps—that Charles was "most likely th' one child of his to grow webbed feet and sprout fins." And some remarked that were it to happen, they wouldn't be that much surprised.

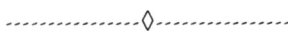

Ebenezer had, on occasion, related to Charles Howard and his friends the tale of the dugout canoe and the journey he and his friends had made down the Kennebec "back when he was a young'un." And though they had searched diligently, the dugout Ebenezer had hidden in the ravine near Hallowell never turned up; they had stashed it away too well.

But the journey his father and his friends had one day intended to take, Charles Howard completed. With a few mates of his own, the lads found a fairly recently felled tree of some goodly size and, with wisdom shared from older residents of Hallowell, proceeded to fashion their own dugout. This required considerable chopping, and then patiently "burning out" the heart of the log with hot coals and then more chopping. Not an easy task, even for stout lads on a determined mission. But after several days of "burnin' 'n gougin'," they had a "seaworthy ship," as Charles Howard called it. They proceeded to carve "USS KENNEBEC" into its side.

Two days later the boys steered their craft down the Kennebec, all the way to the village of Bath, just a couple of miles below the town of Brunswick. It was August 1845 just two weeks past his twelfth year.

Charles knew instinctively they daren't venture too much nearer the point where Ft. Popham sat, as the outbound current into Muscongus Bay would be flowing a bit strong; too strong for three lads in a heavy dugout even with four skillfully crafted wooded oars. Charles Howard had the foresight to make an extra, in the event one broke, or they lost one on their journey. They were all "good seafarin' men," and, as Charles Howard pronounced, "men worthy of their salt."

Charles Howard Packard had tasted th' salt; even this far inland, the salt in the air was unmistakably perceptible. He could taste it on his lips; he could smell it in the air. And he wanted more of it, that he knew for certain.

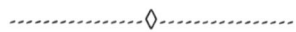

They made no attempt to hide the dugout; they knew this was as far as they should go on such a craft. So they worked it part ways up th' bank and left it for flood waters to one day carry out to sea. Out to sea—for better or worse, it was in his blood. And out to sea was just where he wanted to go and where he wanted to be. To be "on th' salt." Except Charles Howard Packard wanted aboard something a bit larger than a dugout canoe—something a whole lot larger. . . .

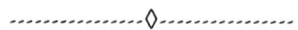

Not long after his fourteenth birthday, a day or two, perhaps, Charles Howard ran away from home—ran away to the sea. In truth, he had already informed his parents of this ambition, and they didn't spend a great deal of effort in trying to talk him out of it. It was in his eyes, this passion that had claimed him and that was especially obvious to Ebenezer. Any attempts on their part, he had explained to his wife, to sway their son to some other "more worthy endeavor," would, as Ebenezer emphasized, fall on deaf ears—completely and totally deaf ears. He knew his son and he knew his determination; he was of age. And so, resigned to this fact, Hannah bravely bid her son a motherly farewell; that is, after she had packed a knapsack with enough provisions to feed him the better part of a week.

He boarded a flatboat that plied the Kennebec between the towns of Augusta and Brunswick, a trade boat, of sorts. He hoped there might be a trading ship or two in the harbor at Brunswick where he might sign on as a deckhand or mess boy, at worst. If not, he knew he had best travel on to th' port of Portland, where large numbers of trading ships dropped anchor.

Brunswick Harbor berthed a two-mast schooner and an even smaller fishing boat. But neither had need of additional crew. Charles Howard's entreaties fell on their deaf ears, as they steered him to the gangplank back onto the dock.

"Maybe next year," the first mate had told him, "when ye have some sea legs 'neath yer arse!" This port didn't have the appearance of good possibilities, not in the' least. It was time to move on to Portland.

He managed to latch on to a dray wagon hauling a load of ships' tackle and hawser rope down to the docks at Portland and found the driver to be of a pleasant sort. He learned a bit about the ships and conditions there on the docks and that just might come in very handy by sunup tomorrow and this night, as well.

The driver showed him a couple of dock sheds where, if a bloke had a bit 'o good luck, he could grab a decent night's sleep 'n not be set upon by th' watchmen. His luck held.

At the first crack of dawn, Charles Howard decided he would try the direct approach to see if he could land a crew job on one of the ships. By mid-morning he had applied at five vessels, without much encouragement. One had considered him as a cabin boy but decided at the last on an older, supposedly more experienced roust-about. It was time to heed the advice of the dray driver. He settled upon a couple of likely ships—neither one anchored next to th' other—and picked up a good-sized coil of rope near some dock crates and started mingling with other roustabouts who were loading supplies aboard the first ship. He made it onboard and was just past the gangplank heading aft when the ship's quartermaster grabbed him by the scruff. "Ere there, mate, an' just where might ye think yer' headin'?"

"Well, I'm haulin' this rope aft to th'...." He never finished the fib he was about to test on th' seaman.

"No, yer not, 'n don't be aimin' to pull no wool o'er me eyes, ye lyin' little swab. It's settin' out as a bloomin' stowaway, that's what yer be headin' out to do." The quartermaster turned him around back to the gangplank and gave him a half-hearted boot in his backside.

"Now haul yer arse 'n this useless bit 'o hawser back to th' docks 'n don't be sneakin' back onboard me ship, er I'll have th' crew keelhaul yer arse under me ship."

As Charles Howard stomped down the gangplank, th' ol' seaman gave a bit of a chuckle and thought to himself: "Now that's a plucky lad, one what's prob'ly gonna wind up on one 'o these ships afore th' day's out." Which is exactly what happened. The second ship that was a couple of berths down the pier, wasn't quite as tight on her security watch. Charles Howard this time hauled a crate on his shoulders and easily moved onboard with the other deckhands. This time he made it to the storage lockers on the starboard side and eased inside one, taking th' crate with him. Inside he pulled the tarps over him just as th' dray driver had told him. And if his luck held, in the next day or so, he would at last be at sea.

Removing his knapsack, he quietly filled himself with stone-baked bread and jerky. Somehow it tasted better than ever he could remember—probably just th' salt air, he thought to himself.

Back up at the pier, the gruff old seaman on the first ship watched as Charles Howard Packard worked his same stunt. With a bit of satisfaction, he noted that this time, th' lad had managed to pull it off.

"Good lad," he muttered to himself, "I 'ope 'e makes it."

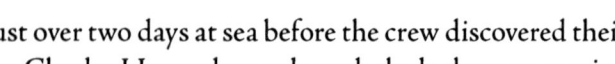

The *Intrepid* was just over two days at sea before the crew discovered their stowaway. In a way, Charles Howard was pleased; the locker was getting to be a bit confining and time to face up for his action.

The skipper, a weathered old salt, gave his stowaway a blistering, spittle-filled round of a tongue-lashing and threatened to throw him overboard. That was just for show; inside, he admired th' boy's spunk, as he, himself, had gone to sea in much the same fashion. But he had no intention of being soft on th' lad;' he would find out soon enough if this stowaway had the makings of a ship's mate.

"Put this bilge rat in th' galley," he said to his first mate, "an' let's just see how he likes earnin' his keep." As Charles Howard was roughly led away, the captain yelled after him, "and if it's a dirty job that needs doin', well, there's yer bloke. . . ."

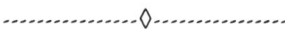

Over the next several years, Charles Howard Packard would earn his keep and more. He proved as determined at sea as he had been ashore.

But those first few voyages, as the *Intrepid* plied its trade routes from New England ports to other ports of call in the West Indies, Charles Howard toiled away in the ship's galley. He was sorely vexed over scrubbing the pots, but he never uttered the first gripe. And well it was, for had he complained, they would have kept him there, and then, likely as not, put him off at some remote port. But he proved his mettle, and by early 1848, he had been made cabin boy, under the eye of the first mate. Leaving the galley bothered him not in the least. Less than a year later, he was one of the deckhands. And as the captain observed, a good 'un to have aboard, yessir, a good mate.

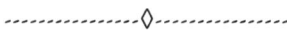

From time to time, the ship's owner would have duty positions open up on other ships in their fleet and word would reach these ship's skippers for likely candidates. They preferred to promote within their own ranks when at all possible.

The *Intrepid's* captain had Charles Howard report to his cabin.

"Howard," the captain began, "I've a bit of good news fer you. Seems our line has need 'o a good first mate on one 'o our steamboats what's makin' th' run 'tween New Awlins 'n St. Looie." Pausing to relight his pipe he continued: "Iff'n this sounds to yer satisfaction I'll be puttin' yer name in." Charles Howard took but a moment to take this all in and responded: "Yessir, Cap'n Danaher, I would like that just fine."

He enjoyed serving under Captain Danaher on the *Intrepid*, but he knew this was a good time to start up the ladder for his own ship. Perhaps, he mused, that won't be so far off—not far at all. . . .

Charles B. Packard

In April 1853 Charles Howard Packard reported at the St. Louis offices of Trafalgar Lines to sign the contract papers for his new position. He would start his duties as first mate on the steamship *Bonaparte* when she docked next Tuesday.

------------------◊------------------

Chapter 7

Charles Howard Packard, Ship's Captain

Timeline: 1853-1868

The crew of the *Bonaparte* dropped her mooring lines smartly on the deck, and with the morning sun's reddish-orange glow creeping ever so furtively across her decks, they backed her slowly out into midstream of the mighty Mississippi. Smoke rolled from her twin stacks creating briefly a dark, wispy cloud bank that hovered above the river. A blast from her foghorns signaled she was underway. Dockworkers glanced up at the *Bonaparte's* graceful departure then turned their attention back to the crates and barrels they were loading into a warehouse.

It was a busy time; and a glorious dawn, that fourteenth day of June 1853.

Standing watch with the wheelhouse crew, Captain Emmitt Hawkins followed every move of his deckhands. Even those on the hurricane deck whose efforts were likewise under the watchful eye of his new First Mate Charles Howard Packard; they, too, came under his piercing gaze. The old skipper missed very little.

Theirs was a seasoned crew. Every seaman aboard stepped lively in carrying out his duties; with th' cap'n, they knew there was little other choice. He gave a fair shake to all, yet demanded and got a full day's effort in return—and sometimes more.

The crew respected the cap'n but it was more a grudgin' respect they paid 'im.

With th' first matey, it were a mite diff'rent. He seemed a good 'un, he did. Yep, he was a bit more like one 'o the tars. They had larned that right away, they had. After only two or three sailin's, they found that the new first matey had th' same tough hide as th' cap'n but held a fair likable way 'bout 'im. More a reg'lar sort, 'e was. 'E'd showed that on their runs.

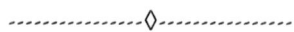

After they had steamed out toward the deeper channel, Charles Howard joined the crew up in the wheelhouse, taking up his station starboard side, right beside Captain Hawkins.

"All ahead two-thirds rudder midship; step lively, now." Captain Hawkins issued his orders in a clear, steady voice: "Easy as she goes. Leadsman, make your sounding." After a few seconds, he sang out: "Mark....Twain ...safe water." They were moving into deeper water now—two fathoms or more—and picking up steam.

The *Bonaparte* had added five more passengers the previous day, giving near full status to the ship's cabins. They had also loaded onboard several kegs of nails and other building hardware, lumber, bundles of fence posts, crates of wrought iron fencing and ornamental gates from foundries in Ohio, and barrels of syrup from Vermont, with full complement bound for the port docks in New Orleans.

The next stop on this trip south was scheduled for the following day at the town of Cape Girardeau in Missouri; they would take onboard livestock for the slaughter yards in Memphis and barrels of beef for New Orleans.

At the small port in Cairo, Illinois a number of barrels of apples, flour from Cairo's grain mills and crates of farm produce would find their way onboard for the marketplace at New Orlean's French Quarter.

The *Bonaparte* would ride a deep draft on this run.

One of the passengers was a young man from Hannibal, Missouri by the name of Sam Clemens who was 17 years of age and busting loose after adventure. What kind didn't much matter to Sam; most anything would beat the last couple of years serving as a printer's apprentice. That had been a dirty, boring job, and one he had shed eagerly

Sam had a presence about him that bespoke an unmistakable air of confidence, mingled with just the right dash of cockiness—and a whole lot of love for river life, Mississippi River life.

There were times the river—well, at times it just seemed so much more than just a river. There were times Samuel Langhorne Clemens wore it, as one would put on a coat; and it fit him well.

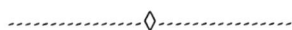

Sam had boarded the *John J. Roe* the previous day in Hannibal, transferring to the *Bonaparte* for the voyage down to New Orleans; and wherever else his itching feet directed him; he had a hunger for life!

Charles Howard had taken a liking to the youngster from the start. Sam was likable, and only a few years younger than he and possessed a great knowledge of steamboats and river life, in general.

After the *Bonaparte* had gotten underway, Charles Howard invited Sam to join him in the wheelhouse. He introduced him to Captain Hawkins and spent the better part of an hour in pleasant conversation with Sam and the captain. Sam shared a lot of his childhood adventure with Charles Howard and the captain.

After awhile, Sam thanked Charles Howard for his hospitality and left the wheelhouse, telling them he wanted to work on an article for his brother's newspaper. "I haven't sent one for some weeks now, and I'm of a mind that Orion's soon to be after my hide." They watched as Sam closed the door and made his way down the portside steps.

Turning to the captain, Charles Howard remarked: "That's a right pleasant fellow and holds a right smart sense of our work on the river—says he hopes to be a river pilot someday."

"He seems smart enough," replied the captain with a nod toward Sam's direction. "If his discipline and skill match his aims, he just could be a good one...."

After a lengthy pause, Captain Hawkins continued. "But there is the other matter, Howard, that does vex me somewhat."

"What's that?" Charles Howard asked.

"That lad holds a load of trouble upon his shoulders—a load he shouldn't be carrying. I don't rightly know what kind, but he has some demons riding in his wake."

Over the next few years, Charles Howard fed on the vast knowledge and skills of Captain Hawkins until he came to anticipate just what his skipper was thinking and just what action they would soon be undertaking. He sometimes carried out the captain's orders before he had even finished expressing them—such was the bond between captain and first mate.

It came as little surprise to most of the crew when First Mate Charles Howard Packard was once again summoned to the shipping line's St. Louis offices. Even Charles Howard anticipated the reason for this summons; he was to be given his first ship.

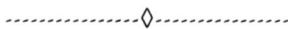

First Mate Charles Howard reported to the St. Louis offices in high spirits, in spite of a cold, driving rain that soaked everyone and everything in sight on that dreary day in late September 1856.

Stepping into the vestibule, Charles Howard shed his slicker and rain cap, and after hanging them on the hall tree, stepped into the outer offices. The office manager, a sometimes dour soul by the name of Huldah Richards, surprised him with a semblance of warmth in her greeting.

"Good morning to you, Mr. Packard, and it's a fine day I hope you be enjoying."

"That it is, Miz Richards; that it is." (They both lied quite easily). . . .

"If you'll be kind enough to give me your papers and satchel, I'll be carrying them for you into Mr. McEachern's office. He's been expecting you."

Thomas McEachern, the General Manager for the Trafalgar Shipping Lines, was, as usual, up to his ears in paperwork and shipping reports for what seemed like far too many ships afloat.

"Come in, 'oward, come in. Grab whatever chair suits your fancy and let's get on with our business." He wasn't the first to call Charles Howard by his middle name, but the way he dropped the "H," pleased Charles Howard no end.

"Or per'aps it's Captain 'oward I should be calling you, now as I think on it. I'm sure by now you've 'eard the rumors what's been out on the the river; the captain on the *City of Baton Rouge* is retiring this coming first of December, and we want you to take command."

Thomas McEachern wasted little time with idle talk and was known to get right to the point. Glancing up from his desk, he locked his gaze with Charles Howard's and inquired: "And I'm presuming that you'll be accepting of our offer?"

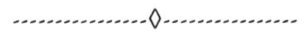

For the next several weeks, Captain Howard Packard stuck like a shadow to Captain Ev Saunders, the retiring captain of the *City of Baton Rouge* steamship. He read the ship's logs for days on end, until he knew every creak and groan the ship had made over the previous 16 months. If a steam valve had blown, Charles Howard made mental note of it; and when a paddle vane broke loose back in February around Keokuk, Iowa, he remembered it. After all, this was now his ship; officially, of course, not until December 1, 1856. But as far as Captain Charles Howard Packard was concerned, this lady of the river belonged to him.

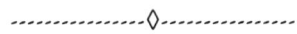

In recent years, Charles Howard had seen many a lovely young woman come aboard his ships and sat at the captains' tables with quite a number of them. In his eyes, they were quite fetching, and some were as charming as any young man could possibly ever desire—if he were looking, that is. But none had had quite the effect on him as the lovely young lady at the Captains' Ball in New Orleans—the annual spring ball held each year at the Hotel Terrebonne to honor the captains and first officers on the Trafalgar Lines' steamships and freighters. This occasion had become a significant social event for New Orleans and in recent years had evolved into more of a "coming-out" gala for many of southern Louisiana's socially prominent young ladies. With so many eligible young captains and first officers to serve as handsome escorts, it truly sparkled in all its glamorous elegance.

Captain Howard Packard stood in the receiving line with all the young officers as each young lady and her chaperone, usually her father, passed down the line for introductions. His manner was most courteous, and he smiled with sincere interest as each young lady was introduced. He had a singular talent for remembering each name and repeated it with a nod and a disarming smile as they glided down the line.

But his true interest—as revealed in his frequent side glances—rested with the lovely fair-haired young woman passing ever close to his posting—closer, but so agonizingly slowly. After what seemed an eternity, she at last stood before him, her blue eyes as lovely as the waters in the Caribbean. To say he was entranced would be a ship's hold of understatement.

"Captain Howard Packard, this is Miss Louisa Cook and her father, Mr. William Cook of Centreville, Louisiana." The attendant escorting Miss Cook and her father had announced them quite properly to Charles Howard and moved down the line to the next young officer without being aware of the immense impact the young lady had just had upon Charles Howard.

Charles Howard had managed, just barely, enough composure to repeat their names and ever so gallantly take her extended hand in his with a gentle, yet firm touch. Even as he courteously nodded toward her, his eyes never left hers.

With considerable reluctance, he released her hand so as to grasp her father's. And with even greater resolve, he managed to tear his gaze from the lovely Miss Louisa Cook and attempted to focus upon the next young lady being introduced. It was a lost cause; Louisa Cook had scuttled him but good.

The Crepe Myrtle

For the next half hour or so, Charles Howard had somehow managed to make it through all the remaining introductions as graciously as possible considering, of course, that only one name was foremost in his thoughts: Louisa Cook.

Louisa, wordlessly, he repeated it over and over, as he strolled through the hotel ballroom scheming as to how best to arrange a second and hopefully longer-lasting introduction to the beautiful young enchantress. Carefully surveying the crowded ballroom for some glimpse of the lady from Centreville—and not quite certain where that magical place was even located—he found himself at the opened glass doors leading out upon one of the many verandas surrounding the glittering ballroom. Stepping onto the veranda, he was immediately immersed in the pleasing fragrances from the honeysuckle and viburnum shrubs surrounding the railings. A magnificent magnolia tree encroaching upon the veranda was resplendent with gigantic white blossoms. Though not given over to such assaults upon his senses, Charles Howard could not but marvel at such a sensual display about him. With the instinct of a true seaman, he glanced up to the heavens, searching out his natural compass, the North Star.

As he did so, he became aware of what a truly glorious night this was—the naturally-perfumed breezes wafting through the foliage; the night sky so radiant with the millions of sparkling diamonds; the soft music drifting from the ballroom; and the sudden realization that the only thing missing from this moment of beauty was someone with whom he. . .

Her voice interrupted the thought. "Are you wishing upon a star or merely gazing at them?" Charles Howard spun around toward the voice, and there stood Louisa and her father. "I beg. . .uh, no-no, I don't believe in wishing for anything, Miss Cook." He flushed, momentarily caught off guard by this unexpected appearance of the sought-after Louisa Cook.

"Please forgive my confusion and loss of manners, Miss Cook. . .Mr. Cook. How do you do, sir?" Regaining his composure, he continued: "I'm sure you've forgotten, what with all the names and faces, but I am Captain Packard, Charles Howard Packard; and, as before, I am delighted to make your acquaintance."

Louisa hadn't forgotten. She very much remembered the handsome young captain's name but most certainly had no intention of letting him know that. "Oh, yes—yes, of course. I do seem to recall that name." "Father, you remember Captain Packard, do you not?"

William Cook smiled at his daughter's little game of "cat and mouse" and replied: "Yes, I certainly do. Good to meet you again, captain."

For the next several minutes they amused themselves in pleasant, lighthearted conversation. Charles Howard spoke little of his circumstances, politely but firmly pressing the issues regarding their lives and wanting to know about their interests and what their home life was like. According to Mr. Cook, he owned a small but thriving plantation in Centreville on which he grew substantial quantities of sugarcane and cotton. After he had learned the general location of Centreville, Charles Howard cleared his throat and addressed Louisa's father. "Mr. Cook, it would mean a lot to me if you would grant me the honor and permission to call upon your daughter, Louisa."

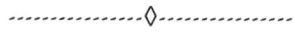

The wedding took place December 9, 1858, at the Old Oak Plantation in Centreville. Officiating was the Reverend W. H. Burton, as Charles Howard Packard and the radiant Louisa Cook exchanged wedding vows beneath a massive oak tree. Charles Howard was 25 years of age; Louisa was one month shy of her nineteenth birthday. She carried a white Bible, inside of which was pressed the magnolia blossom Charles Howard had plucked from the tree the previous year at the ball. For December, it was a great day for a wedding with warm sunshine and family gathered all around filled with their own festive spirits. For Captain Charles Howard Packard, his brightest moment had been two years earlier upon receiving command of his first ship. Standing beside his beautiful, young bride, he realized that that moment had now been surpassed....

They made their home there in St. Mary's Parish not far from the Cook plantation in Centreville; and on November 14, 1860, their first child was born. He was named Willard Howard Packard—the Willard from Louisa's side of the family, and the Howard from his father's name.

His arrival was a great blessing to the young Packard family, and his early years would have been of even greater pleasure had it not been for a particularly harsh and unpleasant circumstance—the onset of this nation's Civil War which began April 12, 1861, with the attack on Ft. Sumter, South Carolina.

In due time, their family would be increased with the arrival of their second son, Chas Elbridge Packard, who came amidst this terrible war on March 1, 1863. When Chas Elbridge was 4 years old, twins were born into the Packard family on November 27, 1867; and they were named Eulalia and Fassitt—both lived just a few days past 8 months. Eulalia died July 29, 1868, Fassitt on July 30, 1868.

Charles Howard had inscribed on their tombstone: "God called these babes to Angels places in Heaven"—it was one of the saddest days of his life.

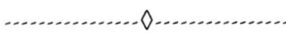

Chapter 8

The Fosters of Texas

Timeline: 1825-1875

By the year 1825 Stephen F. Austin's first colony, the original "Ole Three Hundred" families, was thriving quite well. Later that same year he would settle a second colony not too distant from his first. And by 1831, there would be five of Austin's colonies populating the southern reaches of the Mexican "state" of Texas. Lured by the attraction of cheap land, the settlers streamed in from just about everywhere, seeking to start a new life in this fertile frontier territory. As most of these new colonists came from the southern states, they brought their slaves with them. (Gone to Texas, Randolph B. Campbell, 2003.)

Austin was journeying through a part of his colony along the Brazos and decided to visit with his friends, the Fosters, and discuss a few issues. Arriving at the homestead of Randolph Foster, he rapped on the doorposts and called out: "Randolph, are ye at home this day?"

The heavy oak door creaked open, and Randolph Foster loomed in the doorway, a broad grin on his face. "Come in, Stephen, come in. I've just this very minute put on some water a' boiling for a cup of tea; rest yer bones in that chair and have a cup." The two friends were off on a conversational trail when the door again opened as Isaac Foster came stomping in. "I'm tellin' ye, Randolph, those Injuns are. . . ;" he paused as his gaze lit upon Austin and quickly his scowl recovered into a smile for his friend. "Stephen, what brings this favor of a visit from ye?" he asked. "Have ye nothin' better to be doin'?"

"Isaac, ye'll never be a'changin'; always th' brash one, are ye not?"

The pleasantries over, they sat and talked over some recent news, as Isaac finished his tale of another Indian attack in the colony.

"A rider came in a bit ago, him 'n his horse all lathered up, consarnin' a'nuther Comanche raid, he says, up north a ways. Says the settlers got th' best o' the savages but not til they'd got a few folks kilt and a couple cabins burnt, too. Damn their orn'ry hides!"

Austin spoke up: "That's jest one of th' matters that I've been thinkin' on 'n that consarns yer safety 'n that of yer neighbors. Let me show ye some designs fer protection of yer homes."

The men looked over some sketches and agreed they would quickly make such changes to their cabins' designs. Austin next turned to discussing the arrangements of which Randolph Foster had contributed such a major part, back around 1822 when they began receiving the colonists. Austin had faithfully followed the terms and conditions as set forth in his land grant charter with Mexico; and, with Randolph's considerable land-surveying skills, set about assigning the various sites, as determined by lots drawn by his colonists.

Austin mused: "Ye know, them settlers was sorely anxious t' break ground fer their cabins, t'weren't they?" "That they were, Stephen, that they were," responded Randolph. "'N t'were it not of great advantage t' ye, as well? Seems as I recall, th' fees due ye would not be forthcomin' til them souls had a right smart beginnin' t' their homesteads."

"That be of a fact, Randolph," Austin replied. "That purely be th' truth," he continued. "An' thinkin' back on them days, my friends, I'm considerable of mind that had I put forth a bit more encouragements, why, no tellin' how many settlers might e'en now be hereabouts. I'm a' thinkin' there could'a been thousands of families, thousands, mind ye, 'n not jest them ole' three hundred."

Isaac spoke: "That purely may be so, Stephen, but it's a great task ye've undertaken, an' a great matter what's been done fer th' folks, 'n not jest us Fosters but t' others, as well. Ye've done a right proud thing, helpin' us git some good lands." Truly, John Foster, Sr. and his sons, Randolph and Isaac Foster, had received favorable locations for their homesteads due in no small part to the roles Randolph had played back in 1821 as Austin had begun preparations to settle Texas.

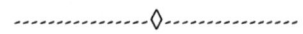

The several Foster homestead sites were situated in what is now Fort Bend County, Waller County, and Matagorda County. These sites at the time encompassed more than 20,000 acres of prime, fertile Texas farming land.

Located along both the Brazos and Colorado Rivers, these were indeed very fertile lands, lands not only for farming and growing of crops but also for herds of livestock to graze upon. When the Fosters first came to Texas, grass grew to their knees and grew wild and tall and in great abundance. The Fosters rolled up their sleeves and set about developing their lands. Cabins and barns were to be constructed and some temporary fencing to hold in what few head of livestock they had brought with them from Mississippi.

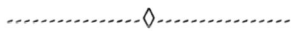

The major difficulty facing the Foster families initially was the actual locations of their homesteads in relation to one another. In more modern times, these distances of just a few miles—perhaps no more than 10 miles from Randolph's land to his father's and some 35 miles to Isaac Foster's site—may seem inconsequential. But in frontier Texas days, marauding bands of Indians made these distances very much a consequence. Apaches from the desert regions of Mexico, as well as from Texas' Davis Mountain wilderness areas, would swoop in for their raids upon settlements in the southwestern reaches; these raids often resulted in fatalities among the settlers, as the Apache could be brutally savage toward the white man. Occasional forays by Mexican bandidos were all too often the cause of concern although the bandidos tended to be more of a nuisance. All of these paled in comparison to what the Comanches brought in their raids upon the settlements. This tribe was truly the devil of the plains, torturing and killing with a ruthlessness not found with any other tribe. The cruelty and savagery of the Comanches was matched only by their bravery; they were easily the most feared and most fierce warriors throughout the southwest. Even the Apaches stayed clear of them.

Understanding this, the Fosters had wisely set up their homes near one another and made this decision soon after completing the cabin of their father, John Foster, Sr. Randolph Foster stood up and moved his chair as he spoke: "I'm of th' opinion we've little choice in this matter. These Injun raids have set our course fer us, 'n we'd best keep our wits close at hand. I propose we build our next cabin, which me 'n Isaac will share, over yonder in that clearin' near th' creek."

John Foster cleared his throat and spoke: "That seems a right smart thing t' do; then when these raids have settled some, well, mebbe we'd best start on you lads' tracts 'n git yer cabins done up proper. But first, reckon as we'd best tend to th' gun ports on this cabin 'n git 'em set in 'n all. Mebbe shore up th' doors, too; if the' Injuns come, we'd best not make things any th' easier fer them."

Isaac stood near his father as he said: "What of our cattle? I'm of a mind as how we'd best be puttin' our fencing' betwixt our cabins; that ways, we kin all keep an eye on 'em better. Least ways, mebbe keep'em out o' the' savages' hands, y' know."

They all agreed and spent the next hour or so going over their plans for their homesteads. After reinforcing John's cabin, they devised a system of warning signals in case of Indian attacks. Their plans were well thought out, and by building temporary cabins and such, would well serve their needs of mutual protection for all their families. The Fosters spent most of 1824 and well into 1825 clearing land and putting up their buildings.

Many of the other colonists did likewise, as they initially set up their cabins in close proximity to each other. A few of the settlements even went so far as to construct a type of community "fort," in which a centrally-located structure was erected for the common defense of the nearby inhabitants. Constructed of heavy timbers, these forts were equipped with several gun ports, and well-stocked with extra muskets, gunpowder, and a parcel of food rations. For the most part, these resourceful pioneers were able to fend off these raids and generally suffered few casualties. By the end of 1826 the settlements were all shaping up well, and Indian troubles seemed less and less.

Charles B. Packard

But their real troubles lay elsewhere; having just recently gained her independence from Spain, Mexico with all her political turmoil would eventually present the Texas colonists with the greater challenges and most assuredly, the gravest danger. . . .

Late in 1823 Austin had established his colony's government seat along the Brazos River in a new town given the name of San Felipe de Austin. And by 1828, the Mexican government had established the four municipalities from which they would govern their Texas "state." These four were located at San Antonio de Bexar, the missions of Goliad and Nacogdoches, and Austin's own San Felipe de Austin. These governing municipalities encompassed, for the most part, the geographical boundaries of what was then the entire territory of frontier Texas. This area today would approximate perhaps one-fourth of modern-day Texas. (Gone to Texas, Randolph B. Campbell, 2003.)

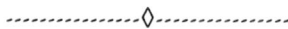

Randolph and a good friend and neighbor, Silas Morton, were riding back from the trading post near Fort Bend and were enjoying the warm sunshine on this nice spring day March 1827. "Ya' know, Silas," Randolph began, "I've a bit o' concern whut th' men said back thar 'bout th' fightin' 'n all."

"Be speakin' o' th' scrapes up Naco'doches way, Randolph?" Silas asked. "'Cause iffen ya' are, well—I've a consarn er two, meself. Seems th' Mex'cans got ther hands on ever'thing more er less in all th' colonies here 'bouts. Jes' don't seem right."

"Thet may be, Silas, but I'm thinkin' more of the matter how sum o' our own settlers jest seem ready t' square off purt' near over ever' bit o' tussle whut rears up. They jest seem t' be spoilin' fer a fight, ya' know?"

"Well, Randolph—ya' members as how last year when we split off'n Coahuila, 'n how they's got, whut, eight er more represent'tives to th' gov'ment house, 'n we's got but one?"

"Yep, I do—'n I reckon as how it got lots o' folks riled a bit, but. . . ."

"But what I'm sayin', Randolph, is thet it jest don't set right, seein' how th' Mex'cans seems t' have one way fer theirselves 'n 'nother fer us settlers."

They rode on a ways, both men quiet for awhile as both chewed on their thoughts and what each had just said.

"Ya' takes slavery, Randolph," Silas opened up again. "Mex'co don't want us havin' them slaves, 'n thet's fine iffen they don't want enny, but they dang well knowed we came here t' Texas with'em, 'n they sure t' hell never said nothin' 'bout them then, now did they?"

"No, yer right, Silas." Randolph and Silas didn't always see eye to eye on everything, but Randolph knew that his friend, while sometimes downright cantankerous, was most times more right than wrong.

"Ya know whut I think, Silas? Sometimes I think us 'n the Mex'cans jest pure don't like one 'nother."

"I 'spects yer right, Randolph, 'n mebbe I'm a'choppin' 'n ther ain't no chips a flyin'. Anyways, I've said my piece, so I'm a'lettin' it be. Th' Mex'cans ain't goin' t' change, 'n I dang shur ain't neither." Not much else was said, and they reached the Fosters' homes shortly after noon. Randolph and Silas set about unloading most of the supplies and provisions they'd obtained at the post. After a few minutes, Randolph's stepmother, Mary, came out to help.

"I heard ya' pull in, Randolph," Mary Foster said. "Here, let me help you with these." They finished unloading the Fosters' provisions, and with a handshake and friendly wave, said goodbye to Silas.

The next few years found quite a few changes taking place in Austin's colony. For one thing, more and more settlers were coming in, and a few new settlements sprung up as these newcomers settled in. And as some wanted more security for their young families, many of the older towns and settlements found their numbers growing, as well. For another, the Fosters were expanding, too, as John Foster and his sons spent a lot more time down south, helping Isaac develop some of his acreage on the bayou lands along the Colorado River. John Foster helped his sons considerably with the clearing of lands and putting up Isaac's buildings and cabin. He helped, that is, as much as he could, taking into consideration that John was moving towards 73 years of age. Not that John couldn't still do a lot of the physical labor which was required—it was more of the case of Randolph and Isaac not letting him do much of the labor.

Much of the enjoyment John Foster derived from these times spent with his sons was in the trip itself. Whether he and his sons were riding south at the crack of dawn or heading back home after long hours spent in labor—most of which John watched from the shade of a huge live oak tree—he always found pleasure in their many hours of conversation along the trail. So far, 1829 had been a good year; and 1830 would have been good, too, had it not been for the cattle drive....

Cattle drives in frontier Texas had not yet become a major part of commerce, but a few drives would occur from time to time, mostly for financial gain and, occasionally, out of necessity. Some remote Texas settlements and military garrisons, in particular, would find themselves in need of beef cattle to restock their food supplies.

Word had reached Austin's first colony that just such a need had arisen. Saddling his horse, Austin set his trail south for John Foster's place. Arriving late that afternoon, he rapped on the door with his cane and called out: "Mr. Foster, sir, it is Stephen Austin and I've a matter to discuss."

John unlatched the catch, slid back the bar and opened the door to welcome his friend. "Come in, Stephen, come in. What brings ye this way?"

Stephen removed his hat, dusted off his coat, and strode into the cabin. Lowering his head as he crossed the threshold, he remarked: "Well, now, Mr. Foster, I see ye have changed yer door frame to a size as I'd suggested. Havin' a bit smaller openin' should make fer a bit more difficulty fer Injuns to break inta', don't ye think?"

John hung Austin's topcoat on a peg and replied: "That I do, Stephen— yep, I surely do; but ye've not come all this way to inquire of my doorway, now have ye?"

"No, indeed I have not. What I have come fer is a matter of beef cattle, Mr. Foster."

"Sit down, Stephen, 'n I'll be gittin' up some tea fer us. Then ya' kin tell me 'bout yer cattle."

Stephen Austin took the cup handed him and said to John: "Th' Mex'can garrison over t' Nuevo Laredo seems t' be low on provisions 'n need some 40 or so head o' cattle; John, do ye know o' any drovers 'n yer area?" Mary Foster brought in a plate of teacakes.

John Foster rubbed his beard and replied: "Ain't too sure of any drovers, Stephen, but I do reckon I know whar ther be 40 er so head o' beeves 'round here." Austin drew a map of where Nuevo Laredo was in Mexico's northern province of Coahuila and explained that the "Alcalde" official from San Antonio de Bexar had sent the requisition along with the best route to take. The beeves were needed as soon as practicable; and payment would be made in gold coin from the Bexar bursary.

John Foster passed the word around the colony and half dozen or so colonists responded to help drive the herd. Two of the men were John's son, Isaac, and his friend, Silas. The Fosters were able to bring 24 head of cattle with the rest coming from a couple other homesteads.

By December 1, 1829, Isaac Foster, his friend and neighbor, Silas, and five other settlers set out on the drive, pushing some 52 head of cattle. As a precaution to possibly losing a few head on the trail, they left the colony with more than the requisition called for.

The drovers had made a wise decision, for they reached the Mexican garrison early in January 1830 with 43 head of cattle. Indians had made off with a few head, and the others had simply wandered off. Cattle drives were seldom begun in the dead of winter, but the drovers figured the southwestern reaches of Texas shouldn't present much of a problem with severe winter weather.

With this in mind, they had decided to make the drive, figuring little more than a month to get the cattle to the garrison. Nuevo Laredo was roughly 300 miles from the Foster homesite; even allowing for a number of rivers they would need to cross, the trip across west Texas and back would take about a month and a half, maybe even a bit more.

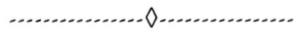

The men headed back home on January 11, 1830. Isaac had the delivery voucher tucked safely in his saddlebags and not having a herd to slow them down figured they ought to arrive home late that month.

So far, everything had gone fairly well. On their westward journey and for much of their return, the weather hadn't been too bad. The drovers had encountered a few wintry days, and some occasional snow flurries had briefly caused them a bit of apprehension. The riders knew only too well that the northern reaches of Mexico could at times turn brutal as winter storms would, on occasion, sweep in from the Rockies and sometimes even into southwest Texas.

In Texas, these winter storms were called "blue northers" and for good reason as they could hit with little warning. The "blue" well described the condition in which once-living things were found following the storm's deadly visit.

One hit Isaac Foster and the settlers riding with him less than a week's ride from home. The men were roughly halfway between the settlements at San Antonio and Goliad, in what then were fairly desolate plains. Late that afternoon, the dark skies turned even darker.

The storm came roaring across the west Texas plains, and temperatures plummeted to well below freezing. The cold, driving rains turned into sleet, and then a bitterly-cold snowstorm ripped into them. "Git yer saddle blankets wrapped 'round ya' 'n use yer rain slicks to wrap ever'thing up in," Isaac yelled to the men. These actions helped a bit—only a little, considering they were all still damp from fording the Guadalupe River but a couple hours earlier. Their plight could not have been much worse; Isaac knew the men had to get to shelter, and they had to do it soon. The weather had turned bitterly cold, and a man would die in no time.

"Stay close t' one 'nother so's we don't get parted in this storm and keep talkin' to each other."

"What th' hell ya' want us t' say, Isaac?" Silas yelled above the storm.

"Whatever th' hell comes t' mind—jest say any damn thing ya' want—but jest keep on talkin'!"

A couple of the settlers started singing some kind of saloon ditty, and Isaac told them all to sing and to sing loudly. With no kind of shelter in sight, Isaac knew their best hope now was to keep riding and hope they would soon ride out of the storm. A few of them prayed that they would do so; prayer was about all they had left.

Shivering and chilled to the bone, they glimpsed ahead through the driving snow what appeared to be a cabin of some sort or were their senses merely playing fiendish tricks on them? No, it was a cabin—abandoned, but nevertheless a cabin, to provide some measure of shelter from this killing storm. Hurriedly, they dismounted and stumbled inside, leading their mounts in with them. The men wanted all the warm bodies they could muster. A few of them gathered all of the snow-covered branches and wood available and soon had a small fire blazing before them that afforded them a newfound hope.

The door was missing as well as two of the three window coverings, but there were no complaints. With a lot of luck maybe most of them would survive this ordeal. Even with the cold winds whipping about the cabin from time to time, they knew this cabin was their only chance to live through this god-awful storm.

Throughout the night and for most of the next day the storm raged with all its fury. Snow had drifted about the cabin, but they had managed to gather up a few more pieces of firewood. The band of drovers gave little thought to their hunger pangs once their meager provisions had given out. Their thoughts were solely on survival and trying to keep their horses fed. The men hoped that the handful of grasses they took turns pulling up would be enough—for these horses might yet be their best hope for survival.

Some of the men had developed wracking coughs; and several were running feverish temperature with bone-shaking chills. One of the men appeared to be worse than the rest, so Isaac took off his own saddle blanket and wrapped it around his neighbor. He moved him up closer to the fire. The neighbor looked up at Isaac and chattered, "I-isaac—keep th' th' blanket—yer shur-shur gonna nee-need it jes' as-as much!"

Isaac flung the blanket back on the man and warned him: "Keep th' damn blanket on, ya' hear? Ever' one o' us is damn shur in a bad way, but it's you what needs it th' most 'n don't ya' be argu'n with me, now!" The men were in poor shape; they all were suffering from severe exposure, and a few had developed frostbite from the frigid winter storm. By late afternoon of January 21, 1830, the sun had burst through. The storm was over.

Still weak from their ordeal, the men arrived back home three days later. Though a few would have health problems for years to come, all would survive—except for Isaac. Having never fully recovered from exposure, Isaac Guilford Foster passed away on January 25, 1830. He died in his father's cabin, and the Foster family buried Isaac there on the family homestead. John Foster, Sr. grieved over his son's grave.

Once he learned of his brother's death, Moses A. Foster came to Texas and made one simple request of his family—when his time came, he wanted to be laid to rest next to his brother, Isaac. . . .

Time heals all wounds—just not immediately when it's most desperately needed. . . .

For the next several months the Fosters grieved the loss of Isaac Guilford Foster and especially did his father and his younger brother, Moses Foster. John Foster sadly recalled the hours spent with Isaac and Randolph as the three of them journeyed down to Isaac's homesite to do construction work, land-clearing, and things such as that. He would be missed.

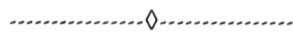

This story of an ancestor "freezing to death on horseback" was told a number of times, not only by our Mother, Ruby Inez Foster Packard, but also by her sister, and my aunt, Audrey Ellen Foster Deavers. They never knew the name of this ancestor, nor do I. But I certainly believe it may have happened.

I chose Isaac Foster due to the fact that Foster family records indicate that "there is no evidence to suggest that Isaac's death resulted from anything other than an accident." (John Foster and Randolph Foster, Gordon Leigh Briscoe, 2003.)

Coincidentally, our Mother used to sing a rather mournful little cowboy tune as I was growing up, and the lyrics had a hauntingly, familiar bearing to this legend of a great-great-ancestor freezing to death. Here's the old tune; judge for yourselves:

Ol' Limpy

"There's an empty bunk, in th' bunkhouse tonight,
There's a pinto with head hangin' low.
His spurs and his chaps, they hang on th' wall,
Limpy's gone, where th' good cowboys go.

He was ridin' the' range, last Saturday night,
When a norther started to blow.
With his head on his chest, headin' in from th' west,
He was stopped, by a voice soft 'n low.

A crazy young calf, had strayed from its maw,
And was lost in th' snow and th' storm.
Limpy stopped just awhile, then headed on home,
With th' maverick held safe in his arms.

He arrived at th' bunkhouse, early next morn,
And put th' li'l maverick to bed.
Limpy fell in his bunk, unable to move,
That mornin' poor Limpy was dead.

There's a place for all good cowboys,
A place where th' good cowboys go.
And someday he'll ride, ol' Pinto again,
On that range, far off that I know."

---◊---

On April 6, 1830, the Mexican Congress, under orders from President Bustamante, enacted a law which would place oppressive hardships upon the

Texas colonists. Of all its provisions, those posing the greatest threat to the Texians' way of life were the ones outlawing slavery and those imposing duties on all goods shipped into and out of the colonies of Texas. The colonists were incensed.

The rules had now been changed; provisions in the laws of Mexico which initially welcomed the settlers to Texas in 1822-1824 now had the effect of a backhanded slap in the face. The rift between the colonists and Mexico now grew even wider with each side firmly entrenched in their positions. There seemed little hope for compromise, and armed conflict appeared to be inevitable.

John Foster and his sons wanted little more than simply to live in peace. The Fosters had spent long months in the clearing of their lands and planting crops. Raising families took up a lot of time.

John leaned his shovel against the fence and wiping his sleeve across his brow, remarked to his two sons: "Been a spell since there's been sight of Injuns around, ya know? Might be soon as how we kin finish work on yer place, Randolph. 'N mebbe next year yourn as well, Moses. . . course, we've a bit o' a ways to go down t' yer bayou lands. Gonna' tak us a mite longer."

"Yep, it will fer a fact; me 'n Randolph figgers its nigh on'ta 30 'er so mile down ther, as th' crow flies. More iffen we take th' road 'n th' backtrails." Moses spoke knowledgeably of his father's lands, well aware that Randolph and his father—as well as Isaac, when he had been alive— knew only too well of the details of the bayou lands of Isaac's along the Colorado.

John Foster, as sole heir to Isaac's land, had deeded some of it to Moses, seeing as how it needed to be worked; and his advancing years placed a bit of a handicap on just how much he could still do. Besides, he knew Moses was the right one to take over some of Isaac's lands. Moses and Isaac had always been close.

Randolph straightened up from his chore and stretching his arms behind him said, "Don't see as how there'd be much trouble finishin' up th' work down thar oe'r th' next year, Moses; like Paw sez, ain't been much sign o' Injuns lately."

Looking around his father's homestead, at all of the sheds they'd erected, Randolph continued: "Seems good t' me, what with all that's been grown on yer lands, Paw—th' crops, our herds, 'n even th' cotton seems t' take to th' soil here."

Randolph paused to drink some water from the leather skin hanging from the fencepost, then commented: "Johnson 'n some o'th'settlers over t' other side o' the' Brazos have planted sugarcane. Seems to me it's doing' right well; mebbe next year we oughta look t' plantin' some ourselves."

John looked about him as though taking inventory of all that Randolph had mentioned and smiled as he spoke: "All thet ye've both spoke on is true 'n all; it's a good start what we've done here with our crops 'n all th' other things what's been bilt."

John turned his gaze toward his sons and fixed them with a piercing look as he spoke: "But yer both shufflin' about th' edges o' whuts bin on yer minds fer a spell, now; I know, 'cause its sorely bin on mine. Ther's a fight a'comin' with Mexico, 'n ye'd best be of a mind wher' ye stand."

"I'm a'standin' with my family—thet's wher' I be standin', 'n I be damned iffen them fancy Mex'cans will take what's our'n. A fight ther' wantin'; it's a fight they'll be gittin'!" These last words Moses spat out as a scowl took charge over his face.

Randolph smiled in the direction of his brother, Moses, thinking how much like Isaac he was. Shoot, they oughta' be, he thought; from th' time they was young'uns, they was like two peas-in-a-pod—twins, almost.

Turning toward his father and speaking in a firm and deliberate tone, he said: "Moses is right, Paw. We've put a right fair bit o' sweat 'n labor inta our lands, 'n seein' as how our family stood up ta' th' British, well—sure'n hell I cain't see us a'turnin' tail now; reckon as how we'll fight, iffen it come t' thet."

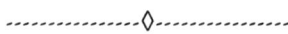

An uneasy truce had settled over Texas despite several armed conflicts that had popped up between 1830 and 1832. For the most part these were more on the order of disagreements and disturbances that were resolved without bloodshed.

Charles B. Packard

Until June 1832....

Armed confrontation occurred at the mouth of the Brazos River which resulted in many casualties, including the deaths of 10 Texans and 5 Mexicans; these were the first known fatalities as Texas moved ever closer to war with Mexico.

Then, in late summer of 1832, another battle took place at the municipality in Nacogdoches. Lasting several days, the Battle of Nacogdoches ended with the surrender of the Mexican garrison. This time 4 Texas settlers were killed and 47 of the Mexican soldiers. With this victory, the Texas volunteers had cleared all Mexican military from Texas with the exception of the garrisons at Goliad and San Antonio de Bexar; these two remained potent forces to reckon with.

And in what seemed merely an ongoing drama, the political and social unrest throughout Mexico was little more than "business as usual." This was particularly true of the military, where coups in Mexico City resulted in leadership changes that occurred with frustrating regularity. And it was equally frustrating for Mexico as well as for the Texas settlements. (Gone to Texas, Randolph B. Campbell, 2003.)

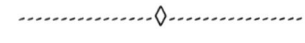

Just such a coup in 1832 resulted in the removal of President Bustamante. His replacement was the ambitious and arrogant young career officer, General Antonio Lopez de Santa Anna. This military revolt afforded the Texans the opportunity to mask their recent clashes with Federalist troops behind the rather questionable support for the new Mexican leader and his brand of government. This subterfuge worked for awhile even though hostilities and resentments between the two factions stayed at a constant simmer. Change was still in the air, and it lacked the feel of peaceful coexistence.

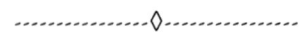

November 17, 1835, was a mild, pleasant fall day; Stephen Austin and a number of the settlers of his first colony decided to hold a meeting so they could "clear th' air" of some things that were troubling many throughout Texas. Most of the Fosters were there, along with the Johnsons from up north, and Randolph's good friend, Silas Morton. Others came, too.

As the settlers milled about the room in the trading post, John Foster stood up near the woodstove in front of the racks of pans and kettles and spoke: "Stephen, d'ye mind iffen I speak a few words?"

Austin smiled at his friend and replied: "Not a'tall, Mr. Foster. Please do." Austin was actually quite pleased to have John Foster address the meeting; most all of the settlers considered him the "patriarch" of Austin's original colony and respected him greatly.

John Foster walked slowly to the front of the group and greeted them warmly: "It's good seein' all of ye again; seems me 'n my boys bin a mite busy th' last year er so, whut with clearin' our lands 'n erectin' our buildin's. I thank ye fer takin' time fer this import'nt meetin' with our Mr. Austin."

John looked around the room and continued: "This year's seen a right angry bit o' bizness from our hosts, th' Mex'can government. . . John paused, as several hoots and rude noises greeted his mention of Mexico.

He continued: "Yes, 'n I understand how ye feel; I'm a bit frustrated with our southern neighbors, myself. But whut ye've got to decide on is th' matter of our takin' a stand, er not, on th' matter of independence from Mexico. An' th' most import'nt issue of someday joinin' up with the United States governm'nt."

John paused and dipped the hollow gourd into the rain barrel for a drink of water. Continuing, he said: "Them's whut I see as bein' yer most import'nt chores on th' table afore ye. 'N afore I forgit, we are most oblig'd to our Stephen Austin fer all th' hardwork 'n negotia'shuns he's labored on fer all our great benefit." A hearty round of applause and cheers directed toward Austin followed John Foster's comments; Austin seemed embarrassed yet obviously quite pleased. John cleared his throat and added: "As I recall, th' convention meetin' back coupl'a years ago, I believe in 1833, brought some angry words 'n threats o' war agin Mexico. 'N th' way I see things a'movin', thet sure may come t' be. But regard'less how we git our freedom from Mexico, yer goin' t' have some hard choices ye've got'ta make as t' leaders 'n repersenta'tives whut will go t' fight fer ye'. I've been talkin' as t' how ye've gotta do this 'n ye've gotta do that. Th' reason is. . .well, it ain't easy to spit it out, but jest t' say it; I'm gonna be headin' back t' my lands and propities back in Mississippi." This revelation brought some groans and pleas to stay, but John shook his head and raised his hands for quiet. "I'm mighty honored t' have friend's like ye are, but me 'n my sons have bin all 'round th' matter, 'n this is whut we think's best. I kin assure ye' thet iffen I thought I could help in a fight, iffen it comes t' thet, I'd shore stay. But I reckon as how we all know thet I'd mos' likely be more a li'bility than I'd be a asset." This brought a polite round of laughter for most all present knew that John Foster, Sr. was edging up on 79 years of age—time for the old warrior to hang it up.

John smiled at his self-effacing humor and spoke up once more: "Wal, reckon ye've heared me talk more t' night than in th' 'leven er so years whut I've bin in Texas." John paused, then turned toward Austin: "Stephen, I've stood here long 'nuff; why'nt ye come 'n see iffen ye kin salvage this meet'in?" John walked away to hearty and grateful applause, and Stephen Austin wisely picked up on John Foster's exit line. "Mr. Foster," Austin said, "ye've stood here t'night t' speak whut's on yer heart, an' I'm of th' opinion thet all here know thet ye've also stood fer what's right and decent. Yer a mighty fine gentle'man, Mr. Foster, 'n I propose thet now we all stand to give ye the tribute whut yer owed."

The applause this time was thunderous in the small room. John Foster, Sr. was visibly moved by the honor and was inundated by well-wishers and grateful neighbors. He had contributed greatly to the colony.

Within two months John Foster, Sr. left Texas. . . .

------------◊------------

Hostilities flared throughout Texas in 1835 as the aroused settlers moved ever closer to war with Mexico. There were skirmishes that summer at Anahuac and a siege at San Antonio in November. With the surrender of the Mexican garrison at San Antonio de Bexar in early December, the Texas colonists no longer believed a peaceful agreement could be reached. The Texans wanted their independence from Mexico and were more than willing to fight for it. The Texas Army grew as more and more settlers and newly-arrived volunteers came onboard.

On December 25, 1835, Foster joined 27 other Texians in signing the Columbia Resolutions, which urged a declaration of ". . .the total and absolute independence of Texas. . . . " (John Foster 1757-1837 and Randolph Foster 1798-1878, Gordon Leigh Briscoe, Revised 2003.)

In 1820 Mexico had eagerly welcomed new settlers to their "state" of Texas; now, 15 years later, they were about to go to war. On both sides, hundreds and hundreds would lose their lives. The reasons for going to war were so many and so varied it would seem impossible to single out just one. But if pressed, one would certainly be the actions of General Santa Anna. This arrogant, ambitious little dictator (often called the Napoleon of the West) took on the self-appointed role as Supreme Dictator over all of Mexico and in the process cancelled out all that which had earlier brought the settlers and colonists to Texas.

Santa Anna would soon reap what was sown. . . .

◊

By the start of 1836 the best that could be said of the "army" of Texians was that organized confusion reigned alongside an ill-advised feeling of over-confidence.

Things began to rapidly deteriorate for this band of settlers, volunteers, and untrained adventure-seekers, beginning late in January 1836. General Sam Houston was desperately attempting to organize and train his regulars into some semblance of disciplined fighting soldiers while Stephen Austin was battling apathetic and chaotic government members in his attempts at forming an effective and cohesive governing body. And for a long while, both men were valiantly waging an uphill battle. A number of Texas settlers spent long hours over the next several weeks carrying messages and various supplies of ammunitions between their forces at Goliad and San Patricio; Moses Foster and in particular Randolph Foster were very actively involved in helping out in these desperate times.

Randolph Foster and his friend, Silas Morton, were carrying supplies from San Felipe to the troops at Gonzales. The two colonists were planning to set up camp for the night when they came upon some men who were just finishing the branches and poles for their camp's lean-to.

Quickly recognizing neither party posed any danger, the men put away their muskets and pistols.

"Hello, th' camp," Randolph called out. "Iffen ye are agree'ble, we'd be much obliged t' join ye."

"Come on in," a voice called out from the camp.

"Come in, 'n set a spell. Spects it's a mite warmer 'round air fire then whar ye be sittin'."

Randolph and Silas dismounted and tied up the reins to the saplings where the other horses were tied and hobbled. They shook hands with the men and joined them around the fire.

"We ain't got enny tea but yer welcome t' share air water 'n some o' th' venison 'n rabbit what's on th' spit." It was th' same voice Silas and Randolph heard when they had ridden in earlier.

"We be grateful to ye," Randolph acknowledged, "'n we have a bit o' jerky whut we'd be pleased t' contribute." The men passed around the food and water and sat quietly for a spell.

The camp voice spoke again. "Whar might ye be headin' fer?" he asked politely.

Randolph replied: "Me 'n Silas heer be headin' t' Gonzales with some provisions fer Col. Moore 'n his men. 'N whar ye 'n yer men goin' ta'?"

The camp voice replied: "We're a'goin' t' Gonzales, as well, but then we be headin' on t' San Antone ta' jine up with th' fellers be at th' Alamo."

"Thet would be Colonel Travis 'n Colonel Bowie, I reckon, as they bein' in charge o' th' men thar," Randolph responded. "So ye vol'unteers helpin' out; 'n whar might ye be from?"

"Cletus o'er thar—th' one whut's red-haired—he be from Kentucky; rest o' us be Tennessean's," the camp voice again answered. Randolph Foster introduced himself and Silas, and the camp voice did the same. As he finished, he held out his hand to Randolph and said: "'N I be Crockett, David Crockett. Reckon as we be ridin' 'longside ye t'morrow mornin', iffen ye don't mind."

After several days Randolph Foster and Silas Morton said goodbye to Crockett and his men and wished them safe journey as the Tennessee volunteers headed on west toward the Alamo. Crockett and his men that morning helped Randolph and Silas load up more provisions and munitions bound for Fannin's Army at Goliad. The date was the fourth of February 1836.

A fortnight later, General Santa Anna and his army of several thousand soldiers crossed the Rio Grande heading for San Antonio de Bexar. Santa Anna had but one aim—to teach the insurgents a lesson....

General Santa Anna's army of more than 1,500 Mexican soldiers stormed the Alamo early the morning of March 6, 1836. The defenders of the Alamo numbered no more than 183 men; of these, Colonel Travis and Colonel Bowie had some 150, maybe 160 experienced fighters and combatants to face Santa Anna. There were a few from Missouri, Kentucky, along with a dozen or so men with David Crockett—his Tennessee Volunteers. The rest were mostly Texians, and a number of Tejanos, those of Mexican descent who considered themselves "Norte Americanos."

Word of the fall of the Alamo reached General Sam Houston toward the middle of March 1836. The survivors—a few women and children—related to the folks at Gonzales what had taken place just a week earlier at the Alamo. "It were horrible, oh dear Lord, it were so cruel 'n horrible," one of the women cried. "They jest slaughter'd 'n butcher'd th' men, jest hack'd 'em ta' pieces." Some of the womenfolk tried to give comfort to the survivors but they could tell the surviving women and children were in shock and nearly hysterical. A captain in Ed Burleson's small army tried to pry more information from the terrified woman but soon gave up to wait for a more opportune time to continue his questioning. The captain pulled a few of the men to one side and instructed them: "Saddle up 'n ride ta' General Houston. Let 'im know that Colonel Travis 'n th' Alamo has fallen." He paused, deep in thought, and continued: "He oughta' still be at Wash'nton-on-th'-Brazos; iffen not, he mebbe at San Felipe. But find 'im 'n let 'im know whut's happn'd 'n hurry!" (The two men left, and the next day encountered General Houston and that army on their way to Gonzales.)

The captain tried questioning the woman that evening and was able to piece together the tale he related to General Sam Houston the next day.

"Th' woman sez th' fight 'n started March 5th er 6th, she weren't too clear. Anyways, she 'members th' men sayin' th' Mex'cans had raised a red flag, sayin' it meant 'no quarter,' no surrendering, fight ta' th' death. Th' Mex'cans kilt all th' men—Colonel Travis 'n Colonel Bowie 'n Crockett 'n his men—all were shot 'n stabbed; some were hacked with bayo'nets 'n sabers, too. She said sum'thin' 'bout all th' bodies were stacked up 'n burnt. That's 'bout all I got 'fore she jest turn'd all quiet 'n her eyes turn'd glassy-like. Gen'rul Houst'n, I ain't never seen one like that. It were spooky, like."

Sam Houston gently laid his hand on the captain's shoulder and spoke quietly: "Thank you, son; you've done a good job. If ye'd be so kind, help th' women 'n children to git settled 'n all. Ask th' other womenfolk 'roun' here to help. They shure need all th' comfortin' 'n encourag'mint what we kin' give 'em." Houston turned away so the young captain wouldn't see the grim, discouraged look on his face. The news he had just received was possibly the most devastating he had received to date and certainly the worst in the short time he had been Commanding General of the Texas Army.

Houston didn't see how it could get much worse.

---------------◊---------------

Some weeks later, a scout caught up with General Houston to bring more bad news. Riding into camp the scout was sent straight to Houston's tent.

"Gene'rul, I've brung word 'bout th' boys whut were with Colonel Johnson down San Patricio way. Word is we lost near 50 er so men; not too many got away, sir. Sorry t' bring th' bad news, Gen'rul."

Houston wiped his hand across his face, wondering how much more bad news would ride his way. He looked up at the scout and asked: "When did this take place—did they say?"

Jest a'fore th' Alamo, sir; reckon 'round th' end o' Feb'wery 'r fust o' March."

"What 'bout Colonel Fannin? Wuz thar enny word 'bout him 'n his men? Enny word o' them?"

"Nossir. Did'n' hear 'nuthin' 'bout them, gen'rul." Houston thanked the scout and told him to go to the mess tent and get something to eat. Houston then called some of his officers together as they discussed their next move. By now, Houston's 400 or so men had nearly doubled with more volunteers and settlers drifting in all the time. He knew they still weren't enough to take on Santa Anna's some 3,000 or 4,000 strong Mexican Army which he believed to be heading his way.

What General Sam Houston would later learn was that Santa Anna had split up his armies as the Mexicans were determined to drive the Anglos out of Texas entirely. That is, they would scatter those who escaped from the slaughter the Mexicans intended to once again bring about.

Earlier, in his obsession to obliterate everything and everyone at the Alamo, Santa Anna had lost more than 600 of his best fighting soldiers to the band of Texans at the Alamo. Santa Anna achieved his victory but at a price that would soon cost him dearly. . . .

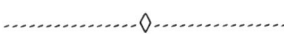

By early April Houston's spirits had improved somewhat, as more and more volunteers and settlers joined up with his army. Randolph, John, Jr., and Moses Foster were among those who joined Houston's forces at their camp along the Brazos. Even the terrible news that most all of Fannin's some 400 men had been killed, did not discourage Houston this time. His army was slowly taking to the discipline and training Houston knew would be crucial if they were to have any success against a much larger Mexican force. The news that Fannin's men had been unarmed when the Mexicans slaughtered and again stacked and burned the bodies only served to enrage General Houston and his men! The Texans were now steeled into a fighting force hell-bent on vengeance for the cruelty Santa Anna had imposed upon their comrades. If General Sam Houston had a problem then, it would have been in holding his army back; Houston knew he could not let them strikeout blindly. This Texas Army needed a more reasonable chance at success.

That presented itself soon enough. Word reached Houston that there was a Mexican Army of some 1,000 or so men south of them around Harrisburg. Houston had his officers seek out one of their best scouts: "Git me sum'one what knows the woods 'n how to recon'noytr' 'n git 'im here quick-like."

"Gen'rul Houston, this here's Foster, Randolph Foster, he's whut hepped Austin scout out th' fust colo'ny, 'n all." It hadn't taken a lot of time for Houston's men to know who was probably the best scout present—maybe the best in all of Texas.

Houston quickly spelled out what he wanted; and soon Randolph and his neighbor, Silas Morton, were on their way south. The two colonists were to be back in "four er five days," Houston had told'em. "So's we kin best know when 'n whar t' set up fer a fight. God-speed t' ya, Foster, 'n hurry back alive!"

Some hard riding brought Foster and Morton back in five days with news of the Mexican Army. Apparently, this Mexican Army was pursuing the leaders of the government down near the San Jacinto Bay, and Houston reasoned they would soon be heading north to come after him.

Randolph Foster had more good news. "Gen'rul Houston, th' folks at Harrisburg told us some cannons was on its way up t' ya. Seems th' folk over Ohio way sent ya' a couple fer our fight agin th' Mex'cans."

On April 21, 1836 General Sam Houston and his Texas Army caught the larger Mexican Army almost completely by surprise. At the Battle of San Jacinto, Houston's Army of some 900 Texans devastated more than 1,300 Mexican soldiers. The Mexican Army lost more than 600 dead with some 730 captured by the Texian Army. Texas lost only 9 men.

April 22, 1836, brought Houston more good news. A prisoner captured the day before proved to be Santa Anna, himself. Enraged, the Texans wanted to "kill 'im on th' spot." But Houston quickly saw the wisdom of keeping Santa Anna alive and forced him to sign documents of surrender. As President of Mexico, Santa Anna's signature guaranteed Texas' independence. The Republic of Texas had her freedom from Mexico! (Gone to Texas, Randolph B. Campbell, 2003.)

---------------◊-----------------

Guarantees, even those written and signed, are often not worth the paper on which they are written; nor, it seems are some words of honor.

So it was for the new Republic of Texas, as first Mexico and then the United States backed off on written and implied promises of support and recognition. No sooner had Santa Anna returned to Mexico following his trouncing by Houston than he and his Mexican government decided to simply ignore Santa Anna's promise of freedom for The Republic of Texas. And in short order, the good intentions of the United States government soon became "a more convenient and wise" decision to delay the hoped for annexation of Texas. The next 10 years would prove to be tumultuous ones in Texas' history. . . .

In spite of these setbacks brought on by the other two nations, Texas managed to move forward socially as well as administratively. The population of Texas boomed as ever-increasing numbers of settlers poured into her lands. The governing body successfully steered Texas toward the election of their first president, General Sam Houston; and over the next several years, Texas would overcome apathy, rejection, internal squabbles, and financial difficulties. In presenting themselves finally as a worthy candidate for statehood, the wheels of government of the United States as well as The Republic of Texas moved slowly but inexorably toward annexation. Finally on December 29, 1845, President James K. Polk signed the Texas Admission Act. Texas became the 28th state admitted to the Union.

---------------◊-----------------

March and April of 1836 had been historic months for the Mexican "state" of Texas with a great deal of action packed into those scant 60 days: early March found the delegates at Washington-on-the-Brazos penning their Declaration of Independence and writing the new Republic's first constitution;

Sam Houston was made commander-in-chief of the entire Texas Army; the interim government voted in their President, David Burnet, and Vice-President, Lorenzo de Zavala; the Alamo fell to Santa Anna's Mexican Army on March 6 while most of Fannin's Army of 400 men was likewise massacred on March 27. By the end of March, the Mexican armies had driven and otherwise intimidated General Houston's Army into the region just north of Buffalo Bayou and Galveston Bay.

As the Mexican Army was soon to discover, the month of April found Santa Anna right where General Sam Houston wanted him . . . .

. . . and on April 21, the Texas Army proved decisively that they had "remembered th' Alamo." (Gone to Texas, Randolph B. Campbell, 2003.)

---------------◊---------------

Having left Texas early in January 1836, John Foster, Sr. and some of his family traveled by boat back to Mississippi. Arriving later that month, John had sought out his son, John Foster, Jr. "John," the senior Foster had begun: "I do consider it wise fer ye t' join up with yer brothers what be homesteadin' back in Texas." The old man settled comfortably in his rocker and continued: "Thar's a fine place whut we've bilt heer, that's fer sure, 'n ye'll always have a home. But I've seen whut is a'takin' place in Texas, 'n I'm of a mind yer opper'tunities fer prosper'ty 'n land own'rship be a consid'rbl' bit better."

John, Jr. shifted his weight and leaned against one of the columns on the front porch where he was sitting. His father's words didn't bother him none; his butt was just itching. He cleared his throat and looking at his father, replied: "Thet may be, Paw, but whut 'bout th' trouble with Mexico? Pears t' me from yer letters thar be fightin' a'loomin' on th' horizon. I be mor'n willing' t' go help Randolph 'n t'others defend air lands thar but I ain't too keen on settin' Deb'rah 'n th' young'uns 'n harm's way."

"No, yer right, son. 'N I reck'n as how we oughta' be discussin on thet matter."

The Crepe Myrtle

For sometime, John Foster, Jr. and his father mulled over the options facing them and eventually decided what would be best for all concerned. The son was going to Texas.

John Foster, Jr. had not been facing an easy decision, as he considered all the many things that could go wrong. Mostly, John didn't want to be away from his wife, Deborah, nor all his young ones. His oldest, Amanda Foster, had turned 16 just a few weeks earlier and would be of considerable help to her maw in looking after the younger ones. Moses, his oldest son, was now 12; he had been named after John's youngest brother, Moses, who was with Randolph in Texas. His sons, Malcolm, age 10, and Lewis, soon to be 8, would be okay. They always seemed to get themselves into some sort of mess or the other. They were just boys; but his youngest, William M., was just going on 2, and John knew he might not get to see him grow up, should he be away in Texas for a couple of years and that would be one problem for him—not seeing his kids for quite awhile. The other problem was the kids would sorely miss their paw, as well.

Getting in the middle of a fight between Mexico and Texas didn't vex him much; his Foster family hadn't yet shied away from a fight, and John, Jr. knew he could and should help his younger brothers, Randolph and Moses. The only problem John, Jr. could see was if he got killed how it might affect his children and that worried on him some.

But John and his father, as well as his older brother, Gibeon, had agreed the family there in Mississippi would look after John, Jr.'s family while he was away. And once the trouble with Mexico was resolved—hopefully, sooner rather than later—he would return for his family and get everyone resettled in Texas.

John Foster, Jr. spent much of February getting his family life in order and making sure his two oldest, Amanda and Moses, knew what he expected of them. He took Moses aside and laid his hand upon his son's shoulder. "Son, it's a right heavy burd'n what I be layin' upon ye, havin' t' be th' man o' th' house 'n all. But yer old 'nuff now 'n I reckon on how I've seen ya' grow up inta' a right fine young man. Ye'll do well. 'N I be much obliged fer yer help th' last day er so helpin' me git my horses packed up fer my trip. Help yer maw like thet whilst I be away, 'n ever'things gonna be fine."

Moses looked up at his father and replied: "Yessir, I will, paw; 'n don't be worryin' none, me 'n Uncle Gibeon 'n Grampa will take good care o' things here. Ya' be safe, 'n say hello t' Uncle Moses 'n Uncle Ran fer me, will ya'?"

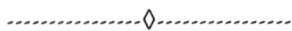

John Foster, Jr. and his pack animals boarded a boat at Natchez on February 22, 1836. A week later he went ashore at Columbia on the lower Brazos; the river was down some, keeping them from stemming the Brazos closer to Fort Bend. He met up with Randolph and Moses the next day, and they quickly caught one another up on the news. Everything was fine back home in Mississippi, John told them. "Paw, 'n Gib 'n all th' kids send ther greetin's 'n said t' tell ya' ever'thing's fine with 'em."

"Wish't we could say th' same heer," Randolph reported. "Jest got word a day er so ago thet th' Mexican Army o' ol' Santa Anna be layin' siege t' th' Alamo. Gonna be fightin' fer sure."

Over the next several weeks the Foster brothers got very little sleep, what with all the talk of war and them trying to keep firm rein over their own property. The Fosters had been more and more occupied of late with hauling munitions and supplies to some of the Texas armies scattered around south Texas. John and his younger brother, Moses, worked a few times unloading supplies from the few boats that came up the Brazos and the Colorado Rivers. Randolph was frequently called upon for special missions what with all his scouting and exploring done earlier before the colonists settled Texas; Randolph was a great asset during the fight with Mexico.

After the great victory at San Jacinto, which, at the time, had appeared to finally resolve things for Texas, life among the Foster's homesteads settled into a much more peaceful and productive routine. The Fosters had built another cabin for John and his young family, should they decide on resettling in Texas.

The Foster brothers labored long hours, getting their fields ready for spring planting. They had decided to plant some sugarcane down on some of the lands that had belonged to Isaac. Fences and buildings were slowly being repaired, considering the recent fights with Mexico had taken a toll on many of the colonists' homesteads; the Texas Army had necessarily caused quite a bit of damage, themselves.

By late June of 1836 peace and prosperity seemed to be permanent residents among the Fosters. Until the day a message found its way to Randolph's door. . .a settler from near Fort Bend had knocked on Randolph's door, calling out: "Ran, hit's me—Abe! Got uh lett'r fer ya."

Randolph opened the door, thanking Abe for bringing the letter which had been in the mail pouch from the recent boat delivery. He closed the door and sat back in his chair at their table. John, Jr. and Moses were still sipping their cups of tea as Randolph slit open the seal.

"It's from Paw; let's see whut he's got ta' say. . . ." His voice trailed off as he began reading the short note.

John noticed a pall had settled upon Randolph's countenance as the letter was slowly placed upon the table. "Randolph. . .whut's th' matter? Is thar somethin' wrong back home?" John was now quite anxious, wondering if something was wrong with one of his children.

Randolph looked up slowly at his brothers and mumbled: "It's Gib. . .he died 'bout two weeks ago."

Gibeon Gibson Foster was their oldest brother, and John Sr.'s first born back in South Carolina. He had been born when this country had declared its independence from England in 1776. He was 60 years of age.

Late in November 1836, John Foster, Jr. returned to his father's home in Mississippi and brought his family back to Texas with him. He would get to see his youngest, William M. Foster, grow up, after all. The three Foster brothers and their families celebrated that Christmas with one another, the first time they had all been together in several years. All had expressed their hopes for a happy, prosperous New Year. 1837 started out that way, as everyone seemed in good health and equally good spirits.

When word reached them that John Foster, Sr. had passed away, the surviving family members were filled with grief; their patriarch was gone. John, Sr. had died on January 26, 1837—at near 80 years of age—he had lived a long and productive life. Not many folks get the opportunity to help settle a new state. . . .

In the ensuing years, some Fosters would pass on into good memories while newborns would take their place—such is the ebb and flow of families.

In 1839 Moses A. Foster (Uncle Moses to little Moses, John, Jr.'s son) passed away, leaving a wife and a son. But around that same time, John, Jr. and his wife, Deborah, brought forth another daughter for Texas. John and Deborah named her Sarah Ann. Two more children were born to John, Jr. and Deborah Foster by 1841.

And in 1843, at age 61, John Foster, Jr. joined his ancestors. He had been a good husband and a very good father. His descendants would remember him kindly.

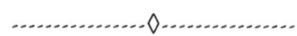

By 1861 as the Civil War was starting, Randolph Foster had managed to outlive all his brothers and his one sister and most of his half-brothers and half-sisters from John, Sr.'s second marriage as well. Randolph was now patriarch of the family.

Ever since February 25, 1850, Randolph had been legal guardian over William M. Foster, the young son of John, Jr. William M. Foster, often called William "Bill" by many of the family, was now 27 years of age. He had rallied to the Confederate cause and returned to his home state of Mississippi early in 1861 to join the Confederacy. William M. Foster was commissioned a Second Lieutenant in Company H, 31st Regiment of the Mississippi Infantry. He served the Confederacy honorably having been wounded in battle at Peachtree Creek in Georgia.

The Crepe Myrtle

When the war between the northern states and the southern states mercifully came to an end, the ex-Second Lieutenant William M. Foster decided to return to his adopted state of Texas. He had acquired a small farm just outside the Wixon Valley community north of Bryan; and soon after he returned, he met and began a courtship with a young southern belle from Louisiana by the name of Martha Ellen Darwin. Her friends called her Mattie.

On October 12, 1865, Mattie and William "Bill" Foster were married by Reverend John Neal, minister of the Gospel. "Mattie," her new bridegroom said, as he took her by the hand, "this heer's gonna be our home; mine 'n yore's 'n all th' young'uns whut we'll have one day." He paused and looking around his place, continued: "H'it ain't thet much now, Mattie, kinda small, I know; but ya' jest wait 'n see—I'm gonna make h'it inta' somethin' whut you 'n th' kids er gonna be proud of. 'N thet's a promise."

For the next few years, William "Bill" Foster proved good at his word as he worked hard to build and develop their farm and the lands they owned. William "Bill" and Mattie slowly built up their land holdings, acquiring small farm acreages from foreclosures, and land sales. By now, their initial farm acreage which totaled some 80 or so acres, had grown to more than 400 acres of good fertile farming soil and another 200 acres of forested woodlands.

With the acquisition of some 200 acres of land in Montgomery County, William "Bill" Foster now owned and controlled more than 800 acres of Texas farmland. Even though some of this land was a bit of a journey for William "Bill" to check on, he nevertheless managed to inspect these acres from time to time.

By 1868, William "Bill" Foster's acreage had grown to more than 1,350 acres, counting the 200 acres down in Montgomery County. Managing this land became a bit of a problem, so when a farmer in Montgomery County offered William "Bill" a good fiddle in exchange, he readily accepted the offer. It was a very well-made fiddle, so William "Bill" felt he had made out pretty good.

Mattie and William "Bill" Foster had begun to feel that they just weren't meant to have children. For more than three years there had been no little ones forthcoming. But that would soon change as Mattie became with child in the spring of 1869.

The day after Christmas of 1869, Ida Foster joined the household, as did Sarah Anne Foster, on June 8, 1871, and Eula Lee Foster, on March 31, 1872. In March of 1874 Reuben M. Foster broke the run of three straight daughters born to William "Bill" and Mattie Foster. The first four children had been born in Brazos County, Texas.

Their second son, John Bradson Foster, would change that as he came into this world in January 1876. John Bradson was born in Bell County, Texas; in his later years he would not exactly be considered one of Bell County's more celebrated citizens.[1]

---

[1] Author's Note: In this family legend of the infamous swap of land for a fiddle, once oil was discovered on this Conroe, Texas land in Montgomery County around the early 1900s, William "Bill" Foster's descendants came to think not too kindly of this old ancestor's "wheelin' 'n dealin'!

Chapter 9

Elbridge–A Favored Grandson

Timeline: 1868-1900

Chas Elbridge was just past 5 years of age when the family buried his little twin brother and sister. Eulalia and Fassitt Packard were born on November 27, 1867, and died only one day apart July 29 and 30 of 1868. The twins were buried in the churchyard cemetery of the family church in Centreville, Louisiana—a very nice little white Presbyterian church where all the Packard children had been christened. On the twins' headstone Charles Howard Packard had these words inscribed: "God called these babes to angels' places in Heaven."

---◊---

The Bayou Teche was a favorite "swimming hole" for young boys in Centreville. From all over St. Mary's Parish they came to cool off in this slow-moving stream and especially so in the hot days of summer. Located less than 15 miles north of the Gulf of Mexico, this southern area of Louisiana could yield some steamy, sweltering days—days that seemed custom-made for boys anxious to peel off their britches and jump headfirst, or otherwise, into any body of cooling, blue water.

The lure of the Bayou Teche in summer was too hard to resist, and Chas Elbridge Packard, still a mere boy, had yet to develop the disciplines for which he would one day be known and usually he was the first one in. Calling back to his friends, he challenged them, "Last one in's a swamp rat!" Flinging his clothes aside, he hit the water as the others were just beginning to undress.

"No fair, Elbie," one of the other boys shouted, "you were already strippin' a'fore we even reached th' bank!"

"Yeh," Andy called out, "iffen any here be a swamp rat, well, it sure be you—'n a big, ugly one, too!" With that, they all let out whoops of laughter.

The debate of who was the swamp rat ended as quickly as it had started; there was too much fun to be had a'splashin' and a'swimmin' to worry 'bout who was first. 'Sides, it'd change from day t' day, anyhows! And somedays there'd be two or three hittin' th' water darn near the same time. The bayou was a great meetin' place for Elbridge's gang.[2]

From his early years in Centreville—except for the four or five years when Captain Howard Packard and his family had lived and worked out of Rockport, Texas—Elbridge and Andy and all his gang had exulted in the pure pleasures of simply being boys. And as much as Elbridge enjoyed having fun, he found similar delight in working and otherwise lollin' 'round his Grandfather Cook's sugarcane plantation in Centreville. His grandfather owned several hundred acres of good farmland near the small downtown area, and Elbridge enjoyed helping the hands chop sugarcane. All the men, including Elbridge, would slice through the sugarcane stalks with their sharp machetes, aiming at the base of each stalk right near the ground. The more he worked at his grandfather's plantation, the better a "caner" he became. When he wasn't swimmin' "nekkid" in th' Bayou Teche, he would be working the cane fields and eatin' syrup 'n bread. His grandmother, Marcelite Cook, would bake up several hot loaves of homemade bread and set out the breadbasket filled to the brim with warm bread 'n butter. And, of course, jars of her warmed-up homemade sugarcane syrup.

Elbridge's maternal grandparents, William H. and Marcelite Hayes Cook, had both been born in southern Louisiana: William on December 30, 1812, and Marcelite on July 10, 1810; they were married July 7, 1836. Their daughter, Louisa Cook, had met and fallen in love with a Mississippi River steamboat captain by the name of Howard Packard— Charles Howard Packard. And they had married right here on Elbridge's

---

[2] Author's Note: Bayou is an American-French word for "small stream;" it comes from the Choctaw Indian word, "bayuk."

The Crepe Myrtle

grandfather's Old Oak Plantation. He knew all this because he'd surely heard his mother tell th' story a coupla' hundred times by now. Well, at least five or six times, maybe. . . .

When Elbridge's father had been "temporarily" assigned to the small port of Rockport, Texas in January 1873, Elbridge had been allowed to stay with his grandparents until they got all settled in at Rockport. Elbridge was almost 10 years old and wasn't too keen on moving away from his grandparents and all his gang, not yet, anyway. His older brother, Willard Howard, had gone to Texas with their parents. Their mother was pregnant with a child (this was a happily anticipated time for Louisa since her last pregnancy in 1867 had eventually resulted in the deaths of her twins; and, in many ways, she had never completely gotten over that loss). . . .

Conrad Elvin Packard was born May 24, 1873; and on December 27, 1875, Leslie Cromwell Packard joined this Packard family. By the summer of 1877, this "temporary" assignment ended for Captain Howard and Louisa Packard, and they came back home to Centreville. During those four years, Elbridge had journeyed by boat—mostly on his father's boat—back and forth from his parents' home to that of his grandparents. And through his early teenage years, Elbridge had become increasingly aware of some difficulties arising in his parent's marriage. He loved both of his parents dearly, but it had become apparent that his mother, Louisa Packard, yearned for more "big city" life and less of the small towns like Rockport, Texas and Centreville, Louisiana. Elbridge knew his father was a well-respected and honorable gentleman who could not bring himself to force a way of life upon Louisa that would deepen her anguish. Howard Packard loved his wife, but he sensed that attempts to force any kind of decision would merely push her farther from his affections; he would perform his duties as usual, bide his time, and pray that things would yet work out. You cannot force someone to love you back. . . .

Howard Packard asked Elbridge to accompany him to the bank where he had some business to take care of. "Elbridge, you're getting on up in years—be 15 soon." They walked a ways, and Elbridge could tell this was not going to be just a casual conversation. "Son, I suspect you already know your mother isn't any too happy right now; truth is, ever since we lost th' twins, not much seems to have gone her way. Least, not as I see it. Your mother and I have,.. well, we've had some long talks, and I'm of a mind she wants to move back to New Orleans."

Elbridge's heart sank with that news, partly from the disturbing news of his parents marriage and partly from knowing he might be leaving Centreville again. "Dad, that's pretty bad news 'bout you 'n mom 'n all." Elbridge hesitated a bit, not too sure he wanted to ask the question that lay on the tip of his tongue. But it was there and didn't appear to want to leave. "Are you...you going with Mom? To New Orleans, I mean...will you both be moving there?"

"I hope so, son." The old man's shoulders seemed to droop a bit with these words. "I do pray so."

Shortly after Elbridge's fifteenth birthday, his mother and father moved to New Orleans. The shipping company readily approved the move, as Captain Howard Packard would be in a much more favorable location for the company's benefit, not only for shipping assignments on the Mississippi but for any international shipping voyages, as well. As for his parents, Elbridge hoped they would be able to work through their difficulties and keep the family intact.

As for Elbridge, his grandfather and his parents had come to a decision that pleased all concerned: Elbridge would live on his grandparents' plantation and earn his keep working the fields. Elbridge would be staying in Centreville....

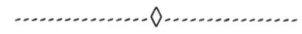

Elbridge worked tirelessly on his grandfather's plantation and over the next few years had acquired a considerable knowledge on successfully managing such a sizable operation. William Cook's own son was a fairly good worker but was not cut from the same cloth as Elbridge. Elbridge just had the proper touch for getting things done and in such a way as to gain the most effort from their field hands. By his eighteenth birthday, Chas Elbridge Packard was made overseer for his grandfather's plantation. This position was not given him; he had earned it.

The Crepe Myrtle

In the year of 1883 following his twentieth birthday, Chas Elbridge Packard made his first purchase of some parcels of land. Some were lands owned by his Grandfather Cook but most were acquired from neighboring landowners willing to sell. And south of Centreville, along the old Bayou Sallie, Elbridge began buying small parcels of land for a mere $.10 an acre. At the time it wasn't considered very valuable property, seeing as how most of it was little more than swampland. But at these low prices, one really would not be putting a lot of money at risk. And worthless or not, owning land was not a bad thing to do; it was good speculation. . . .

Most of Elbridge's lands were on, or near, his grandfather's holdings and certainly considered good farmlands for raising crops. And in this part of Louisiana, the crops to grow were sugarcane and cotton—King Cotton. One couldn't go wrong with these growing in their fields; Elbridge planted them, as well.

Sugarcane was, and still is, a major part of Louisiana's industry. First brought to Louisiana in 1751 by colonists from the Caribbean, sugarcane continues to help drive The Pelican State's economy, provide work for field hands and gives children even today a nice snack to cut right out of a field. Many sugarcane products are shipped from Louisiana, most notably cane syrup, and sugar. The latter had a well-known 1950's ad which labeled its product, "pure cane sugar" (Louisiana, Off the Beaten Path, Gay Martin, 2003.)

William H. Cook died on July 15, 1886. Elbridge had lost his grandmother, Marcelite Cook, in 1882, and now his beloved grandfather was gone; it was a sad time.

The family buried William H. Cook next to his wife, Marcelite, in the same Presbyterian church cemetery in Centreville, along with all the other family members who had passed into the pages of time: Packards, Queens, and Cooks; Moffitts and Footes, and a number more, as well, quite a number more.

. . .A haunting presence lingers here. . . .

----------------◊-----------------

Charles B. Packard

When William H. Cook's will was read to all of the assembled family, Chas Elbridge Packard was practically the first to voice his dissent—not because he had not received generous consideration but rather because he believed he had received too generous a bequeathal. His grandfather had left him most of the estate: lands, buildings, and funds. Chas Elbridge Packard assumed ownership of a fair share of the property lying immediately south of the road to Franklin, Louisiana. And less than 500 feet from the banks of the small stream flowing parallel to this road—The Bayou Teche....

At church service one Sunday morning, a certain young lady surprisingly caught his eye. Surprisingly, because Elbridge had long known of this young Irish lass whose family also lived in Centreville. But he didn't remember her looking so. . .well, so very pretty. As he was leaving following the church service, he caught the attention of his childhood pal, Andy.

"Andy, good morning to you, friend."

"Good mornin' to ya' as well, Elbie. And how are ya' this foine mornin'?" Andy still had a bit of his Irish brogue to his speech; and it was one that always brought a smile to Elbridge's face.

"Andy, me foine Irish lad, 'n it's a bit o' a favor what I be needing," Elbridge mocked Andy's speech, largely exaggerating the Irish accent.

"Elbie, that is quite likely th' worst Irish accent that I ever be a'heerin'. I'd give it a rest if I were you, ya' crazy Cajun!" They both knew that neither had the Cajun blood in them, as neither of their ancestors had come to Louisiana with the Acadians from Nova Scotia, many years ago.

"An' just what favor might I be considerin' for ya', Elbie?"

Elbridge colored a bit, for he knew that most likely his response would elicit a bit of good-natured ribbing from his friend. "The young lady in the white lace dress—would that be Mary Margaret?"

A sly grin spread across Andy's face, and now Elbridge knew for a fact he was in for it. "Oh," Andy stepped back a bit as he responded, "so now ye've finally takin' notice o' th' poor lass, 'n her what's been castin' glances yer way all these many years 'n all." Andy made no attempt to hide his pleasure at seeing his friend squirm in embarrassment.

Elbridge ignored the reference to her noticing him and asked straightforwardly: "Andy, do you know if she be courting anybody just now?" "No, not t' me knowledge. No, I be fairly certain that tis not th' case. Th' poor lass," Andy said so mockingly. "'N tell me, young lad, would it be of int'rest t' ya if I offers me services of matchmaker?"

Chuckling wickedly, Andy ducked as Elbridge playfully swung a hand as though to cuff him one.

Elbridge had no need of matchmaking from anyone; in most every aspect of his being, courage was not a trait in which he was lacking. He had it in abundance.

He went to the Moffitt home that next week and politely introduced himself to Mary Margaret's mother, Mary Adeline Foote, even though Elbridge was already well known throughout Centreville's rather small community. He asked Mary Margaret's widowed mother for permission to call upon her daughter; Mary Foote Moffitt's husband, Enders Ernest Moffitt, had passed away the previous year on July 23, 1888. Enders was only 40 years old. Chas Elbridge and Mary Margaret began courting in the fall of 1889. As they both attended services at the Presbyterian church, seeing them together became a common occurrence among the parishioners. Chas Elbridge began setting aside more time for Mary Margaret which meant he no longer spent 16 hours or more working his farmlands. Some of the credit for the change in his workload Mary attributed to what Andy had told his friend that day at church. "Elbie, it's small wonder ya' haven't seen how little Mary Margaret has growed up right a'fore yer eyes, seein' as how yer head is stuck workin' on yer books, or out slavin' in th' fields. If it's a'tryin' ta'kill yerself what ya' be aimin' fer, well, yer doin' a right foine job."

Andy's words had a certain ring of truth to them as Elbridge sometimes had recurring bouts of pneumonia which frequently laid him low. He had been experiencing just such coughing spells the past several days as he stubbornly persisted in working long hours in the cold barns. Late that October of 1891, Elbridge was finishing up work on his stockyards and slaughter pens. He had expanded his farm, having decided earlier in 1890 to process beef cattle on his property. His farmhands found him as they were finishing work for the day. He started another coughing spell, only this time he began coughing up blood. He stumbled against the feed trough just as his workers came in to say they were heading home. Quickly, they helped him up and brought in a pail of water. He washed up a bit and took a long drink. "Missuh Packard, suh, ya needs t' see a doctah," said his field foreman, old Jeremiah, one of his most trusted men.

"Yes. I believe I will, Jeremiah, first thing tomorrow." Elbridge meant what he said.

Dr. Ira Bowman had just started his practice the previous year, having completed his medical training at LSU Medical School. He hung his shingle just above the outside stairs going up to his second-floor offices; he had the sign company inscribe the words "DR. IRA BOWMAN, PHYSICIAN—MEDICINES—TOOTH EXTRACTIONS." Dr. Bowman had become accustomed to visits by Elbridge Packard, just as he had become knowledgeable as to the reasons for these visits. Elbridge often pushed himself too far and simply did not take very good care of his health. Dr. Bowman worked up a mustard poultice in bandages and wrapped Elbridge's bare chest in it. He then applied hot towels and had Elbridge lie down. "Elbridge, I want you to drink this; it tastes pretty bad, but it will help you rest for a few hours. I want you to lie quietly for awhile. I'll wake you when it's time to go home." He brought a pillow and a blanket; and after he had Elbridge well-secured, he spoke quietly: "You know, I think what you need most of all is a good little wife to take care of you."

Drowsily, Elbridge mumbled: "You may be right, Doc; you just may be right."

Chas Elbridge Packard and Mary Margaret Moffitt were married on March 5, 1892. Elbridge had just turned 29 years old four days earlier, while Mary Margaret was but a few months past her twenty-first birthday. They were certainly a young couple and very much in love. Their engagement had been a mere seven months long.

Nevertheless, it was one of the most unusal weddings ever. . . .

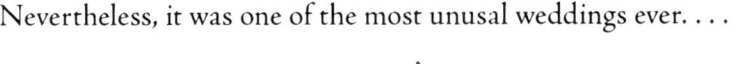

Elbridge had been living at the Franklin Boarding House which was some 5 miles from his farmlands in Centreville. He had been there for sometime as he was building a new home for a wife and children he hoped to someday have.

Several days earlier, he had started having coughing spells; he had been working late again, pushing himself to complete his house. But this time, his coughing attacks became worse, and Dr. Bowman insisted he go right to bed and get some rest. Dr. Bowman stopped by the Moffitt home to speak to Mary Margaret and her mother.

"I've just put Elbridge to bed rest. I'm afraid this attack of pneumonia is worse than the others, and he needs more care than what I can give him. He needs a good, warm home, a lot of rest, and the care that only a wife can provide. I strongly recommend you and Mrs. Moffitt go see him tonight, if possible. I thank you for your time, and I'll be bidding the both of you good evening." Dr. Bowman walked down the steps and climbed into his buggy; he tugged on the reins, turning out into the dirt road toward his boarding rooms; he felt pleased with himself. *Not too bad, Ira, not too bad; you'd make a right fair Cupid*, he mused to himself. . . .

The next day Mary Margaret and her mother went to Elbridge's room. Accompanying them was their pastor, the Reverend C. M. Atkinson, from the Centreville Presbyterian Church—it was March 5th.

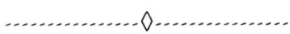

Immediately following the wedding in Elbridge's room, Dr. Bowman and Reverend Atkinson helped Mrs. Mary Moffitt and her daughter, the new Mary Margaret Moffitt Packard, assist Elbridge into the carriage. Upon arriving at the Moffitt home, Elbridge was immediately settled into a bed with a stern warning from his new mother-in-law: "You now be in me care, 'n ye'll be payin' mind ta me, now, young man. It's rest ye be needin', and it's rest ye'll be getting'; it's not a widow what ye'll be makin' o' me daughter. Not yet, ya' hear?"

All Centreville knew that the Moffitt's were a proud honorable family, steeped in the traditions of their Irish ancestry. And as much as Elbridge's life depended on their care, Mary Moffitt knew that no young man would be moving into her home unless he was a husband to her young daughter. And now that that small matter had been taken care of, next would come the care and healing that she well knew would be provided.

Elbridge was nursed back to health, and promising not to over-exert himself, managed to complete his and Mary Margaret's new home, which they moved into early in May 1892. They had a well-attended housewarming with a blessing prayed upon the entire gathering by Reverend Atkinson.

And on April 15, 1893, Eulalia Packard blessed the young family, as did Lucille Packard on July 4, 1894, and Mary Packard on June 3, 1896—three lovely, bright and charming young lasses.

Their first son was born February 8, 1897; proudly, Elbridge now moved himself up to Elbridge Packard, Sr., as he named his new son Chas Elbridge Packard, Jr. On September 21, 1898, his second son arrived. In honor of his good friend who also happened to be the Packard family doctor, Elbridge named this young lad Ira Bowman Packard. Chas Elbridge Packard, Sr. and Mary Margaret Packard had now been married 6 years and had 5 healthy children—it was a very productive home.

Chapter 10

Mary Margaret Moffitt of Irish Bend

Timeline: 1845-1900

Immigrants from Ireland had begun settling in southern Louisiana late in the 1700s and spread throughout the area although many chose the fertile lands along the Bayou Teche, just north of present-day Franklin. This region came to be known as Irish Bend.

A few decades earlier, around 1755, the French Acadians were forced by the English to leave their homes in Nova Scotia. Most of these Acadians (slangily changed to "Cajuns") settled farther north in the settlement of St. Martinville, also along the banks of the Bayou Teche.

Among the early Irish-English settlers were two families who would figure prominently in our story: The Footes and the Moffitts. . . . (Louisiana, Off the Beaten Path, Gay Martin, 2003.)

Rich in their individual cultures and traditions, these two peoples inspired customs and disciplines that blended well in those that came after them. Those who followed also chose to plant their roots along the Bayou Teche (pronounced "Tesh"—a Native Indian word meaning serpentine or meandering.)

Nezerat Ezekial Moffitt was born in 1823 near Irish Bend, the son of one of the Moffitt families immigrating from Ireland. He, too, grew up near the Bayou Teche. Another family of immigrants from Ireland—the Footes—also settled in this new land. One Foote family settled in southern Louisiana's Irish Bend while another Foote family remained in the New England region. These New England Footes produced a son, early in 1800, who would one day ply waters considerably deeper than those of the Bayou Teche. . . .

In 1848 Nezerat Moffitt and his wife settled near Centreville where their son, Enders Moffitt, was born on November 14. The Teche called to him, too. Enders grew up, married Mary A. Foote, and they started their family. Mary Margaret Moffitt, born on September 22, 1871, was as pretty an Irish lass as Centreville had seen. Enders and Mary Moffitt thought so, too.

Mary Margaret was a bright student; studious, disciplined and born with a hunger for learning. She greatly admired many of her teachers at Centreville's Parish School. Mary Margaret also became smitten with an older boy in St. Mary's Higher Grade Academy, a boy by the name of Chas Elbridge Packard. Mary Margaret was only 10 years old but she knew the young man—some 8 years older—had a certain presence about him that she admired. He was polite and treated most everyone he met with an engaging smile. Mary Margaret was too young to comprehend all the emotions clutching at her, but she knew she was most fond of this young man.

Mary Margaret completed her schooling in 1887 and went on to advanced education for her teaching certificate. She commenced teaching elementary classes in 1889 at the same school she had attended as a child—an accomplishment that brought her much satisfaction and a small monthly paycheck. With her first pay Mary Margaret spent most of it on a platform rocking chair that was a lovely possession she would cherish through the years and an heirloom she would pass on to her family in the years to come. The rest of her first pay she gave to her mother.[3]

Mary Margaret derived great pleasure from her work and quite possibly the only matter she considered less than ideal was the lack of attention from the handsome young man who attended the same Presbyterian

---

[3] Author's Note: Grandmother Mary Margaret Packard would pass this rocker to one of her daughters-in-law, the wife of her son, Frank Packard. Today, the chair resides in the home of a dear cousin, Frank Packard, Jr., a retired attorney living in Alabama. Many of the photographs and family tales in our story have been passed to my hands from this gentleman cousin, a nephew of our father, Ira Bowman Packard, Sr. Family ties are truly an enduring treasure.

church. That young man was Elbridge Packard; most days when they happened to cross paths, it seemed to her as though Elbridge was walking with his head in the clouds. At least, that would explain the seeming indifference and lack of acknowledgement even of her presence. Her strict upbringing precluded any sort of opening move on her part—heavens knew her family would have absolutely been on their heads had she done so—but Mary Margaret experienced certain days when she felt compelled to rap Elbridge Packard upside his noggin just to see if that might have some sort of desirable effect upon this befuddled, would-be swain.

And then, just when Mary Margaret had all but concluded that her Mr. Packard was a hopelessly lost cause, word reached her ear that Elbridge Packard had inquired if anyone were courting her. Upon hearing this, she thought back to the recent church services and had, on a few occasions, felt that Elbridge had been looking in her direction. But past experience had told her this was merely a figment of her imagination, and so she had abandoned that train of thought and resumed her study of the scriptures.

But now this was exceedingly joyful news for the young school teacher, news that made the beautiful fall day even more glorious. Mary Margaret headed home, barely aware that there was actually solid ground beneath her feet. But when, she pondered, just when would her Elbridge Packard come around to ask permission to call on her. "Hmmph," she snorted, "the way that rapscallion has moved of late, it may be next year before he ever gets around to darkening my door." She reddened, as she realized she was talking to herself and out loud, at that. "Oooh, and just what sort of hold has this person on me that makes me carry on like some star-struck school girl," she mused. And that, she thought, is but a rhetorical question. When and how he comes around, if ever, is solely at his discretion and now requires of me considerable patience and certainly diligence in carrying out my teaching duties. Mary Margaret knew she was mightily involved in a massive rationalization; and deep inside, she knew only too well that she cared and cared deeply that one Chas Elbridge Packard come around, and soon, to call on her.

Mary Margaret needn't have worried. Later that week Elbridge Packard knocked upon the Moffitt's door. Bravely, if a bit awkwardly, Elbridge Packard asked for permission to call upon their young school teacher.

---◊---

Theirs was a most unusual wedding and a timely one, at that. Chas Elbridge Packard was dangerously near death on their wedding day, March 5, 1892. Mary Margaret Moffitt and her mother, Mary A. Moffitt saved his life. Quite literally, they saved his life that perilous day in his boarding room. Immediately after the wedding in his room, the new bride and her mother took him into their home and successfully nursed Chas Elbridge Packard back to good health.

Future generations would ever be grateful. . . .

---◊---

Chapter 11

Rosie Alice Hawkins, Cherokee Child

Timeline: 1846-1876

The travelers had crossed the river a ways into Alabama, some 30 miles or so from Fort Oglethorpe. The weather was surprisingly warm for late March of 1876 but the water was still quite cold.

Just a few miles downstream was a well-used ferry crossing, one that most travelers in these parts used with regularity and had they been white folks, they, too, could have crossed the Tennessee in a matter of minutes. But these travelers were Cherokee from her mother's tribe in south central Tennessee—save for Esther Ellen, who was a half-breed—and they knew the "white-eyes" would not allow Indians the use of this ferry, though this land had once been their land and this river had once been their river; all this mattered little. Prejudice seldom respects traditions unless it is its own. The men of her tribe had spent the better part of the pleasant afternoon gathering logs and cutting saplings for their raft and pulling vines from the trees to use in lashing their raft together with strips of leather thongs. When completed, their raft would hold up well. Esther had helped the others as they lashed the logs and saplings into a crude but sturdy raft. The raft would have to be very sturdy as they set out to cross the sometimes turbulent Tennessee River.

Quietly, they led their horses into the river, calming them for the long swim across and pulled their raft in after them. Esther Ellen climbed on as the raft drifted slowly out into the current. The water was rather cold but no one complained. Reaching the opposite bank just before dusk and carefully concealing the raft, their journey resumed eastward. A mile or so from the river, the travelers made camp and fed and hobbled their horses for the night. The warm campfire felt good.

Esther lay quietly in her blankets, contemplating the days and weeks ahead and what she was about to do. What was within her belly reminded her of one thing she would do and that was to give birth to her child, hers and Hiram's. Bringing a child into the world in these circumstances was not the way she had once imagined things would be. As a young woman, she simply desired the comfort and security of a family and her own man with whom to share that family life. Esther Ellen cared little about the color of skin of her man; he could be white, like her paw, or Indian, like her mother. What mattered was that he be good to her and their children....

Esther had been born in 1846; the daughter of a Cherokee squaw and a white trader, she grew up among her mother's tribe learning many of their ways. When Hiram had first claimed her as his woman, Esther had been quite pleased. He had a decent place a few miles away from the village where the sun rose up over the trees. In his dealings with the Cherokee of the village, Hiram had seemed to be a fair and decent man. She moved into Hiram's cabin shortly after her twenty-sixth summer and very soon was with child; and she felt very proud.

But not long after she became pregnant, Hiram staggered home roaring drunk one night and in a particularly foul mood. He was suddenly like some crazed animal gone berserk, striking Esther repeatedly. Even after she had crashed to the floor, bleeding from cuts to her face, he continued striking her with most anything he could lay his hands on. Esther lay crumpled in a heap on the dirt floor, bleeding and drifting in and out of consciousness. The only thing that likely spared her life was Hiram's passing out in a drunken stupor.

Esther survived but not her unborn. The savagery of the beating ended the life before it had barely begun. She had grieved for many months afterward, and even Hiram had at times shown a measure of regret but Hiram's regret had not ended the violence. Somehow, in his twisted mind, he saw it as all Esther's fault. This violence toward her had gone on for a few years, and Esther had almost resigned herself to this just being a painful part of life; until the winter of 1875-76 when once again she found that she was with child. Esther had once sworn an oath to her mother that she would not again allow a child to be taken like the other one—a blood oath she swore to her mother's tribal ancestors. *Two days after Hiram left on a trading journey, Esther left, too. This child would be given every chance of survival....*

Esther and her Cherokee companions—blood kin to her mother—were five in number: three Cherokee braves, one squaw, and the half-breed, Esther Ellen. By the first of April they had reached another tribe of her people, those who lived in the foothills of the Chattahooche Forest in northern Georgia. Their village was scattered about both banks of what is now Moccasin Creek; here, Esther Ellen and her baby would be safe. Nearby was a small abandoned cabin that all helped in cleaning up for the baby's birthing; with the blankets and pelts they brought with them, the cabin was soon as comfortable as possible. Esther Ellen smiled a contented smile; everything would be just fine. The baby stirred softly in her belly as though to echo its agreement....

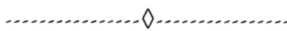

On July 1, 1876, Esther Ellen gave birth to her baby—a little girl with black hair and bronze skin, just like that of its grandmother. Esther Ellen knew her mother would be proud; she gave the baby girl a name she had long wanted to name a daughter if she had ever had one. Smiling up at her companions, she responded to their question: "What name you give little one?" They had spoken in Cherokee and Esther responded in kind: "Her name Rose...Rose Alice."

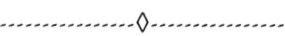

Ironically, Esther Ellen gave birth to her baby, Rose Alice, less than six days of travel from where her own mother had birthed her some 30 summers ago. She had been born just a few days' ride from Tennessee in the Smoky Mountain region of western North Carolina. Her mother's tribe had moved their village several times over the next 12 summers finally settling near the trading post at Wartrace, Tennessee in 1858. Here, Esther Ellen blossomed into a handsome young half-breed, and 14 summers later she would come to endure abuse at the hands of a white man.

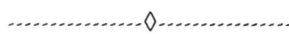

In 1878 two years after Rose Alice was born, Esther Ellen left northern Georgia to return near her mother's tribe in Tennessee. She had learned from her tribal family that Hiram would never bother her again, nor anyone else for that matter. Hiram had never returned from a trip up to Franklin, Tennessee, where he had journeyed on a trading venture less than a year earlier. Esther learned that Hiram had been shot to death in a drunken brawl over a poker hand. Hiram lived violently, and he had died violently.

As a child Rose Alice often had a song sung to her by her mother. Unmistakably, this song spoke of tribal origins and was a song her mother sang to her at birth and throughout her childhood years—a song she would often sing to her grandchildren years later in the farm community in Central Texas, called Oenaville. Her grandson, Foster Wayne Packard, recalled the words to Grandma Foster's song which she sang to her grandchildren from the mid-1940s to the early 1950s:

> "Way over in th' Loo-Tinky-Loo;
> Way over in th' Loo-Tinky-Loo;
> Nee-Hi-Lo, Nee-Hi-Lo, Nee-Hi-Lo."

Chapter 12

The Natchez Trace, Journey to Texas

Timeline: 1846-1900

Alexander Hawkins could see that things were gonna be lean agin' much like last year; most of this crop was just not gonna make it either. Alexander picked up a handful of dusty soil and watched as it trickled out, and then flung it in disgust at his feet. This part of Tennessee was mostly rocky soil with heavy growths of juniper and cedars—pretty country, but not much for farmland.

He walked back along the hillside, passing among the juniper trees which dotted his land. Alexander knew dang good'n well it weren't 'cause he didn't work hard; many days he worked from sunup to sundown tryin' to scratch out a livin' for Esther 'n the kids. Some years he'd had good crops, dang good crops. He know'd ther wuz a goodly number o' farms 'n homesteads what had rich, fertile lands fer farmin'. But his'n weren't one o' 'em. . . .

Alexander headed down toward their house, his shoulders drooped more in defeat than in fatigue. He weren't no quitter, nosiree—but enuf's enuf, he thought. He and Esther had sold off or traded much of their livestock just to take care of their family's needs and were down to a couple of cows, a few hogs, and several dozen chickens. The past few years had been pretty rough. Hard to make a go of it, even with Esther's help th' past year. Alexander thought on this awhile, knowin' full well he had a powerful big decision facin' him.

Some 40 miles or so west was Th' Natchez Trace, a wagon trail that had been in use for nigh on t' a hunnert years. He know'd it went plumb down to Natchez, smack on th' Mississippi River. Roughly about 400 miles away—about 26 days' journey by wagon—figger a month to allow how wheels got busted an' maybe bad weather'd slow 'em some.

Once they cross'd the Mississip by ferry, he knowed they'd have about another 400 miles to where he was thinkin' on. Prob'ly another month there—mebbe more—dependin' on what he'd face goin' cross Louiseann. He'd heard there'd be some swamps 'n such he'd have 'ta steer clear of. Gettin' bogged down wouldn' help none. With decent weather 'n such, he knowed he'd have a good two t' two-and-a-half months to allow for finishin' the trip. He'd need reach there a'fore December; they'd better plan on headin' out 'bout th' end of August. By then they oughta have most of th' crops in, figger'n as how dad-blamed little they'd be, he thought disgustedly.

Esther could can up some corn 'n greens, and he'd have 'ta butcher a few hogs for smokin'. That'd give'em a right smart bit of food for the trip and with any luck he knowed he 'n Junior could shoot some game along th' way. He thought about his son, Alexander Hawkins, Jr.; th' boy was only 11. He'd have some growin' up to do 'n pretty durned quick. Be good for 'em. He were a good boy anyway and make a good man someday.

He'd work somethin' out with his cuzzin over'n the valley for the covered wagon they own'd; he'd told Alexander he'd swap it to 'em for his land and mebbe a couple hogs or such. Seemed like a fair trade, considerin' he didn't hisself think much of th' land, no how. He'd do right by Willie, though. . . . But th' land he was thinkin' on now was s'posed to be fair to middlin' farmland, good fer crops like cott'n 'n corn 'n such. Decent land if you worked it good. Folks coming back this way'd told him that they'd heard tell th' land grants weren't as big as they'd once been, but they was still 100 or so acres if a person could qualify fer 'em.

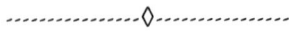

The General Land Office was established in Austin, Texas in 1836 when Texas was still a Republic. The early grants, called Headrights Grants back then, were awarded by the Land Commissioners to homesteaders in parcels of as much as 4,400 acres. Most were of 1,000 acres or less.

After Texas was admitted to the Union as the 28th state on December 29, 1845, and for several years after, the General Land Office continued awarding grants of 320 acres. This changed toward the late 1800s. Later grants, called pre-emption or homestead grants, were of half parcels or 160 acres. Each county had its Board of Land Commissioners; it would have been to this board to which a settler coming into Texas would have made his presentation or appeal for such land grants. One hundred and seventy-two years later, it remains the Texas General Land Office. ("Texas Land Grants," Information Brochure from Texas General Land Office, Archives and Records Division, 1994.)

He walked in th' front door, pullin' it shut a'hind 'im. Good smells comin' from Esther's kitchen. "Supper's ready—git the kids warsh'd up," Esther said. He stood ther fer a moment, watchin' Esther; she was still a right smart lookin' woman with her coal black hair 'n dark eyes. She had th' same copper colorin' as her mother who'd been a full-blood Cherokee—same's lil Rose Alice—same blood wuz in her, too.

Feelin' his eyes on her, Esther turned and asked, "got somethin' on yer mind, Alexander?" She'd knowed fer sometime, now—she just wanted to hear 'im say it.

"We're goin' to Texas, Esther."

---------◊---------

Alexander Hawkins had gone to the trading post over at Wartrace about a year earlier and saw Esther and her little girl looking at some dresses. Alexander had lost his wife a couple or so years previous, long 'bout 1878; she had died of something th' doctor had called consump'sun, or some such name. He didn't much cotton t' raisin' his boy all by hisself, so he had asked 'round 'bout th' woman named Esther. He learned she'd been widowed herself, 'n wuz a half-breed a 'living' with her family at th' Cherokee village over east o' ther. He know'd ther wuzn't much sense t' beat' 'bout th' bush so with his hat 'n his hand, he ask'd Esther if she thought it mebbe wuz a proper thing in all if she'd give sum thought t' livin' with him; her 'n the' little girl, of course. Esther at first was taken aback by such a direct approach but soon realized this man had been very straightforward and didn't seem afraid to speak his mind. She told him she would think on it some. If she decided it would be a good thing, well, then she'd leave word for him there at the post. Sometimes you did what was practical just to survive.

In the summer of 1879 she and little Rose Alice had moved west a ways into Alexander's cabin. He was neat in his ways and proved to be a decent person to be around. Maybe this arrangement would work out, after all. Time would tell. . . .

Alexander and Esther loaded the last of their goods on the wagon and tightened the cinch ropes securely. Junior and little Rose Alice, who had just turned 5, checked the water barrels; they were full. They pulled out from the homestead with 3 cows, 4 or 5 hogs, and their dog, Boy, trailing along behind. The horse 'n mule team weren't used to pulling this much of a load; they were more accustomed to the much lighter plow rigs. Alexander had to encourage 'em from time to time. He and Esther never once looked back; they had a long trip ahead of them, but somehow they were looking forward to it. The date was August 6, 1881.

Five days later they reached The Natchez Trace and turned south toward the Alabama stateline. Those first few days had taken getting used to and the heat had caused a few delays. Rose Alice had suffered a bit from heat exhaustion, and Alexander found it necessary to rest his family and the team, as well, when it got plumb swelterin'. Two days runnin' they'd camped near a cool stream as they slowly adjusted to the rigors of wagon travel. This was at Garrison's Creek not too far south of Nashville. They'd pick th' pace up soon enough; of that, Alexander was certain. Couldn' push his family too hard—not with the long days ahead.

The Hawkins' wagon crossed into Alabama early in September; they had now covered 74 miles. Much of the trip across the northern corner of Alabama and through most of Mississippi had been somewhat uneventful; they were making good time now. Both the team and the family were settlin' in to a good pace as they got their trail legs under them. They had lost only one hog, somewhere along the trace about three days into Mississippi. Other'n that, they'd had few difficulties.

Just a ways north of Jackson, they'd busted a wheel, and it took Alexander an' Junior almost two whole days to repair it. The rest of their trip through Mississippi went well; they were about two days journey this side of Natchez. It was late September and the Hawkins family had now journeyed some 460 miles in less than 2 months; they were nearly halfway there. . . .

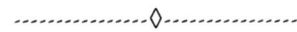

Natchez was a bustling port along the Mississippi River and a melting pot of gamblers, rogues, and saloon women. It was taming down some but not enough to suit Alexander. The Hawkins' wagon was nestled down about a half mile out of town in a thick grove of trees. They planned on camping there for a few day's rest before heading across the Mississippi River with another month in crossing Louisiana on their journey to Texas.

The hardest part of their trip was facing them.

Alexander had ridden into town the next morning to load up supplies— flour, beans, some axle grease, and a few other staples for the trail. He rode down along the river road to check on ferry runs across the river. Counting the wagon, his family, and the few head of livestock, the crossing would cost him $.35 in toll fees.

He loaded his supplies in his trail pouches and stood there along the dock pilings watching boat traffic passing up and down the river. A good-sized paddle wheeler was steamin' upriver on its way t' Memphis. She was loaded with spices, rice, 'n barrels of sugarcane syrup from th' Louisiana cane fields. Rice was becoming a big commodity of trade in recent years, as barrels of rice sometimes outnumbered the barrels of syrup. The steamboat rode low in the water; she was loaded to the gunnels.

Just a few days earlier another steamboat had stopped in Natchez to unload cargo. This boat was making a return trip to New Orleans; by now she was riding high in the water, as most of her cargo was gone. The captain of this paddle wheeler was a 48 year old seaman from New Orleans, whose family had in recent years moved from the small town of Centreville, Louisiana. His name was Howard Packard, Captain Charles Howard Packard.

Early next morning the Hawkins family crossed the Mississippi River—wagon, livestock, and ol' Boy. The sun hadn't yet burned off the mists rising from the granddaddy of rivers, so Alexander and his family were treated to the somewhat unsettling river sounds of clanging bells, shouted-out depth soundings, and the piercing boom of the foghorns—very unsettling, except to Rose Alice who slept undisturbed.

Their trip across the ol' Mississippi was long and very nerve-wracking as the dense fog slowed things considerably. The ferry barge came dangerously close on a few occasions to colliding with two larger boats that were traveling at too fast a clip for these weather conditions. Only the experienced hand of the barge skipper saved the Hawkins from almost certain harm. After what seemed like hours, Alexander's family, finally set foot once more on solid ground, very solid ground. The trip over had only taken 46 minutes.

----------◊----------

Getting across Louisiana would prove even more hazardous and very costly. The swamplands were bad enough, as several times they had to backtrack in order to bypass some sucking marshy bogs that sought to keep their wagon for all time, and, on at least one occasion, very nearly did. But this cost was merely one of time lost. The milk cow lost to a treacherous quicksand, while sad, would merely be a temporary inconvenience, as would the loss of two more hogs which had either stumbled into a similar fate or else had just aimlessly wandered off along the way. These losses, while unfortunate, could eventually be made up. But some never would. . . .

During a particularly difficult time, as Alexander and his son labored in the stifling, bug-infested humidity in attempting to work the wagon out of yet another marshy swamp, the heavy limb which Junior was leveraging under a mired wheel snapped and the splintered ends punctured his side and part of his thigh. These weren't real bad wounds so after cleaning them off best they could and dabbing some coal oil to ward off infections, Esther wrapped a torn rag on them; and the menfolk resumed their labors.

Several days later, Alexander, Jr. came down with shaking chills and a fever that just wouldn't loosen its grip. Some sort of infection had developed, and Esther tried every remedy she knew in trying to help their son. For several days Junior lay in feverish semi-consciousness, perspiration soaking his clothing. His breathing grew more labored with each passing hour.

In late October more than 25 days after crossing the Mississippi River, Alexander and Esther buried their son near a large live oak shrouded with hanging moss, like huge grey veils. Taking a piece of wood from the wagon, Alexander scratched these words on it:

> Alexander Hawkins, Jr.
> Died October 1881
> "He were a good man"

The Hawkins' wagon crossed the Sabine River into Texas late October 1881; they had traveled over 800 miles from central Tennessee in 2 months and 18 days. With them were 2 milk cows, 2 hogs, and the family dog, Boy; Esther, Alexander, and little Rose Alice were in their new home state. In November 1881 the Hawkins family moved westward on their way to some land near Little River, Texas; they were making their last trip in the covered wagon they brought from Tennessee.

Three days travel west of Livingston found them topping a small rise. As they paused, Alexander spied a small band of Indians less than a mile away. The Indians were slowly approaching, causing Esther and Alexander a bit of concern. Alexander had little Rose Alice crawl under the bench seat and covered her with blankets. He told Rose Alice to take the dog with her and to keep him quiet. Alexander removed his rifle from its leather case just to be on the safe side. Rose Alice sensed the danger from her parent's actions and buried her face in the blanket to muffle her cries. Esther spoke: "Hush, now, Rose; ever'things gonna be fine. Jest you keep th' dog quiet."

About a quarter mile away, the Indians turned slowly towards the south, disappearing harmlessly into a stand of live oaks. The danger had passed....

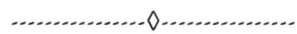

Charles B. Packard

Additional inquiries to the Archives Office of the Texas State Library in Austin have revealed these rather pertinent items of information:

- *Although some covered wagons could complete 20 to 25 miles per day, this was the exception; records reveal that 12 to 15 miles per day traveled was the reality in the late 1800s.*

- *While western and north central regions of 1870s Texas were still roamed by hostile Comanche Indian tribes, the parts of southeast Texas along the Brazos River Basin were, for the most part, inhabited by members of either the Twakoni or Tonkawa Indian tribes who were a rather peaceful people. (Gone to Texas, Randolph B. Campbell, 2003.)*

--------◊--------

The Hawkins settled temporarily near Belton while Alexander prepared the papers for his request for a land grant. Not many land grant parcels were left but Esther Ellen and Alexander remained hopeful. Hopeful for some good farmland.

While in Belton one day, Alexander filed a request for a marriage license; and on June 15, 1882, they were married. Three weeks later, Rose Alice turned 6 years old.

A short time later Alexander built them a small cabin and started clearing a few acres for farming. They had finally settled at Rogers, Texas, where they would start their family. Mary F. Hawkins was born May of 1883; then, Minnie Hawkins followed in March 1885; and Lizzie Hawkins was born in January 1888.

Alexander walked his land one afternoon and was pleased with what he and Esther Ellen had done. They had a nice farm and a growing young family. He stooped to pick up a handful of dirt; it was good, black soil. He would work it[4] good. . . .

---

[4] Author's Note: As a small boy, I delighted in some of the stories Grandma Rosie Alice Foster would tell me, especially about the Indians approaching their wagon and how terrified she had been. She could not recall all the circumstances of their journey, just that she and her parents were somewhere in Texas. This was a story I asked her to tell me over and over.

The Crepe Myrtle

----------------◊----------------

Many of our Foster relatives were born in Rogers, Texas. Many times Mom took me with her to visit with her Aunt Minnie and Aunt Lizzie who both lived in Rogers. Aunt Lizzie is the one who gave Mom the crepe myrtle that grew beside our front porch when we lived at the pump station, a few miles from the farm community of Oenaville, Texas. This crepe myrtle grows there still and is all that remains from when we grew up along with it—more than half a century ago....

----------------◊----------------

Chapter 13

John Bradson Foster, Scoundrel

Timeline: 1876-1900

William "Bill" and Mattie Foster were hard workers and took very good care of their farm. The land in the north part of Brazos County was good, fertile farmland and produced for them a number of bumper crops. For the most part, the Fosters stuck with what everyone else was growing: corn and their leader, cotton. Cotton was a major crop in Central Texas and a leading export to other states.

Their crop of kids was growing, as well. Ida had come along in 1869, Sarah Anne in 1871, and Eula Lee in 1872. Reuben, their first son, was born in 1874, and John Bradson Foster had joined the family in January 1876. Mattie Foster had a difficult delivery with little John Bradson; it was a sign of things to come. . . .

--------◊--------

John Bradson was 5 years old when his father died. William M. Foster died of pneumonia early February of 1881. Although his wounds from the Civil War had pretty much healed, he would occasionally have serious breathing problems; mostly, these occurred if he exerted himself physically and especially in cold, damp weather. He had worked hard building up their farm and helping Mattie raise their kids. Now, she would have to carry on without him and that would not be easy. Her oldest two daughters, Ida and Sara Anne, would have to grow up fast and they would be needed in helping her raise the young'uns—especially, the two youngest, John Bradson and Alonzo; Alonzo was just a little more than 3 years old. Fortunately, John Bradson and Alonzo would not be grieving their father's passing' as they were too young to have really known him.

--------◊--------

Mattie had some help from William's family, as his younger sister, Sarah Ann Foster, took the youngest boys for awhile. Sarah Ann and her husband were living in Fort Bend County, close to her mother's home on the John Foster, Jr. lands. (John Bradson had been named after his grandfather, John Foster, Jr., and his great-grandfather, John, Sr.). Sarah Ann and her husband kept the two boys most of 1881 and returned them to their mother just before Christmas. Life was pretty unsettled for John Bradson and, for awhile at least, not likely to get much better. At least Aunt Sarah had sent them home with some Christmas gifts for th' family.

---◊---

Back home, John Bradson found his life ruled by women; between his mother, Mattie Foster, and his two older sisters, they kept him on th' go. At least they tried to. John Bradson felt like there were enough women on th' farm to get things done. He just didn't see no reason t' get all worked up over chores 'n things. Hell, he wuz almos' 10 years old 'n helped with th' plowin' 'n plantin'. Whut more do they want from me, anyways? To him, he wuz doin' mor than 'nuf.

---◊---

John Bradson was 12 when his mother died; she was only 44 years old, and this made for troubling times for William and Mattie's children. His older sisters were now running things on th' farm, 'n they continued makin' life pret' near mis'rable fer him. Some o' ther uncles came up from time t' time t' check on things 'n help out when they could. Their Aunt Sarah Foster's husband, Uncle John Lauraine, had come to help out with the spring plantin' and had gone up t' th' house fer sum water. He plunged th' dipper inta' th' water well bucket, gulped it down, 'n hung th' dipper on its hook and continued: "Don't rightly see whut good th' boy's gonna be 'round here, 'xcept mebbe to eat'cha outa house 'n home. Would'n blame ya'll enny iffen ya tossed 'im out on his ear."

Ida walked over t' th' well and turnin' toward her Uncle John, replied: "Thet may be so, Uncle John, 'cept it ain't gonna happen. I know John's 'bout th' laziest boy a'round, but he's still my bruther, 'n I know fer certain momma 'n poppa woulda thrashed us good if'n we wuz t' kick 'im out." Ida turned toward th' fields wher sum o' th' others wuz workin' and said: "'Sides, I've figgered out how ta' keep th' boy workin', least ways, workin' a little bit. It's in th' Bible, Unca' John: Ya' don't eat, iffen ya' don't work!"

Shortly after he had turned 18, 'bout th' end of May, John Bradson started hanging out 'round th' saloon. Didn't require a lot of effort as everyone else there was a lot like him; well, most were a lot like him. Biggest difference was that near everyone else had some money to buy beer and whisky; John seldom did. He had taken over a small piece of land as a sharecropper, seeing as how the owner couldn't find anyone willing to care for such a small place; and when John found the energy to put in some time working, he would earn a few dollars off some crops and produce what he sold. Most times he did some odd jobs 'round th' county earnin' a few dollars here'n there; and most times the odd jobs were legal. . . .

John Bradson eventually ran afoul of the law but when no witnesses came forward he was allowed to go free. The county sheriff warned him to find some place else to live; he didn't want no bootleggin' hoss thief in his county. John Bradson may have been lazy but he wasn't stupid. He decided Bell County would be good a place as any; he was packed and ready to ride out next morning. Seeing as how he'd very little t' pack, didn't take no time at all to git out of town. In September of 1894 John Bradson Foster was 18 years old and takin' a powerful amount of time growin' up. He swung up in th' saddle 'n headed west toward Bell County.

John Bradson got himself a part-time job at th' feed store in Little River just a ways south of Temple. He found a cabin outside of the community that was halfway decent, and he managed to clean it up some. Rent was cheap enough so long as he took care of some of the stock herds on th' 20-acre farm; it wasn't much but it gave him a living. For once in his shiftless life, John Bradson was startin' to acquire a bit of a sense of responsibility. He even cleaned himself up ever' once in awhile and started to learn what it was like t' stay sober—fer th' most part, that is. He still took a drink ever' now 'n then.

John Bradson was a farmer; he just wasn't a very good one. But he was good at drinking and brawling. Problem was, neither one paid anything. 'Bout th' only good thing he had goin' fer him was his dark, good looks and his curly hair. Wimmen seemed t' be taken by his appearance 'n easy goin' manner. Had they been able to see through him, they'd have known his easy going manner masked a pretty wide streak of shiftlessness. But sometimes people see what they want to see; and sometimes there are persons who think they are capable of changing troublesome ways. Such a person was Rose Alice Hawkins.

Rose and John had met at the Bell County Fair and Rodeo held that summer in Belton. Rose Alice and her mother had canned some dewberry preserves and some pickles, and Esther Ellen had made a quilt to sell. This event had become an annual occasion for the Hawkins family, and all looked forward to it with considerable pleasure. Alexander had once again entered a hog in the judging contests, as he had each year for the past five years. He kept tellin' hisself, "mebbe one o' these days' ya jest never know." Rose Alice was helping her mother set up their pickles and preserves when John Bradson stopped to say hello. "Those shore look good. Air ya' sellin' 'em when th' judgin's over?" Rose Alice turned at the question and looked into the stranger's handsome face. His eyes sparkled with merriment, and Rose Alice thought she would never get her voice to work. "Why, yes. . .yes, of course, we'll be a'sellin' 'em; to those wha's got money, of course. Air ya' inter'sted 'n buyin' some?" She had recovered sufficiently.

"Mebbe," John replied, "jest mebbe I will. 'N would ya be interest'd in sharin' em with me, iffen I was ta' buy a jar?"

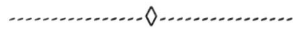

John Bradson began his courting of Rose Alice, riding over to Rogers about every two weeks or so. Rose Alice was becoming taken with John Bradson's ways and was growing very fond of him, which was a good thing, because Esther Ellen wasn't. She told Rose Alice what she thought of him but of course the young Miss Hawkins figured her mother just didn't understand him. The problem was Esther Ellen Hawkins had him pegged dead to rights; too bad Rose Alice was blinded by his charm. Sure would have saved her a lot of heartache and grief farther on down the road....

Rose Alice Hawkins and John Bradson Foster were married on September 24, 1896, in Belton, Texas. Officiating at his church was Reverend G. W. Hill, and he joined the young couple in holy matrimony. They settled on a small farm near her parents' home in Rogers, Texas. It wasn't a big farm like her parents', but it was her first home and Rose Alice was very proud of it. She especially liked the way her new bridegroom called her "Rosie" Alice Foster; she just liked th' sound of it.

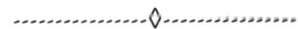

Their first child was born on August 3, 1899; they named her Lola Pearl Foster. A year later, in May of 1900, they birthed their second child, another little girl they named Lorena. Sadly, Lorena only lived a few months—a sad moment for Rosie Alice. Two years later, in May of 1902, Audrey Ellen Foster was born, and in 1903 Eula Lee Foster was born. While visiting some of their family up in Cleburne on December 16, 1904, the baby of their family was born. Rosie Alice named this little girl Ruby Inez Foster.

Chapter 14

Early Bell County, Texas

Timeline: 1900-1930

The mid-1800s was a colorful time in Bell County's past. Even as Texas was declaring its independence from Mexico, some adventurous settlers had already moved into Bell County, striving to establish their farm homes. These homesteaders were trying to set down roots more than 14 years before Bell County was officially established in 1850. In this same year of 1850 the community of Oenaville was founded, 30 years before Temple. Today, the pioneer community that once was Oenaville has all but disappeared, just like the Indian tribes who had first lived there.

Comanche Indian raids once were a deadly reality throughout Central Texas with the last known savage attack occurring in the western reaches of Bell County in 1859. But as more and more pioneers began settling in Bell County, the Indian raids became fewer and farther between. The Texas Rangers played an even greater role in forcing the Comanches from Central Texas, as the Rangers' raids against these Indian camps caused the fierce Comanches to question the wisdom of remaining in these parts of Texas. Pulling up their tent poles, the Comanches moved back into more remote regions of west Central Texas.

This rich, fertile area—geographically known throughout Texas as the Blackland Region—was perhaps the best farming soil in the Lone Star State. The prairie grass, growing wild and relatively untouched, reached waist-high on the settlers. This black soil would one day produce bountiful crops.

But the towering prairie grass also would one day present quite a challenge to the plows of the early farmers. . . . (Around & About Oenaville, Freddie Lee Whitlow & Mae Greenway; Oenaville, Vicki Ewing Montgomery, Oenaville Community Association.)

---------◊---------

The year 1900 had initially brought good news for the Fosters living near Rogers; their second child, a baby girl named Lorena, was born in May, and their farm was beginning to show some signs of healthy crop growth. John Bradson and Rosie Alice Foster were very poor having very few possessions to their name, but they had all the makings of a growing young family.

Then, tragedy struck as baby Lorena passed away just a few months later. While John Bradson seemed to take it in stride, Rosie Alice was devastated. She thought back on the baby her own mother, Esther Ellen, had lost back in Tennessee. In time, the pain had healed, and Rosie Alice and John Bradson resumed running their farm.

Two years later, Rose Alice gave birth to another baby girl who they named Audrey Ellen; Audrey Ellen was also born in May, but she survived. Rose Alice had given her mother's name of Ellen to this new child of theirs; the Fosters now had two daughters.

A year later, in 1903, another child was born into this Foster family—another little girl, Eula Lee—and named after John Bradson's older sister. John Bradson expressed his disappointment that he still didn't have a son to someday help out on th' farm. (To herself, Rose Alice thought, you mean a son t' do all th' work; she knew John only too well.)

Earlier that summer of 1904, Rose Alice knew she was again pregnant. After harvesting the crops that fall, they left Rogers for a short visit with some of John's family up near Cleburne; the Fosters arrived late November 1904. A few weeks later, the baby girl in their family was born and they named her Ruby Inez Foster. Ruby was born on December 16, 1904—another daughter for John and still no sons.

John Bradson was easily frustrated, and all the more so because he had not yet fathered a son. He now had a wife and four daughters to feed and care for, as well as a farm to run. To John Bradson Foster, this was becoming a lot like work. And work was something he was not overly fond of. John began spending more and more time in the saloons, getting drunk and just generally raisin' hell. This was something he enjoyed a lot; raising a family and taking on responsibilities required a certain amount of discipline. Discipline was not something John Bradson had a whole lot of; shiftless people seldom do.

The surprising thing, which most everyone eventually came to agree on, was that John Bradson hung around as long as he did. The family figgered him t' be gone a lot sooner.

One warm spring day in 1910, John Bradson left home and never returned. Lola Pearl was 11, Audrey Ellen was 9, Eula Lee was 7, and Ruby Inez was 6; and Rosie Alice Foster was left to take care of all that which John Bradson had turned his back on. The care and feeding of four little girls was probably the most disheartening and terrifying thing Rosie Alice had ever encountered—probably even more so than the time when she was only 5 years old and her family encountered a small band of Indians soon after bringing their covered wagon into Texas. That was terrifying enough for a little 5 year old child. But now Rosie Alice was a grown woman with her own small children—four of them, in fact—and no visible means of support—not to mention a small farm to tend. After a few days had passed, and the initial shock had worn off, Rosie Alice did the only thing she knew how to do in order to support her family—she picked cotton.

All th' Foster girls picked cotton. From Lola Pearl, th' oldest, down to Ruby Inez, th' baby. All th' Foster young'uns wuz out in th' fields before sunup, when th' mornin' dew wuz heavy on th' plants. Folks like th' Fosters, who depended on picking cotton to support themselves, had long ago learned to hit th' fields early. Some pickers could bring in several hundred pounds of cotton if they got into th' fields before th' sun came up 'n burned off th' dew.

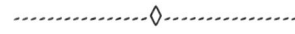

For several months that summer of 1910, Rosie Alice 'n th' girls survived. Just barely, but the family survived. All of 'em picked cotton six days a week 'n rested on Sunday. Th' girls purt near wore out their shoes 'n had t' make do with whut they had—weren't no money fer lux'ries like shoes 'n dresses. Rosie Alice made th' girls dresses from th' flour sacks once't they wuz empty; flour sacks back then were right purty, all decorated with flowers 'n patterns 'n things like that. Th' shoes she stitched up 'n patch'd th' best she could. Once't th' girls were home, Rosie Alice made 'em go barefoot so's ta' make th' shoes last longer. Whut little money they made mostly went fer food. Rosie Alice 'n th' girls lived on red beans 'n cornbread 'n whut veg'tables were picked from th' garden. Th' cow didn't give much milk, but whut she gave wuz shared by all th' family. Once a month or so Rosie would kill a chicken so's th' family could have some meat, but she couldn't fry up too many—Rose Alice needed th' hens fer whut few eggs they laid. 'N roosters wuz too tough t' eat; but th' Fosters would, if it came t' that.

Towards th' end of August, Rosie Alice Foster knew she had t' make a hard decision 'bout whut t' do with th' girls. Pickin' cotton had helped thru most o' th' summer, 'n Rosie Alice had worked on a few farms 'round their place, doin' whatever she could to make some sort o' livin'. But with fall 'n then winter comin' on, she knew there'd be little money—certainly not 'nuff t' feed n' clothe four young'uns. Makin' this decision was prob'bly th' hardest Rosie had ever made, but she knew she had no choice; th' kids'd have t' go somewhere's else t' live. . . .

Lola Pearl went to live with her Aunt Annie Foster Thompson and Uncle Thomas Thompson over near Little River in September; her Aunt Annie was John Bradson's older sister. Audrey Ellen moved in with her Aunt Ida Foster Silvers and Uncle George Silvers near Belton; Aunt Ida was John Bradson's oldest sister. Audrey left home early in October to live with them. Eula Lee went to Brownwood, Texas in late October to live with her aunt and uncle, Lonzo and Clara Foster. Lonzo Foster was John's younger brother. Ruby Inez stayed with her mother in a little cabin near Rogers. The cabin only had a dirt floor but it was given to them to live in until they could somehow get back on their feet. Some days all they had to eat was a single potato between them; Rosie Alice and little Ruby held on the best they could. For the first time in their young lives, the four Foster sisters were separated and living with other relatives. The sisters missed each other.

Ruby Inez Foster had a lot of spunk and even more feistiness. Rosie Alice and her youngest daughter were barely making a living and most of the time Rosie Alice felt that little Ruby was doing all she could to make it a lot more difficult than was necessary. . . .

Ruby had a pet dog named Jack who followed her everywhere she went; Jack even slept at the foot of her bed and wouldn't let anyone lay a hand on his young mistress—not even her mother. Whenever Ruby would do something that called for a paddling, Rosie Alice would go after Ruby with a switch only to find Jack growling at her. Ruby would climb up in the tree in their yard and when Rosie Alice would go out into the yard after her, Ruby would sic Jack on her own mother. Jack would chase Rosie Alice back into their cabin, barking and growling at her all the way to the door. (If orneriness could be bottled, Ruby would have been wealthy.)

As they got older, the Foster sisters began spending more time with each other since they weren't that many miles apart, except for Eula Lee who was living with her aunt and uncle up in Brownwood. But Lola, Audrey, and Ruby saw one another most every month. The girls were growing up and longed for each other's company.

Very little had changed for Rosie Alice and her four daughters; the other three sisters were still living with relatives. Rosie Alice and Ruby had sometimes been forced to move in temporarily with other family members, either Rosie's sisters or some of John Bradson's sisters. John had abandoned his family in 1910; by 1915 Rosie Alice and Ruby Inez had been forced to live wherever they could. (Years later, Mom and her sisters—Lola and Audrey—would tell how harsh and bitter their childhood years had been.[5] As small children, these sisters endured the painful experience of picking cotton for a living. With little or no money they just survived having very little to eat. Possibly, even more traumatic, was being separated from one another as their mother, Rosie Alice, found it necessary to farm the girls out to live with other relatives. John Bradson had tried very hard to ruin their lives. . .he very nearly succeeded.

---

[5] Author's Note: I never had the opportunity to talk with or get to know Aunt Eula, she died of tetanus when I was 2 years old.

By 1921, two of the Foster sisters were married. Lola Pearl had married Frank Luttrell, and Audrey Ellen married Willie Deavers. Lola moved to Dallas where Frank Luttrell had his home. Audrey Ellen and Willie Deavers moved into the log cabin he owned near Taylor's Valley. Eula Lee and Frank Corbett would marry two years later, in 1923, and live in Brownwood. But in 1921, Ruby would have a truly bizarre experience. . . .Ruby Inez was going on her first date. Two boys from Belton had invited Ruby to go on a ride in the country. The two young men had told Ruby another girl was going with them, and they would be picking her up on the way. Ruby was 17 and had trusted the two young men. The only problem was that there was not another girl going with them. The two young men intended to take advantage of Ruby. As the three of them headed out of Belton, Ruby knew their intentions were less than honorable. In fact, she was told what was going to happen; the two men told her they intended to have their way with her. Ruby could not jump out of the car; the men were driving too fast, and she was seated between them. As the men drove the car into the woods west of Belton, Ruby for the first time began fearing for her safety. She knew the men intended to rape her; but she feared it could be even worse. She feared for her life. The men parked the car and told Ruby to take her clothes off. She told them she damned sure wouldn't and that they had better not try to do it, either. This had a startling effect on the men and Ruby sensed they weren't as dangerous as she had feared. The men pulled her from the car and taking some rope, proceeded to tie her to a tree. The men then informed her that, "If she didn't give in, we'll jest drive off and leave you tied to the damn tree."

Ruby told the men they could just go to hell and to leave her tied to the tree. She said she'd rather die in the woods than to give in to their threats. The men climbed back in their car and drove away leaving Ruby bound tightly to the tree.

For a long time, Ruby Inez feared the men actually intended to leave her just the way she was—all alone and tied to the tree; mebbe they really wuz just pure mean, she thought to herself.

About an hour later—as Ruby cried and called out for help—the men drove back to where they had left her. One of the men walked up to the tree and took out a knife. He approached Ruby and opening the blade, reached out. . .and cut the rope. The man commented: "Ruby, yer damn sure th' contrar'est woman whut I've ever met. Git back in th' car, girl' we ain't gonna hurt ya." The men drove Ruby home; she never saw either of them again.

In 1923 Eula Lee married Frank Corbett and moved in with him in Brownwood, Texas. Ruby Inez Foster also married in 1923. She had met a rancher from Regina, New Mexico when he had come to Belton for the annual rodeo and to look over some livestock. Ruby Inez Foster became Ruby Inez Gay, marrying the young rancher, Bob Gay. The small ranch Bob Gay owned was just outside Regina, a small community just south of Albuquerque, New Mexico. The ranch was nestled in the foothills and mountains in a small valley called a "rain cone." Ruby Inez now lived in a real home. . .with a real floor. . . .

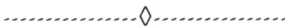

On August 13, 1924, a son was born to Bob and Ruby Inez Gay; the little boy was named Robert J. Gay. Ruby was now a young mother with a husband and her own home. As she thought back on how her young life had started out, she now had every reason to be happy. But she wasn't. A husband, and a house—even one with a floor—did not necessarily make a home, much less a happy one. Ruby's first two years of marriage had revealed some troubling flaws in her young husband's character. Bob Gay had a good job with the Santa Fe Railroad and made decent money. The problem was, he gambled and drank most of it away. Once again in Ruby's young life, she found herself hungry. And as little Robert approached his first birthday, Ruby experienced anew some days when all she and her little boy had to eat was a single potato between them. Ruby knew she would find some way to survive; she had long ago proven that. But to see her child go hungry was more than she could bear.

Ruby Inez had another problem, as well; she knew she was pregnant with her second child. If Bob Gay could not properly feed and care for a wife and child, how would a wife and two children fare under his responsibility? Sadly, Ruby Inez Gay already knew the answer to that self-imposed question. She had no choice but to leave this irresponsible man; he was too much like her own father.

Ruby wrote to her sister Eula Corbett, and a few months later, Frank and Eula Corbett pulled up to Bob Gay's ranch. Ruby loaded her son and her few clothes and headed back to Texas. She would live with her sister until her baby was born. After that...well, Ruby thought to herself, I'll just have ta' cross thet bridge when I get t' it. Ruby, little Robert, and her sister, Eula, and her husband arrived in Brownwood on November 16, 1925. The day was cold and blustery but for the first time in several years, a calming sense of relief embraced Ruby Inez. In spite of her recent troubles, Ruby actually began to feel good about herself. Ruby had survived before; she would again.

----------◊----------

Ruby Inez Foster Gay gave birth to a baby girl on March 4, 1926. The baby was also named Ruby Inez Foster Gay and was born in Brownwood, Brown County, Texas. In later years, as the younger Ruby Inez grew into an adult, others would not always be able to tell mother and daughter apart. Discounting the age difference, the mother and daughter were much alike in personality and temperament. Ruby Inez, the mother, had long been known to be spunky, stubborn, and sometimes just plain ornery.

The younger Ruby Inez would be even more so....

----------◊----------

Eula Corbett was having a cup of coffee in the kitchen with her sister, Ruby; Robert and little Inez were playing on the living room rug. "Ruby," Eula began, "I know you 'n th' kids wanta' be on your own, but honey, Frank an' I just want ya' t' know you 'n th' little ones can stay here long as you want. Lord knows we got plenty o' room."

Ruby smiled at her older sister and reached over to squeeze her hand. "Sweetheart, you are th' dearest sister a body could want' but me 'n th' kids have done been here morn' a year now, 'n its time t' move on." Ruby paused to take a sip of her coffee and continued: "'Sides, Audrey wrote me thet I could prob'ly git a decent place fer me 'n th' kids there in Temple—mebbe even git a fairly good job there at th' laundry. Audrey says she shore would like t' see me 'n th' kids; we ain't seen one 'nother in more'n three years, goin' on four. 'N she says mother misses me, too, 'n shure wants t' see her gran' kids."

Eula smiled at her sister and got up t' pour 'em more coffee. "Ruby, honey—if yer gonna go, I just want ya' t' know me 'n Frank sure gonna miss you 'n th' kids. Least ya' can let me 'n Frank drive you down t' Temple 'n there ain't no argu'ng 'bout that."

Ruby and Eula were both crying as they stood up to hug each other; they held their embrace a long time. The sisters knew they were gonna miss each other.

Ruby Inez and Robert and Little Inez moved into a little duplex in Temple on a nice, sunny spring day. The apartment was small but very clean. Ruby looked down at the floor and thought out loud: "Lord, thank you for this little home, 'n I hope you won't ever let me wind up livin' on a dirt floor agin, not ever." May 12, 1927 was a special time for Ruby; she had just spent more than a year with her dear sister, Eula Lee. Now, Ruby would get to spend some time with her sister, Audrey Ellen, and her mother, Rosie Alice Foster. Ruby enjoyed her time with Eula and Frank up in Brownwood, 'cause her sister had looked after her 'n th' kids real good. But she was back home, now. Bell County was where most of her family lived. Bell County was just home. . . .

Ruby Inez Foster and her two children, Robert Gay and little Inez Foster Gay, had very good neighbors, and many of the neighbors helped look out for the kids. One of Ruby's neighbors knew that Ruby was working very hard at the laundry ('course, Ruby knew only too well that nothing was as hard as pickin' cotton), and she suggested that Ruby give some thought t' doin' warshin' 'n ironin' ther in her own place. "That way, Ruby, you would be with th' kids, 'n still make good money, mebbe even more'n you'd make workin' fer someone else."

Less than a year later, Ruby was doing laundry and ironing clothes for many of her neighbors. Word had spread around the neighborhood, and Ruby's business was doing very well. Some stores around Temple allowed Ruby to post her business address and phone number. These new customers were bringing in a good living for Ruby and her children. The year 1928 was her best year. The work was pretty hard but for the first time in a long time, Ruby was happy. And her kids were well fed. Robert and little Inez were good kids, seldom giving Ruby any reason to paddle them. Robert was now 6 years old, and his little sister was 4; and they were respectful, well-behaved children. And most of the other kids in the neighborhood were. . .well, most of the other kids were just kids. When the children played together, everyone seemed to get along pretty well. Except for little Johnny. . . .

Johnny was 7 years old, and for the most part got along well with all the other kids. But whatever the reason, Johnny seemed to enjoy teasing and picking on little Inez and most times this tormenting really never got out of hand. But this one day, little Johnny just could not resist picking on Inez; he kept up his teasing and taunting until finally he made her cry. The kids were playing on Ruby's porch, and Robert had had enough of Johnny's ways; Robert got up, grabbed Johnny by the neck and back of his shirt, and threw him down the steps out 'o the sidewalk. Little Robert was furious! "Don't you ever pick on my sister again—you hear me!" Johnny looked up, bewildered by this angry outburst and not really sure what had just happened. Inez looked up at her brother—she had never seen her brother this angry, either; he looked ready to bite a nail in half. After a few moments, all the kids resumed the games they had been playing, and everything returned to normal. Children don't stay mad for long. But Johnny never again picked on Robert's little sister.

-----------------◊-----------------

Chapter 15

Cajun Country, Centreville, Louisiana

Timeline: 1900-1926

The Floating Gallery returned to Centreville during the summer of 1900. Those wanting family pictures would line up along the Bayou Teche awaiting their turn to board the photographer's barge. Word would spread throughout the towns of Franklin and Centreville, and families would gather up their young'uns and then try to pose the squirming tykes into a successful sitting.

Small towns like Franklin and Centreville lacked the populations to support an intown studio; back in those days, a local photographer likely would have starved. An enterprising photographer in Lafayette determined that if those prospects along the southern reaches of the Bayou couldn't come to him, then he would just have to go to them. Outfitting a small barge with living quarters and studio equipment, the photographer would then visit all of the towns and communities between Lafayette and Morgan City. Sometimes he would be gone several weeks.

The Floating Gallery had just completed a very successful couple of days up in the town of Franklin. The photographer headed on downstream toward the smaller community of Centreville; he knew of at least one family that would show up. Over the years, this family had proven to be a very good customer; and the family was still growing.

The Packards came, just as the photographer knew they would. Chas Elbridge and Mary Margaret Packard rounded up their kids and headed for the Teche. Elbridge, Jr. had grumbled some when his mother made him wash his face and comb his unruly hair. The youngest, little Ira Bowman, had fussed a bit when his father changed his gown, but a lump of sugar completely took Ira's concentration off the clothing issue. The girls—Eulalia, Lucille, and Mary—couldn't wait; the three sisters loved having their pictures taken. Especially since their mother had just recently bought them new dresses that were identical, as this precluded the girls arguing over colors and styles.

The Packard family moved up the boarding ramp onto the barge, and the photographer seated the parents in front of the backdrop screen. As Chas Elbridge and his wife, Maggie, took their seats, the photographer had the three girls stand between and slightly behind their parents. He picked up little Ira to place him on his mother's lap when Chas Elbridge stopped him. "No, I want little Elbridge there beside his mother and hand me the baby; I'll hold Ira on my knee. Yep. That's how I…does this look alright?" He asked. The photographer responded, "Yessir. That looks jest fine. OK. Everyone look up here—gimme a big smile—hold it!"

The photographer took two more poses, and the Packards were free to go. He told Elbridge the proofs would be mailed, and the family could pick out the ones they wanted which sometimes took three weeks.

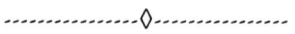

Chas Elbridge and Maggie owned three carriages. Actually, they owned two carriages and a small cart. The parents had a large, black shiny carriage which was mostly used for church and other such formal occasions. Their other carriage was for the girls; this was a surrey with fringe along the cover. The girls would take turns handling this surrey as well as the single pony their father allowed them to harness to this rig. The small cart was for the two boys, little Elbridge and Ira Bowman, their two-year old. Chas Elbridge would hitch one of their goats to this cart, as he held the reins and walked the goat in a circle; the two little boys got a great deal of enjoyment from this ride in the sideyard.

When Ira Bowman was a child—maybe 5 or 6 years old—Mary Margaret (Maggie) Packard would prepare him a lunch and pack it in a half-gallon syrup can. The syrup can had a wire handle with which to carry it around. Maggie would also prepare a second lunch pail in another empty syrup can for little Thomas, the son of Elbridge Packard's foreman, old Jeremiah Brown. Jeremiah's family worked in the Packard fields; as field foreman, Jeremiah was one of Elbridge Packard's most loyal and trusted employees. And like many of the field hands who worked there, Jeremiah's family was black. Maggie Packard told this story many years later: "Little Ira Bowman and Thomas would sit on a big log in our backyard, eating their food out of the pails. Most times Thomas would reach over and take some food from Bowman's pail, and Bowman would take food from Thomas' pail. The boys would sit there, laughing and eating out of one another's lunch pail."

---◊---

In 1899 another son was born to the Packards; he was named Isaac William Packard. Isaac William only lived five months; he died in April 1900.

---◊---

On Christmas Eve 1900, Maggie wrote a letter to her sister, Kate, who was in the hospital at Lafayette. Her letter read like this:

Dear Kate

> For a wonder I am all alone. (That is Bo and Elbie are here but they are asleep.) The others have gone to that long talked of Christmas house. Eula has been on her head all day almost. She came to me about two o'clock and told (me) she had gone to see what time it was and she thought I had better dress them as she thought it was ten minutes to five. Nell and Chester have taken them to the hall. Elbridge is in town to. I am rather tired as I have been very busy all day. I cooked my turkey this evening and had so many other things to do. Allways the way on Monday you know. Tell Isaac if he wants a piece of that turkey he had better get Elbridge to express it to him. As you know turkeys don't last long when Elbridge is around. We kept the largest one for N.Y.s so you all will get your share yet. Mama was here with Maggie Sunday evening. She did look to sweet, with her hood and that little blue sacque Mrs. Packard made for her and her cheeks were like to pink roses. Mama says she is good as

she can be. Dr. Bowman's baby has had spasms again, and he is better now. I am glad I had a chance to write to you tonight as I know it would be an impossibility tomorrow. Such times as these young ones expect to have tomorrow. I am glad to hear you are improving and hope you will continue to do so until you are entirely well. Chester and Nell came in with the children, talked awhile, and have gone home. I thought I wasn't going to get Eula and Lucille to bed they talked so much. Mary as well said was so over-joyed she was dumb for once. Elbridge teased Eula told her while they were at the hall Santa Claus stopped here said well as they were not at home he would not leave anything. She did not put much faith in what he said however. Even Maggie went to the Christmas house. I wonder what she thought of it. The chimney was red boxes made like a brick. They were filled with candy. Lucille wants her Papa to build one like it. Elbridge and I just finished fixing the children's toys. What a hubbub there will be here tomorrow for awhile. It gives me a headache almost to think about it. I wish you and Isaac could be with us tomorrow. Not to enjoy the noise but the dinner. Well, I must stop as I am tired. I wish you both a happy pleasant time tomorrow. I know you must be glad to think you will be home so soon. Good night.

Your loving sister
Maggie P.[6]

---

[6] Author's Note: This was a very interesting letter in so many ways. First of all, I was intrigued by the way Grandmother Mary Margaret Packard used the word "to"—intrigued because Grandmother Packard had been a school teacher when she met and married our grandfather. And so many of her expressions confounded me initially. Let's just say I was most fortunate when, in 1996, I drove to this part of southern Louisiana and had the opportunity to sit down with Aunt Mary. This wonderful lady interpreted all of the letter, as Aunt Mary had been 4 years old when Grandmother Packard wrote to her sister, Kate. I sat down with this surviving older sister of my father when Aunt Mary was 99 years old! Here are her "translations": The Christmas house was built for the children inside the little Centreville Presbyterian Church of which the Packard family were parishioners. Chas Elbridge Packard, and his father, Captain Chas Howard Packard, constructed the house out of wood and made the "red brick" chimney out of red boxes. The boxes were filled with candy for the kids.

The Crepe Myrtle

Harry Packard was born on February 12, 1901. His full Christian name was Harrison Cooke Packard with his middle name coming from his Great-grandfather William Cook (their old English name had been Cooke.) From the time he was born, Harry was a scrapper. Harry just loved a good fight. . . .

Caroline Packard was born April 17, 1902; she only lived three months, dying in June of 1902. Marcelita Packard was born November 2, 1903; her little brother, Franklin Packard, was born August 24, 1905. Leslie Packard was born October 13, 1906 and died June 25, 1907.

Alexander Packard joined the Packard family on the fourth of November, 1907. Alexander and Ira Bowman would develop very close brotherly ties. . . .

----------------◊----------------

    Grandmother Maggie Packard said she "kept the largest turkey for N.Y.s"—that is New Years. The other Maggie mentioned was little Maggie (Margaret) Wooster, our Grandmother Packard's niece, and the daughter mentioned of Kate and Isaac Wooster.
    The Mrs. Packard mentioned was Great-grandmother Louisa Packard, wife of Captain Chas Howard Packard. Bo, of course, would be my father, Ira Bowman Packard; and Dr. Bowman was the family doctor and dentist after whom my father was named.
    Aunt Mary said her sister Eula "had been on her head all day," meaning she was very excited about Christmas. She was bouncing around the house all day—"on her head," anxious to go see the Christmas house.
    Grandmother Packard instructed her sister, Kate, to have Isaac get in touch with Elbridge to let him know if Kate and Isaac wanted some of the turkey; in other words, Isaac needed to "express" to Elbridge if they wanted some turkey.
    And finally, Aunt Mary explained why her mother, Maggie Packard, had written "Mary was 'dumb' for once." It seems that when the little 4 year old Mary arrived at church, she saw Santa Claus sitting up front near the Christmas house, and she said, "he was dressed all in red and had big white hair and white beard, and I became afraid he would steal me or kidnap me. She said a lot of kids in those days loved pictures of Santa, but in person he could be terrifying! And she was terrified of him and more or less speechless or "dumb" for once.I have added this letter to the reference section so you can try to read it in its original form. The letter was written on Grandfather Packard's business letterhead:
                      Packard & Dugas, Dealers in Fresh Meats
       Centreville, St. Mary, La.   December 24 ~~189~~ 1900
(the 189 had been scratched out because the year now was 1900)

Charles B. Packard

By 1908 the Packard boys were spending many of their leisure hours swimming in Bayou Teche. Only the older boys—Harry, Bowman, and Elbridge, Jr.—were allowed to swim in the Bayou. The others were still too little, for now; but their time would soon come. And in this same year, the older girls—Eula, Lucille, and Mary—were allowed to wear heels to church. The girls would walk to church on Sunday mornings by themselves; but on Sunday nights, even though their church was just a few hundred feet or so from their home, their father and grandfather would always escort them. Their poppa, Chas Elbridge Packard, would walk in front, carrying a coal oil lantern, and their grandfather, Chas Howard Packard, would bring up the rear; he also carried a glowing lantern. The girls would be in the middle, walking single file. This procession would walk down the middle of the dirt road, all the way to church, never once using the nearby sidewalks. When asked many years later, why the sidewalks were not used, Mary replied: "Because, the sidewalks back in those days were made of wooden slats; they were maybe one-half inch apart, and our heels would have become stuck. We had no other choice; we had to walk in the road."

----------◊----------

For her twelfth birthday on June 3, 1908, Mary Packard was gifted with a horse by her father. Chas Elbridge handed the reins to Mary and spoke: "Mary, I expect you to take good care of this animal; you must see to it that he's fed and watered daily. Do you understand?"

"Yes, Poppa," Mary replied. "I'll take such good care of him; you just wait 'n see." Mary was so excited to have her own horse and was impatiently waiting for her father to complete his instructions to her so she could jump on this magnificent beast and ride off across their fields.

Chas Elbridge continued: "You also must see that he's brushed and combed; a horse requires a great deal of attention, Mary." Elbridge paused a moment and again spoke: "And one other thing—I absolutely expect of you proper behavior in the way you ride your horse. You are not to straddle him like men do; you will behave ladylike and ride sidesaddle. You understand me, Mary?"

"Yes, Poppa. I will be very careful, 'n I will ride as you say." Mary paused to catch her breath, she was so excited. "Poppa, can I ride him. . .can I ride 'ol Nick, now? Please, can I?"

Chas Elbridge smiled at his daughter and asked: "Nick? Is that what you've named him, already?"

"Yes, Poppa, this is my good boy, ol' Nick!" (In later years Aunt Mary would tell me that she would "ride ol' Nick across th' fields with his mane and tail flying and my long auburn hair streaming back of me, as well!" She said sometimes her poppa would catch her astraddle Nick, and he would really scold her. After sternly lecturing her on how she was to ride, she would sit sidesaddle and ride off at a slow trot. Once she could see that her Poppa was out of sight, Aunt Mary would swing her leg across the saddle and away they would go. Aunt Mary said when she was out with ol' Nick, she knew she would rather ride her horse, than eat.)

The year 1910 had started out well for the Packard family. Everyone was in good health, and Elbridge's business was growing extremely well. And by spring, Maggie Packard knew she was again with child. Dr. Bowman had reasoned that this baby would most likely come around September, maybe even October.

Then out of nowhere a real tragedy struck the family that summer. Lucille Packard had been on an outing with her church group, and they had paused for a lunch break. Lucille walked over to the water pump to get a cool drink of water. At the time, nothing appeared to be wrong with the pump, or with the water, as Lucille pumped some cool well water and drank.

Within a few weeks, Lucille had been diagnosed with dreaded typhoid fever. Dr. Bowman did all that medical science allowed, but Lucille grew weaker. Most of the Packard family had gathered around Lucille's bed; several of her sisters were crying. Elbridge was beside himself with grief. Lucille looked at her family standing by her bed and spoke softly: "Oh, please don't cry. Don't grieve over me, don't you know that soon I'll be in a far better place? Just please don't cry." Lucille passed away June 12, 1910; she was 16 years old.[7]

---

[7] Author's Note: Aunt Mary was one of the girls beside Lucille's deathbed. She said Lucille was such a strong believer in God; Lucille died very peacefully. But Elbridge grieved over the loss of this daughter for many months afterward.

Hyland Packard was born into the family on October 5, 1910. The Packard Clan had now grown to 3 girls and 6 boys; the family was already in a holiday mood, what with their newest birth and Christmas just around the corner. And most all of the family, except Elbridge, had moved on from the pain of losing Lucille.

A year later, the youngest girl in the family was born. Catherine Packard was born September 26, 1911, five days after the thirteenth birthday of Ira Bowman Packard.

Late in November of 1912, Maggie Packard called two of her sons into the kitchen. Bowman, who was now 14, and Alex, who had just had his fifth birthday, came inside to see what their mother wanted. "You wanted us, Mama?" Bowman asked.

"Yes, son; I need you t' take your little brother t' see Doc Bowman. Alex has a tooth needin' looked at." Alex made a face at this pronouncement; he purely didn' wanta do anything but stay outside 'n play. 'N he 'specially didn' wanna see no doctor.

Alex protested: "Aw, Mama, I don't wanna go see Doc Bowman; can't I go nex' week? My tooth ain't hurtin', anyways."

"Isn't hurting, Alex; th' word is isn't, not ain't; and no, you're not going next week. You're going right now. And you're going because I say you're going. Now go!" Turning toward her older son, Maggie Packard said: "Bowman, you make him go and stay with him to be sure Doc Bowman looks at that tooth."

Bowman looked over at Alex and jerked his head toward the door, letting Alex know it was time to get moving. The two brothers walked across their big frontyard, heading down the road aways toward Dr. Bowman's offices. Crossing the dirt road, they climbed the stairs up to Dr. Bowman's and walked in. Dr. Bowman looked up from his patient in the chair and spoke: "Hello, boys, Bowman, you and Alex take a seat. I'll be with you lads in a minute or two."

The two brothers sat down and almost immediately Alex started fidgeting in his chair. "Alex, sit still 'n be quiet, or I'll tie a knot in yer ear!" Alex wasn't sure if his older brother could really tie a knot in his ear, or not; but he sure didn't plan to find out. Sometimes his big brother had a bit of a temper.

After Bowman and Alex had been waiting in the outer office awhile, a loud yell came from the patient in th' chair. "Dang it, Doc, that hurt!"

Less than two seconds later, Alex bolted from his seat, shoved the screen door open, and went sailing down the backstairs. The screen door had just slammed shut as Alex was clearing the bottom steps. Bowman reached the door just as Alex went flying around the corner of the building. Bowman shook his head and thought out loud: "Boy, Mama sure ain't gonna be happy 'bout this; that kid's gonna get a paddlin', sure as shootin'."[8]

---◊---

On February 13, 1913, Chas Elbridge died from pneumonia—double pneumonia, actually. His death, while tragic and devastating to his young family, should not have come as too great a surprise. Elbridge had long suffered from bouts with pneumonia, and because of his work habits, Elbridge kept putting himself and his health in vulnerable positions. He worked very hard.

But what was tragic about his death was the set of circumstances put into play almost immediately after his death. Those circumstances changed forever the lives of two families: the Packard family of Chas Elbridge and Mary Margaret Packard, and the other family, whose name cannot and will not be revealed.[9]

---

[8] Author's Note: In 1994 I sat with Uncle Alex in his small house in Centreville while he told me this story about the doctor visit and other stories, as well, involving him and our dad. In 1994 Uncle Alex was 87 years old and possessed a sharp memory. Alex said when that patient yelled out, he was out of his chair and down the stairs in a flash. And he said he never went back to see about his tooth. He figured his Mama must have forgotten about it, since there were so many kids in the family to keep track of.

[9] Author's Note: Because of a promise I made to three of Dad's sisters—Aunt Mary, Aunt Marcy, and Aunt K.C.—I must change the name of the individual whose

Charles B. Packard

Here, in the words of Aunt Mary, is the story. . . .

"Poppa had come down with pneumonia, 'cause he'd been working awfully hard in his store and his stockyards. Doctor Bowman had finally put him in bed for some rest, but Poppa just kept getting worse. The family was by his bed, we were all cryin', 'cause we knew Poppa was dying. I became frantic, running across th' street into the grocery store, pleading with someone to come help my Poppa, 'cause he was dyin', and I just wanted someone to help save Poppa.

After awhile I ran back home, but Poppa had already died. Oh, it was so sad; 'n we were just crying and standing around Poppa—we just didn't know what to do. About that time, this old uncle came across the street with a couple of his hired hands, old Uncle Zeke, th' mean ol' devil, told Momma not to worry that he'd take care of everything and that we didn't have to worry about money. He told Momma he'd take Poppa's safe to keep everything taken care of. This mean uncle took th' safe; his hired hands carried it back across th' street to where he and Momma's sister lived. They lived across th' street in the house which Poppa had built for them; and old Uncle Zeke had never repaid Poppa for building him a house.

Uncle Zeke ran th' bank next to th' grocery store, you see, and he 'n a coupla attorneys took over all th' money Poppa had in his bank and all the land deeds that Poppa had been buying up for a long time. This old uncle gave Momma and all of us some money over the next several years but it was nothing compared to what we'd had if Poppa had lived. Old Uncle Zeke cheated us out of several thousand dollars and title to all the hundreds and hundreds of acres Poppa and our family had owned."

When asked why Grandmother Packard hadn't kept the safe and tended to the family's business herself, Aunt Mary replied, almost in a surprised tone: "Why honey, Momma couldn't do that; women weren't allowed

---

duplicity and outright theft left the Packard family in 1913, in precarious financial circumstances. Most all of the descendants of Elbridge and Maggie Packard know the name of this person; however, I promised not to reveal his name in our family story. Suffice it to say our Packard families have survived quite successfully and quite extensively. Grandmother Packard and Grandfather Packard would have been proud.

to do business back then. We couldn't conduct banking matters or sign contracts or papers 'n things like that; we just weren't allowed to."

As this story unfolded, more and more circumstances came to be known. For one thing, Chas Elbridge had continued buying land south of Franklin and Centreville, in the area around Bayou Sallie road. This land was bought by Chas Elbridge for $.10 an acre, as it was mostly swampland. During the mid-1930s substantial oil reserves were discovered on these swamplands.

Our uncle, Marvin Morris, who was married to Dad's sister, Marcelita Packard Morris, told the family some years later that he conservatively estimated this oil fortune at more than $35,000,000. Uncle Marvin Morris was a very successful and well-educated businessman; he was not given to making exaggerated claims.

For another thing, Chas Elbridge had well over $13,000 in the bank—quite a lot of money in 1913 and title to his meat market and stockyards.

Also, the Packard family owned several hundred acres in the lands around Chas Elbridge's meat market and stock pens. These were rich, fertile acres near the Bayou Teche, acres which were planted in sugarcane and cotton.

While he was alive, Chas Elbridge Packard had worked hard and amassed sizable holdings in the Centreville area. The Packard family was quite well-to-do and one of the wealthiest families in town.

With the death of Charles Elbridge, the safe and all of its contents were now in the hands of old Zeke Forrester, the banker. With the help of his lawyer cronies, Zeke could now begin conversion of all the Packard holdings into his own name and could, himself, become even wealthier.

Only one circumstance stood in his way: that circumstance was named Chas Elbridge Packard, Jr.

On the death of his father on February 13, 1913, Chas Elbridge Packard, Jr. became "head" of the family. At 16 years of age and over 6 feet tall, Chas Elbridge Packard, Jr. was a strapping young man and potentially a dangerous adversary for the schemes of the old uncle, Zeke Forrester. Something had to be done by Zeke and his accomplices if they wanted to safely circumvent any retaliation from this son of Chas Elbridge Packard, Sr. That "something" was World War I.

----------◊----------

Aunt Mary continued with her story: "Not long after World War I started in 1914, this old Uncle Zeke began encouraging Elbridge to join the Army. At first no one in our family thought much of it, as old Uncle Zeke provided Momma with some money from time to time so we weren't starvin' or nothin' like that. You see, this ol' uncle had not started taking over Poppa's money and land just yet, 'cause he knew Elbridge woulda gone after him, for sure. But Elbridge didn't turn 18 'til 1915, an' Momma wanted him to stay home an' see to things in Poppa's place." When asked about Elbridge staying home to take care of things, Aunt Mary replied: "That's just how folks did it back then; when the father of a family died, th' oldest son was expected to stay home to help see to things, don't ya' see? And in 1914, your daddy, Bowman, was only 16, so Momma wanted Elbridge to stay home a mite longer. Anyways, not long after the year 1915 started, your daddy was about to turn 17, so Momma let Elbridge enlist in th' Army.

At that time, Elbridge believed his Uncle Zeke was just givin' him good advice as to his future; Uncle Zeke told him th' Army would give him good trainin' 'n a good education for his future 'n all. We didn't figure out 'til sometime later that ol' Uncle Zeke wanted Elbridge in the Army so's he would be in the fightin' during' th' war 'n git himself killed. When asked how the family came to realize that, Aunt Mary said: "Oh, honey, when somethin' that evil is takin' place, there's always someone what's goin' to let a word or two out, and before too long, we knew—we just knew. People that worked in ol' Uncle Zeke's bank; maybe some secretary in one o' his lawyer cronies' offices, who knows—but word just got out 'n we wrote to Elbridge to inform him 'n he was hoppin' mad; least, that's the tone in his letters what we received from him. Elbridge said if he survived th' war, he'd take care of ol' Uncle Zeke, when he got home. He meant it, too; I knew my brother pretty well. I'm sure he meant to shoot that mean ol' devil."

We had to pause while I put a new blank tape in my recorder; Aunt Mary made us some sweetened ice tea, and then we all sat back down. Aunt Mary continued: "Time passed 'n before long the War ended around 1918, an' we were all lookin' forward to havin' Elbridge back home. All except ol' Zeke; that mean ol' cuss knew he'd best disappear quick like if he didn't wanta git hisself killed by my brother. Th' word we got was that some of ol' Zeke's friends told him he'd' best disappear for a year or so, 'cause they said: 'Thet boy's gonna come after ya', sure as shootin' 'n he means ta' kill you, Zeke, kill ya' dead!'"

Well, ol' uncle Zeke disappeared, alright; folks said he'd gone to New Aw'lins on some bus'ness, or somethin'; 'n sure enough, when Elbridge got back home, he got one of Poppa's pistols 'n went lookin' for Zeke. After a coupla weeks, Momma sat down with Elbridge 'n convinced him that wasn't too smart, goin' after his uncle like that, even if he did deserve t' be shot. She said most everybody knew about it, 'n as prominent as ol' Zeke was, the law'd have to arrest Elbridge 'n at least put him in prison. So after a bit, Elbridge 'n all the' rest of us just sorta' got on with things 'n let it slide. We figgered sooner or later, things'd catch up with that mean ol' devil." Aunt Mary paused a moment, as she 'remembered on something,' she said: "Your daddy, Bowman Packard, was just about ready to join Elbridge in the' war, when it ended. Momma had told your daddy he could enlist, 'cause your daddy had just turned 20 in 1918; 'n Harry was now 17, so Momma said Harry could look after things at home. Your daddy was on th' train to New Aw'lins to board a troop ship, I guess on its way to Europe. We wuz all glad Elbridge had made it, 'n we didn't want no more brothers having' to' go to war, y' know?"

The Packard boys enjoyed fighting, not because they disliked each other, for the Packard brothers were very close; rather, the brothers simply enjoyed boxing. Elbridge had given the boys several pairs of boxing gloves the past Christmas, saying they needed to learn how to defend themselves. Elbridge wouldn't allow the two youngest, Frank and Alex, to fight with the older brothers. But Elbridge, Jr., Bowman, and Harry could go at it any time they wanted. Harry never got his fill of boxing; he was ready to go with anyone who'd put on the gloves with him. Harry never could whip his two older brothers—especially his brother, Elbie—but he always got in some good licks against 'em. Elbie and Bowman got to th' point where they sorta' dreaded taking on Harry; Harry had a way of punishing his opponents regardless of their age or size. Harry was never without two pairs of boxing gloves, one for him, and one for whoever would put 'em on against him. Harry was said to have even slept with 'em on his bed.

----------------◊----------------

Christmas gatherings at the Centreville Presbyterian Church continued to bring festive excitement for the Packard children; in particular, the younger ones looked forward to these with youthful anticipation.

Their grandfather, Charles Howard Packard, especially relished these moments with the children, as he tried to carry on with the traditions which his son, Charles Elbridge, had begun before his death in 1913.

This Christmas of 1916 held the promise of holiday joy for all, and spirits were high as the children were led into the church. Once all were seated, the pastor invited all the children "to come down front for a visit with dear ol' Santa." The baby of the family, little Daniel Packard, was 3 years old, and the next oldest, Catherine (K.C.) Packard, was now 5 years of age. Several of the Packard children headed down the aisle, when some sort of fear gripped K.C. The sight of "Santa Claus," with his vivid red suit and all the massive white hair and beard suddenly terrified her, and she yelled out: "Dan, stop! Don't go up there, Dan! If you sit on his lap he's gonna take you away 'n kidnap you, Dan!"[10]

With that, the entire congregation erupted in fits of laughter! Even the pastor and dear ol' Santa could not contain themselves, and it was several minutes before the laughing subsided.

---

[10] Author's Note: Aunt K.C. told me how frightened she had been that Christmas—somehow she just knew ol' Santa Claus was going to kidnap little Dan. And in her joy at getting "something special" from her grand-poppa she had gotten all tongue-twisted that day at school. Christmas of 1916 was the last Charles Howard Packard shared with all his grandchildren. He died in 1917 at the age of 84.

The Crepe Myrtle

---◊---

Early in 1917 K.C. Packard was sitting on her grandfather's lap as he told K.C. of an upcoming voyage he was going on. "Catherine," Chas Howard began: "I'm going overseas to Morocco, and when I return, I'll have a gift for you."

This pleased K.C. immensely, and she asked her grandfather what he was bringing her. "Catherine, I'm going to bring you some pretty white cotton socks and a pair of red Moroccan leather shoes."

K.C. couldn't wait to tell her classmates at school! Next day at class, she announced: "My grand-poppa is bringin' me some white cotton shoes and red leather socks!"

She had gotten it all backwards, and the kids all laughed and teased her for the longest time!

---◊---

Harry still loved to fight; he'd put on th' gloves with anyone, anywhere. 'N every chance he got, he'd either challenge one of his brothers, or else he'd make one of them fight with some of their friends. By now Harry was 18, Bowman was 21, Frank was 14, and their younger brother Alex was 12. Alex had just got out of school that day and was on his way home. The day was bright 'n sunny 'n already pretty warm for March of 1919. Alex was walkin' down the wood sidewalk towards home when he heard his brother, Harry, yell at him, "Alex! Git yer ass over here, right now." Alex saw his brother standin' across the road with another fella 'bout th' same size as Harry. As Alex walked over to them, he could see that the other guy was a bit bigger'n Harry 'n sure bigger'n hisself. "What ya' want, Harry?" Alex asked.

"Yer gonna fight this fella; that's what I want. 'N yer gonna whip 'im, or else I'm gonna whip yer ass when we git home. Ya got that?"

"But he's bigger'n me, Harry. S'pose he whips me? Alex didn't care much for his odds.

"Don't matter; yer gonna fight 'im; 'n if ya' don't, I'm gonna whip yer ass; 'n if ya lose, I'm gonna whip you, too!" When asked how he did, Alex replied: "Oh, I fought 'im whipped 'im, too. Didn't have too much choice, seein' as how Harry was gonna whip me one way or t'other."

Alex told about another time a year or two later when he and Harry were over in Franklin; they were standing on a corner, leaning up against this building when a big, shiny black automobile pulled up to th' curb. The car had Texas license plates 'n looked fairly expensive. A pretty husky fella got out of th' car and spoke to th' brothers: "How ya' do? I seen you had some boxin' gloves; you fellers boxers?" The stranger asked.

"We sure are," Harry shot right back. "You be inter'sted in puttin' 'em on?"

The big fella replied: "Well, reckon as I jest might; lemme git outa my coat 'n we'll jest go a round er two."

Harry and th' big stranger put on the gloves, laced 'em up 'n started circlin' one 'nother. Quick as a snake strike, th' big stranger shot out a right and caught Harry pretty good aside his head. Harry staggered back a coupla steps 'n fell against th' building. "How'd you like that 'un?" the stranger asked with a grin on his face. Harry stood up, rubbing a glove to his cheek. "Yeah," Harry said, "you got me pretty good." They circled each other, jabbin 'n feintin' at each other for a bit, 'n then Harry shot out with a hook that caught th' big fella smack on th' jaw 'n sent th' stranger sprawlin' across th' hood of his own car. Harry got a big grin himself and asked: "'N how'd ya' like that 'un, sport?" Th' big stranger at first just scowled at Harry 'n then slowly a big grin just sorta grew on his face. "Yep," the stranger agreed, "ya dang sure popped me good, kid."

Harry and th' stranger sparred around a bit longer with neither landing another solid blow. The big stranger dropped his gloves 'n said: "Well, boys, reckon as I got to get back on th' road; gotta be in "Nawlins by t'morrow." Harry took off his own gloves and asked: "What'cha headin' t' New Awlins fer, mister? Got some bus'ness over there er something?"

"Sure have," th' stranger said. "I've got a match over there t'morrow night; that's how I make my livin'. I'm a professional prizefighter, kid. 'N ya' just gave me a helluva good scrap. You'd make a right fair prizefighter, yerself. Ya' got a helluva right hook!" The big stranger got in his car and slowly drove away from the two brothers. . . .

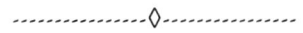

Frank Queen and his wife, Kate, were uncle and aunt to Mary Margaret Packard and great-uncle and great-aunt to all the Packard children. Frank Queen was a retired U.S. Marshall who had served the southern district of Louisiana for a long period of time during the late 1800s, having retired around the turn of the century. In his retirement, Frank Queen bought a good-sized farm south of Centreville in the southern part of St. Mary's Parish. Old man Queen had mostly planted sugarcane on his lands and cultivated a very large parcel near the house for his garden. He and his wife lived comfortably, enjoying the produce that came from this large vegetable garden. Frank Queen was a stern, crusty old warrior and didn't put up with a lot of nonsense from folks and most especially not from his own family—in particular, not from Alexander Packard. So for a period of time during the World War I years, when his great-nephew, Frank, was around the age of 12, and his great-nephew, Alex, was about 10, Frank Queen would frequently hire these two brothers for odd jobs around his farm. At least, Frank Queen tried to hire them to work. . . .

These are stories told by Uncle Alex Packard:

"Old Uncle Queen would hire me'n Frank to work sometimes cuttin' sugarcane 'n other chores 'round his place, but mostly we'd work in his garden. One time he told me 'n Frank we wuz t' plant these flower bulbs in Aunt Kate's flower garden 'round the house. He told Frank, anyways, since he wuz th' oldest, so he wuz in charge." Uncle Alex would hesitate from time to time, as though he was recalling those long ago memories. And sometimes he'd even grin a bit, as he was now. "So Frank brought th' basket with th' bulbs 'n he started turnin' up th' soil for me t' plant 'em. He'd dig up a coupla' feet with th' spade fork 'n I'd stick 'em in th' dirt. Frank musta' stopped t' take a breather, 'cause he yelled, 'Alex, durn yer hide; yer plantin' em upside down! Hell fire, they won't grow like that. Now we'll hav 'ta go back 'n dig 'em all up, 'n this time ya' better do 'em right!' Alex paused a moment, then said: "Guess Frank didn't have much sense o' humor."

"'Nother time," Alex volunteered, "ol' Uncle Queen had us come out t' dig potatoes. Frank got us a couple o' spade forks, 'n we headed t' th' garden. Frank started on th' first row, spadin' up th' soil 'n the potatoes; I was followin' behind him, coverin' 'em back up. Ol' man Queen musta seen me, 'cause he yelled: 'Alex, git over here!' Boy, wuz he hot. I walked over to him, 'n he asked me what th' hell I wuz doin', 'n I said, Uncle Queen, I'm coverin' up yer potatoes. He looked at me a coupla seconds 'n said: 'Alex, I want ya ta run back ta town.' When I asked Uncle Queen why, he just said: "Cause when ya git ther, th' first thing I want ya' to do is to tell 'em I jest fired yer ass.'" (Uncle Alex just chuckled for a second or two; I figured he was remembering what his old Uncle Queen's expression must have been, as the young Alex had confessed so brazenly to covering up the potatoes!)

By 1922, many of the Packard children were grown and married like Eula, Mary, even Marcelite, who was 19; Elbridge, the oldest son, was married and working at a power utility plant. Bowman and Harry were working for Western Union, stringing lines for the telegraph system throughout southern Louisiana; Bowman and Harry were still single and living in Franklin in the same boardinghouse in which their father had once lived.

The children still living at home with Mary Margaret Packard were Frank, who now was 17, and Alex, who was 15. Hyland was now 12, K.C., the only daughter still at home was 11, and the youngest, Daniel Packard, was now 9. Dan had been born late in 1913, the same year his father died. Dan was never held by Chas Elbridge Packard as his youngest would not be born until months after Elbridge had died from pneumonia.

In 1922 tragedy once more darkened the doorway of the Packard family. The youngest son, Dan Packard, and some friends were swimming in the Bayou Teche. With these young men was little Thomas, Jr., the son of Thomas Brown. Little Thomas was 8 years old and was the grandson of old Jeremiah Brown, who had been the field foreman for Chas Elbridge for several years.

The boys were playing water tag, and several long minutes had passed before little Thomas was missed. The boys frantically began searching for him, diving repeatedly into the Teche, desperately trying to locate th' boy. Some half hour later the little boy was found, entwined among some underwater plants. His limp body was pulled to the surface, and Doctor Bowman was brought to the Bayou Teche banks. It was too late to save the little boy. He had died in the waters where so many hundreds of little boys like him had spent their warm summer days. (Many years later, Aunt Mary would tell me this story, and how grief-stricken Dan had been. Just as our father, Bowman Packard, had been close friends with Thomas Brown, having shared many snacks out of empty syrup pails, so had Dan Packard become close friends with Thomas, Jr. Aunt Mary said Dan grieved for a very long time. . . .)

---◊---

And in 1926, Bowman Packard and Alex Packard moved to Temple, Texas; Bowman had taken a new job with the Atlantic Oil Company out of Dallas, Texas.

---◊---

Chapter 16

Ruby and Bo–Temple, Texas Years

Timeline: 1926-1940

Bowman Packard started working for railroads back in Franklin, Louisiana around 1920; he and a younger brother, Harry Packard, had both worked for the Texas/Western Union Lines in the southern Louisiana region. Not long after, Bowman and a close friend, Boots, had begun stringing telegraph lines for the Western Union Company. Bowman, Boots, and Harry ran in close circles; many of their friends said Boots was almost as much a brother to Bowman as his true brothers. Packard blood was the difference....

In 1926 Bowman Packard accepted an offer to go to work for the Atlantic Oil & Pipeline Company that was headquartered in Dallas, Texas. The company wanted Bowman Packard to fill the post of foreman of their telephone-line system throughout the general area of Central Texas; this area stretched from Navasota to Huntsville to Palestine, Hillsboro, Gatesville, Lampasas, and over to Rockdale. Bowman's job was to keep all the telephone lines in this area repaired and in good working order and was to headquarter out of Temple, Texas. Alex Packard followed his older brother to Texas....

--------◊--------

Ruby Inez Foster Gay had moved to Temple with her two small children, little Robert and her namesake, little Inez, in 1927. Robert was 3 years old; Inez was a 1-year old toddler. Ruby had taken up residence in a nice clean duplex, where she would eventually set up an in-house laundry and ironing business to support her young family. Ruby worked very hard, and at times she struggled to make ends meet. But she and the children had a comfortable place to live and most of the time enough to eat.

--------◊--------

The Crepe Myrtle

Little Inez Foster Gay was 2 years old when her father, Bob Gay, came to Temple; he planned to take little Robert and Inez back to New Mexico with him. Ruby had left the children under the care of a good neighbor while she rode the bus into downtown to take care of some business. Ruby had to draw some money from her savings to pay rent and buy some food. Bob Gay drove up to their house, parked his car, and knocked on th' door. When the neighbor lady opened the door, Bob Gay said: "I'm here for m' kids; I'm their daddy." The neighbor lady was momentarily caught off guard and stammered: "Why, these. . .these are Ruby's kids. Who'd you. . .you say you're their pa? Does Ruby know you're coming for 'em?" Bob Gay walked on in th' house 'n told little Robert t' git his clothes 'n help Inez git hers. "'N hurry up; we gotta git movin'; got a long ride ahead of us, Robert."

Meanwhile, the neighbor lady realized none of this seemed right; there was just somethin' wrong 'bout the way this stranger was behavin'. She went next door to her side of the duplex 'n called th' police; then she went back t' Ruby's to try t' stall the fella what said he was the kids' daddy. She kept questioning Bob Gay, trying to interfere with whatever plans he may have had for taking Ruby's kids. "If you're here fer th' kids, how come Ruby never said nothin' 'bout you comin'?" The neighbor lady was pacing around, all nervous-like; 'n she was sure gettin' on Bob Gay's nerves. "'Cause," Bob Gay replied, "Ruby jest prob'ly forgot; I called her from Albuquerque 'n told her I wuz comin' over. Now would ya' quit botherin' me? These are my kids, too, 'n if ya' want, I'll call th' police." The neighbor lady smiled and said: "No need t' get all worked up, mister'; 'sides I done saved ya' th' trouble. Th' police are already on th' way; I called 'em awhile ago and should be here any minute." The look on Bob Gay's face told the neighbor lady all she wanted to know; he was lying and had the look of someone what just been punched in the stomach 'n was huntin' desper'tly for some air t' breathe.

About that time, two police cars pulled up in front, and two officers walked up to the door. One of the officers asked, to no one in particular: "OK, how 'bout somebody tellin' me what th' hell's goin' on here?" Bob Gay and th' neighbor lady both started talkin' 'bout th' same time; th' officer quieted 'em down and started askin' questions. After a few minutes of gettin' some good answers from th' neighbor lady and some vague ones from th' fella from New Mexico, the police officers began getting a pretty clear picture of what was going on.

And the picture got really clear as Ruby came to th' door, carryin' two sacks of groceries. Seein' th' police cars had at first scared Ruby, thinkin' maybe somethin' had happened t' th' children. When she saw the neighbor lady holding Robert's and Inez's hands, Ruby breathed a sigh of relief. Ruby told th' police officers in a matter of minutes all they needed to know. Thanking Ruby and th' neighbor lady, the' officers took Bob Gay by th' arm and escorted him to th' street. One of th' officers removed his cap and wiped his forehead with a handkerchief.

"Fella," th' officer said, in a quiet, but threatening voice, "I'm gonna let ya' go." The officer then looked at his watch and continued: "It's now 'bout 2:30; 'n since you came in from New Mexico, I'm sure ya' know th' way back. Ya' got 'bout 10 minutes t' get outta Temple afore I throw yer butt in jail. 'N ya' got maybe til sundown t' get outta Texas. Do I

make myself clear?" Th' officer turned toward his squad car 'n turned suddenly and said: "By th' way. . .don't come back this way any time soon, 'cause if ya' do, I'm gonna figger ya' fer bein' stupid 'n around here we put stupid in jail."

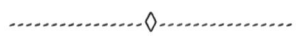

Bowman and his brother, Alex Packard, had a room at the old Stegall Hotel on the southside of the square. Temple had several fairly good places to eat but the one Bowman and Alex liked best was located next to the hotel. The dining room served supper family-style, and the price was more than reasonable—$.50 a person, all ya' could eat. The two brothers looked forward to ending their workday with a good, hot meal. This particular day was one they both looked forward to as they already knew what would be served. . . .

Uncle Alex told this story:

"Me 'n yer daddy had worked hard that day, stringin' phone line from Temple up towards Waco; we wuz lookin' forward to th' day's special—liver 'n onions. Yer daddy really liked liver 'n onions, 'n I was rather fond of it, myself. We walked into th' dinin' room 'n sat down next t' each other. This big ol' boy sat across from yer daddy 'n prob'bly weighed more'n three hunnerd pounds. He was th' manager of th' dry goods store across th' square 'n most times seemed a bit uppity. Anyhow, th' waiters brought out th' food 'n set down a big ol' platter of liver 'n onions. They started th' platter on one end o' the' table 'n not more'n two or three fellas had taken a servin' when it reached th' big ol' boy 'cross from yer daddy. He picked up th' platter 'n raked all the liver 'n onions onto his plate. Everyone jest sorta looked like they couldn' believe what they'd jest seen. But yer daddy didn' say a word, he jest reached 'cross th' table 'n grabbed that big ol' boy by th' throat with his right hand 'n started chokin' him. Ya know yer daddy had a mighty powr'ful grip, what with stringin' phone line 'n climbin' poles 'n all. I mean, a powr'ful grip. Anyways, thet ol' boy started turnin' blue, 'n some of th' men could see yer daddy wuz chokin' him t' death. Coupla' guys tried t' loosen yer daddy's grip, but Bowman wuz jest so strong." When asked if Dad had killed the man, Alex replied: "No, yer daddy didn't kill 'im, but he came close. It took three or four of us t' pry yer daddy's grip from thet ol' boy's throat." Alex chuckled a bit, and then said: "Ya know, that ol' boy'n yer daddy became pretty close friends; but he didn't ever again hog all th' food; I can tell ya' that."

----------◊----------

In 1930, Bowman Packard married a Temple girl by the name of Naomi. Uncle Alex told this story:"Yer daddy married this Naomi, 'n I wuz his best man; they got married by a Justice o' th' Peace. Didn' care too much for her, myself, but yer daddy said he loved her. Yer daddy took Naomi t' Louisiana t' meet Momma 'n the' rest of our family; they didn' take t' Naomi, either. Somethin' 'bout thet girl just...well, she just didn't seem t' be one of us. Yer daddy 'peared t' be th' only one who liked her." Uncle Alex paused for a second or two, then continued: "Yer daddy 'n Naomi fought a lot, almost from the' start. They just didn' seem to be right for each other; least they didn' seem that way t' me. I wuz livin' with yer daddy 'n Naomi in this little house yer daddy wuz rentin' 'n they wuz in their bedroom arguin' 'bout somethin' or other. I wuz in their livin' room trying t' lissen t' th' radio program. Naomi started yellin' at yer daddy 'n all of a sudden there was a gunshot. I ran into their bedroom just as yer daddy wuz takin' a pistol away from Naomi. There on th' pillow where yer daddy's head had been wuz a bullet hole. Naomi had tried t' kill yer daddy."

Uncle Alex said Dad filed for divorce and at the hearing, the judge granted Dad's petition for divorcement and ordered no alimony was due Naomi under the circumstances. But Uncle Alex said Dad spoke up and said: "No, your honor, I want to pay her some settlement; I'd just as soon give her $25 a month for six months until she can get her life back in order."

Uncle Alex said their marriage lasted less than a year. She was acquitted of assault with a deadly weapon; Dad and Alex never saw her again.

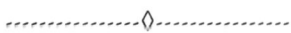

By 1932 Ruby Foster Gay had a thriving business taking in washing and ironing in her home. Robert was 8 years old and little Ruby Inez was 6. Ruby had a lot of regular customers, who steadily provided the business that allowed her to properly care for her small family. Ruby's family was far from wealthy but she and her two children lived comfortably enough.

One day a new customer knocked on her door with a sack full of shirts and clothing he needed to have cleaned. He introduced himself as Bowman Packard, and the man with him as his brother, Alex Packard. Bowman told Ruby that the clerk at the grocery store had suggested Ruby's as a good place to get shirts and trousers cleaned and pressed. "She does a good job," the clerk had told Bowman. "'N she really gets a good crease on th' trousers." So Bowman and Alex had gathered up most of their dirty shirts 'n trousers 'n taken 'em t' Ruby. Bowman handed th' sack of dirty clothes over 'n asked Ruby: "M'am, when do you s'pose we can pick 'em up?" Ruby smiled and replied: "I'll have 'em ready fer ya' by day after tomorrow. Will thet be soon enuf?"

As Bowman and Alex walked down th' sidewalk towards their pickup, Bowman turned t' Alex and said: "Ya' know, Alex, that's th' kinda woman I need; one who'll be a good wife 'n take good care of me. Did 'ja see how clean 'n neat she keeps her house? And those kids, they sure were clean-lookin' and well-mannered, weren't they?"

―――――◊―――――

Bowman came by himself t' pick up his clothes 'n spent a coupla' minutes on th' porch talkin' to Ruby. He noticed Ruby looked rather pretty 'n had on a nice pink 'n yellow dress. Bowman shifted his feet using th' toe of his right boot to scuff at nothin' in particular 'n said: "Ruby, there's a new picture show playin' at th' theatre, 'n I wuz wonderin' if you'd like t' go with me this weekend if ya' can get a babysitter 'n all." Ruby smiled real big 'n replied: "Why, yes, yes, I think thet'd be fine. You come by Saturday evening, 'n I'll go with ya."

Ruby and Bowman dated pretty steadily th' rest of 1932, mostly goin' t' picture shows, or to th' Moss Rose Café to get supper. Occasionally, they'd go to one of th' nightclubs in Temple, along with some other couples, for an evening of dancing. One of their friends was now th' Chief of Police; he was th' same police officer who'd run Bob Gay out of town.

Ruby told this story:

"Me 'n Bowman had gone t' th' nightclub with some of our friends, 'n we wuz dancin' 'n havin' a real good time. Roy, our Chief of Police, had asked me t' dance 'n Bowman had said, 'sure—go ahead, Ruby. So Roy 'n I wuz dancin'; 'n all of a sudden yer daddy walked out on th' dance floor 'n grabbed Roy by th' arm 'n spun him aroun' 'n said, 'Roy, you're dancing' too damn close t' Ruby—treat her respect'fully, or I'm gonna bust ya' one.' Well, Roy just looked at yer daddy all innocent-like 'n said, 'Bo, I didn' mean nothin' by it; of course, I treat Ruby proper-like.' So yer daddy 'n Roy 'n me walked back t' our table, 'n nothin' more was said." When asked if the Police Chief had been acting improperly, Mom replied: "No, of course not. Honey, your daddy just had a bad temper, 'n he wuz always very jealous of me. Your daddy didn' want no man holdin' me, dancin' or otherwise." Mom smiled at me and added: "Truth is, I didn' either; once't I'd met yer daddy, ther' jest wasn' any man good enuf but Bowman Packard."

―――――◊―――――

Bowman Packard and Ruby Inez Foster Gay were married in Cameron, Texas on November 7, 1933. Alex Packard was Bowman's best man, and

Audrey Ellen was Ruby's maid of honor. There were few others there at th' Justice of th' Peace; little Robert Gay 'n little Inez were with some of Ruby's kinfolk. Robert was now 9 years old, and Inez was 7. By the end of November 1933 Bowman Packard had adopted Ruby's children; they were now officially Robert G. Packard and Ruby Inez Packard. (Court records would actually show that Inez's legal name was Ruby Inez Foster Gay Packard.)

In 1934 Bowman, Ruby, and the two children moved into a small white house on Temple's southside. The address was 1309 South 25th, across the street from a small neighborhood grocery store, and this would be their home for the next five years.

----------------()----------------

Bowman took his new bride, Ruby Packard, and their two children to Centreville to meet Bowman's mother and the rest of his family. Alex said the Packard's loved Ruby from the moment they met her. Ruby was now one of the family. But Bowman very nearly wasn't; he made a teasing comment which didn't quite sit well with their mother, Mary Margaret Packard.

Ruby told me this story:

"We went to Bowman's hometown of Centreville t' see all his family; Bowman said he wanted me t' meet all his brothers 'n sisters 'n his Momma. I didn't know I'd be a'meetin' 'em all at once. I was sure gettin' nervous, wonderin' what they'd think of me. Bowman's brother, Alex, had told me none of 'em cared a lick fer Naomi, 'n I was afraid they wouldn' like me, neither. Anyways, we pulled up t' his Momma's little house, 'n me'n the kids got out of th' car t' go inside."

"Well, all of 'em were there; I never saw so many folks what looked like one another a'gathered there in one place. So your daddy started inter'ducing me t' everyone 'n everyone t' me. 'N then he inter'duced me t' his Momma. She was just so pretty 'n tiny 'n had the prettiest white hair. I smiled at her 'n said: 'How ya' do Missus Packard; I sure am glad t' meet ya.' Well, everyone jest got t' talkin' 'n carryin' on, an' 'fore ya' know it, yer daddy hushed ever'body 'n said he wanted t' tell'em somethin' 'bout his wife, Ruby. Well, I guess ever'thing wuz goin' so well; I jest thought

The Crepe Myrtle

he'd prob'bly say somethin' nice 'bout me. Then, yer daddy told'em thet when he met me, I was so poor 'n all, thet the first pair of shoes he bought me, I backed off inta the'river, lookin' at my tracks! Oh, Lord, I wuz so embarrassed, 'n all; I jest wanted t' die! 'N all your daddy's sisters 'n brothers wuz laughin' so hard—except for yer Grandmother Packard. She was so mad; ya could see fire in her eyes. She jumped up outta her rockin' chair 'n walked over t' hug me 'n said: 'Bowman

Packard, if I ever hear you talk about this girl that way again, I don't care how old you are, I'll take a razor strap to ya, the same way yer daddy used to when he wuz alive! Do you understand me?' Well, yer daddy was jest grinnin' at me, 'n then I knew he wuz jest pullin' my leg. 'N all his brothers 'n sisters came t' me 'n hugged me 'n said don't pay no attention t' Bowman, he's always pulling stuff like thet. Don't worry—you'll get used t' him, sooner or later."[11]

---◊---

In 1936 Ruby and Bowman had their first child together, a little baby boy. He only lived a few days...a deep sadness filled their home....

---◊---

By the summer of 1938 Ruby Packard had another baby growing inside her. Ruby and Bowman were cautiously optimistic; they sure didn't want to get their hopes up like before. Robert and Inez were likewise excited over the prospect of having a baby sister or baby brother to help look after. Inez was now 12 years old, and Robert was almost 14—'least, he would be 14 in another month as his birthday was August 13.

Ruby Packard gave birth to a baby boy on December 24, 1938. At first, Bowman wanted to name his newborn after himself; but after giving some thought to the matter, he decided to name his new son after his own father and grandfather. The boy's middle name, he decided, would be the same as his own middle name, Bowman. The newest member of the Packard family was named Charles Bowman Packard.

---

[11] Author's Note: This, too, was a true story. Mom said when Dad pulled this stunt, she thought he was serious at first because she and her sisters had truly been raised "dirt poor." As Dad would say, he got a kick out of "hoorahing" someone.

Like a number of families back then, the Packards decided to birth this child in their own home. Ruby said that Bowman mopped and scrubbed their floors for two days prior to the birthing. Ruby said no germs could possibly have survived Bowman's onslaught with the mop.

Bowman called Dr. A. H. Alsup early that morning to report the baby was coming; Dr. Alsup delivered their baby at 5:45 a.m. on Christmas Eve morning.

Early in 1939 Bowman, Ruby, Robert, Inez, and the baby went to Centreville, Louisiana to have the baby christened in the Packard family church. Charles Bowman Packard was now 4 months old. All of the Packard children had been christened in this little white Presbyterian church. Now, Bowman's son was also."

A year later the Packard family—Bowman, Ruby, and their three children—moved to a larger house closer to downtown; the new house was three blocks from Temple High School on Elm Avenue. The house had a nice fenced backyard and a wide front porch with two white columns that someone could easily cling to. Our house was about halfway between the high school and Woodson Field where the Temple Wildcats played football. . . .

The first memory I have of this house on Elm Avenue involved Bob and Inez coming home from school. The year was 1941 when I was about 2½ years old. Mom would allow me to stand on our front porch where I would hold onto one of the columns waiting to catch sight of my brother and sister.

Once they came into sight I could run to meet them and walk home with them. Actually, I guess I "swung" home with them as each would take my hand and swing me between them. Mom said this was a big highlight to my day.

Easter of 1941 brought the only other memory regarding this house. Mother and Dad had taken me for a ride in Dad's company truck, and I would stand up in the seat between them. We had just passed over a small creek on the west side of Temple when Dad called out: "Look at that! Did you see that rabbit?" I looked all around but didn't see anything—let alone, a rabbit. Mom then distracted me, saying: "Charles, I'll bet that wuz th' Easter Bunny!"

By now I was probably on pins and needles and that's when Dad brought his left arm back inside the cab holding a big Easter basket, almost as big as me, with a big chocolate rabbit, 'n a small cake with colored icing all over, 'n jelly beans, 'n candy Easter eggs. . .and Mom wouldn't let me eat any of it and said it'd spoil my supper. Pleading did no good; Mom said I would just have to wait, 'n I could have some after our supper. I didn't want any supper; I wanted that big ol' chocolate rabbit.

When we got back home, I remember Mom telling me to put th' basket on th' buffet; I reached up, put th' basket on top, 'n pushed it back like Mom said. I also remember th' smell of 'taters fryin' 'n that's all. I don't remember eatin' supper and more importantly, I sure don't remember eatin' a single bite of all that candy!

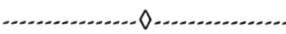

Chapter 17

Bob and Inez

Timeline: 1924-1943

Robert G. Packard was born in Regina, New Mexico in August of 1924. Ruby Inez Packard was born in Brownwood, Texas in March of 1926. Their father was Bob Gay, a rancher and Santa Fe Railroad worker. They may have been born Robert J. Gay and Ruby Inez Foster Gay, but to me they will always be Robert G. Packard and Ruby Inez Packard; and they will always be my big brother and my big sister.

In the early 1930s grade school was first through sixth grades; junior high was seventh and eighth grades; and high school was ninth grade through eleventh grade. In the latter part of 1930 a state law was passed making high school as it is now—ninth grade, freshmen; tenth grade, sophomores; eleventh grade, juniors; and twelfth grade, seniors. Students going from the eighth grade would skip the ninth grade if they had been enrolled under the older 11-year program and enter the tenth grade. Bob Packard was in this transitional class. But because of having a severe case of mumps, Bob started high school at mid-term in January 1939; he was enrolled in the tenth grade starting his sophomore year. I was barely one month old.

Bob completed high school in December 1942 but elected to take extra courses to make up for the transitional year from the eighth to the tenth grade. Consequently, he completed 11½ years of school, graduating in June of 1943 as President of the Senior Class and possessed the highest Grade-Point Average of Temple High School. Bob had actually begun his senior year on December 8, 1941, one day after Japan attacked Pearl Harbor on Sunday, December 7th. Inez had entered her freshman year in September of 1941; and in October of 1941 Inez was dating the quarterback for the Temple Wildcat football team.

For as much as Bob Packard excelled in academics, Inez Packard excelled in mischief; and frequently, this was a source of great embarrassment to her older brother. Inez often claimed that Bob was so smart and such a perfect student that even had she focused her energies more on her studies, measuring up to Bob still would have been an impossibility. And yet, as much as Inez frustrated her brother, Bob, she brought a wealth of amusement, intrigue, and, in some perverse way, a certain admiration from others in our family for her "creative" schemes. (Mom told me of some of Inez's pranks):

One fall evening in 1941 Inez had asked Dad if she could go out with some of her friends; Dad had told her no, because it was a school night. Inez persisted, but to no avail; Dad stood firm. However, he told Inez she could have her friends come over for awhile. Mom and Dad soon left as they were going out for a bite to eat. When they returned home, Dad had commented to Mom about the great number of cars parked along their street. Mom and Dad entered their very noisy home to find some 30 or 40 high school students; most were Temple Wildcat football players! Inez had called her boyfriend, the team quarterback, and told him to round up all his teammates and come over to the house. Mom said she and Dad walked into their kitchen, and Dad remarked: "Ruby, that's th' last time I try to discipline our daughter; she's just too dad-blamed clever for me. You are going to have to do it if it's gonna get done."

Inez had several girlfriends, many of them from prominent, well-to-do Temple families. Mom often said that she just figured Inez's friends had so much money—or at least the parents did—that they became easily bored. If that was the case, they soon had the perfect ringleader in Inez Packard. Inez, herself, told me this tale:

"Me 'n my friends were at the Hawn Hotel Coffee Shop right next to the Arcadia Theater; we often went there to have lunch during school. Anyway, we were bored 'n decided to have a little fun. Me 'n one of the girls went to th' phone booth in th' hotel lobby 'n called th' Temple Fire Station 'n told 'em there was a fire at Stavinoha's Hardware just up the street. Then, we all went back 'n sat at th' lunch counter waitin' for the fire trucks. Two of 'em came up th' street, red lights flashin' and sirens blaring somethin' fierce. We knew this was wrong, but oh, golly, it was so exciting!"

Early in 1942 Dad took me with him to Johnson's Chevrolet which was catty-cornered from old man Huggin's Gulf Service Station. Dad was having his company truck serviced, and he drove up the ramp to the second floor where the mechanic's service bays were located. Dad had my red kiddie-car in the truck bed, and the service manager had apparently arranged this with Dad. Dad told me what took place next:

"Th' service foreman told me to bring your kiddie-car, 'n they'd let you drive it up th' service ramp. This mechanic picked up your car 'n walked you back down th' ramp. He then had you peddle your car up th' ramp 'n told you they were gonna service your car, too. (Can you just see some car dealer in 2008 letting a 3 year old peddle a kiddie-car into their service bay?) Once you rode your car up, they took it 'n said they'd service it, just like your Daddy's. Over on one of the huge concrete posts there was a big poster of a Japanese soldier; one of those war things that warned about saying things that'd help th' enemy. I suppose you musta' heard us talk of how cruel 'n merciless th' Japs were, 'cause you walked over t' one of th' mechanic's tool boxes 'n picked up a big wrench. Some of th' mechanics were a bit puzzled at first until you started smashing that poster with th' wrench. All of th' mechanics started laughin'; and a few had tears from laughin' so hard." Some years later I asked Dad if I'd broken the guy's wrench 'n he replied: "No, but you sure tore th' hell outta that Jap poster and probably took a chunk or two out of the concrete post"....

By April of 1942, Dad and all of our family moved from Temple, Texas to live at the pump station which was just a few miles from Oenaville, Texas. Oenaville at the time was still a vibrant farming community about 12 miles or so east of Temple.

The reason for the move was quite extraordinary, and dramatically altered what I had always believed. My older brother, Dr. Robert Packard, recently told me what had actually occurred; here is his explanation:

"I was a Senior at Temple High, and Inez was a Sophomore, so you can see how devastating this was to us. This move meant that our High School social life and school activities ceased to exist. But because out country was at war, Mom and Dad had no choice; we had to move to the Atlantic Oil Company's pump station for national security reasons. You see, our government knew that any would-be saboteurs would most likely target our oil refining plants, which included oil pipelines and pumping station such as this one just outside Oenaville. Moving to Oenaville's pump station was not in the least for financial reasons; it was simply a mandatory move which our family had to make to increase the employee staffing at this potentially-vulnerable oil pump station."

This move not only distanced Bob and Inez some 15 miles from high school, but also moved them light years away from their friends and classmates. This was a painful and discouraging time for both of them, and especially for Bob. For him, this was about the worst thing that could possibly happen.

At the same time, on Bob's horizon loomed the prospect of having to go into the military and likely face the very real possibility of going into combat and maybe losing his life. . . .

---------------◊---------------

Chapter 18

World War II and Bubble Gum

Timeline: 1941-1946

In June of 1943 Robert G. Packard finished Temple High School with the highest Grade-Point Average of all the senior class. Bob had overcome a number of difficulties in accomplishing this honor, not the least of which was the somewhat traumatic move to Oenaville in 1942. Bob had endured the emotional loss of his Temple friends and high school classmates, the loss of ready access to the school's library and science labs, and a general sense of separation from his teachers and study groups. And he frequently had to walk the 15 miles to and from high school.

Despite these setbacks Bob had achieved the grades to be class Valedictorian. But this was not one of his goals; what was a goal was to earn straight As in his classes. In 11½ years of schooling Bob had achieved that goal, making all As in his classes.

His high school counselors had urged him to take more balanced subjects his senior year so he would be named class Valedictorian. But Bob declined, thanking them for their advice; he instead chose only those subjects he wanted to take, physics, math courses, and the like. He said his enjoyment was in achieving certain goals but never particularly cared for gathering the honors that accompanied the achievement.

Bob had been working at a local gas service station throughout most of his senior year. Because of the ongoing World War II, Bob would be giving a lot of thought to joining the military. A number of circumstances led Bob to enlist in the Army that summer of 1943. For one, he had completed school with highest honors and would likely be placed in a key military position. Secondly, by waiting he ran the risk of being drafted and most likely placed in a combat zone. And lastly, Bob and Dad had some trifling disagreements, mostly from Dad's over-protective attitude about me. Bob said he would push me on my tricycle, and Dad would object to Bob's overly-aggressive play. Bob said he would never have allowed anyone to harm me—and particularly himself—but I'm sure Dad was over-reacting. Regardless of the reasons, Bob enlisted and was soon on his way to San Antonio to start basic training at Fort Sam Houston Induction Center.

Early in World War II, we were still living in Temple, and due to gasoline rationing, Mom and I would ride the bus into Temple to shop. Mom said she and Dad had bought an Army outfit for me to wear as we took bus trips and just to wear in general. As Temple was so close to Fort Hood, most of the bus passengers were soldiers from all parts of the United States. Mom said that regardless of what I weighed when we boarded the bus, by the time we got back home I would always be heavier from all the dimes, nickels, and quarters stuffed in my pockets. Apparently, the real soldiers would hold me on their laps, and Mom said they taught me the Army "caisson" song.

In later years I've thought of these young soldiers who sat me on their laps and stuffed my pockets with coins. It is possible that some of those who taught me their Army song lie in some graves across the seas. I'll probably never know, since I was too young to really get to know them.

Even today, I can only hope that all of them, wherever they were from, were able to return to their families and hometowns, when that awful war ended.

And if some of them did not. . .then I'm grateful I was not old enough to have known them. . . .

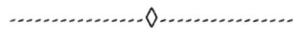

Rationing coupons became a way of life in the early 1940s. I remember Mom and Dad having to produce coupons for coffee, sugar, and gasoline. Other commodities were on the rationed list but I only remember these. And indirectly, I remember the impact that sugar rationing had on something dear to kids' hearts—bubble gum. Fleer's Bubble Gum disappeared from the shelves of stores; and though it sounds extremely trite to say so now, that was how a lot of us kids came to view World War II. We lost our bubble gum. Thousands of American families lost their sons, daughters, brothers, dads, loved ones; and we lost our bubble gum. Our nation lost these young heroes and heroines, young people who would never return home, and we lost our bubble gum. As selfish and self-centered as that sounds, when you are 3 and 4 and 5 years old, it seems there must be some reference point on which you might possibly make sense of all that is going on around you. For us, it was bubble gum—that was our reference point. . . .

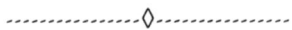

Death was something that I really could not comprehend when I was young. Sometime during 1942 Mom received a call from a very good friend named Dorothy Williams; she asked Mom to please come over; she needed a friend to talk to in the worst way. Mom tried to explain what had happened but I apparently just could not grasp what she was telling me. When we reached the Williams' home, she fell into Mom's arms, crying and sobbing uncontrollably. She said she just received a telegram; Wendell had been killed in the Pacific. I admit that most of these words—"telegram," "Pacific"—had no meaning to me. She showed Mom and me Wendell's picture (I had asked Mom who Wendell was) that sat on the dresser in his room. I can vaguely recall that Wendell was dressed in his dress Marine's uniform, with the navy blue coat, and the gold shiny buttons and what was called a cover (to me it looked like a cap!). The cover was a brilliant white color, all so pretty and clean. And I could see that Wendell, although I knew he was much older than me, was young. He just looked so young. . .and I could not understand how someone so young could possibly be dead. . . .

Mom's favorite aunt was Aunt Ida, a sister to Mom's father, John Bradson Foster. Mom and I used to drive out to Aunt Ida's farm somewhere near Belton. I'm ashamed to admit this but what I most clearly remember about this dear old great-aunt had to do with food. When Aunt Ida made us red beans and cornbread, she cooked on her woodstove in her kitchen. This always left an incredibly delicious taste and aroma of wood smoke in her food. Years later, I can attest it was incomparable. And watermelons—Aunt Ida and her son, George Silver, would always let me go out to their melon patch to pick out a nice juicy watermelon. George even tried to teach me how to tell when they were ripe.

To say the least, it seems to me that "goin' to visit Aunt Ida" was one of my very favorite things to do; and many times the only way I remember seeing her outside her house was wearing a big, puffy dress that went to her shoe tops and a pretty blue and white sunbonnet. (Mom had a can of something in her kitchen cabinets—Old Dutch Cleanser, I think—that always reminded me of Aunt Ida.) I guess the sunbonnet didn't help Aunt Ida, as she died of something Mom said was a heat stroke. Mom and Dad and I went to the funeral home to see Aunt Ida; this was in the summer of 1944. The funeral home was dimly lit, and there was an eerie coolness inside. And it was quiet, very still, and quiet. Here and there I could hear muffled cries, and people quietly sobbing in their handkerchiefs. And then Mom led me up to it—the casket. And lying inside was Aunt Ida. She didn't have on her sunbonnet, and somehow she looked so different. But it was Aunt Ida; at least, someone who looked like Aunt Ida. I was now 2 years older than when I had seen Wendell's picture in his Marine uniform. And I still could not really understand death. But somehow with all my confusion about living and dying, I knew that I would not be seein' Aunt Ida again. . . .

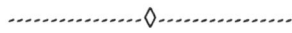

Sometime around 1943 a Japanese fighter plane made its way to Temple, a captured Japanese fighter plane. The Jap plane was set up on display in some sort of big showroom floor in a building just a few blocks from a drugstore on Temple's near southside. Mom and Dad took me to see it; and when it was our turn to look at it, they lifted me up to the cockpit. Everything was written in Japanese, so I wouldn't have been able to read it; of course, since I was only 4 or 5, the writings could have been in English, and I still would not have been able to read the words!

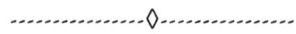

Just out past the Veteran's Administration Hospital on Temple's far southside and alongside the highway toward the Sunset Drive-in Theatre, stood a large prisoner-of-war camp. Mom and Dad said the prisoners were either Germans or probably Italians. Dad said the government wouldn't dare put Japanese prisoners in Texas. Dad said: "Get some of these Texans liquored up on moonshine 'n there wouldn't be any need for th' prison; there wouldn't be any Japs left to keep in a P.O.W. camp!" May have been some truth in what Dad said....

------------◊------------

Another favorite aunt of mine was Aunt Lola, Mom's oldest sister. Aunt Lola and her husband, Uncle Walter Shull, lived in Dallas; and Mom and Dad would put me on the Katy train (Missouri, Kansas & Texas Line) to Dallas. I was 5 years old in 1944, and I was put in the custody of the conductor for the trip north. The trip probably only took 3 or 4 hours, as Dallas was only about 100 or so miles from Temple. I don't remember wandering around the train so the conductor must have kept a pretty close watch on me.

But what I do remember is Uncle Walter. Uncle Walter Shull was in the Navy during the war, and he served aboard submarines. Submarines! I must have asked Uncle Walter a thousand questions about submarines, and I'm sure he answered every one. One question in particular received a very demonstrative reply. I had asked: "Uncle Walter, what's it like at sea? Do you see a lot of sharks 'n whales 'n things like that?" Uncle Walter replied: "Oh, we see all kinds of things, especially whales; let me show you something 'bout whales." Uncle Walter walked into Aunt Lola's kitchen and came back into their living room with a glass of water. "Let me show you what whales do," Uncle Walter said. With that, he sat down on the carpet, took a mouthful of water and lay down on his back. He looked up at me 'n spurted his mouthful of water about 2 feet into th' air! Th' water splashed back down on him, his uniform, 'n all over Aunt Lola's carpet! Boy, was Aunt Lola mad! She came stomping into the room, red-faced 'n yellin' at Uncle Walter. And I was laughin' my head off! I don't remember ever seeing anything so funny. Of course, I didn't see any future to askin' Uncle Walter to do it again.

Another thing about Dallas I liked a lot was something I'd never seen in Temple, at least, not in 1944. That was ice cream trucks. This white truck came to Aunt Lola's street 'bout every day around 2 o'clock in th' afternoon. Aunt Lola would give me a nickel so I could buy something off the' truck. 'N ya always knew when he was comin' down th' street.

You could hear his bell jingling half a block away. These trucks didn't play music; just jingling bells ringing let you know he was comin'. 'N sometimes Aunt Lola would give me a dime 'n said to buy Sherry one, too. Sherry was a little red-haired girl who lived a few houses from Aunt Lola; Sherry was about my age, 'n Aunt Lola always told me "to be nice to Sherry; I think she likes you." Well, when Aunt Lola gave me a dime, I'd let Sherry pick out an ice cream bar, too; 'n I recall that I was nice to her, too. Least I didn't pull her hair, or pick on her, or anything like that. Otherwise, I kinda avoided Sherry; after all, when your aunt tells ya' a neighbor girl likes you. . .well, I don't ever remember of any 5- or 6-year old boy liking any girl, except maybe his mother or sister. . .well, a mother, anyway. . . .

--------◊--------

The Atlantic Oil Refining Company contacted Dad, and informed him that, for national security reasons, he would have to relocate to the pump station outside the Oenaville farming community. Dad was a telephone lineman, and would have no pump station duties, as his work required him to travel throughout Central Texas maintaining his telephone lines.

There were three houses at this pump station facility — the middle house was occupied by the station chief, Charlie Porter and his family; the end house by the Chapmans, and older couple who had no children; and our house, which was nearest to the pump station.

We moved that April, and in the process, pretty much ruined my older brother's life. . . .

--------◊--------

Chapter 19

The Oenaville Years

Timeline: 1942-1952

"*A young man, Cullen Johnson, moved to the area reportedly from Florida and formed a partnership with an old man, Rev. Hiram Thompson (Uncle Hiram, as he was familiarly known.) They hired Joseph Bray in 1871 to build them a store, a stone structure, the first business in the area, bordering on the Bray land just east of Big Elm Creek. Cullen Johnson later married one of Ben Shipp's daughters.*

In 1872 a Post Office was located in the store necessitating naming the small village; and there are no absolutes in how Oenaville got her name. One source attributes naming her after the first baby born here, Oena Griffin, while another suggested she was named for the Indian girl named Oena found on the banks of Big Elm Creek by the first settlers. L. C. Williams, at the Old Settlers' Association reunion in 1904, gave yet a different slant on the origin of Oenaville's name. When Cullen Johnson was appointed the first Postmaster, he went to Belton to arrange matters. They presented him with a list of suggested names for the town, all of which he rejected, finally settling on Oenaville after the town of his origin in Alabama, Mr. Williams thought. The most popular and generally accepted legend, however, gives Cullen Johnson credit for naming the town after the Seminole Indian girl he'd left back in Florida. His partner, Hiram Thompson, added the "ville" onto it. Mr. Williams, as did others, felt disappointed with the choice of a name, but Oenaville it became and remains to this day. (Oenaville, Vicki Ewing Montgomery, Oenaville Community Association.)

By 1884 the town had 150 inhabitants, 3 churches, 2 mills and gins, 2 saloons, a cooperative association, and a school. At that time Oenaville shipped primarily cotton. By 1890 the population rose to 200 and remained at about that level through the 1940s. By 1949 Oenaville had declined to 150 residents, 5 businesses, 2 churches, and a school. . . ." (The New Handbook of Texas, Vol. 4, The Quarterly of Texas State Historical Association.)

---------◊---------

In the early 1940s Oenaville had 2 cotton gins, a blacksmith shop, a small Post Office/store, a gas service station, a general store, a red brick school, and 3 churches. On one corner stood a crumbling frame building that had allegedly once been a barber shop. Oenaville had, at one time, been quite a bit larger and much more heavily populated than Temple. But then the railroads came through Temple, and everything changed almost overnight. Temple grew into a thriving, bustling community, and by 1940 was populated by some 20,000 residents.

---------◊---------

Meanwhile, Oenaville had declined to a little more than 150 inhabitants—150 friendly, hardworking folks, who seldom had to lock their doors. In 1942 I was too young to appreciate Oenaville; time would change all that.

---------◊---------

Growing up in the country back in those days was the best thing that a young boy could hope for, and the pump station was probably the best place to be. This property owned by the Atlantic Oil & Refining Company was situated among some 6 or 7 farms, every one of which had raised boys. There were probably 15 or 16 boys, most of them around my age. In time the adventures we would come to share would be limited only by the boundaries of our imaginations.

---------◊---------

Several changes occurred in our household in 1942, but I do not remember how or when these changes took place. Mom said that when Inez finished the tenth grade that summer, Sis had had enough of living in the country and away from all her friends. Inez was yearning for big city lights and all that would represent. Inez left home that summer for Austin, where she went to work at the downtown Austin Grill; waiting tables during the day and going dancing with her friends after work became her routine. Soon after Sis left home, another family member moved in. Grandma Foster, my Mother's mother, came to live with us at the pump station. In more ways than one, Grandma Foster brought a lot of wonderful memories to my life.

Grandma Foster had a very dark complexion and coal-black hair; she seemed to always have a healthy tan. At the time I didn't realize this, but her appearance was simply the result of Cherokee Indian blood in her. This Indian bloodline was passed down through a number of our relatives: my older brother, Bob; my youngest brother, Ira B. Packard, Jr.; and his daughter, Lisa; Aunt Audrey Ellen Deavers; and a couple of her sons; a cousin, Dick Luttrell, son of my Aunt Lola Luttrell; and Dick's son, Donnie Luttrell. All of these descendants of Grandma Foster were born with dark, bronze skin and jet black hair. Such was the heritage of Indian bloodlines she passed on to her children and grandchildren.

From time to time Grandma Foster would sing songs to me, songs that had unusual words and sounds, songs that she said her mother had sung to her although she could not say where or when she had first heard them. She also taught me games which she said were probably passed down from some of her mother's Cherokee kinfolk.

In the summertime, Grandma Foster woud make ice-cold lemonade; and in the winter, she would make me hot lemonade. I liked the hot lemonade the best.

But the very best thing she did for me was to tell me the story of her journey in a covered wagon in 1881 when she was 5 years old. Her parents had left Tennessee in a covered wagon on their way to Texas. Shortly after arriving in Texas, somewhere in the southeastern regions near Livingston in Polk County, the Hawkins' wagon had stopped atop a small rise. In the distance they saw a small band of Indians; not knowing whether these Indians were friendly or hostile, the Hawkins had Rose Alice hide under some blankets beneath the wagon's bench seat. Grandma Foster said she had been terrified, as Indian attacks still occurred throughout parts of Texas. But these Indians must have been from a friendly tribe, possibly the Alabama-Coushatta Tribe. The Indians soon rode off, and the Hawkins were safe; and Grandma crawled out from under th' blankets. Grandma Foster would tell me this story, 'n she said that within a short time I would ask her to tell it again. Over the years, I guess I asked Grandma Foster maybe a hundred times to tell me this story. She probably grew tired of telling this story, but I never tired of hearing her tell it. . .never.

--------◊--------

Christmas of 1942 should have been a wonderful and magical time for a 4 year old; but it wasn't for me; I had the mumps. . . .

Our family had started a tradition the previous year in shooting off fireworks on Christmas Eve. We were living in Temple at the time, and Bob and Inez were still living at home. I wasn't allowed to handle fireworks just yet, but Mom 'n Dad said we all had a lot of fun, lighting off Roman candles, skyrockets, 'n strings of Chinese Black Cat Firecrackers. Mom said I liked the sparklers the best. So I was looking forward to possibly getting to light some off—and just maybe getting to at least hold some sparklers. A week before Christmas Dad had bought a big sack of fireworks, and I kept eyeing that bag like it was filled with Hershey bars. I couldn't wait to help shoot 'em off. Then I came down with th' mumps.

"Son," Mom said, "you sit here near th' stove, 'n you can look out th' window 'n watch." "But Mom," I had whined, "thet ain't gonna be no fun. Let me go out just for a few minutes, OK, just a few minutes?"

"No, you've got th' mumps, 'n you're stayin' here where its warm by th' stove; 'n I want ya' to drink your tomato juice. You've hardly touched it."

I guess tomato juice must a' had some sort of cure for th' mumps, but I never learned for sure. I was all bundled up in my pajamas, robe, 'n house slippers 'n had a big glass of tomato juice sittin' on th' counter next t'me. I had to give it one more try:

"Mom, ya'll are goin' outside; why can't I go out just to watch? 'N I'll drink all this tomato juice so that should make it OK. . .OK?" Mom closed off that pathetic appeal of mine pretty quick. "No," Mom said, "you're not going out with th' mumps, 'n that's that. We don't have th' mumps 'n you do. Now sit here 'n be quiet, or I'll put ya ta' bed 'n you won't even get t' watch. Now which do ya' wanna do?" I lost that argument 'n I knew it; so I sat there and watched while they had all th' fun. But I didn't drink that tomato juice....

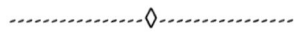

Where we lived was right next to old man Ernest Lancaster's cornfield. He told all of the grown-ups who lived in the three pump-station houses that we could pick all th' ears of corn we wanted but to be careful not to trample any of his cornstalks. Inez had come home for the weekend, 'n she 'n Bob were goin' t' pick some ears of corn for dinner. This was in Late summer of 1942. I wanted t' go with 'em to help, but Bob 'n Inez told me I needed to stay home. I guess I put up a fuss, because Sis said: "Honey, you really need to stay here with Mom 'n Dad, so the Green Giant won't get you." This was th' first I had heard of any giant, and I asked: "What giant? What giant are you talkin' 'bout?" Inez went to Mom's cabinet 'n took down a can of corn 'n pointed to th' label. "This giant, honey; th' Green Giant. Didn't you know he lives out there in th' cornfield?" I lost all interest in going with 'em; I wasn't really sure whether or not that giant lived out in the field, but I knew I didn't wanna find out.

From the time we moved to Oenaville and for the next few years, Mom and I would sometimes get to travel with Dad when he had "a case of trouble" on his telephone lines. Lots of circumstances would cause the telephone lines to break, usually bad storms. High winds, lightning strikes to the telephone poles, and occasional tornadoes would cause a lot of downed lines, or a "case of trouble," as Dad called it. And sometimes falling trees over toward the East Texas forests would really mess up Dad's telephone lines. When the lines were damaged badly, Dad would sometimes be gone for 3 or 4 days until he had located 'n repaired th' damage. So we'd get t' travel with him. Mom and Dad 'n me'd stay in different little towns all over Central Texas. Th' names became a part of my vocabulary: Hearne, Shiro, Evant, Palestine, Hillsboro; we'd travel with Dad to first one, then th' other. And th' part I liked best was eatin' breakfast with Mom 'n Dad in those little out-of-the-way cafés that Texas used to have (unfortunately, these quaint little diners have gone the way of so many other good things.) Anyway, Dad would order his coffee; 'n when th' waitress brought it, Dad would pour in the little glass bottle of cream, stir in some sugar, and then refill the glass bottle with some of his coffee. This would be mine to drink. That was always special to me. Too bad you can't get those little bottles any more.

One time, Dad spent a week or so in King's Daughters Hospital with several broken ribs and some bad bruises. Lightning had struck the telephone pole he was working on, and he had fallen some 15 feet to the ground. Mom 'n I visited him every day during his hospital stay. Dad said it had hurt pretty bad when he fell, 'n he thought he'd been unconscious for awhile. I guess that might have prompted the reply I'd give whenever someone asked me what my Daddy did for a living. Or at least that may have been part of my response. Mom said I'd get this pained expression on my face, slowly shake my head from side to side, 'n say: "My Daddy's a telephone lineman, a troubleshooter—bless his heart." How this actually started, I'll never know....

A few years later, little brothers made their appearance, 'n Mom had t' stay home to care for 'em. Dad would sometimes continue taking me with him on some of his trouble-shootin' trips throughout Central Texas; and I suppose that one day I just outgrew these times with my Dad. But now, as I look back on those trips, I remember th' good times we had. I miss them. And I miss Dad, too....

Shortly after Christmas of 1942 Inez came home for th' weekend and to bring Mom 'n Dad some news; she had fallen in love with a young aviator stationed at Bergstrom Airfield. His name was Chuck Walters, and at the time he was a flight sergeant going through pilot training. And he was a Yankee, from St. Paul, Minnesota. On top of that, Inez told Mom that she'n Chuck had had a disagreement 'bout something or other, 'n he hadn't called her for several days. Sis told Mom she thought since Chuck hadn't called, maybe she should call him. Mom said she told Inez: "Honey, don't do it; don't cha' dare do it. Wait 'n let him call you." "But Mom," Sis wailed, "I love him, 'n I don't want him to stay mad at me; I just want him to come back." "Then wait, sweetheart," Mom had told her. "Wait, 'n let him call you. If you call him, he may not ever come back. Trust me, darlin'; if he really loves ya', he'll be callin' in a day or two."

Chuck called Sis two days later. He said: "Pee Wee, I'm driving up to Temple tomorrow. I'd like to meet your Mom 'n Dad." Inez was ecstatic. Mom said Chuck drove up the next day 'n came out to th' pump station to see Inez—or Pee Wee, as he used t' call her—and to meet Mom 'n Dad. Chuck reached out to shake Dad's hand, Mom said Dad at first wouldn't shake his hand. Wasn't so much that Dad didn't like Chuck; it was simply that Mom said Dad didn't think any man was good enough for his daughter even if she had been a real handful growin' up!

A lot happened in 1943. Bob enlisted in the Army on July 14, 1943, and left by train for Fort Sam Houston in San Antonio to begin Army Basic Training. And on July 29, 1943, Inez Foster Packard married 2nd Lieutenant Charles Anton Walters. The wedding took place in the Texas State Capitol in Austin. Inez wore a white gardenia in her hair; gardenias were always her favorite flower. Chuck Walters, now a commissioned pilot, wore his Army Air Corps uniform. Mom said they were a very striking couple. Sis had finally managed to "ground" her pilot at least long enough to marry him. As far as Chuck Walters—well, let's just say if our family had already been well-stocked with characters and certified pranksters, adding Chuck Walters into our family qualified having him near the top of our list—probably the dean of pranksters.

Not long after their wedding that summer of 1943, Inez continued begging Chuck to take her up in his C-47. Previously, Chuck had managed to put her off by saying "it wasn't permitted" or "regulations don't allow civilians on military aircraft" 'n arguments such as those which, of course, had absolutely no effect on my sister. This is the story Sis told me about her flight:

"Chuck finally agreed to take me up in his plane; so on a beautiful, sunshiny Sunday afternoon we climbed aboard his plane 'n he got me all buckled into my parachute 'n strapped in th' co-pilot's seat. He started through his preflight checklist, saying a pilot always has to follow that procedure, 'n then he started th' engines. Boy, was it loud in th' cockpit! He taxied out to th' runway 'n off we went.

As he climbed up over Austin 'n out over th' countryside, I could see it was even more of a beautiful summer day than what I saw from ground level; the sky was as blue as any I had ever seen. It was simply gorgeous! He motioned to me to put on th' headset, 'n he asked me over the headphones how I liked it up here in his highway. I told him it was just breathtakin'! He turned to me 'n smiled and said: 'Pee Wee, you wanta fly this bird for awhile?' I asked him if he was kidding—you mean I can really fly your plane? He said: 'Sure, just take hold of the yoke and hold er steady; that's all there is to it.' "Well, I grabbed hold of the wheel (yoke), and all of a sudden I'm flying this big ol' plane. That was so incredible! I mean, here we are, 'bout 3,000 or 4,000 feet up, 'n I'm flying this plane! I'm lookin' all around the skies 'n so proud of myself. Everything's so great, 'n I glanced over at Chuck so he could see how happy I was—and he's asleep! I mean, he's asleep with his flight cap pulled down over his eyes, his arms were folded across his chest, 'n he had his seat back, 'n that damned fool is asleep! I started screamin' 'n yellin', Chuck—Chuck , take this damn wheel before we crash! Chuck, wake up! All of a sudden, I can see his grin under his cap bill; and he sat up 'n said: 'Sweetheart, don't worry. We aren't gonna crash. We can't crash, Pee Wee; I've had th' flight controls on auto pilot th' whole time.' Well, Chuck sure had a lot of fun, scared the hell out of me, that's what he'd done. He said there wasn't anything I could have done to override the auto pilot. And that may be, but I'm here to tell ya' that at 5,000 feet up in th' sky, he may have known that; I sure as hell didn't!"[12]

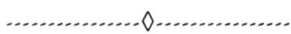

Not long after this episode, Chuck was reassigned to China where he and hundreds of other pilots in the Far East would be based in that country, ferrying men, planes, 'n supplies to the Nationalist Chinese forces as they waged war against the Japanese throughout Southeast Asia. Chuck was one of the many pilots who flew what was termed "The Burma Hump," in which these American pilots flew over the mountain ranges to keep the Allies in that region well-supplied. Chuck said a number of times his plane was attacked—as well as the other C-47s—by Jap fighters, as the

---

[12] Author's Note: Of all my remembrances of Chuck 'n Inez, this is far and away my favorite; this was a classic Chuck Walters!

Japs fought to keep the American pilots from making these supply runs. Chuck said thanks to American fighter escort, they didn't lose many of these "Goony Birds," the pilots' affectionate name for these lumbering C-47s—C-47s that had no armaments. . . .

By late 1943 Chuck was in th' Far East, ferrying supplies in his C-47; and Bob would soon be in th' Philippines. Bob was in the Army Signal Corps as a radio intercept operator and serving as a Japanese interpreter. Bob would write home to Mom 'n Dad, sometimes weekly, at least lettin' 'em know he was OK. He couldn't say much as all mail was carefully screened to make sure classified information didn't inadvertently get past the censors; we didn't know he had been in th' Philippines until after th' war. Same with Chuck's mail; even officers had their mail read by military censors. War was going on, and a slip of the tongue could cost lives, American lives. And on the home front, I was now old enough to understand the fear and anxiety that Mom and Sis would show from time to time, worrying about Bob and Chuck. I'm sure Mom 'n Sis tried to keep their worries from me, so as to not unnecessarily frighten me. But from time to time, their worry showed on their faces. And whether Mom and Sis knew it or not, all of us kids talked about things like th' war—at least as far as we could understand it—and from time to time, we overheard other grown-ups talking about it, as well. So we had our worries, too. As far as Chuck Walters, I hadn't yet gotten to know him real well, as he was still a bit of a "mystery person" to me; but I knew my brother, Bob, and I did miss him. And somehow, I knew he was "somewhere" in harm's way. And I worried, too. . . .

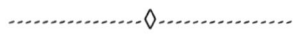

Something curious happened to Private Robert Packard when he was completing basic training. I would have said 'humorous,' but being assigned to overseas duty during World War II would strain credibility to label most anything similar as being "humorous." Bob can best explain what happened to him:

"We were nearing completion of training, and men were receiving assignments to different theaters of operation: Pacific, European, or Advanced Training Schools. The OIC called me in and said there was a problem. The officer explained: 'Private, I need to assign you to your next post but the problem is this. You are shown on my records under two different names. You are listed as Robert James Packard and as Robert G. Packard. Here's the deal, Private, if you are Robert G. Packard, then you're slated for Army Engineers at Camp Claiborne, Louisiana. If you are Robert James Packard, you will be assigned to the Army Air Corps in California. Which one are you?' Bob responded: "Sir, I am Private Robert G. Packard."

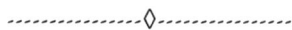

Bob departed Fort Sam Houston Army Induction Center on August 10, 1943. On August 11, 1943, he was assigned to Army Engineers, 361st Engineering Regiment at Camp Claiborne, Louisiana. After completion of this Army Technical School, Bob was then assigned to a posting at the University of Illinois on December 8, 1943. He was enrolled in the Army Specialized Training Program (ASTP) for military officers training. Upon completion of this officer training on March 27, 1944, Bob was then assigned to the Signal Corps, 842nd Signal Training Battalion, leaving July 14, 1944, for Hawaii. From there he served in the Philippines from November 22, 1944, in the 4025th Signal Group until the end of the war. By now Sergeant Robert G. Packard was ready for his next assignment: Army Signal Corps specialist in Japanese languages with his posting to Japan on October 31, 1945, to serve as Japanese interpreter for the Army Occupational Forces.

Meanwhile in 1944 I got a baby brother. Foster Wayne Packard was born at King's Daughters Hospital on September 27, 1944. My reign as only child in the house was coming to an end and with its demise, all the perks and privileges that I had long enjoyed. By now, First Lt. Charles A. Walters had returned from China and was frequently home on short leaves of absence. Which would explain the appearance in 1945 of Charles A. Walters, Jr., my sister's first born. And in 1946, Mom and Dad contributed another little brother. Three baby boys in three years. Wayne in 1944, Charles A., Jr. on July 9, 1945, and Ira Bowman Packard, Jr. on June 18, 1946. The kids were coming fast and furious, and I could sense my empire beginning to crumble. When Inez gave birth to Donna

K. Walters on August 19, 1947, the crumbling walls of Jericho had nothing on me. My time as resident "spoiled brat" was over. But there was at least one bright shining moment in this era of rugrat downpours; in 1946, Fleer's Bubble Gum was back on th' shelves!

-----------◊-----------

Mom and Dad always made Christmas a joyous time for all! As the years went by, this holiday became such an exciting, festive occasion, I'm sure others figured we had a lot more money than we really did. Mom and Dad just had a way of "creating" Christmas excitement in our home without havin' to spend a lot of money. The Christmas in 1943 was no exception. Chuck Walters and my brother, Bob, were away at war, and Sis had come back home to be with us until, hopefully, her husband returned from that God-awful war. Christmas Eve night at th' pump station found Mom, Sis, and me in our small living room, listening to the radio playing Christmas carols. December 24th was my fifth birthday, and Sis had bought me a Hershey almond candy bar, one of my childhood favorites. I don't remember where my Dad was, but he wasn't there at the moment. I was just about to unwrap my candy bar when there was a noise from th' other part of the house. "What was that?" Mother asked. Sis piped up: "Oh my gosh! I'll bet it's Santa Claus; 'n if he catches you still up, he won't leave you any toys!" Mom said: "Quick, get under th' coffee table 'n shut your eyes real tight. Maybe he won't see you. Hurry!" I was under th' coffee table in maybe two seconds flat; 'n I'd completely lost th' notion of eatin' my Hershey bar or anything else that might make a noise. My eyes were shut so tight, they actually hurt. A few minutes must have gone by when Dad walked in, 'n said: "Did ya'll hear that? Somethin' was up on the roof, but I couldn't see who it was." I didn't have to see; I knew who it was! Mom said: "We think it might 'uv been Santa, but we don't know for sure." And Inez said: "Let's go back in th' Christmas Room, just in case!" (The Christmas Room was the front bedroom that was always—at that time—kept as a spare room. A couple of weeks before Christmas, a tree appeared and got decorated up, and no kids were allowed in until Christmas morning, and it was kept locked!) Sis opened th' door, and there under th' tree was a Lionel Train Set! I always loved trains 'n I really liked traveling on trains. I just like everything about trains. I forgot all about my Hershey bar; I had a new Lionel Train!

I was 6 years old on Christmas of 1944; my little brother, Wayne, was 3 months old, and our soldiers had landed earlier that summer at Normandy. All the radio talked of was th' war coming to an end 'n all our troops coming home. Mom 'n Dad 'n Sis were gettin' more excited by th' day. I remember there was such a change all around, and mostly it was good.

That spring of 1945 I got to drive a farm tractor. The Schwake family had a farm just past old man Ernest Lancaster's farm, 'n one of th' older Schwake men sat me on his lap 'n told me t' keep th' tractor tires in th' furrows. That tractor bucked 'n twisted, 'n I wound up making a bunch o' new rows, for awhile at least, until I got fired. He said he'd wait 'til I got bigger 'n stronger. That suited me just fine.

That summer, I was playing on th' floor with a toy truck when our phone rang our three sharp rings (we were on a party line 'n had one of those big old wall crank phones.) Mom answered, 'n I heard her start crying. I ran into the back bedroom n' asked: "Mom, what's th' matter?" Mom looked at me 'n sobbed: "Oh, honey, our little President is dead; President Roosevelt just died!"

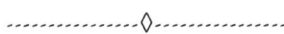

On July 9, 1945, my little nephew, Charles A. Walters, Jr., was born. In time, my brother, Wayne, would have a little playmate—a very close, family-member playmate. A few months later, I started first grade at Oenaville Schools. Actually, I started school in a church, a Baptist church, at that.

The Oenaville community leaders learned the old school building was unsafe, so earlier that summer it was being torn down; and a new red brick school building was under construction. So for a few months, all th' Oenaville kids were divided up among the three churches. As I recall, first through third grade was at the Baptist church, fourth through sixth at the Methodist church, and th' big kids, seventh through ninth grades at the Church of Christ. At least, that's how I remember things.

Just behind our Baptist church was a storm cellar in the event of tornadoes. One day a bunch of us boys were playing at recess, 'n a couple of third graders put me in the cellar 'n closed th' doors. There was just enough light comin' through th' cracks to where I could see this big ol' tarantula crawlin' along th' top shelf. We knew their bite couldn't kill you, but their big, hairy bodies made you think they could. My yelling didn't get th' cellar doors open

but slammin' my shoulders against the doors did. I had now been in that cellar twice; my first time 'n my last time.

Oenaville Baptist Church also played a big part in my family's enjoyment of Christmas. Ever since Dad had joined th' Baptist church in 1943, Mom 'n Dad 'n me 'n all my brothers, once they'd come along, would join with this church congregation in celebrating Jesus' birth. Our pastor, usually a very young Baptist fresh out of Baylor University, would schedule this church service on Christmas Eve whenever possible. We would gather early in th' evening, and after an opening prayer, sing all th' traditional church carols: *Away in the Manger, Hark, th' Herald, Silent Night, O, Little Town of Bethlehem* 'n many more. Then, th' pastor would read from the Gospel of Luke about the shepherds in the fields and Jesus' birth in the manger in Bethlehem. Th' grown-ups would have their eyes fixed on their hymnals; we kids would have our eyes on th' Christmas tree just off to th' side of th' pulpit. Th' church ladies would have th' tree all shiny 'n sparklin' bright from th' strings of Christmas lights, icicles, 'n angel's hair all over th' tree. Underneath were the gifts we would get each other, and the Christmas stockings filled with fruit, nuts, and candy (the church ladies would have us kids draw names 'n buy a gift of no more than $.25 to be wrapped and placed under th' tree—and $.25 would buy a nice little gift back in th' '40s.) The stockings held the usual mix of walnuts, almonds, and pecans, Christmas candy, and an orange, an apple, 'n sometimes a banana. These were the red mesh stockin's found in most all grocery and drugstores back then; no need to go out lookin'—you won't find 'em like those any more. . . .

Christmas Eve, December 24, 1945, was a wonderful time.

The Crepe Myrtle

The part of the pump-station acreage where the three employees' families lived was some 12 or 13 acres; the entire Atlantic Pipeline land was more than 40 acres, we were told. So each family had 2 or 3 acres where their house sat and the rest could be for a garden or whatever they wanted to use it for, within reason, of course. Mom and Dad fenced in most of ours, putting up chicken wire for a large flock of chickens and a small hen house. The rest was enclosed for a cowshed, with a cow, a calf, and a hog Mom 'n Dad had bought. So there on our part of the pump-station land, amidst all the farmers surrounding us, we had our own small farm. . .our own very small farm.

I never could manage to get th' knack for gatherin' eggs. I could pick up snakes, even poisonous ones; I could butt heads with th' calf until I got headaches; 'n I could chunk huge yellow jackets' nests 'n get stung 10 or 12 times at once, but I could not get th' eggs like Mom could. Too tentative, I suppose. Mom would just reach in 'n get th' eggs. Most times I could, too, but every now 'n then if I didn't reach in quickly, I'd get a hen peck on my hand, 'n then I'd smack th' ol' hen. Boy, could they squawk!

I learned to milk th' cow, too. Sometimes our cat would walk to th' milkin' shed with us, knowing he was goin' to get some warm milk. Mom would be milkin' away 'n she'd aim a stream of fresh, warm milk toward ol' Panther 'n that cat rarely let any of th' milk stream hit th' ground. And one day we had a "Moo Cow" moment!

Charles A. was barely a year old that summer of 1946; 'n my brother, Wayne, was almost two. Mom, Sis 'n me 'n th' two little kids headed out towards the milkshed with little Charles A. being pulled in his red wagon. Mom 'n Sis had stopped by th' fence so Charles A. could see his first Moo Cow. Sis pulled his wagon up next to th' fence; just th' other side of th' fence, our milk cow was grazin' on grass. The cow looked up and having finished grazing she let out the deepest, most rumbling, longest-lasting mooing sound I've ever heard. Charles A. let out th' loudest shriek I've ever heard! Tears 'n saliva 'n water were streamin' from that little guy, and I mean streamin' from everywhere; he was absolutely terrified, 'n I don't blame him. That was one big Moo Cow 'n one huge bellow. . .and one very wet little nephew! (But that was then; Charles A. today enjoys all the good things that "Moo Cows" provide, I just don't think he trusts them!)

Mom had my newest baby brother that same summer. Ira Bowman Packard, Jr. was born June 18, 1946. He had Grandma Foster's Indian blood, too; even as a small boy, you could see his dark complexion and his dark hair, just like Grandma's. His skin seemed to always hold a deep, bronzed tan, 'n he probably would have looked natural wearing breech cloths 'n carrying a bow 'n arrow. And he was one tough little cookie; when Mom would take a switch to him for doing something bad—which was quite often—she would grasp him with one hand and switch his legs with her other hand. Around and around they would go, Mom switchin' his legs, 'n I.B. just laughin' at her! And th' more he laughed, th' madder Mom would get. And usually, after a coupla minutes of this, Mom would wear down 'n she'd start laughin', too. You just couldn't help it; I.B. would walk away, rubbing his legs, 'cause you knew it had to hurt. But he never cried.

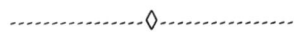

Bob came home that Christmas, in 1946; the war, at last, was over. Chuck was home, as well. Our two war heroes had safely returned, and our house was brimming with joy and happiness and with family members. Mom and Dad 'n Grandma Foster were hovering over all, helping to keep the festivities moving along. All of us kids provided the spontaneity and unbridled energy for this holiest of holidays. Foster Wayne was just past 2 years of age while Charles A. was about 1½; and our baby brother, I.B., Jr., was a robust 6 months old. Summed up, our entire family had gathered to celebrate Jesus' birthday.

As we began opening gifts, Bob took me to one side and handed me a present. As he did so, he said: "Charles, this is not a toy. And I want you to understand something—I will never give you a toy for Christmas. Anything I give you will always be educational. I do not believe in toys for children, as I want to see you focused on educational things." The gift was a crystal radio set that Bob helped me assemble. True to his word, over the next few years Bob gave me a Gilbert Erector Set, a chemistry lab (which Mom came to deeply regret), and a six-volume set of books about adventure and explorations. He never gave me a toy.

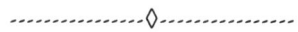

That next year Bob enrolled at The University of Texas, compliments of the G.I. Bill. Chuck Walters, now an Air Force Captain, was assigned to Sheppard Air Force Base in Wichita Falls, Texas. Of course, Inez and Charles A. went with him. And early that spring of 1947, my friend, Tommy Anderson and I would hear one of the biggest whoppers ever told!

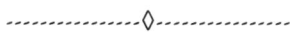

Tommy Anderson and his parents lived less than half a mile down the road from us on a little farm that became probably my best and favorite playground and definitely a place that gave us our greatest adventures ever.

We were just a month or so from summer vacation, and Tommy and I were going to walk home from school; our homes were less than 3 miles away. We had stopped at Cumbee Allen's General Store to get a soda pop, and a couple of local farmers were sittin' on th' bench out front of th' store. As we walked past, we heard ol' man Ernest Lancaster say to th' other farmer: "I'll tell ya, it was hotter 'n hell last summer why, I'd hitched up two of my ol' mules to haul some corn from th' fields," he paused to spit tobacco juice out toward th' road 'n then continued, "so th' mules are standin' there hitched t' my corn wagon, 'n it just kept getting' hotter 'n hotter. Well, afore ya know it, all that corn started poppin' 'n with all that popped corn fallin' around, them crazy mules thought it was snowin' 'n they stood there 'n plumb froze t' death!" Both old men started laughin' 'n slappin' their knees, 'n Tommy 'n I just looked at each other. We took a few swigs of our pop 'n started walkin' home. We both knew that any stories told on that bench was mostly gonna be lies, anyhow.

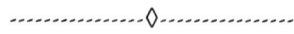

A bunch of us boys were hanging around Otis Jones' farm when Garlon Rea's parents drove up 'n let him out. Now there were 7 of us; me, Garlon, 'n the 5 Jones boys: Lynn, the oldest, then G.R., Noel Ray, Butch, 'n th' youngest, Booger Red. Booger Red had hair as red as his father's 'n twice as many freckles. He was as feisty 'n spirited as his name. So we decided to divide up 'n play Cowboys 'n Indians. About that time, Garlon remembered his new six shooters 'n ran to his Mom's car to get 'em. Man, they were fantastic—the new, red-handled Gene Autry gun 'n holster set. We were all pretty jealous, as none of us had any toy guns that nice. I needed me a new six-shooter, too!

That next week, Mom and I were in town, 'n I saw th' best lookin' cap pistol ever. It had an authentic-lookin' leather belt 'n holster with bullet loops, 'n th' gun had a shiny silvered finish with pearl grips. But th' best feature was th' bullets came apart, so you could load the new round single caps, one to each bullet. I had to have it, if for nothing else than to keep up with Garlon Rea; and it was only $6.

Mom said no. No way was she 'n Dad going t' pay $6 for a toy gun. Not in 1947, she said that was way too much money. Fussing and grouching wasn't getting me anywhere, so for th' next few days I tried pleadin', beggin', trying' t' bribe her by doin' extra chores 'n stuff. That didn't work, either. Fed up, Mom finally said: "Son, if you want that gun, you're gonna hav'ta get yourself a job." Now out in th' country, there aren't too many grocery stores or drugstores or places that would hire someone who was only 8½ years old. 'N then I remem'bered—Tommy Anderson's dad was startin' t' hire cotton pickers for his fields. Mr. Anderson said: "Sure, I'll let ya pick cotton; pay is $.50 a hundred pounds, same as ever'one else." Man, I figured I'd earn that $6 in one day! Mr. Anderson told me t' show up early, since th' cotton would be wet with early mornin' dew, 'n you can get twice as much weight those first couple of cotton sacks if ya' picked fast enough. He said by 8:00 a.m. th' sun would burn off th' dew.

Mom fixed me a lunch 'n a Mason Jar of iced tea 'n told me all 'bout pickin' cotton. She 'n her sisters had had t' pick cotton for a livin' when they were just little girls, so she knew all th' tricks of th' trade.

I was up at 5:00 a.m. 'n headed down th' road t' the Anderson's fields. When I got there, there musta' been 12 or mor pickers already in th' field. Man, they musta' really got up early.

By 9:30 I'd just managed t' pick my first sack, 'n it weighed a little more'n a hundred pounds. This was gonna be harder than I thought....

When I headed home at dusk, I had no idea how much I'd picked; I was too blamed tired t' really care. 'N I was ready to give up on that Colt 45 gun. But I knew I couldn't face Mom 'n Dad to tell 'em I was quittin'. I just couldn't let myself admit this job was too tough. Even if it took me 3 or 4 days, I was goin' to get that dad-blamed gun. I knew that for sure.

I was up at 5:00 again 'n determined to pick a lot faster. Around noon I'd already turned in another two of those long, white canvas cotton sacks 'n I was on a pretty good roll. I was maybe workin' on a good half-filled third sack when I heard a car horn. Ol' man Anderson yelled: "Charles, yer Mom 'n Dad are honkin', better run see what they want."

When I reached th' car, Mom asked me to go see how much I'd already earned. Mr. Anderson said: "Well, let's see." He pulled a little blue notepad outta his top pocket of his coveralls 'n said: "Well, looks like ya got 'bout $3 or so." Three dollars! Is that all, I thought, as I walked back t' th' car. I'd already worn holes in one pair of jeans from th' day before, 'n my hands had bad cuts from the sharp spines of th' dried cotton boll, 'n I'd been stung a time or two by yellow jackets. But I thought, shoot, Mom did this when she was younger 'n me, 'n she had t' do it. When I told Mom 'n Dad how much I'd earned, she said: "Well, go tell Mr. Anderson you're through. We'll get you that gun; we just wanted ya' t' see how hard it can be t' earn money."

I suppose I should have learned a lot of lessons from that experience, especially about having to work hard for a living 'n things like that. Maybe I did 'n maybe I didn't; but one thing I can assure you I learned—I didn't ever want to pick cotton for a living.

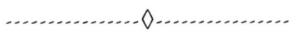

Earlier in 1947 we'd lost track of Dad for a few days, 'n Mom sure was worried. Dad had gone down toward Huntsville on a case of trouble with some lines down between Huntsville 'n Navasota. Mom always worried when Dad was around Huntsville, what with th' State Penitentiary there. Mom always worried an escaped prisoner would come upon my Dad (Mom should a' worried about the convict; if Dad got his hands on 'im the fella would probably wish he was back in th' prison. Dad sure had a mean grip.)

Anyway, there'd been a lot of heavy rains 'n some floodin' along th' Brazos 'n th' Navasota Rivers, so we had every reason t' worry. Especially Mom, she just seemed t' worry about most everything.

We got a call from Tommy Hart, Dad's boss up in Dallas; he told Mom there still had been no word from Dad. He said soon as they'd heard somethin', they'd let Mom know. That sure didn't ease her mind.

Next day Dad called, 'n Mom 'n I sure were relieved. Dad said soon as they could get his truck out of th' creek bed 'n get it cleaned up, he'd be home. The floods had caught him on th'wrong side of th' creek, 'n Dad said a real nice ol' Aunt 'n Uncle (that's what Dad called older black folks) had pulled his truck part way out of th' creek with their mules 'n had put Dad up for a few nights until th' floodin' let up. Dad told me later: "That ol' Auntie made th' best biscuits 'n coffee I've ever tasted but don't tell your mother—she'd just be jealous of another cook fixin' me somethin' to eat." Dad said he practically had to force th' old couple t' accept the $10 he offered for all their trouble. When he told 'em the Atlantic Oil Company would reimburse him, he said they accepted the money—but very reluctantly. Dad said they sure were kind old folks and kept a clean little cabin out in the piney woods near Navasota. And they were mighty proud people.

Dad had a real problem; whenever someone would "goose" him, he'd just absolutely go nuts. Mom said when she 'n my Aunt Lola had introduced their husbands to each other, Mom had stood slightly behind my Dad, 'n Aunt Lola had done th' same with my Uncle Frank Luttrell. Just as th' two men had reached to shake hands, th' women goosed 'em! Mom said Dad 'n Uncle Frank grabbed each other by th' throat and slapped th' hell out of each other with their other hand! Mom said she 'n Aunt Lola almost fell t' th' floor, they were laughin' so hard. (I never met Uncle Frank Luttrell; he was killed in a car wreck before I was born. . . .)

Dad would sometimes work with one of th' pipeline gangs if they were working on a pipe leak near where Dad would be workin' on his telephone lines. One such gang was run by Dee Hunt, a really tough, hard-nosed gang boss who happened to have this really deep, gravelly-soundin' voice. And Dee Hunt 'n his wife, Huldy, just happened to be some of Mom 'n Dad's best friends (Dee Hunt's gang was who built the big wooden swing set that was in our backyard at th' pump station all those years; his gang built it for me when we first moved out to the country near Oenaville.)

During th' summer of 1947, Dee Hunt's gang was digging up th' pipeline that ran real close t' th' Brazos River outside Bryan; they had traced th' oil leak to this site. Dad happened t' be close by; so when he'd repaired his downed lines, he'd come over t' help Dee's gang dig up th' damaged pipe. Dad said it was mighty hot that day, 'n he 'n most of th' men had taken off their shirts 'n tool belts. Dad's lineman's belt was heavy with all th' pliers 'n tools he wore on his belt—and he 'n Dee Hunt had stopped t' have a cigarette 'n cool off some. They were standin' on th' riverbank when one of Dee Hunt's men walked up behind Dad 'n goosed him. Dad jumped 'n went right into th' Brazos! Dad said he was glad he had removed his lineman's belt. "That," he said, "would've added another 20 or so pounds; but aside from all that weight, I'd probably have ruined some of th' tools."

-----------------◊-----------------

Before school started at Oenaville that fall, we had a tragedy occur with one of our classmates. That summer one of th' Billeck boys came in contact with a rabid skunk, and sadly, he became infected with rabies; Tommy Anderson, a friend of th' Billeck boy, went to visit him in th' hospital before he died. Tommy was there when our classmate died. Tommy said th' death was th' most horrible thing he'd ever seen. The boy had to be strapped to his bed so he couldn't infect anyone else when he went into convulsions 'n choked to death. (Rabies is an infectious viral disease that attacks the central nervous system. In more than 65 years, I've only heard of one single case in which an infected person survived; fatality is almost certain.)

That fall of 1947 found Tommy Anderson and me involved with a skunk-like critter of our own in one of his Dad's sheds. Tommy and I were playing near their barnyard when we saw an animal run into their small hay shed. We went in to see what kind of creature we had just spotted. Tommy and I started pulling bales of hay out of th' shed until we were down to about 3 or 4 bales. Tommy said: "Wait, 'n let me run git my .22; we'll shoot 'im if it's a skunk or somethin'."

When he came back, I picked up a hay-bale hook 'n said: "OK, I'll start pullin' th' bales one at a time, so you can shoot 'im 'n make damn sure ya' shoot him 'n not me!" "Don't worry," Tommy said. "I ain't gonna hit you."

As I hooked the next t' last bale 'n hauled it out, we both saw th' critter run behind th' last bale. We quickly worked out how we'd move th' last bale so Tommy would have a clear shot. (Now, I need to tell you this hay shed was small—maybe 20 feet deep and about 12 feet wide—a fairly tight space.) I hooked th' last bale. Just as Tommy moved t' th' left side of th' shed, I jerked th' bale to th' right, as Tommy yelled: "It's a damned polecat!"

Tommy shot th' skunk-like critter. Almost instantly, th' shed was filled with this pungent, stinkin', eye-waterin' spray! Choking 'n gaggin', we stumbled out of th' shed. . . .

Tommy's mother burned our clothes, fussin' at us th' entire time. She set out two big galvanized tubs she used to wash clothes 'n made us each sit in one. Mrs. Anderson scrubbed us both down with lye soap 'n tomato juice to try to remove th' smell; and I can tell ya' she was none too gentle. She was still pretty riled at us. I went home wearin' some of Tommy's brother, J.D.'s, clothes; mine had been burned.

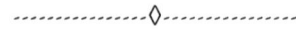

In October of 1947 Mom drove into the parking lot at Oenaville School 'n honked th' horn for me to come to th' car. As I approached, she said: "Come see what I got ya'; I think you're gonna like this." Was it a new cap gun or some Hershey bars? I wondered. "Look up in back," Mom said. Lying up on th' deck behind th' rear seat was a dog. . .a dog! Was that all she'd brought me? Mom could see my disappointed look and said: "Well, honey—I thought you'd like a little dog." She hugged me 'n closed th' door. "I'll see ya' when ya' get home; maybe you 'n your dog can play some. Right now he's a bit scared 'n a little timid. But maybe by th' time you get home he'll be ready t' play with ya. Given 'im a chance—I think you're gonna have a good time together."

King would become the best little dog we ever had. Mom had gone to th' dog pound that morning while she was in Temple grocery shopping, and even years later, could not explain what motivated her to go look at the animal shelter. An Army captain from Ft. Hood was being reassigned to Germany but could not take his pet with him. Mom said when she walked to the cages to look over the abandoned strays, all of the dogs were jumping upon the cage fencing, barking and yelping, as though to say "pick me"—all except King. Mom said he was sitting off to the side and looked so sad; Mom said he even looked like he'd been crying (I don't even know if dogs can cry but Mom thought he looked like it.)

Anyway, Mom said she couldn't resist this little black and white dog and so he came home with us. When I got home from school, I noticed that the dog was mostly white and on his back were two black splotches of hair that were almost perfectly shaped like a king's crown. My favorite radio program in those years was th' one about Sgt. Preston of th' Yukon 'n his dog, King. I thought this little dog looked like a small version of the celebrated Huskie so that became his name—King.

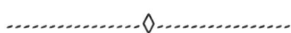

A year or two earlier Dad's company had constructed a big oil-storage tank up near th' pump-house office with big steel steps reaching to th' top. This big white 'n black oil tank looked like a great place to get a good look all around th' farmlands, so King 'n I went up. Th' view was pretty great, 'n King 'n I ran around th' top. Seemed t' be a great place t' play until Mom spotted us from her kitchen window. Boy, did she yell at me. "Charles Packard, you 'n King get down from there 'n I mean right now if you don't want me to take a switch to ya!" (A few days later, King 'n I went up again; and Mom threatened a whippin' once more. This time I was told firmly not to ever go up there again. And just in case, a gate with a lock was placed at th' bottom of th' steps so that pretty well ended that bit of fun.)

Rabbit hunting was one of our favorites, and one which King really got into. Whenever we would flush one from th' tall grass, off they would go, th' rabbit bounding away and King in hot pursuit. Once in awhile I would snap off a quick shot with my .22; fortunately, I never killed one 'n King never caught one. Good thing, too, 'cause Dad said if I killed an animal, I would have t' eat it—not only eat it, but Dad said I'd have ta' clean it 'n cook it (good thing Dad's rule didn't apply t' that polecat me 'n Tommy Anderson killed.)

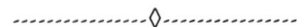

Like most other dogs in the country, King really liked chasing cars and pickup trucks. Whenever he heard one comin' down th' road, King would rip out across our yard, leap through th' gap in our frontyard fence 'n go after th' tires. Luckily, King never bit th' tires 'n caught one of th' cars, either; but he chased every car 'n pickup that ventured down th' gravel road—except Dad's. When Dad would come home from work out on his telephone lines, Dad would first drive his truck up to th' pump-house office to check in for th' day. King would always recognize th' sound of Dad's pickup (we never could understand how), 'n off he would go; but this time King'd head out th' back gate 'n go tearin' up th' path he'd worn in th' tall grass. King would race Dad up to the pump house having some 200 or 300 yards of open field to cover. Sometimes Dad would win but not very often. When Dad would head home, half th' time King would race him home; th' rest of th' time King would ride back in th' front seat with Dad. King enjoyed this 'n I really believe Dad did, too (we almost lost King years later in Port Arthur, Texas—but that's later in another story....)

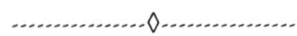

Donald Davis called me and asked if I wanted to go fishing with him. Donald Davis, two years older than me, and by far the best athlete in Oenaville Grade School, called me and asked if I wanted to go fishing. In 1948, this invitation probably made my whole year! I walked to Oenaville to the Davis' home, and Donald and I gathered up our fishin' gear 'n headed to one of th' farm tanks to do our fishin'. A few hours later we had hooked a nice string of some 7 or 8 good-sized perch. Don said: "Let's go home 'n fry these up, 'n I'll make us some biscuits." Biscuits! I didn't know anyone but mothers knew how to make biscuits. I knew Don could probably do anything he wanted, and now I realized that this childhood hero of mine could also make biscuits. I was really impressed....

When we reached his house, Don instructed: "You clean 'n rinse off th' fish, 'n I'll go start th' biscuits." After I finished scraping off the scales 'n cleanin' 'em, I walked in th' kitchen. Don was mixin' stuff 'n rollin' out th' dough just like I'd seen Mom do. Wow, I thought; this guy knows just about everything! We popped th' biscuits in th' oven, and Don got out his mother's skillet. We fixed a milk 'n egg dip 'n rolled th' fish in cornmeal. As th' fish were sizzlin' in th' skillet, I said: "Boy, these sure smell good! 'N your biscuits smell good, too." Don said: "Yep! Oughta' be some good eatin'."

Don got out some plates. I got the forks, and we took his biscuits outta th' oven. They were golden brown 'n sure looked good. We sat down t' eat 'n broke open a biscuit—'n it was bright yellow 'n hard as a rock! Don said somethin' unflattering about his biscuits, ending with "I musta left out th' bakin' soda!" We took th' biscuits outside 'n threw 'em at th' chickens. Th' chickens wouldn't eat 'em, either....

Donald Davis would go on to star for the Temple Wildcats from the 1952 through 1954 seasons. He married his high school sweetheart and went on to play college football. Don had a few coaching stops before he joined Head Coach Bob McQueen as Bob's Assistant Coach with the Fightin' Temple Wildcats. Over the years, Temple had come close to a State Championship but had never reached the throne room.

In 1979 this changed, as Head Coach Bob McQueen—Co-Captain and All-District End with the 1955 Wildcat team—and his Assistant Coach Donald Davis—Co-Captain and All-District Running Back with the 1953-1954 Wildcat teams—led the Temple Wildcats to their first Division 5-A State Championship. This was the first ever State Championship for "The' Fightin' Temple Wildcats"! (And just to prove this was no fluke, these coaches—and personal friends—did it again in 1985. In 5 years, Coach Bob McQueen and Coach Don Davis brought Temple two State Championships.)

---------◊---------

One day Garlon Rea had asked me over 'n I was lookin' forward to this visit; not so much about gettin' t' play with my friend, as much as what I knew his Mom would probably make for us—her famous 'n very tasty homemade potato chips. Her chips were almost worth killin' for; all th' boys in Oenaville School practically fought over who would get t' sit with Garlon at lunchtime t' help him eat those potato chips (usually Noel Ray Jones won this prize.)

Anyway, we were playin' around his Dad's farm 'n pickin' peaches 'n plums off their fruit trees. Garlon spotted a big, juicy-lookin' purple plum way up in th' tree 'n he said: "There's a good 'n why don't cha climb up 'n git it?" Gullible as I was, I started up th' tree—'n that's when Garlon shot me in th' butt with his BB gun! Boy, that stung like I'd just been popped by half a dozen yellow jackets 'n all in the' same spot! But Garlon committed one very serious mistake—he dropped th' BB gun 'n took off for his house. I was down from th' tree in about a split second, picked up his Red Ryder lever-action BB gun 'n peppered him in th' back two or three times 'fore he reached th' door (Garlon is retired now and lives out in Arizona; I called him 4 or 5 years ago and reminded him of his infamous shot. We both laughed about that moment but I admitted to Garlon he really got me good!)

----------◊----------

Christmas of 1948 was going to be just as wonderful as all th' others even if some of th' family couldn't make it home. Bob was goin' t' be busy with studies at The University of Texas (he always seemed to be busy with studies), 'n Chuck 'n Inez 'n their two kids would stay at their home on Sheppard Air Force Base. So our Christmas would just be Grandma Foster, Mom 'n Dad, 'n me 'n my two little brothers.

Christmas Eve mornin' around th' kitchen table was lively, 'n all of us were enjoyin' our breakfast. Dad said to me: "Son, I've gotta go into town on some errands 'n I might need your help; I want you t' ride in with me." This sounded good to me; besides, I knew we'd be pickin' out th' fireworks t' shoot that evening 'n I wanted to help pick 'em out.

Dad 'n I climbed in his truck 'n headed in t' Temple. On th' way he explained: "Son, I don't have a lot of chores t' do, just gas up my truck. I wanted you t' come with me 'cause I've ordered a ring for your mother; I want you to run up t' the Post Office 'n get it for me." To this day, I can't explain why this made me so excited, but it did. Somehow, th' thought of Dad getting Mom a ring for Christmas was…well, it was just so great. I really could not wait to see Mom's expression when she opened Dad's present 'n found her ring.

We drove into Temple 'n Dad pulled into Mr. Huggins' Gulf Service Station which was catty-cornered to th' Johnson Chevrolet dealership. Dad and Mr. Huggins were talkin' while they were gassing up Dad's truck, 'n Dad tossed me th' Post Office box key. "Here, son," Dad said. "Run up 'n see if your Mother's ring is in." I took off up th' sidewalk 'n didn't even stop at th' feedstore next door to look at th' baby rabbits 'n chicks that were usually kept in cages. I took th' Post Office steps two at a time and went inside. I grabbed th' wooden stool which was kept along th' wall 'n stood on it to unlock our box. I reached in—and it was empty! I couldn't believe it. Mom wasn't gonna get her ring under th' tree. I was pretty disappointed.

This time I walked back, not sure how I was going to tell Dad th' ring hadn't come in. "Dad," I said, "th' box was empty; Mom's ring wasn't there!" Dad seemed to take this news a whole lot better than I thought he would. He said: "Well, that's OK. I guess it'll be in next week 'n we'll give it to her then."

Th' ride back to Oenaville was pretty quiet; I was just in one of those moods, dis-appointed 'n all. Dad spoke up: "I'm gonna stop at Cumbee Allen's 'n call your Mother to see if needs anything." That was strange — Dad seldom called ahead. Dad gave me $5 'n told me to pick out some fireworks while he called home.

A few minutes later, we were once again on our way to the pump station. My mood had improved a little; at least I had a big sack of fireworks for later that evening.

We pulled in behind our house 'n I hopped out of Dad's truck 'n was headin' up th' wooden plank sidewalk when out from th' side of our house streamed about 20 kids from th' pump station, Oenaville, 'n all around our many neighbors shoutin' "Happy Birthday" 'n yellin' 'n laughin' 'n.

...'n I was speechless! I remember I was just simply so surprised; I was just speechless. I had never had a birthday party before; this was my very first (and it was one I will never forget; Mom 'n Dad had given me th' greatest Christmas gift ever.)

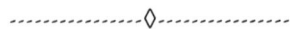

In 1949 my brother, Wayne, and my nephew, Charles A., went hunting. Wayne was 5 years old 'n Charles A. was 4; they had a small BB gun that Charles A. had gotten from his dad. The boys were young but Charles A. and Wayne had been thoroughly coached by Chuck Walters on how to handle a gun—any type of gun. And this BB gun wasn't all that powerful. Th' boys had only been gone for maybe 40 minutes when they walked in th' house, claiming they had killed a bird. "What!" I exclaimed. I couldn't believe it; that BB gun simply was not powerful enough. "Lemme see that bird," I demanded. The boys handed it over; th' bird was stiff as a board! I could tell that bird had been dead at least a week. I didn't doubt they had shot it; heck, they could have put th' gun barrel right up against the birds beak 'n it wouldn't have flown anywhere. It couldn't have flown, period. It was already dead. (Even many, many years later, these two still maintain they killed that bird. I should have made 'em cook it 'n eat it, like Dad would have done.)

In 1949 I broke my arm swingin' like Tarzan off our front porch. I swung out too far 'n lost my grip and landed on my rear end next to Mom's crepe myrtle bush 'n sat stunned for a few seconds. My right arm felt funny 'n when I looked down at it, I could see it looked a bit zig-zagged—it was broken alright.

Grandma Foster was sittin' on th' far end of th' porch, rockin' in her rocker 'n crocheting or something. I yelled at her, "Grandma, I think I broke my arm!" Grandma kept on rockin' 'n said: "Ah, lil Bowman, now don't pshaw me!" I'd never heard that word before but it must have meant she didn't believe me, so I said: "Well, look, Grandma, look at this!" She turned around 'n when she saw my bent arm I was holdin' up, she blurted out: "Oh, land sakes, oh, my God." Now she believed me. She threw her sewing basket to th' side 'n came down our front porch steps quicker'n I'd ever seen her move.

The Crepe Myrtle

Ruby Porter, our neighbor, drove me 'n Grandma Foster into Temple to th' doctor to see Dr. Howell. While I was at Dr. Howell's clinic, Janice Porter's mother went lookin' for Mom 'n Dad. She found my parents at Spot Cash Grocery on th' southside. Mom said Mrs. Porter walked in 'n said: "Now, Ruby, I don't want you 'n Bowman to be nervous," which automatically meant that Mom became very nervous as Mrs. Porter said: "Just don't be nervous 'cause Charles Bowman is OK, but he's broken his arm!" Mom said Ruby Porter was so nervous, as she was trying to reassure my Mother that I was really OK. And I learned from Dr. Howell that I would be able to play sports again, just not for a couple of months. (Ruby and Charlie Porter were good neighbors and good friends to my Mom and Dad. It's just that their daughter, Janice, and I didn't always get along; that's because Janice and I were more like brother and sister, and we fought like brother and sister. We're still like brother and sister; but now she is one of my very best friends. . .and she remembers those pump station years, too. . . .)

---------------◊----------------

Chuck and Inez had just recently returned from Germany where Chuck had been stationed for about a year and a half. We had really missed all of 'em, but Wayne said he remembered being devastated in early 1949 when Charles A. and Donna Kay, his little nephew and niece, had moved overseas with their parents. So their return was cause for great celebration. To add to th' festivities, some friends of Mom and Dad's had given Mom about a dozen baked apples. This neighbor had even dyed th' apples some really pretty colors; they were red, blue, yellow, green 'n looked as tasty 'n as tempting as any dessert I had ever seen. Th' four young'uns—Wayne, Charles A., I.B., Jr. and Donna Kay—were practically droolin' over th' prospects of diggin' into these juicy-lookin' desserts. In fact, each little one had already picked out a color 'n to everyone's surprise, they were all different. But first they had to eat all of their dinner. I had never seen those guys eat their dinner so quickly. Mom and Inez cleared th' table 'n got out four bowls for these baked apples. You could see th' anticipation on their faces. . . .

(Now, I must first tell you that these were not candied baked apples; th' neighbor had forgotten to add sugar 'n cinnamon spice flavoring. They were as tart as anything you've ever tasted.) Mom 'n Inez knew this, as they'd earlier tasted one. But they were waitin' to see th' kids' reactions. Th' four kids dug into the apples at about th' same time. Th' looks that came over their faces told th' story: th' four kids twisted their faces into some of the yuckiest, most unpleasant-lookin' scowls I've ever seen. Mom 'n Inez started laughin' so hard Mom choked on her food! Mom was really chokin' 'n could easily have choked t' death, but Dad 'n Sis started slappin' Mom on th' back and soon she was OK. But that was a very close call. That was sort of a practical joke that nearly backfired tragically. But it was funny.

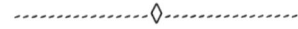

Over the next few years, fun 'n games continued for all of our family, as well as for many of our friends and neighbors.

Tommy Anderson and I continued ridin' their farm mules into one of their farm tanks (some farmers called 'em ponds), buck-naked as we'd go skinny-dippin'. Sometimes Tommy 'n I would be allowed to sleep in th' cottonseed bin; this was some sort of "risky" adventure, especially since Tommy's mother told us t' be careful th' barn rats didn't chew off our toes. Thankfully, they never did. Tommy 'n I would wake up at sunrise when th' barnyard rooster "alarm" went off. Besides, even if th' rooster's crowin' hadn't awakened us, Mrs. Anderson's cookin' would've. Just smellin' her homemade, smoke-house cured bacon fryin' 'n her made-from-scratch biscuits brownin' in th' oven wouldn't let any normal person stay asleep. Those were incredibly great breakfasts.

Hide 'n seek at Otis Jones' farm was another of our favorites; th' Jones boys—Lynn, G.R., Noel Ray, Butch, 'n little Booger Red—would rearrange bales of hay in th' hayloft 'n create a "hidden" secret passage which led to a hideout. When I'd come over to play, they'd tell me: "Wait here 'n count slowly t' a hunnerd, 'n then see if ya' can find our hideout." Th' guys would take off for th' barn 'n before long I'd be lookin' for th' loose straw which would be th' giveaway. Sometimes it was well-disguised 'n might take me a minute or two. I'd always find it but sometimes it was really well-hidden. Then th' next time over, there would be another secret hideout with another secret passageway to be discovered.

So many times it seemed all of us boys were meant to share endless days of summer and endless times of fun. But they did come to an end. My brothers and I didn't know it at the time—back then it seemed parents wanted to spare their kids all the unpleasantness of bad news—but our Dad had developed heart trouble. The doctors had recommended a change of climate and especially a change of jobs; climbing telephone poles and lugging the heavy lineman's belt and tools was putting too much strain on Dad's heart. So Atlantic Oil Company found a desk job for Dad at one of their refineries in Port Arthur. We would have to move.

The day we finally drove away from the pump station and from Oenaville was just about the worst day of my life. . .the worst day was yet to come. . . .

---------------◊-----------------

Chapter 20

Three-Point Landing

Timeline: 1943-1993

The muffled drums sounded a muted beat as the Air Force Honor Guard stepped out in their slow, measured cadence. As the airmen lined up behind the hearse, the Master Sergeant barked the command, "Ten-hut!" Somewhere out of sight a solitary bugle began the mournful sound of taps.

In crisp military fashion six pairs of spit-shined shoes snapped their heels smartly to attention. Almost simultaneously, slightly behind me and to my right, I heard one of our family snap his heels, as well.

I sensed it was I.B, or Buddy. . .maybe both. Seconds later, and almost subconsciously, I brought my heels slightly together, not so much as a military courtesy but something deeper and much more personal. . .most likely the same sentiment that gripped my brother. We both shared deep feelings for this man we were burying today. . . .

Then, moving once again in their slow, measured military paces, the young airmen advanced toward Chuck's coffin.

In that intensely emotional moment, the realization came flooding upon me that during our overlapping years in the Air Force, Chuck's as a distinguished command officer and pilot, and mine as an enlisted radar technician—I had never once had the opportunity to extend to this brother-in-law the military courtesy of a salute.

What I had never been able to render him during his lifetime, I now slowly raised in this, our last few moments together.

The solemn dignity and precise military discipline which filled that space and time for all of us who had gathered at Quantico National Cemetery will forever grace our memories of this man. . . .

And yet, in my mind, there remain many other memories of Chuck Walters—memories, and places of long, long ago. . . .

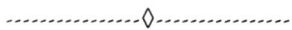

I do not remember the circumstances leading up to our trip to Draughon-Miller Airfield in Temple, Texas; all I can remember is sitting in the backseat as our car pulled into the parking lot and proceeded through the gate. Mom and Inez were in the front seat, and I heard Inez say something about "meeting" someone "landing on this airfield." Mom drove through the gate and pulled up next to the landing field. That summer day was hot.

Mom and Inez had fried up several chickens and put the fried chicken in a picnic basket; they also brought a washtub filled with iced cold beer. The year was 1943 and we were in the middle of World War II. And as I would learn years later, Lt. Charles A. Walters would be landing a C-47 on this airfield.

The pilot of this C-47 was coming to see my sister, but I seem to remember this plane's crew was also soon to enjoy a very special "picnic." (Since all of these participants, except me, have now passed on, I can easily defend that which occurred upon that tarmac. First of all, a war was going on, and even so, there were no hard, fast rules prohibiting a civilian vehicle from parking near the airfield. Secondly, because a war was going on, there were no guarantees these crew members would even be alive the next day; consequently, eating fried chicken and drinking cold beer was the least I believe our family could have contributed for this crew of young airmen.) Seeing an airplane land on this runway was nothing new; Mom and Dad had brought me out here several times "to see planes land." And it was thrilling.

Inez suddenly became very excited, and I quickly realized why. I had seen several airplanes land but nothing like this huge aircraft approaching our car. The big brown plane with a yellow nose taxied toward us, and for a brief second I thought it was going to run over our car! At the last moment the airplane turned to one side and painted on its nose was a big bird, a big seagull. (I didn't know it at the time, but this was a cartoon seagull drawn by Walt Disney and made available to aircraft commanders for reproduction as their ship's logo.) This was a really big plane, easily bigger than any I had seen before. I had seen pictures of these and had even seen them in the movies! But this one was real. This one was right in front of me. And boy, was it huge! The big twin engines changed pitch, and I knew they were stopping.

The fuselage door opened and down the steps came the pilot, the man she called, "Chuck!" Sis ran to meet him and jumped into his arms. This "Chuck" was in his tan-colored flight suit and still had his radio headset cords dangling down his side. This pilot's airplane was just like those I'd seen in the movies; this pilot was just like those I'd seen in the movies. But I wasn't sitting in a seat in a movie theater. This adventure was happening to me in real life, in real time, and I was really impressed! I just stood there, rooted to the ground and almost speechless! (Later, as Mom and Sis and I drove back to our home near Oenaville, I realized I had just witnessed something that was almost beyond my youthful comprehension...and I had a new hero!)

Years later, Chuck Walters would teach me how to safely use and care for firearms. When I would fire my .22 rifle and later my .410 shotgun, Chuck would inspect my guns after I had cleaned them. And likely as not, he would make me clean them all over again. Cleaning solvent and cotton cleaning patches were things I came to hate—and his "intense" inspections.

Chuck showed me how to rub down the gunstocks with linseed oil and how to "bake" this oiled gunstock in the oven. When he would take me on real hunting trips, I learned from him how to carry my rifle or shotgun; he said: "Never carry them with the barrel pointing to the ground—always point them in the air." But the highlights of my arms experience occurred when he let me fire his 20-gauge shotgun, his .270 hunting rifle, and the prized possessions in his extensive arsenal: his double-action .38 pistol and especially his authentic Colt 45 western revolver! This was the real version of the toy pistol which I had picked cotton for some 4 or 5 years earlier. And the interesting thing about all of these sidearms—Chuck loaded and made all of his own bullets—lead molds, and all.

The Crepe Myrtle

The longer I knew this Air Force officer, the more I became convinced that his talents had no bounds....

To me, his most exciting accomplishment was the one that I only vaguely recall but one that was witnessed and confirmed by many that cold, foggy evening in Waco, Texas; and it was the stuff of legends. (Most of these details were given me by Inez years later:)

Inez was home from Austin where she was working and living. Her new pilot boyfriend, someone named Chuck Walters, was flying in to Texas from somewhere out of state and would be landing that evening—with an ETA of 6:00 p.m.—at the Army Air Corps Base in Waco, named Connally Airfield. Chuck had asked Inez if she would be able to meet him at the air base as he had maybe a half hour or so before he had to take off after refueling. The weather in Central Texas was cold that February of 1943, and as I was told years later, already becoming socked in by fog.

We left Temple early that afternoon, driving up to Waco. Mom and Dad were in the front seat, and Sis and I were in the back. I vaguely recall that the grownups seemed to be somewhat on edge, as very little was spoken on the trip north.

We reached the airfield, just east of downtown Waco, and Mom and Inez went in the flight center while Dad parked our car. The control tower wasn't very big, maybe three stories high, and the flight control center was adjacent, in a small, smoke-filled office building. The flight control sergeant was talking to my sister as Dad and I walked in.

The wall speaker just behind the office counter occasionally crackled statically with brief announcements and commentary that came from somewhere outside this room. Some half dozen enlisted men, a few sergeants, and a couple of corporals—manned the various desks and workstations in the office. A couple of wooden benches lined the two walls opposite the flight counter, and in one corner was a Coke machine, a cigarette vending machine, and a gumball machine. The gumball machine became my main focus the rest of the evening.

Inez and my parents ignored my pleas for a few pennies, as they seemed intensely involved in conversation with the flight control sergeant. He told my sister: "Miss, Lt. Walters just reached us on his radio, and he's coming on in; he's maybe an hour out." He paused as though to give more weight to his pronouncement: "But we've radioed Lt. Walters about our weather; as you probably noticed as you drove in, we've had fog most all day. It has only gotten worse. Right now, the field is completely socked in with zero visibility. Not really ideal at all for a landing."

Mom, Dad, and Sis sat down to wait, and from time to time, handed me pennies for the gumball machine. Mom and Dad sat calmly for most of the time; Sis, however, paced nervously for much of that evening.

Some long minutes later, the sergeant spoke to my sister: "Ma'am, we've just got word from Lt. Walters; he's about 10 minutes from the field. The flight control officer just ordered all the field-landing lights and runway lights turned on; we're going to do all we can to help the Lieutenant land that bird."

(Many years later at their home in Alexandria, Virginia, I was sitting with Chuck in the basement rec room, watching football and just generally shooting the breeze. I asked Chuck specifically how, in his own descriptive words, he had accomplished that incredible three-point landing in all that fog. This was his reply:)

"It was simple," he said. "As I neared the field there at Connally, they radioed me that they were turning on all the runway and landing lights so I might have some indication of where the field was. I honed in on their radio signal and could just make out the runway from the faint glow of the parallel runway lights." Chuck then explained the technical data he employed which I do not recall. He had immediately turned so many degrees to his left and flew on that specific heading for a precise number of minutes and then banked sharply to the right, and again for an exact number of minutes, on a specific heading. At the end of this precise number of minutes, Chuck said he banked sharply to the right again, on a heading that would trigonometrically put him on an exact heading toward the airfield. And after so many minutes, he said he would be exactly over the airfield. He didn't say approximately over the field, he said exactly over the airfield. "Then," he continued, "it was merely a matter of maintaining my heading and coming in on the correct approach. The rest was easy."

Probably most other pilots would have said that under those weather conditions, at best it would be a difficult landing. But as Chuck Walters would say: "It was simple."

---◊---

After World War II, Captain Charles A. Walters, Sr. was among the hundreds of pilots given the critical assignment of ferrying coal, clothing, and food supplies to the citizens of West Berlin, thanks to Communist East Berlin trying to isolate and starve into submission their fellow countrymen on the other side of the Communist-erected barricades. Chuck Walters and these other heroes flew into and out of the Berlin Airfield to thwart the communist schemes. Many times, Chuck said, some of the C-47s like his were so heavily loaded with cargo, they would barely clear the end of the runways on takeoff.

During World War II, Chuck had flown into combat zones, as he and other "Goony Bird" pilots had flown the Burma Hump in war efforts against the Japanese; now, after the war, he was among those pilots flying the Berlin Airlift, again delivering critical supplies into hostile environments.

Chuck Walters was born in Chicago, Cook County, Illinois on May 22, 1919. He was the only child of a widowed mother, Anna Walters; Mrs. Walters and her son moved to St. Paul, Minnesota where he spent his childhood years. Chuck used to tell me about hunting snowshoe rabbits in the cold northwoods and ice fishing on frozen lakes. Both of these were foreign to me. We had rabbits in Texas, mostly gangly jackrabbits, that farmers hated. We had some things become frozen in Texas during cold winters, and we had lots of lakes, but to my knowledge, I had never encountered a frozen lake. Must have been awfully cold up there in St. Paul!

---◊---

Chuck and Inez had married on July 29, 1943, in Austin, Texas. On July 29, 1993, they observed their 50th Wedding Anniversary in Alexandria, Virginia. In attendance were Charles A. Walters, Jr., their son, and his wife, Terry; their daughter, Donna Walters Firkin, and her husband, Buddy, were there, as well. And all of Chuck and Inez's grandchildren: Steven Walters, Tracy Walters, and the twins, Kristen and Kelly Walters, David Charles Firkin, Karrie Inez Firkin, and Charles Christian Firkin were there, also. My brother and his wife, Ira B. Packard, Jr., and Debbie Packard, and their daughter, Lisa Packard, had come to join in this time of celebration. And I was there with my wife, Bobbie, my son, Clay, and my youngest daughter, Kelly. Clay was, at the time, Lance Corporal Clay Packard, a member of the U.S. Marine Corps. Dressed in his Marine Corps dress blues, he stood at the door to welcome them into the surprise gathering of Chuck and Inez's family.

Chuck and Inez were led to believe that only their children and their spouses were joining them at Sir Walter Raleigh's for a prime-rib dinner. As the maitre d' led them to the specially-reserved banquet room, Lance Corporal Clay Edward Packard snapped smartly to attention, presenting a Marine Corps salute to Colonel Charles A. Walters, U.S.A.F., retired. Chuck returned the salute, although he and Inez gazed quizzically at this young Marine. The doors opened to a cheering, festive mob of family members who applauded and cheered this amazing couple: Chuck and Inez Walters.

A few minutes later, my sister asked: "Who is that young Marine?" She and Chuck had not recognized their own nephew. Understandably so, as Clay had only been 12 years old the last time they had seen him, and Kelly had been 10.

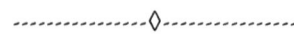

Chuck and Inez lie buried together in the same grave, one coffin above the other, at Quantico National Cemetery in Virginia.

Chuck and Inez's family—their children, grandchildren, brothers and brothers-in-law—all joke from time to time about where, and what, their spirits are up to; to a person, we pretty much agree they are probably sharing a cold beer somewhere, and, just as they once did, most likely circling once more over the Central Texas skies in Chuck's C-47. And Chuck is probably letting "Pee Wee" fly his plane while he pretends to be asleep. . . .

(This chapter is dedicated to all the grandchildren and great-grandchildren of Col. Chas. A. Walters, Sr., a man who most of us knew as Chuck. And for those of you who were there at his funeral. . .to you, he was simply "Poppaw".)

Chapter 21

Port Arthur Years

Timeline: 1952-1954

Our family made some good friends in Port Arthur and a few very good friends. The boys within a couple of blocks radius of where we lived were of all ages: mine, Wayne's, and I.B.'s. We went to school with them, played all the kids' games with them, and, on a few occasions, even fought with them. All in all, Port Arthur probably was as good a place as any other.

But none of this could equal what we left behind. Our friends, our home, even the countryside where we had lived—for as friendly as Port Arthur was, this Gulf Coast city could not match that which was back in Bell County.

The home we had to live in was little more than a half-way decent shack. We weren't quite at poverty level but we had to be close. We hadn't exactly come down a peg or two in our lifestyles; half a dozen pegs or more might better describe our circumstances.

And as I eventually came to realize, the one person most affected by this move was my Dad. Years later, Mom would tell me that Dad had to take a significant pay cut—almost cut in half. Economics dictated this situation. As a highly-skilled lineman, Dad would obviously be in great demand and warrant a very good income—not near that of professional pay levels, but for the 1940s, a good income, nevertheless. As an office dispatcher logging in oil tankers pulling into the Atlantic Oil Refinery in Port Arthur…well, this was not a highly-skilled assignment. Dad was compensated accordingly; we all had to learn to do without. Needless to say, this was a very hard lesson.

Probably one of my best friends was a boy about a year older than me, who lived a half a block away. Buddy Marchand's family had a good-sized garden in their backyard, and his Dad planted a big variety of vegetables and strawberries. Even though Buddy's Dad seldom allowed us to pick his strawberries, Buddy and I had all we wanted. We'd just wait until it got dark, and we'd crawl into the back of this garden; lying on our backs, we'd scoot along like mechanics on a creeper, eating strawberries left and right. Buddy and I were midnight plunderers.

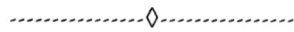

Having just started junior high school as an eighth grader, I quickly learned how different my classmates were in this huge new school. Pranks were still played on one another, but these pranks were more punishing and harsher in nature. Some older boys and I locked a seventh grader in a locker in metal shop one day, and half an hour later, the shop teacher heard him and let him out. In fact, many of my classes seemed to have almost as many kids as we had in the entire Oenaville School. One year, the ninth grade (the highest grade) at Oenaville School consisted of Gary Ewing. That was it; the entire ninth grade class was one student. Woodrow Wilson Junior High School in Port Arthur had almost a thousand students. To say I was overwhelmed would be a classic understatement. And early in 1952, boys in Port Arthur started wearing ducktails; I grew one, as well. Mom thought it looked like hell 'n pretty well said so.

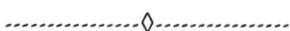

I was on the receiving end of a prank one afternoon while riding the bus home from school. Four or five ninth graders—all bigger than me—let me know I was going to ride the bus all the way to the last stop on the route which was some 3 miles away from our house. I didn't put up much argument as I could tell it would be simpler to ride along and walk home. Sitting a few seats away were Jimmy Tibbets and Harvey Johnson, two tenth graders at Thomas Jefferson High School. Jimmy and Harvey were also well-known throughout our neighborhood as two of the toughest kids on the block. I played tackle football with them a lot but never really hung out with them; they were high schoolers while I was a mere eighth grader.

Our bus reached my stop, but I just stayed in my seat, resigned to having a long walk home. Jimmy and Harvey got up to depart the bus, but Harvey stopped in the middle of the aisle, facing the guys who were keeping me on board. Jimmy stopped at the back exit doors and spoke to me, although he was looking intently at the ninth graders: "C'mon, Charles, you're getting off here. 'N I can guarantee there ain't nobody gonna stop ya'!" (When I got off th' bus, in some odd way I felt like I knew just how settlers must have felt when the cavalry came riding in just as the Indians started attacking!)

----------◊----------

We almost lost King late in 1953; I had just started the ninth grade and though I still wasn't very happy in Port Arthur, at least I had my family and my dog.

Before I saw the "accident," I heard it; screeching tires and horns honking told me something had just happened, and it didn't sound good. And then, one of my friends came running up and breathlessly uttered the words I had secretly dreaded for so many years: "Charles, come quick; King's been hit by a car." He paused as though not sure he wanted to say it; in a softer voice, he said: "'N I think he's been killed."

I knew now what people meant when they would say: "His heart was in his throat," 'cause that was exactly how I felt also, like I'd just been punched in the stomach and had the wind knocked out of me. I felt all of that, and more. As I reached Procter Drive, I saw King lying alongside the curb across the street. He wasn't moving.

As I reached King, tears were already blurring my sight; he was so still. Just the way he was lying, I was sure he truly was dead. My little dog was gone. I stooped and gently lifted him up, sadly wondering what you do when your pet has been killed—and that's when he moved his head! King was still alive! King gingerly turned his head and licked my hand, but other than that, he wasn't moving very much. That was OK with me; and I started breathing again, as well.

Less than an hour later, he was walking around OK, just not his usually alert, aggressive self. He was back to his old ways in another day or so. We figured he had been struck a glancing blow and probably just knocked unconscious.

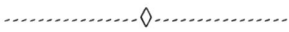

And then we did lose him. At least, he didn't show up after 2 or 3 days. Sometimes he would disappear for a day or so but he'd always come back home. This time did not feel like the others; after a week, I was sure that he wasn't coming back. This time, he wasn't going to be lying in the street for me to pick up and have him come to in my arms. I had no idea where he was or if he was even alive. This time, he was truly gone.

I was nearing the end of my ninth grade and would be starting high school next fall. Spring of 1954 was very nice in Port Arthur but I was miserable. I would sit in class and gaze out of windows, wondering where King was and if there was any chance of ever seeing him again. In those moments, I would remember how things were at the pump station, and I could see us running in those fields chasing rabbits that we could never catch. (And I would think that if only we were back there, then maybe King. . . .)

I knew I had to stop doing this; we would not be going back to the pump station. We were here in Port Arthur. And King was really gone. That was the real world, not that place in my memory, nor in my fantasy; he was gone.

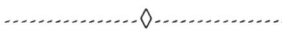

Buddy Marchand came over to my house, riding his bike up into the gravel road we shared with five other tenant families. As he dismounted, he said: "I saw King the other day; me 'n this guy were ridin' our bikes in this other neighborhood, 'n I'm pretty sure it was King. "Least," he said, "it sure looked like 'im."

Next morning, maybe an hour before school would start, Mom and I left in our car to look for King. Buddy told me pretty much how to find this neighborhood, so Mom said we'd drive around and try to find him.

This was the happiest I'd been in more than two weeks. At least, I held out hope that King really was out there somewhere and just maybe. . . .

Mom turned up the first street, and we agreed that she would look to the left side, and I'd take the right. Mom drove slowly as we checked out every single house. "Mom," I said, "suppose King's locked up in someone's backyard; how'd we know which one?"

"Well, honey," she replied, "there's just no way we can know; we'll just have t' hope he's even alive, let alone if he's in someone's backyard." That sure didn't sound encouraging. In fact, as we cruised up the fourth street, I was getting pretty discouraged. All the houses looked so much alike; small, like the one we lived in at the pump station. And the one we now lived in was even smaller. Mom broke my train of thought. "Honey," she said, "it's getting late, 'n I need t' get you t' school."

"OK, Mom, but could we just do two more? 'N then we'll go." I was OK with that because even if we didn't find King on this search, I knew we could come back on Saturday. We went down the next street—nothing.

We were slowly cruising the last street when I caught a glimpse of—was it a dog? "Mom," I yelled, "stop! I thought I saw—back up, back there, that house with the two big bushes—on the porch." Mom backed up and sure enough, there was a little white dog. But I wasn't real sure it was King. Mom stopped, and I was almost afraid to whistle in case it wasn't King. "I whistled and called out: "King!" The little black and white head raised up, and—it was King! It really was King!

He leaped from the porch as I opened the car door and was in our car in less than two seconds. Mom was crying; I was crying and King was licking my face. Then, Mom's and mine, again and again...that may have been the wettest welcome either of us had ever experienced! (That day at school was absolutely the happiest day of my teenage years!)

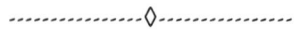

June 25, 1954 was the worst day of my life....

Wayne, I.B., Jr. and I slept in the same bed; it was a very small house. About 5:15 that morning I was awakened by Mom shaking me awake, and she was crying: "Charles, Charles, honey, come quick; I think our little Daddy's dead!" With that, I leaped out of bed, and in a foggy stupor, I remember hoping this was a bad dream. And I had a god-awful sick feeling in the pit of my stomach as I thought, oh, please God, don't let this be happening!

I walked into Mom and Dad's bedroom, and Dad was lying on his back with eyes shut and his mouth slightly open, as though he were snoring. But he wasn't' snoring. I gently shook him, saying: "Dad, Dad, wake up! Dad, please, wake up!"

Dad had died sometime earlier that morning of a heart attack. The rest of the morning is still a blur and probably always will be. I remember Mom sitting slumped by the front screen door, sobbing and softly crying. I also remember thinking, in some pathetic way, that Mom was the grown-up; I should be the one crying. I remember an ambulance pulling in the driveway.

And sometime later that morning I remember sitting in the small living room with some neighbors, and I think there were some relatives there, as well. Then, I remember someone holding smelling salts under my nose; they said I had blacked out. I know a lot of things happened but I do not remember them. But what I do remember is that throughout that day I did not cry. I was devastated on the inside, but I did not cry. . .I wanted to, so very much. But I just couldn't. . . .

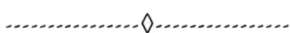

The next day or two were also a blur, as Mom said there was a funeral service in the Baptist church, and then Dad's coffin was put on a train for Temple. Mom wanted him buried in our hometown, near our other family members. . . .

At some point, Mom, Wayne, I.B., Jr. and I were gathered by ourselves in that small living room. In a subdued voice, Mom spoke: "I just wanted to ask you kids what you'd like t' do. We can stay here, or we can move back to Temple. You just need to. . . ." Mom did not complete the sentence before I had interrupted her: "Temple. We're moving back to Temple," I said emphatically. "No way in hell I want ta' stay here. I'm ready to move now."

I hadn't responded with a suggestion; Mom said I had spoken as though I were giving orders. I meant no disrespect. I had lost my Dad here in Port Arthur, and I just wanted to go home....

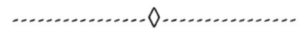

Two days later, Chuck and Inez drove over to Port Arthur and loaded our few things into both cars. We were going to live with Chuck, Inez, and their kids for awhile, as Mom and Sis looked for a house in Temple. At this time, Chuck was now Captain Charles A. Walters and stationed at Kelly Air Force Base in San Antonio. I knew Wayne was going to be happy because when Chuck and Inez and the kids had first gone to Germany in 1949, Wayne had missed his nephew and niece terribly. The Walters were only gone a year and a half, but to my brother it had seemed an eternity.

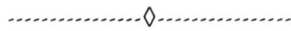

The day after we arrived at Kelly AFB, I got a haircut. Maybe the accurate phrase is I was ordered to get a haircut. My sister wasn't officially military, but she could bark orders like any old grizzled First Sergeant. As we got in her car, my sister lit into me: "Brother, I want you to know that crap you call a ducktail is the worst looking mess I've ever seen! I'm ashamed of how my brother looks, and I'll be damned if I'm going to let you dishonor our Dad by looking like that! And Charles, after we get that cut off, don't you dare grow that crap back, or I'll come cut it off again! Now, do you understand what I'm saying?" I felt almost like coming to attention and saluting her. I said: "Yes, and don't worry; I'll never grow it back again." I meant it, too. Somehow, the ducktail reminded me of all that had occurred in Port Arthur, and I wanted all of that to just go away.

Mom found a little house in Temple, and she and Inez bought some furniture there in San Antonio. We spent a few weeks sanding and repainting this used furniture until it looked fairly nice. Mom didn't have a lot from Dad's company insurance, but she and Inez made it cover most of these costs. For the remaining summer of 1954, we enjoyed milkshakes Chuck and Inez made for us kids each night, and we would watch Charlie Chan movies until almost midnight. Under different circumstances, those summer days with Chuck and Inez would have lingered pleasantly in my memories. Truthfully, I do believe that those less-than-halcyon days were made quite a bit more endurable because of what my sister and brother-in-law did in helping us to cope.

---------------◊----------------

Mom, my brothers, and I moved from San Antonio to Temple in August of 1954. The little house Mom had bought for us was on the far northside of Temple, at 913 Crockett Courts. It was a very nice, clean little house, and had a nice, big fenced-in backyard. I walked with King all around the perimeter, checking for any gaps through which he might possibly escape (I remember thinking how ridiculous that was, since this was the first fenced-in yard he had ever seen. He had always roamed as a free spirit, and I found my concerns to be just a bit ludicrous; why, I asked myself, are you all of a sudden so all-fired worried about King's being loose to run free? Of course, I already knew why: King had almost been killed by a car and had seemingly wandered off never to return. Those days were over.)

King and I finished our fence inspection, and I snapped a padlock on the gate by the back corner of our house. I reached down to hug King and promised him he would never again chase a car, much less get run over by one. "King, this is your new home, and this is your backyard. You will be safe here." (Mom had rescued King when he was 2 years old in 1947. Seven years later, King was home to stay; he would live comfortably in this place until he died in 1961 of old age. King was 16 years old. . . .)

I started high school in Temple that September of 1954. Bill Valigura was Assistant Principal and a very good friend of Mom and Dad's. Mom used to tell me "Bill Valigura was like a son to me 'n your Dad; you show him respect, now." I assured her I would. Bill Valigura's mother-in-law, Mrs. Babe Lancaster was my Sunday School teacher at the Baptist church in Oenaville, Texas. I had looked around the Temple High School grounds, cognizant of the fact that at last I was now attending the same high school which Bob and Inez, my brother and sister, had once attended. Hopefully, my two younger brothers would attend here, also. (Mrs. Babe Lancaster had taught our Sunday School class a poem—a poem that, through the years, had hovered over me, constantly nagging at my conscience whenever I tried to take a shortcut or to do some task only half-heartedly. Her poem simply said:

> "Things that you do,
> Do with your might.
> Things done by halves,
> Are never done right."
> Mrs. Babe Lancaster, Oenaville Baptist Church, 1945.)

---◊---

Throughout the fall of 1954 I determined to buy a nice Lionel Train for Wayne and I.B.; I reasoned that since Dad would not be with us, then just maybe a really fine Lionel Train Set would be a nice Christmas gift for my two little brothers. Working at Spot Cash Grocery enabled me to buy an extra car, or crossing signal, or some station building each week when I got my paycheck. Half of my check went to Mom for helping on expenses, and about a fourth went for the kids train. By late November, I had invested $170 in a very elaborate train layout. This was an amount that far exceeded any train set I had ever received—many times over.

---◊---

Christmas Eve of 1954 I turned 16 and faced with the daunting task of assembling this vast train set alone, I had invited my very good friend, Tommy Anderson, to spend the night and help on this project. By 9:00 p.m. Wayne and I.B. had gone to bed, and we carried all the boxes and train set packages to the living room. I checked on my brothers one more time and convinced they were asleep, Tommy and I started opening boxes. By 10:30 we had all the track pieces laid out in a huge oval with two inner loops and a siding. By midnight we had some of the station houses and the water tank wired in and strategically placed and realized we were both hungry. Mom had placed a box of chocolates under the tree for Wayne, a Whitman's Sampler; at 12:30 a.m. the box of candy began looking more and more appealing to us laborers. We opened the candy, rationalizing we had earned at least a couple of pieces for the work we were doing.

By 6:00 a.m. Christmas morning, Tommy and I had finished the train set project; we had also finished Wayne's box of candy.

Wayne and I.B. played with the train set that morning for perhaps 30 minutes. A few years later, after I had enlisted in the Air Force, my brothers took down the train set boxes from the closet and set it up for a second time and the last time, as it turned out. Mom sold it for $110 a year and a half later. I guess Wayne and I.B. just weren't railroaders. But Wayne sure grumbled over not getting his box of candy....

Many years later I came to realize that most likely I had subconsciously purchased that train layout to somehow assuage my own grief and not necessarily that of my two little brothers. I had always been the one who loved trains, whether the real ones I rode on, or the toy ones I played with.

And the box of candy: in 2004 I sent Wayne a fresh box of Whitman's Sampler, along with a note in which once again I apologized for the theft of his 1954 candy. I told Wayne that the good news was that for the next 50 years I would be sending him an annual box of candy to compensate for all of those 50 intervening years.

But the bad news, I explained, was that I would not live that long!

----------◊----------

Chapter 22

The Fightin' Temple Wildcats

Timeline: 1943-1985

Football has long been important to our family, maybe even as important as food. Well. . . maybe not quite that important but at least a fairly close second, and in particular, Temple Wildcats' football. Before I had the privilege of wearing Wildcat Blue and White, Temple High School football was a big part of our family's history. Even before I was born, Mom and Dad would frequently attend Wildcat home games at Woodson Field. Mom said Dad had long followed Temple Wildcat games, as far back as the late 1920s; this was even before they had met and started dating. They were Wildcat fans, pure and simple.

Mom had once described in detail a game between Temple and Waco, a game which Mom and Dad had attended sometime during the mid-1930s. Temple and Waco were playing for some type of championship, and the Wildcats were inside Waco's 5-yard line and apparently on the way to defeating Waco. The Wildcats had called for a pitchout to a wingback who was seemingly wide open for a game-clinching touchdown when a Waco player picked off the pitchout; the Waco player went 95 yards for the winning touchdown. This was told to me on two separate occasions: once, when I was about 10 years old and again when I had first made the Wildcat team in 1955. Twenty-some years later, the disappointment in Mom's voice still showed.

In 1941 my sister, Inez, had obeyed Dad by staying home on a school night and instead of going out with her friends as she had wanted, called them up to come over as Dad had suggested. The only problem with that was the fact that she had invited the entire Temple Wildcat football team to our house! And Dad could only stand there, shaking his head. . . .

Sometime in the early 1940s and after we had moved to Oenaville, I had begun listening to the Friday night Wildcat games. These football games became a much anticipated part of my week, and I remember hanging on every word from the radio announcer.

One game in particular sticks out in my memory: Temple was involved in a very close game—I believe the opponent was Corsicana—and the second half kickoff was about to start with Temple kicking off. The opposing team's return back fielded the ball and took it all the way for a touchdown. I remember being really angry. Then, the other team kicked off to the Wildcats, and the return back, a star player named Earl Black, fielded the ball on about the 10-yard line and started up the right sideline. Once Earl Black had cleared the first wave of would-be tacklers, the radio announcer really became excited: "Earl Black is up to the 30, the 35, th' 40—two Temple linemen are now escortin' him—Earl's down to the 35, th' 30—he's goin' all th' way for a touchdown! Folks, that just put th' Wildcats back in th' lead! What a run—90 yards for a Wildcat touchdown!" Just like that, my frustration switched to total elation. (That was probably the most exciting radio play-by-play I have ever heard. I don't recall who won the game but I believe the Wildcats won.)

Dad took me to a lot of Temple Wildcat games; he even took me to some of the out-of-town games. One game we attended was in Bryan, Texas, maybe an hour or so drive from Temple. Dad and I stopped that afternoon at a popular café to get something to eat before the game. We hadn't been there long when in walked the entire Temple Wildcat football team. Apparently, the Wildcats were having their pre-game meal there.

Some of the Wildcat players spoke to Dad; being at such an impressionable age, I guess I thought that was so special, my Dad "knowing" some of these gridiron "heroes" and vice-versa. (Strangely, I remember nothing of the game. All I remember is being with Dad as the Temple Wildcats walked in . . . .)

The fall of 1946 brought about a big change in my grade school routines at Oenaville; for th' first time, th' older boys were letting me play touch football with them at recess (actually, we played "touch" football when th' teachers were around; otherwise, we played tackle.) I was almost 8 years old and among the youngest allowed to play. I loved football but hadn't yet learned all of the rules; rules that I soon would learn th' hard way.

We had quite a few good athletes in our school, but none were more talented nor more athletic than Donald Davis and Buddy Lewis. These two were the fastest and best football players in our school.

Two of th' older boys chose up sides; I was th' last one chosen. Actually, I don't even think I was chosen; I think one of the captains said: "You get him." So much for how I impressed th' guys....

We kicked off, and the other guys lined up for their first play; they threw a pass and somehow or other...I intercepted it...my first play!

And then I just stood there; I did not know which way to run! Everybody was yelling, "run this way; no, run this way," and so I just stood there, totally and absolutely confused. Someone tagged me, and th' play was mercifully over. About that time, Donald Davis came over 'n said: "C'mere, kid, 'n let me teach ya' something!"

Donald proceeded to educate me on at least one of the many rules I would learn from him and Buddy Lewis over th' next several years. Thanks to their teachings, I would like to think I at least became a fairly good football player—not great, but fairly good.

Over the next few years, Dad and I would often talk about th' Wildcats 'n how someday maybe I could play for them; 'n he could come watch me play. Dad said he would, although at th' time probably neither of us knew if I would be good enough to make th' team. But that was sort of a dream, or ambition, perhaps, in which we both could bond as father and son.

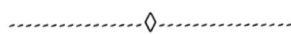

In 1952 Dad's health necessitated a move to a different climate and a job that would not place such a strain on his heart. And for all intents and purposes, my dreams of playing for th' Temple Wildcats ended and along with them, any hopes I had of Dad coming to watch me play.

And in June of 1954 when Dad passed away from a heart attack, any hopes of him witnessing anything, passed away with him. Dad's heart condition left him no chance of survival. Cigarette smoking had claimed another victim. Many years later, when I felt like I had finally worked my way through this loss, I came to realize that, in many ways, his death was a blessing. Dad was very unhappy those last two years; I believe he knew he was dying, and I believe this removed a lot off his shoulders. Having to take this desk job killed him, I believe, as much as did the heart attack. And finally, this inevitable heart attack allowed our family to return to Temple and gave me the chance to tryout one day for the Temple Wildcats.)

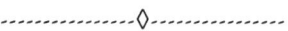

In the fall of 1954, I ventured down to the practice field to watch the Wildcats scrimmage. By then, Donald Davis was the star running back for the Wildcat Varsity, and in many ways, I felt a lot of satisfaction seeing one of my childhood "heroes" perform so well. Donald was even better than I had remembered. I walked over to the field and watched the "B" team or Junior Varsity, as they practiced for their upcoming game against Gatesville. And although the desire to play for the Wildcats had somehow lost a little of its luster, the desire was nevertheless still there. All the Wildcats looked really talented, but I thought, at least give it a try.

A few days later, I walked into Coach Anderson's office in the gym and told him I'd like to play for the "B" team. Coach Anderson asked me if I'd played any junior high football, and I told him no, I hadn't. We talked a few minutes, and he convinced me I should wait until next year. So I walked away.

(What I am going to reveal next is simply an object lesson I later came to learn from this experience and that is: "never give up on your dreams or ambitions—never." You see, I let this kind gentleman make the decision for me. I gave up too soon. Several months later, Erwin Owens told me that Coach Anderson was watching our gym class play flag football, and the Coach said to Erwin: "That Packard kid is fairly good; maybe I should've let him play, after all.")

Charles B. Packard

In 1955 I went out for spring football and made the "B" team. Coach John Connell at first put me at fullback then moved me to defensive back. I started every game at this position and led our "B" team with 7 interceptions that fall. I also returned a punt about 85 yards for a touchdown. That play was truly a thing of beauty but not because of my run. What made this such a "textbook" play, was the way all of our team performed on that one outstanding play.

Here's how the play unfolded: the Palestine Wildcats "B" team was about to punt to us on fourth down. We were already up 13-6, and Palestine was punting from near midfield. Bucky Stevens was back at left return back, and I was at right return back. Marvin Wall had turned with his back to the Palestine huddle and signaled a number "1" return. That meant a return around our left end, so regardless of which one of us fielded the punt, I would end up with the ball. If Bucky fielded th' punt, he would hand off to me; if I fielded it, I would fake a hand-off to Bucky. The punt was absolutely perfect as far as we were concerned. . . high and deep, about a 35- or 40-yard punt and coming to me. I fielded the punt cleanly and turned to cross in front of Bucky as we executed a fake hand-off. I should say, as Bucky executed a fake. Naturally, I couldn't see Bucky's fake because I was busy "pretending" I didn't have the ball, as I tried to hide the football on my backside. As Bucky and I crossed, out of the corner of my right eye, I could see a big lineman coming at me, and I hoped he would take the fake and go after Bucky; if not, he would possibly stop me before I could even turn the corner. I continued toward the left side, and the Palestine player pushed off on my shoulder pads and took off after Bucky! For a wild split second, I wanted to turn and look at Bucky because he had to be executing th' best damned fake ever!

Meanwhile, our punt return linemen and linebackers had made their hard contact hits on the Palestine linemen and drifted over to the leftside, forming the hoped-for screen of blockers. I turned th' corner and for some 40 or 50 yards downfield, all I could see was a beautiful line of Blue and White Wildcat uniforms as our guys were lined up perfectly, each man about 8 to 10 yards from each other. To my memory, there was not a Palestine player in sight. I cruised down the sideline, as Marvin Wall and another Temple boy formed up next to me as escorts. Marvin had this menacing look on his face as though to dare any Palestine player to head our way.

We went on to win convincingly, 26-6. And after our wild, exuberant after-game meal, our old bus, *Th' Blue Goose*, broke down. We were stranded somewhere out in the East Texas piney woods, at an out-of-the way gas station. Some cowboys came in with a big possum in a towsack; and with half of us still too wound-up to sleep and way too bored, we decided to put th' possum in our thick helmet duffel bag. And we threw th' possum on th' bus with the other half of th' team and coaches, trying to sleep. All hell broke loose and we watched as players and coaches climbed across the tops of the seats, trying to escape this hissing, snarling "thing" in the duffel bag (more than 50 years have passed since we committed this mindless prank so hopefully the statute of limitations has long passed. But Lord, was it ever funny! And we refers to John Gill, Bucky Stevens, Bobby Winnett, and a few others. I was not the only one involved but let's just say I helped....) We reached Temple about 3:00 a.m. that morning.

We were allowed to "sleep in" the next day and to be in class after lunch. As I walked to school, I have to admit the previous evening's adventures were still very much in my thoughts. Crossing North Third Street, I headed towards Northside Drug. Billy Walker, Robert "Smitty" Smith, and half a dozen guys 'n girls came out, cheering 'n whistling. I know my head must have swelled a size or two as I admit I enjoyed th' moment. (Anyone who has scored a touchdown for his team and says the praise and recognition doesn't really matter is either an emotionless ice cube or a liar. For that moment, I was on top of the world. But after reading my description of that punt return play, you would have to recognize that that perfectly-executed play was carried out by 11 Wildcats and not just one... Besides, turning that corner and seeing that perfect blocking wall of Temple Wildcats, I'm not so sure but what my Grandma Foster couldn't have scored that TD.)

(From 1950 to 1953 the Temple Wildcats had some truly awesome teams. Led by All-State Quarterback Doyle Traylor and a host of talented athletes, Temple advanced to two State Championship games in Class AAA, playing

the Breckenridge team two years in a row. We lost both games in close, well-played contests, but regardless, we lost and that hurt.

Nevertheless, once a Wildcat fan, always a fan. When we moved to Port Arthur, Texas that summer of 1952, I good-naturedly did some bragging about my Temple Wildcats. One of my new friends in Port Arthur was a guy named S.I. Pellerin—"Brother" was his nickname—and he enjoyed mocking my hometown. "Brother" would exaggerate the name "Temple," by pronouncing it over and over, as "Tem-pul, Tem-pul." Remember this mocking reference by S.I. "Brother" Pellerin, because 4 years later, we would play his team. . . .)

---◊---

Starting my senior year in September of 1956 our Wildcat team learned that Temple was being moved up to Texas footballs' highest classification: AAAA! For several years, Temple had pretty well handled our District AAA, winning District Championships for some 5 or 6 years running. Now, we would be in th' Big Boy league, playing teams like Waco, Austin, Houston San Jacinto, and Houston Bellaire as well as other highly-regarded and established programs like Killeen, Brownwood, Cleburne, and the team my "mocking" friend from Port Arthur was attending. I couldn't wait until we faced Brother's team!

We played Houston San Jacinto a tough game but lost. They were big and fast and very good—but we lost. Our next few games went our way, as we beat Killeen, Houston Bellaire, and lost a tough one to Cleburne, the eventual Class AAA State Champion. The Cleburne Yellow Jackets were really good; you have to be good to win a State Championship in Texas. But our Temple Wildcats had a 90-yard touchdown run by Bill Bryant, one of our team's captains, called back by a bad call from one of the officials. After the game, this official came to our bus and admitted he had made a bad call. The other coaches and some of the players had to restrain Coach Cottle; he was ready to literally strangle that referee. And in the Killeen game, I had a fumble recovery I made inside the Killeen 25-yard line which led to one of our touchdowns. Even though the first half of our Killeen game had the Kangaroos badly outplaying us, we still went in at halftime, up 12-6. In the second half, a weird series of goofs by Killeen led to a 46-yard punt return by me to put us up 18-6. In all of our home games, I had never heard the Wildcat Fight Song, as all of us Wildcats were too involved in the game to really hear cheers and fight songs. But as I circled into the end zone on that punt return, for the first time I heard this stirring fight song; and it sends a chill through you.

We were close to halfway through our season and stood only 2-2; and up next was the game I had been waiting for: Port Arthur Bishop Byrne, a big Catholic high school; and Bishop Byrne was the school attended by S.I. "Brother" Pellerin, a very good, close friend from my Port Arthur years. Regardless, I wanted to see our Temple Wildcats throttle this team. I wanted Brother Pellerin to recognize just who, and what, Temple, Texas was all about. We pounded 'em, 46-6. We were now 3-2 and had regained some momentum. And I was fairly sure that my friend at last knew how to pronounce the name of Temple.

We journeyed to Brownwood the next week and extracted revenge for the previous year's loss, 22-6, which Brownwood hung on our "Cats." We beat Brownwood, 12-6; and the game wasn't really that close. Our record now stood at 4-2, and the next week the big, fast, and very talented Austin Maroons were coming to our place. And Friday night was going to be Dad's Night. All of the fathers of our Wildcat players would be wearing their son's jersey number. Mom had contacted Jimmy and Mildred Faulkner, two of Mom and Dad's good friends and asked Mr. Faulkner if he would wear my jersey (Jimmy and Mildred Faulkner were the parents of Patricia Faulkner; and Patricia is now the wife of a very good Oenaville friend and childhood playmate, Buddy Lewis.)

We took the field that night, well aware that Austin had been listed as 12-point favorites over our smaller bunch of Temple Wildcats. When the game ended, our Wildcats were on Austin's 4-yard line; Austin was lucky to get out of Temple with a 12-12 tie. We kicked them all over Woodson Field. Bill Zaleski, Pat Cuba, Dale Glasscock, James Houston, and I were all over that backfield. Austin's All-State Quarterback, Mike Cotton, saw more of our Wildcat defensive line than he did of his own running backs. I had two sacks of Mr. Cotton, and I know "Big Bill" Zaleski hammered him a time or two. (Mike Cotton would go on to play for the Texas Longhorns, and lead the 'Horns to SWC Championships.)

We played two more Austin teams the following two weeks and though both of them were scrappy teams, we came out with hard-fought wins. And speaking of scrappy, our Wildcat team had a couple of scrappers ourselves. Don Mraz, our sophomore quarterback, and Bill Bryant, our senior captain running back, defined the word scrappy (interestingly, these two wore very famous Wildcat uniform numbers: Don Mraz wore number "11," which had been worn years earlier by Doyle Traylor, Temple's All-State Quarterback; and Bill wore number "43," which was worn by Donald Davis, Temple's All-District Senior Running Back from the mid-1950s. And Donald Davis was godfather to Bill's first son, some years later.)

The 1956 Temple Wildcats' record now stood at a respectable 6-2-1, and all of us knew we could have been 8-1. So we were new to AAAA football; so what? We were Temple Wildcats. But the reality was, we were 6-2-1, and about to face our perennial foe, the Waco Tigers. Waco was just as fast, tough, and talented as Austin—and maybe even more so. We knew we would be in for a tough home game to close our season. (The 1956 Temple Wildcats had no All-State players but we probably should have. We had some outstanding football players who, game after game, gave their full share of "110%," and more: ; players like Bill Zaleski, Dale Glasscock, Bill Bryant, Pat Cuba, Marvin Wall, Dan Malin, Don Mraz, and Danny Bryant. We had other good players like Tommy Wright, Don Cannon, Billy Walker, James Houston, Jay Seastrunk, Bucky Stevens, Frank Roberts, Bill Machalek, Milton Carver, David Jernigan, and me. Our team came up against some very good opponents, and for the most part, we played good, solid football. We won some games in which we were underdogs, and we won not so much because of our talent but because we played just a little bit tougher and more determinedly than did our opponents. But we lost a few because some of our games went against us due to mistakes and penalties. One of those losses would be the one we wanted the most—against the Waco Tigers. That game was tough and close pretty much all the way. One of our junior players failed to cover the sideline on a kick, and the Waco return back ran all the way for a touchdown. We lost to Waco, 20-14.)

Getting to play for the Temple Wildcats remains as one of my life's greatest accomplishments. And though I grieved the loss of my father and agonized over not having him there to watch me play, I still believe I played fairly well. I had a few really good games in which I made some very good plays. And I had a few games in which I know I could have played better. The problem is, you can't get do-overs, not for the 1956 Temple Wildcats, nor in life. You give it your best shot, and sometimes that is enough. I have recognized that I was a good football player—not a great one, but a good one. And occasionally, I made memorable plays.

Our entire family loved the Temple Wildcats and followed their progress closely. And I was the only member of my family to wear Temple's Blue and White. I am still very

proud of accomplishing that. And I know my Dad would have been proud, too....[13]

----------------◊----------------

For as much as our family had loved the Temple Wildcats, that same passion, in later years, would lead to a rather remarkable change in loyalties.

By the mid-1970s, our immediate family members totaled 26 and included our Mother, Chuck and Inez and their offspring, me and all my brothers and all of our children. And our allegiances gravitated toward two NFL teams—the Dallas Cowboys and the Washington Redskins! You could not have orchestrated two more natural nor volatile rivalries had you tried. These were antagonists in the strictest sense. And strangely enough, even though our teams greatly disliked each other, our family rivalries actually led to many of my fondest memories of these clashes between the 'Skins and 'Boys!

---

[13] Author's Note: In 1941 Mom and Dad returned home to find their house filled with some 40 Temple Wildcats due to my sister "out-foxing" my Dad. In the fall of 1956, following an all-night poker game at my house after one of our football games, Mom woke up Saturday morning to find some 6 or 7 Temple Wildcats sleeping on the carpet, the sofa, and in recliners. She said that brought back memories of 1941. And because Mom always was a Wildcat fan, she fixed breakfast for all of us...it was the least she could do....

Just before Dallas embarked on their run of three Super Bowl victories in four years, the Cowboys were unquestionably one of the worst teams in 1989, going 1-15 in that season. And the lone victory?—it was against the hated Washington Redskins who, coincidentally, were the defending Super Bowl victors of the previous year. Such was the rivalry between these two teams.

Another time, my wife and I had gone to visit our Redskin family members, and on our return trip back to Indiana had encountered some rather odd behavior from passing motorists. As the motorists passed us, the occupants would smile and wave enthusiastically as though we were long, lost friends. The only noticeable oddity was that most of the passing vehicles sported Washington Redskin bumper stickers; and we knew that we had an Indiana license plate.

A stop in Frederick, Maryland to gas up cleared up the mystery: someone (who to this day remains unknown) had stuck a detestable Redskin bumper sticker on our car! All those traveling 'Skins fans thought we were Redskin fans, too! But the most endearing, yet most frustrating memory of our years of rivalry involves my sister, Inez. This beloved sister, who succumbed to cancer in 1999, proved to be the all-time champion of payback!

Whenever the Cowboys would whip her Redskins, my brother, I.B., and I would phone her and harass her mercilessly.

But when the tables were turned, with her 'Skins beating up on the 'Boys, Sis wouldn't call us right away to extract vengeance; Inez would wait until about 2:30 in the morning before calling us! Not yet awake, I would have to sleepily listen to her singing that hated "Hail To The Redskins"! Inez was brutal.

Our family rivalry with the Redskins and Cowboys endures. But without Inez around to stir the pot, it will probably never be quite the same....

----------------◊----------------

[*As I recall those wonderful years of listening on the radio to Wildcat games, and especially those occasions when I accompanied Dad as we attended several games, I realize now that probably none of that compared to the honor*

The Crepe Myrtle

and satisfaction I got from the privilege of simply putting on that blue and white uniform as a Temple Wildcat. Even if Dad weren't around to see me play. . . .

That 1956 Temple Wildcat team, though undersized, and probably a bit short of the athletic talent with which many of the 4-AAAA schools we faced were blessed, was nevertheless loaded with a dedicated bunch of over-achievers. Guys like these:

Dan Malin, a ferocious junior tackle on that team, went on to play college ball at Rice University; in Texas, Rice University is considered "the MIT of the Southwest."

Danny "D.B." Bryant, a solid, talented sophomore guard, started all three of his years for the Wildcats and went on to play his college ball at Oregon State.

Don, "mighty Mite" Mraz—to my knowledge the only Temple player talented enough to wear the Number 11 of the legendary All-State, All-American quarterback, Doyle Traylor—led the Temple Wildcats all three years as our starting quarterback. Don packed a lot of dynamite in his 5'7" frame. Don was our spark plug. . .a true Wildcat!

Tommy Wright, our junior quarterback, half back, and "Mr. Everything" football player, attended The University of Texas and became a very successful and wealthy financial executive and business manager. He and my younger brother, Foster Wayne Packard, have crossed business paths numerous times in Texas.

Bucky Stevens was the very talented and very dedicated junior running back who, in his sophomore year (1955) on our "B" team (Junior Varsity) executed the (probably flawless) fake hand-off that allowed me to run back that punt against the Palestine Wildcats for a Temple touchdown.

Marvin Wall, a senior linebacker-defensive back on our 1956 team, won the Most Valuable Defensive Back Award at our banquet. Marvin was also the guy who provided "escort duty" during my punt return, and judging from his intense scowl, dared any Palestine player to try and stop us.

Don Cannon, also a senior guard on our '56 squad, went on to attend The University of Texas and became an equally well-known and financially successful Certified Public Accountant in Texas, managing, operating, and steering any number of companies and corporations toward financial success.

Senior fullback, David Jernigan, was a sight to behold at most of our games as Dale Glasscock recently reminded me. After a play, this fiery running back would return to the huddle, all smeared with blood! And like Dale said, it just seemed to match his red hair and bright red freckles! David just seemed to like the red blood—usually from his nose, and an opponent's to coordinate with the rest of who he was.

Pat Cuba, another senior on our team, absolutely played "lights out" football on our defense; Pat had only one playing speed—and that was "destroy"! Pat graduated from The University of Texas and became a millionaire through his numerous real estate ventures in Texas until his untimely death back in the 80s.

Wilbur "Bo" Meier was another senior guard on the Wildcats, and in 1956 Bo and I were guests on the sidelines at the rivalry game between Kilgore Junior College and Tyler Junior College. When the Kilgore Rangerettes came onto the field at half time, I can assure you Bo and I thought seriously of accepting that little 1-year scholarship offer! Bo obtained his PhD in Engineering and went on to become head of the School of Industrial Engineering at Purdue University and years later assumed the position of Dean of the Engineering Department at Penn State University, and chairman of Industrial Engineering at Iowa State. Eventually, Bo went back to Texas and assumed the position of Chancellor at The University of Houston. At the time of his death, he was a professor of Industrial Engineering at North Carolina State University where he had also served as dean. He was selected a member of the Academy of Distinguished Alumni and a Distinguished Engineering Graduate of the University of Texas at Austin. We lost a good friend and a brilliant scholar in Bo on October 13, 2008.

This brings me to our three senior Wildcat captains, Bill Zaleski, Dale Glasscock, and Bill Bryant. It is probably a good thing that I am running out of words because I doubt there are enough left to adequately describe the talent, leadership, and skill which these three Wildcats brought to our team.

"Big Bill" Zaleski was the biggest guy on our team but back then that was only 200 lbs.; high school teams in Texas nowadays have running backs who weigh that much! But back then, Bill played like a 400 lb. terror! "Big Bill" played his college ball at Tulsa and today he and his wife, Linda, successfully own and run a thriving business, Data Projections, Inc., in Houston. Bill was abundantly gifted and successful throughout his football years; it's good to see he is still the same...

Dale Glasscock was our senior starting tight end and like Bill Zaleski and Bill Bryant, played both ways; they were just too good and too valuable to not be out there on the battlefield. Of all my Wildcat teammates, Dale would be the one I would label a gritty, hard-nosed true Texas cowboy! Dale played his college ball at TCU under the legendary old Abe Martin, and following many successful and profitable years in the insurance business, took over the operational management of a ranch deep in southwest Texas. Located some 50 miles west of San Antonio, Dale's ranch lies not too far from the route our Foster ancestors would have traveled in that fictional cattle drive in 1830. And interestingly enough, Dale told me there is still a very old, run-down line shack out on the plains, probably a leftover from authentic cattle drives from the 1800s. A very dear friend, Dale, (unfortunately for me) played on the TCU team that beat my Texas Longhorns 6-0 in a hard-fought game.

And lastly, we come to Bill Bryant. When we would purchase copies of the Temple Daily Telegram early Saturday mornings to see if our names had been mentioned, we always knew we could read about #43—Bill Bryant. The sportswriters went into overdrive writing about our senior running back, with phrases like "the scrappy Bill Bryant"; "Scooter Bryant broke off a 23-yard TD run"; "from there, the scrappy #43 ripped his way to pay dirt." Much like Don Mraz, Bill Bryant also was endowed with a legendary number, #43, that of Donald Davis, my own hero from those Oenaville years. Don was godfather to Bill's first son. After Temple High School, Bill went to Texas A&M, simply because he wanted to play under Paul "Bear" Bryant. Disappointed when Bear Bryant left to take over the program at Alabama, Bill and his wife, Joyce, transferred to Abilene Christian College, where, in typical Bill Bryant fashion, he played, starred, and co-captained his Abilene Christian football team.

Charles B. Packard

And over the ensuing 45 plus years, Bill Bryant coached high school football across the wide expanse of Texas, from 3-AAA programs up to 5-AAAAA big time Texas football powerhouses.

And in July of 2008, our ex-Wildcat teammate was honored with his induction into the Texas High School Football Coaches Hall of Fame.

As for me? Well, for two years I got to play alongside this scrappy, hard-nosed bunch of over-achievers, and was privileged to wear the Royal Blue and White Wildcat uniform which we all cherished.

And my senior year, I started at defensive half back alongside Bucky Stevens. He was a true Wildcat.

After serving honorably for 6 years in the U.S. Air Force as a Radar-electronics Technician, I was encouraged to "try out" for college football. I had been stationed for 4 years at Sweetwater AFS, Texas where we had a small but intense football program organized and ramrodded by the Base C.O., Bird Colonel T. L. Donohoo. A fighter pilot in World War II, Col. Donohoo was as tough and cantankerous as that part of West Texas in which he was born. A personal letter from him earned me an invitation to walk on at Texas Tech.

I guess I just wasn't mentally tough enough to handle riding the bench; I had been told by a few coaches I would get a football scholarship that next spring but in the meantime we had no money; we were pretty much starving and I knew I needed to get a real job. Dropping out of college and walking away from football was a huge disappointment. I felt like a real failure....

Failures? I had several, including not being able to play a single down as a college player.

My first two marriages failed, even though they successfully produced the three children whom I adore.

My first attempt at starting a business failed, resulting in having my car repossessed, losing all my money, and the indignity of being evicted from an apartment.

Other than the year in which I lost my Dad, I suppose 1985-1986 was as low a "failing" period as I ever endured. And about the time I felt like just giving *up, I believe God reminded me of what it meant to never quit. Somehow I began to think back to those Wildcat years. Those guys never quit. We always believed we would win every game. The legend on the wall of that long-ago locker room said it all: "A Winner never quits—and a Quitter never wins."*

Things began turning around in 1991 when I met my wife, Bobbie—a girl I've been married to approaching 18 years. In 1996 we started our own company, and in January 2005 we sold it which has afforded me the opportunity to retire and have the time to finish this family story.

Throughout Texas, most all high school football locker rooms will display another well-known motto, but I truly believe that the version on the Temple Wildcat wall filled that bunch of guys from 1956 with the will to over-achieve: "It's not the size of the dog in the Fight; it's the size of Fight in the Dog!"]

Chapter 23

Remembrances

As we near the end of our story, I have recalled a few special stories and tales which I believe you will find interesting; I enjoyed writing them and hope you enjoy reading them:

---◊---

Dad's younger brother, Alex Packard, landed at Normandy on D-Day, June 6, 1944; Uncle Alex was in the Engineering Battalion assigned the extremely dangerous job of clearing the steel barriers and hedgehogs from the landing beaches. These obstacles had been erected on the beaches by the Germans to prevent the Allies from bringing ashore their tanks, trucks, and supplies. Uncle Alex was seriously wounded during this landing and received combat disability pay. Uncle Alex never married.

Uncle Alex had a newspaper photo of Dad and Dad's friend, Boots, made into an oil painting, and he gave me this canvas during my visit to Centreville during the 1990s. I tried to convince Uncle Alex he needed to keep this memento of his big brother, but he handed it back to me, insisting: "No, you need to keep it; I'm an old man and won't be around many more years. This needs to go to one of Bowman's sons."

I was finally grasping the depth of this brother-to-brother relationship when Uncle Alex told me of working in Temple with our Dad. Dad and Uncle Alex were stringing telephone lines between Temple and Waco, and Uncle Alex mentioned he wasn't being paid by the Atlantic Oil Company for his efforts. This puzzled me so I asked Uncle Alex: "I don't understand, Uncle Alex, why would you want to work so hard without being paid?"

I will never forget the look Uncle Alex gave me; you would have thought I had just sprouted horns or something as he responded in exasperated tones: "Why, boy—I just wanted to be with your Daddy!"

Aunt Mary told me of her last visit with our father. We had once again gone to Louisiana to visit with all of Dad's family, and Dad had stopped at Aunt Mary's to say good-bye. Aunt Mary knew this was going to be a very brief visit because Mom and we three boys had stayed in the car. This would have been in the summer of 1948.

Dad and Aunt Mary had sat in the kitchen for a few minutes drinking a cup of coffee. Aunt Mary had sensed an unusually somber tone in Dad's words, because she had always found Dad to be very upbeat and cheerful. As they hugged good-bye, Dad stood up and pushed open the screen door. Aunt Mary followed Dad outside and waving good-bye to Mom, called out: "Good-bye, Bowman, reckon I'll see you next year." Aunt Mary said Dad turned and with the saddest look she had ever seen on his face, he replied: "No, Mary, I don't think so. This may be our last trip."

Aunt Mary told me she believes that Dad already knew his health was bad and didn't want to alarm her or anyone. She said somehow Dad knew he would not be back.

Dad died in 1954. . . .

In 1947 I stole something; I stole a couple of meaningless items from The Woolworth Store in Temple. And the memory has never faded. . .nor the guilt. I was 9 years old and sitting next to a kid at the Bell Theater in a Saturday morning matinee. I didn't know this kid next to me except that he said he was a couple of years older 'n me, and he looked to be part Indian or something like that. He talked a lot about how brave and daring he was but mostly he just talked a lot.

Before long he bragged how he could steal things and never get caught. He looked at me and said: "Bet you couldn't do that!" Foolishly, I let my pride answer for me: "Oh, yes, I could. I could take something if I wanted to; I ain't scared of getting' caught."

When the matinee ended, he dared me to go with him to Woolworth's across the street and prove what I had just said. I felt a strange knot in the pit of my stomach, but I went with him. He had challenged something inside me that I just could not at the time explain. So, I went. We both walked around several aisles, as I watched him take a couple of things. I was picking up a kind of toy flower that had a long tube and squirt bulb attached. Nervously, I put it in my pocket. A minute or two later, I picked up a cheap-looking leather coin purse with some kind of stitching and that went into my jeans, as well.

When the other kid and I walked outside, he asked to see what I had taken. His only response was: "Well, that sure ain't much but I guess you're OK." And he walked away. I sure didn't feel OK; it's funny now but at the time I just felt like I had eaten a lot of candy 'n junk 'n just wanted to throw up. I truly felt sick.

Mom and Dad picked me up later on the street corner by the Star Barbershop; and on the way out to th' pump station, Mom turned and said: "Son, are you OK? You act like you don't feel good." "Nah, I'm OK," I answered. "Maybe just somethin' I ate at th' show."

How did Mom know? I wondered to myself. Does she know I'm just a thief? A lot of these thoughts rattled around inside me, and I somehow felt dirty 'n cheap, and I knew absolutely that what I had done was wrong.

Later that afternoon, Mom 'n I were alone, and Mom said: "Charles, honey—I know somethin's bothering you. I can just tell; why don't cha' get it off your chest?" I felt like a floodgate had opened as I poured out th' whole sordid story.

Mom placed her hand on my shoulder 'n said: "Son, what you've done is very wrong—and what you're feelin' is a whole lot of guilt. And you should! Charles, you've been raised better'n that 'n what you've done is let some kid who hasn't been raised right show you how to be dishonest." Everything Mom said to me rang so painfully true. . . .

Monday morning Mom took me into Temple to the Woolworth Store and asked for the manager. She told him I had stolen some things and that I wanted to return them. And then I had to apologize.

I've made a whole bunch of mistakes since that time but stealing hasn't been one of them. . . .

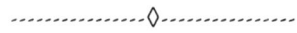

I have complained loud and long about the changes that the four kids (Wayne, I.B., Jr., Chas A. and Donna) brought into our family during our Oenaville years; essentially, how they ended forever my reign of being the only child in our family and how all of the spoiling and perks which that status had brought me was now transferred to them.

And yet, in recalling those wonderful, long-ago years, I can still see the kids in my mind's eye, as they played all their child's games. Everywhere they went, it seems they marched single-file in stairstep order: Wayne first, then Chas A., I.B. Jr., and little Donna Kay bringing up the rear. And as they marched around our yard or out on the trails of the tall grass of the adjacent fields, this tune played over and over in my thoughts: "Hi-ho, hi-ho, it's off to work we go." These were our little dwarves—our four little Oenaville dwarves! And at times, they were just that comical—but they were endearingly comical.

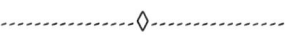

But the three boys—well, they were just boys. Like the time Mom and Sis wanted the four kids to come in for their baths before going to bed. Donna came in readily—little girls always seem to be so obedient. But Wayne, Chas A., and I.B., Jr. stubbornly stayed on our swing set, time after time ignoring Mom and Inez's threats to come inside or else. Dusk was settling in, and the boys continued swinging back and forth, back and forth. . . .

I told Mom I'd get 'em to come in, as I took a white sheet out of the closet. I went out the front door and quietly slipped the sheet over me as I stepped onto the sideyard. It was now almost completely dark outside; I carefully peeked around the corner and could see the three boys on their swings in the corner of our backyard. They were laughing and having a grand old time as I pulled the sheet completely over me and stepped out to where I knew they would be able to see me clearly.

I let out the spookiest moaning sound I could make and waited to hear their shrieks and yells. Nothing! Not one sound came from them. This was really disappointing, and I raised the sheet to see why my ghostly presence had not... What I saw was three empty swings, slowly swaying back 'n forth. I started laughing so hard, I literally collapsed to the ground....

I.B., Jr. was 4 or 5 years old when Mom and Dad would have company come over to play cards. Everything was very pleasant as Mom, Dad and their friends would play card games throughout the evening hours until around 8:30 at night. That was when I.B., Jr. normally went to bed. So he would just walk over to the card table and in a calm, even voice, announce to Mom and Dad's friends: "It's getting late; hadn't ya'll better go home now?"

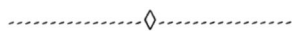

In 1961 my brother, Wayne Packard, graduated from Temple High School with the highest GPA of all the boys. My brother also was awarded a scholarship jacket. His jacket looked almost identical to the football jacket I had earned playing for the Temple Wildcats some five years earlier.

I was very proud of my little brother....

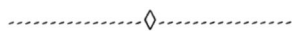

During those years after my brothers, Wayne and I.B., Jr., came along, I would continue riding with Dad in his company pickup on many of his line-repair trips. Mom, naturally, stayed home to care for our two newcomers. These trips were great fun, and I very much enjoyed those times and adventures shared with my Dad.

Even the apple-eating horse....

We would be riding along through the Texas countryside, and Dad would ask, innocently enough: "Son—do you know how a horse eats an apple?"

That's when I would twist and contort in a sudden paroxysm of shrieks and laughter as I fought valiantly, yet hopelessly, in futile efforts at keeping Dad from grabbing one of my knees!

Just as Dad was incredibly vulnerable at being goosed and losing all semblance of control, so, too, was I when anyone grabbed my knees (I.B., Jr. is the same way!) And to further compound my plight, once Dad's steel grip locked on one of my knees, I was captive until he decided to turn loose. Then, I would collapse against the seat, simultaneously laughing and gasping for air! (Dad didn't just have a powerful grip—he had an incredibly powerful grip...no wonder that old store manager was turning blue when Dad had him by the throat!!)

----------------◊----------------

Genius borders on insanity.

I've probably heard this axiom a dozen times or more throughout my lifetime. And at no time was this truth more evident than on those occasions when our big brother, Bob, would come home on the weekends from The University of Texas and regale us with some of his warped "inspirations."

As I think back on those visits, I am of the opinion Bob came home not so much to visit with his family as he did to enjoy Mom's wonderful cooking.

This particular weekend Mom had prepared one of her marvelous roasts, and we hungrily parked ourselves around the dining table; Mom and Dad occupied their usual spots at the ends of the table with little Wayne and I.B., Jr. seated along one side and me and our brother, Bob, on the other. Dad began carving the roast, having already asked the blessing.

Bob was in his third year at Texas that summer of 1949. And already he was warming up for the lecture his three younger brothers were about to receive on the merits of eating meat. Clearing his throat, Bob tapped his fork on his water glass and began: "Children, there are certain conditions you must be aware of before you plunge your forks into a morsel of meat. First of all, if you stab your fork directly at the meat, this frontal assault tends to alarm the piece of meat, and it immediately goes into shock and thereby becomes too tough to chew." By now we were all giving Bob our full attention, puzzled but paying rapt attention.

"Consequently, you must distract the morsel of meat," Bob continued, "so it will remain tender and delicious. Therefore, I would suggest you switch the fork to your left-hand and carefully and slowly maneuver the fork around behind the meat, all the while waggling your fingers of your righthand as a distraction. Then you quickly pounce on the meat before it catches on." Bob did this, impaled the meat, and thrust it into his mouth.

By now Wayne and I.B., Jr. were gazing wide-eyed at Bob while Mom and Dad were laughing and slowly shaking their heads from side to side. As for me? At 11 years of age, I was old enough to realize that either World War II or The University of Texas had probably caused irreversible damage to my big brother's senses. . . .

And maybe it was both. . . .

-----------◊-----------

Not long after obtaining his Ph.D. in Physics from The University of Texas and perhaps shortly after joining the teaching ranks at Baylor University, Robert G. Packard was being considered for a top-secret assignment by the United States Government. Of course, at the time, none of our family knew about this, nor was Bob able to divulge this interesting bit of information. In fact, it was probably awhile before he was informed of this background check by the F.B.I. And it was some 35 or 40 years after the fact before Bob was allowed under the National Security and Secrecy Act to reveal details of the project he had worked on (naturally, we heard Mom's version—that our brother was working on some atomic submarine project at the Bremerton Naval Yard at Bremerton, Washington on Puget Sound.) Only after the project had been declassified could Bob finally clear up all the mystery. Actually, Mom hadn't been too far off: Bob's work involved magnetic explosive mines that were set adrift in the seas.

The Crepe Myrtle

For sometime, I have enjoyed telling my version of this true story: that in spite of the findings by the F.B.I. regarding all the shady characters in our family—they hired Bob, anyway!

--------◊--------

The following tale is about a circumstance which, at the time, was quite risky, highly questionable, and one hell of a lot of fun—especially considering the part that one of my best friends played in this little drama. But, as I look back, I can see where the consequences for our actions could have far outweighed the enjoyment we shared. Perhaps our only lame excuse is that some of us were simply mindless, immature teenage boys with way too much time on our hands. Building model airplanes was once one of my very favorite hobbies. Having watched a real pilot build them for years, I quite naturally followed in Chuck Walters' footsteps in this enjoyable pastime. Not quite as skilled as he, but nevertheless I was pretty good.

And so it was that when I read a model magazine ad for a propless, authentic jet aircraft with a true jet engine propulsion system, I immediately sent off for this bit of model airplane wizardry. The ad said the "solid fuel engine was about the size of a thimble."

A few weeks later, it arrived. The aircraft body—fuselage, wings, rudder, etc.—wasn't all that spectacular; but the jet engine was a true piece of genius. A few simple wire clips held the "engine" underneath the fuselage belly, but the solid fuel pellet was the secret to this little jet aircraft's performance. I fastened the clips, inserted the solid fuel pellet—roughly the size of the old-time candy root beer barrels—shoved the piece of fuse behind the asbestos screen up against the fuel pellet, snapped the aluminum engine-housing cap shut and lit the fuse protruding from the hole in the cap.

Holding the aircraft as the instructions said, I watched as the lit fuse ignited the fuel pellet and smoke started slowly streaming out of the tiny hole in the rear of the engine. And then the smoke exhaust really shot out of the hole as the jet plane literally pulled away from my grasp. Trailing a tiny jet-stream of smoke, the lightweight aircraft shot across our backyard at maybe 5 feet off the ground, finally running out of "steam" some 40 or 50 feet away.

This thing was great!

Out of curiosity, I took another fuel pellet—I had a supply of about 15 more—set it on the ground and ignited it. The smoke volume it gave off was awesome...and that's when I had an idea....

Next morning I headed to school with a fuel pellet and piece of fuse in my jeans. Joining my Wildcat teammates outside the boiler room in the basement hallway, I clued several of them in on my idea. Most of them thought it was a good idea. Except for our pal, Robert Smith, Smitty thought it was a great idea and said: "C'mon—let's light that sucker!" Smitty and I walked a ways down the hallway looking for an empty locker. Locating one just a ways from Miss Black's classroom, Smitty held the locker door open as I placed the fuel pellet inside and lit the fuse. Smitty calmly closed the locker, and we walked back to our Wildcat buddies.

(At this point I need to tell you about Miss Black; she was one very sweet little old lady and much loved by her students. Miss Black was also very high-strung, quite nervous, and not in the least prepared for what was about to occur....)

At first, very little smoke came out from the locker and several of the guys commented: "Ah, that's nothing—what a bunch of _____." And that's when the smoke started pouring out from the vents and around the door. And then the "artist" went to work. Smitty ran to the locker, yanked the door open, and at the top of his lungs started yelling: "Fire! Fire!" Smoke billowed into the hallway. Grabbing the fire extinguisher outside Miss Black's classroom, Smitty started spraying the walls, the lockers, the floor, the ceiling—everything in sight *except* for the locker with the smoke pellet!

Miss Black came out into the hallway and for a moment or two I thought she was going to have a seizure. She was yelling at Smitty: "Put that down! Quit spraying!" And Smitty kept yelling: "There's fire! It's on fire! We've gotta put out th' fire!" Girls started screaming; our guys were laughing 'n yelling, and pandemonium reigned!

Several more teachers showed up and before long order had been restored. All of us students were sent to our next class, and the smoke had finally started dissipating. Calm again descended upon our hallways.

I was sitting in the library when a girl from the office handed me a yellow slip and said: "Charles, Mr. Valigura wants to see you."

I felt my life flashing before my eyes. . . .

Bill Valigura was our Assistant Principal, a World War II hero—having been shot down with his bomber crew and imprisoned by the Germans—and was someone my parents had considered "just like one of their own sons," and I was about to face him to explain my recent actions. As I headed down the hallway to the office, I wondered who had squealed.

Outside the school the weather that early spring day was absolutely glorious. We were but a few months away from graduation for our senior class of 1957. And I was surely on my way to face the executioner. All sorts of thoughts assailed my senses: Mom would disown me; as poor as we were, she would nevertheless drum me out of the family; my big brother would be livid (he and Bill Valigura had known each other for years and were friends); Mrs. Babe Lancaster was Bill Valigura's mother-in-law and had been my Sunday School teacher at Oenaville. How could I ever face her again? And at the very least, I would probably face suspension and even more embarrassment than what I was already drowning in! My prank was coming home to roost.

Bill Valigura motioned me into his office and closed the door. "Come on in, Charles, and have a seat." I looked at the chair and for a moment wondered what an electric chair looked like. As I sat down, I had already decided during my walk down the hallway that if he asked, I was going to readily admit my part in this prank. I knew I would not lie to Bill Valigura. I would not do that to Bill nor to myself.

"Charles," Bill began, "were you down in the basement where all the trouble occurred?"

"Yessir, Mr. Valigura," I replied, "I was down there."

"Well, some of the girls who were there said Smitty had grabbed a fire extinguisher and was spraying all over the hallway with the liquid. They think he may have sprayed some on you. Did he get any on your shirt?"

That was it? Fire extinguisher spray on my shirt? I wasn't facing certain death? This can't be all there is, I thought to myself. Regaining my composure, I looked over my shirt and replied: "Nossir, I don't think so, Mr. Valigura. I don't see anything." I was still having a hard time maintaining a poker face in light of what I was hearing... As Bill Valigura walked me out of his office, he said: "Charles, if you find out later that there is some damage, you let me know, and we'll have Smitty pay for you a new shirt!"

As I walked back to the library, even today I still cannot accurately express the depth of relief I felt; Mom and brother, Bob, would not be embarrassed over this stupid prank. Bill Valigura would not have to pull the handle on the gallows' trap door. I would not be expelled!

But all these years later, I've replayed this whole thing over in my mind and would it not have been the crowning touch to all this to have said: "Yessir—Smitty has ruined my shirt—make him buy me a new one??!!"

(Early in 2000, or maybe 2001, I wrote to Bill Valigura, who still lived in Temple. I reminded him of the foolish prank concerning the smoke bomb set off that long-ago spring of 1957 and confessed that I was the one who lit it off.

I saw Bill Valigura at our 45th Class Reunion that summer of 2002. He still looked just as fit and dignified as he had back when he was Assistant Principal at Temple High School in the mid-1950s.

Bill thanked me for my letter.

To this day I still have this sense that Bill knew or at least suspected that I had been behind the smoke-bomb prank. And if so, then he had simply not taken action on his suspicions, probably out of respect for my parents and my brother, Bob. And lacking any substantive proof, he wisely chose to let the matter lie....

In my letter, I expressed to Bill my hope that the statute of limitations had lapsed on my dumb stunt. At the reunion, he assured me it had. . . .)

Our senior year was drawing to a close and since many of us would be joining the service or heading off to college, we planned our last weekend blast at the lake. The Boy Scout encampment at Lake Belton was a perfect spot for just such revelry; situated on a point some 400 yards across the lake from the main shore, this campsite had a big stone firepit, a large lean-to shelter, and wooden picnic table and benches. The camp lay nestled at the edge of the woods rising up the grassy slope some hundred yards from the water's edge and was perhaps 20 feet higher elevation than the lake. Some 30 or 40 feet down the slope from the camp was a 35-foot tall flagpole from which Boy Scout troops would hoist the American flag.

We would often bring food—staples such as eggs, bacon, bread, and lunch meat—but mostly we brought beer—and a big cast-iron skillet and decks of playing cards. Sometimes, we actually ate. This was probably our last hoorah so each of us brought a fifth of something or other along with all the cases of beer. And on this particular outing, the "us" consisted of Billy Walker, Garlon Rea, Fred Heine, Bobby Winnett, Dickie Gibson, and me.

After setting up camp early that evening and anchoring the boats, we made some sandwiches and started playing poker. Since most of what little money we had went for food and beer, nobody usually lost more than $10 or $15. By nightfall, most all of us had made money, and then managed to lose it to somebody else. We hung a Coleman lantern and kept on playing cards 'til well past midnight—and drinking, of course.

Around 2:00 a.m. most of us were asleep or passed out, except for me and Fred. He said he had to see a man about a horse and headed back into the woods. And then I noticed Garlon was snoring away in his sleeping bag with his hand limply draped across his mostly-full fifth of Canadian Club.

That's when a gem of a prank occurred to me: I'd take his bottle of whisky, bury it in the woods, dig it up in a couple of weeks, and then all of us would share it, compliments of Garlon Rea. Besides, Garlon had drunk beer, scotch, and all sorts of stuff; probably he wouldn't even remember he had brought a bottle of Canadian Club. Carefully removing his bottle, I headed back into the woods until I came upon a huge liveoak tree. Wobbling a bit, I very carefully stepped off 20 paces to a rather large bush, and with a dead tree limb as a shovel, buried Garlon's bottle of whiskey. Thinking I was so clever, I even covered the buried treasure with sticks and leaves. This large bush would be easy to find. . . .

Next morning, in spite of big hangovers, we somehow managed to whip up a pretty good breakfast before heading back across the lake for our homes.

A few days later, it started raining. And raining. . .and then it rained some more. A week later, Central Texas had experienced one of its worst floods ever. Fred and I went out to the lake and found the Boy Scout camp under some 10 or 12 feet of water (Fred only agreed to take his boat after I told him—without revealing its exact location—what I had done with Garlon's whiskey). The flood waters still hadn't receded much two weeks later when I left Temple for Lackland Air Force Base to start Basic Training. . . .

Throughout Basic Training at Lackland and Phase I of Radar School at Keesler AFB in Biloxi, Mississippi, I had entertained my buddies about "pilfering" my friend Garlon's whiskey and how I planned to dig it up during leave.

October 1957 finally rolled around, and I went home for a two-weeks leave. I already knew Fred would go to the Boy Scout camp with me, and we'd dig up the loot. This time we brought real shovels and after tying up Fred's boat, headed up the slope for the big liveoak tree. This wasn't exactly R. L. Stevenson's Treasure Island, but after being under several feet of water for more than 4½ months what I was seeking was, to me at least, almost as exciting!

We quickly found the large bush—although by now there were quite a number more as the heavy rains caused several more to spring up—and proceded to dig. After 10 or 15 minutes we had found nothing. Fred suggested another bush close by, so we started on that one, and awhile later, still another one. Half an hour later, having dug around 4 or 5 bushes, I became aware of Fred leaning up against the big liveoak, laughing his butt off. By then, I was sweating pretty good and was not in a very humorous mood.

"OK, Heine—what th' hell's so funny?" Still laughing, Fred replied: "Pack', ya ain't gonna find no whiskey; I was back here when you came up with Garlon's bottle of whiskey 'n I watched as you buried it so carefully. Me 'n Garlon came out the next day 'n dug it up. We drank it months ago."

For a couple of seconds I was really ticked off; but watching Fred chuckle as only he could, I saw how really funny this whole thing was. We started laughing so hard, we both had to go see a man about a horse. . . .

----------------◊----------------

I joined the U.S. Air Force in 1957 and after completing the Air Force's one-year Radar Maintenance Tech School at Keesler AFB in Biloxi, Mississippi, five of us from the graduating class were assigned to the Alaskan Air Command. Four of us joined up in Salt Lake City, Utah (Jim Brown's hometown) and set out for Tacoma, Washington to catch our MATS flight to Anchorage. The four of us—Phillip Payne from Elgin, Illinois, Michael Pallone from Pennsylvania; Jim Brown from Utah; and me from Temple, Texas—drove from Salt Lake City to Tacoma, Washington in Phil Payne's old rattle-trap Plymouth. We arrived in Tacoma in April 1958. After spending two weeks in processing and pulling K.P., we were all assigned to Ohlson Mt. Air Force Station, just up the mountains near Homer, Alaska.

Two enlisted airmen drove up to Anchorage and picked us up for the 225 mile trip to our A.F. Station. On the way, we passed near a place appropriately named Moose Pass, and our driver stopped and yelled to us: "There's a big moose!" The four of us were in the back of this small troop transport called a Weapons Carrier and were dressed very warmly in our thick, heavily insulated Arctic clothing—complete with Parka, Mukluks (heavy boots) and Arctic flight pants—all very warm and cumbersome.

Sure enough, just about 100 feet from the gravel road and off to the left side of our truck, we saw this big moose chomping on some tundra. Throwing caution to the wind, Michael and I, wanting a closer look, jumped down from the truck. Phil Payne and Jim Brown wisely stayed on the truck. Michael and I trotted across the road, jumped across a fairly-shallow ditch, and ran up a slight rise between the woods and the gravel road. The old cow moose started a slow trot deeper into the woods with Michael and me trotting after her. And that's when we realized we just might be in trouble!

Off to our left, at the bottom of the rise, was the old cow's calf. The calf wasn't running and suddenly, neither were we. But the old cow was; only now she was turning to her left, in a long, slow lope, her massive head turning back towards me and Michael. And she was picking up speed.

Michael and I did the same, only back towards the truck! As fast as our clothing-encumbered bodies, and the foot-deep tundra would allow us—which wasn't all that fast! Michael's version later that evening at our new base told the tale:

"Packard was between me 'n the moose and I wanted to keep it that way; we both turned, and ran as fast as we could until I stumbled and fell. I heard something stomping 'n crashing behind me—not sure if it was Packard or th' moose. But I wasn't waiting to find out. I fell to the ground and was instantly back on my feet with my feet and adrenaline both pumping like crazy. Me and Packard flew down the rise, cleared the ditch in one leap, and dove, one behind the other, under the truck! We turned from underneath the safety of the truck 'n saw that old moose standing at the edge of the road, snorting her defiance." Pretty soon, she turned and trotted back to her calf. And pretty soon—maybe the next day—our hearts stopped pounding!

Two things about this story, and both of them true: first, if you find a similarity between this tale, and the one involving Ebenezer Packard and his friend, Michael, in the Maine woods around 1808, it's because I "loaned" our ancestor this adventure. I don't know if Ebenezer actually experienced being chased by a moose, but I know that Michael and I certainly did. One hundred and fifty years after I had Ebenezer and Michael getting chased by a moose in Maine, Michael Pallone and I darned sure were chased by one in the then Territory of Alaska. But I can well imagine that a lot of young boys living in Maine could very likely have been, and most probably were chased by a moose.

Secondly, Phil Payne—who unlike certain others, wisely stayed on the truck—was an accomplished photographer. And around his neck, suspended by a camera strap, was a very expensive 35mm camera. Phil Payne never snapped a single picture of this harrowing adventure; he said he had been too spellbound to remember to film the action!

During the summer of 1963, we came close to losing both of my younger brothers; here are those stories:

When I joined the Air Force in 1957, I held the record (at least among my siblings) for having the most stitches on my body. Falls on broken glass, stepping on a jagged bottle in a creek, cuts with a pocket knife by a good (?) friend, etc., etc., resulted in some 6 or 7 visits to doctors' offices which left me with some 30 stitches. I held this "stitch" record until 1963. . . .

That summer my youngest brother, I.B., Jr., and some of his Temple High School friends were water skiing at Lake Belton. . .and drinking. I.B. was in the water, putting on his skis when his good (?) friend steered the ski boat around to drop off the ski rope. . .and ran over him!

Fortunately, they didn't kill my little brother, but the propellers managed to turn his back, legs, and butt into ground round! And I.B., Jr.'s resulting 160+ stitches clobbered my 30. (Curiously, as I.B. lay on the operating table, the surgeon doing embroidery work on him, asked: "Packard, do you have any brothers?" "Three of 'em," I.B. responded, "and all older." When the surgeon learned that Dr. Robert Packard was I.B.'s oldest brother, the surgeon commented: "I went to school with your brother. . . ."

Recalling our pump station growing-up years and remembering Mom's seemingly-futile switchings of little I.B.'s legs, I just figured that kid had too tough a hide and was just almost indestructible. . .I figured wrong!

Sometime later that summer of 1963 Wayne stopped off in Sweetwater at my apartment before driving on to Lubbock. He was starting his sophomore year at Texas Tech, while I was nearing the end of my six years of service in the Air Force. I had played service football for the Sweetwater A.F.S. Hawks and had decided to walk on at Tech to see if I could earn a scholarship.

With my brother there, I figured Texas Tech was a good Southwest Conference school for my shot at college football; and in Wayne, at least I'd have a one-man cheering section!

Wayne was working a summer job in Temple for a neighbor who owned a road construction company. The work was hot, dirty, and very exhausting—even for a healthy, workaholic 18 year old like Wayne. And when they did paving work, the road surface temperatures were brutal—exactly what Wayne had been doing that weekend in Temple.

He walked into our small apartment, and I could see the look of exhaustion on his grimy, sweat-streaked face. Wayne sat down heavily on the sofa and asked for a glass of water. When asked if he'd like us to warm something for him to eat, Wayne replied he wasn't at all hungry. Not hungry? One of my brothers not hungry? Right then I should have known something was wrong. . . .

After awhile Wayne said he was cold and asked for a blanket. At first, I couldn't believe he could possibly be cold—this was summer in West Texas with temperatures in the mid-90s! And then Wayne started shaking uncontrollably and mumbled something about being sick at his stomach. That's when I finally realized my little brother was seriously ill, and I needed to get him to a hospital immediately. The hospital was maybe 20 minutes away—I think we made it in 10!

An hour later the doctors had stabilized my brother, and I apologized to the nurses for being so impatient with them when I first got Wayne to the emergency room. I suppose they were moving as fast as they could—but it hadn' seemed like it at the time.

Wayne had not taken any salt tablets and drank very little water, so consequently he had become very dehydrated soon after leaving Temple.

The doctors said that Wayne was in a near-critical state, and another hour or so and he would have been gone....

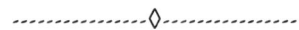

Shortly after my brother-in-law, Col. Charles A. Walters, had passed away, Inez said she needed to talk to me. Sitting in the large family room of the house where Sis lived with Buddy and Donna, Inez asked me if there were any items that had belonged to Chuck that I might want. I told Sis: "The only thing that probably I've coveted all these years would be that chess set Chuck brought back from China; you know, the one with the Nationalist Chinese logo that Chuck had on his uniform."

The chess set wasn't all that spectacular, nor very expensive, but for some reason this chess set held an almost-mystical quality about it. Chuck had brought this back from serving in China during World War II when he had flown what was termed the "Burma Hump." For more than 50 years, I had seen this chess set throughout their apartments, homes, and townhouses—all the many places where they had been stationed during their military career—some of which I had visited.

Sis gave me this chess set so it would always remind me of the Colonel. But not just him alone, but the two of them, actually; for some odd reason, this chess set was but one of so many things that through the years represented a part of Chuck and Inez.

Years later I would learn that Chuck Walters' first grandchild, Steven Walters, had asked as to the whereabouts of his grandfather's chess set. And just like Uncle Alex's wish that I have the oil painting of my Dad, so, too, did I feel it fitting that this chess set rightfully belonged in the Walters family. . . I sent it to Steven in 2005. . . .)

Isn't it strange how we can have something for so many years and don't really miss it until it is gone? It's as though we simply take things for granted. Actually, it isn't "as though"—taking things for granted is precisely what so many of us do.

Things like best friends from high school. Those guys I ran with—Dickie Gibson, Robert Smith, Bobby Winnett, Billy Walker—all have passed away, except for Smitty, and I haven't seen him since 1957. The wonderfully crazy things we did back in those days... Lord, how I miss them—and B; especially B. Most everyone called him Billy; a few merely called him Billy Walker, but to all his friends, he was just B.

B and I frequently had study hall together, and when we had Coach Fikes that fall of 1956, Coach would let us take his car out to the fieldhouse to watch game film of our next opponent. And that first day when Don Mraz, Dickie Gibson, and Danny Bryant were moving to the varsity, it was B and I who really messed with their practice uniform, pads, shoes—everything!

Our Wildcat team had maybe 15 minutes to put on the practice gear for workout—B and I had taken all their laces out, tied their socks, t-shirt, jock strap, whatever, into knots, stuffed this into their helmets and wrapped tape all around the helmet. Then, we taped their pads, cleats, laces, together. (Dickie Gibson laughingly told us that when Don and Danny discovered the mess, Danny had roared: "What th' hell is this? Who in th' hell..." And right away, Dickie replied: "Hell, you know as well as I who did this. Packard and Walker—this is their handiwork and it has their names all over it!")

We all ran together but B and I, as seniors, had more occasions to do things together. B and I double-dated a lot, switching off as to who drove and who got the back seat for necking. Funny thing is, I don't even remember the girls names....

Friday nights after our games, it was just we guys cruising the neighborhoods and drinking beer. Boy, how B loved his beer. Even years later, after we had all grown-up and moved on to other things, B still wanted to ride around and drink. This just wasn't fun anymore but on the few occasions when I would make it back to Texas, maybe just once more with B for old times sake...you know? I never did, but like now, I sort of wish I had....

As the years passed, I saw less and less of B. I guess living in places like Seattle, Kansas City, and Indianapolis were part of the reason. But the truth was, B just kind of wandered off into his own grim destructive lifestyle and more or less allowed his health to go into the tank. One of the Wildcat linemen from the earlier '50s—probably around Donald Davis' or Tom Jenkins' years—had helped B with a job and some money and then that ended with the death of this kindhearted Wildcat benefactor.

It wasn't until early in 2002 that I finally learned from Don and Diana Cannon of B's whereabouts. (The Cannons have pretty much held our Class of 1957 together, as Alumni Coordinators, Den Mother, Pack Leaders, and in general, Tracers of Lost Persons! They know everybody! Don was a senior Wildcat in 1956, and Diana was involved in everything else!)

Diana sadly informed me that B was in the Veteran's Hospital with terminal cancer of the throat. B was no longer ambulatory and had pretty much lost all speech. She warned me to not expect to find B as I remembered him. . . .

In high school B had been a healthy, robust 160-lb. Temple Wildcat running back—ol' number 20—and always had a smile on his face. With bowed legs, B always walked in that jaunty, swaggering manner so typical of speedy halfbacks.

But I was totally unprepared for what I found when I finally came to Temple to see my friend. If B weighed 100 lbs., I would have been astounded. He was now a gaunt, frail little old man, with medical bags and tubes around his throat and chest area. He had very little of the brown close-cropped hair he used to be so proud of. His color was so pale and sallow, I had a hard time believing this was really B.

Over the next several months, several of B's friends came with me to visit: Diana Cannon, Janis Porter Marckstein, and even my brother, Wayne, would accompany me as we gathered with our good friend. And most times B was in as good of spirit as he could manage, under the circumstances. B would give us the best smile he could muster—just like old times. . . .

B passed away October 23, 2002. I think of him often. In particular, I recall our youth, as this is how I like to remember him.

But the moments I shared with him on one particular visit are ones which best speak of his gentle ways and his thoughtfulness of others. B liked nothing more than the nurses to help him into a wheelchair and take him downstairs for a stroll in the courtyard. On this particular visit, the nurse had asked B if he would like to do this, and when he vigorously nodded yes, I asked if they would allow me to take him. I was a bit surprised when the nurses said yes. They showed me how to get B into his wheelchair—actually, they did most of it—and off we went.

Once we were in the courtyard, I could readily see why B liked this place so much. Everything was green and growing, and there were fragrant flowers and plants all about. We talked of old times—well, I talked of old times, and B would nod his head and occasionally make a sort of gurgling laugh, as that told me he remembered.

B half turned toward me and tried to say something, but of course, he could not speak very clearly. Finally, he reached in his pocket and took out a small tablet and pencil and tried so hard to write what he could not say. Even this was so pitifully scrawled, as B had very little motor control in his hands. His slurred speech and his pitiful scratching on the paper made no sense to me at all. After several long minutes, as he fought to get out a word or two, and desperately scratched a semblance of a word or some sort of meaning, it dawned on me what he was asking. B wanted to know if I was OK; he wanted to know if I was comfortable wheeling him around in his wheelchair. B wanted to know if I minded walking him around.

For a crazy moment, I wanted to shout: "No, I'm not OK—and no, I'm not comfortable with this!" I just wanted to pick him up in my arms and say: "B—get the hell out of that damn chair and walk and be cured of this damn cancer." I just wanted us both to be young and alive and not to have to look at my friend and know that soon he, too, would be gone—gone, like Dickie Gibson and gone, like Bobby Winnett.

Instead, I just leaned down and hugged him and said: "No, B—I'm fine; I'm just fine. . . ." And as I straightened up, I used my sleeve to wipe my eyes. . . .

The Crepe Myrtle

Every now and then, as I think of that day with B, I reflect on the strength of character he had. B was the one who was sick and dying. B was the one who could no longer speak or walk or even write. And B wanted to know if I was OK....

Yes, I suppose those of us who are still here are OK...but B—it is so gratifying to know that now you are so much better....

(Sometime after my friend B had passed away, our Class of 1957 was holding a fund drive for one of our very needy classmates. After several conversations with Diana and Don Cannon, we thought perhaps selling some "special" baseball caps might be a good way to raise a few hundred dollars for this very worthwhile effort.

Bobbie and I purchased 100 baseball caps for this project. The caps were navy blue with a white snarling Wildcat. The lettering around the Wildcat mascot read simply: "1956-57 Temple Wildcats." These caps were just a way to pay a special tribute to our friend, B. On the back of the cap was the numeral "20"—that was B's number as a Fightin' Temple Wildcat....)

---------------◊---------------

I will close this chapter with two revelations:

The first concerns an Irish boy first mentioned in Chapter 10. He was the Foote lad cryptically identified who would "one day move on to much deeper waters..." He was a relative of our Grandmother Mary Margaret Moffitt Packard—perhaps a grandfather....

Our Packard relative in Alabama, my cousin, Frank Packard, Jr., the retired attorney, told me of this Foote ancestor who was Rear-Admiral Andrew Hull Foote and during the Civil War was commanding admiral over all the Union fleet serving on the Mississippi River.

The last episode concerns the identity of the evil, scheming uncle who confiscated the safe with all of Charles Elbridge Packard's deeds and business records upon our grandfather's death on February 13, 1913. In keeping my word to Dad's sisters—Aunt Mary, Aunt Marcelite, and Aunt K.C.—I still shall not directly mention him by name. But if you are thorough and diligent, you just might "unearth" his identity....

In recent times I have enjoyed renewing my friendships with a number of my friends from those long-ago Oenaville years.

Donald Davis has retired from coaching and lives with his wife, Carolyn, in Temple. Carolyn told me Donald is a very good cook (according to him!) but still doesn't know much about biscuits.

Tom Anderson graduated from Baylor University with an accounting degree and retired from Exxon Corp. and lives with his wife in Houston. Tom likes to travel and spends a lot of time at his favorite resort in Belize. Unlike our youthful years spent riding naked on his Dad's mules and skinny dipping in their farm tanks, Tom says he now wears swim trunks.

Garlon Rea worked for several years in Houston finally retiring from his engineering position with Houston's city government. Garlon and his wife live in Prescott, Arizona. The last time we talked, Garlon assured me I was the only one he shot in the butt with a BB gun. Good thing... and very charitable of Garlon, I'm sure. That hurt like hell!

Janice Porter is married and living with her husband in San Antonio. Janice is now Janis Marckstein, a very talented artist. Her husband, Jack, is a management executive with a hotel chain. Janis and I no longer fight like brother and sister. Thankfully, we outgrew all that....

Buddy Lewis and his wife, Patricia Faulkner Lewis, still live near Oenaville. Buddy is retired. Patricia Lewis' father, Jimmy Faulkner, is the kindly gentleman who agreed to wear my Wildcat jersey on Father's Night when we played the Austin Maroons.

Cumbee Allen, who at one time owned Cumbee Allen's General Store in Oenaville, had two sons—Jan Allen and Tim Allen. These brothers and their families own several farms in and around where the Atlantic Oil Company pump station used to be. I had the pleasure of introducing my son, Clay, and my niece, Donna Kay, to both of these childhood friends.

Epilogue

A few days before Mom passed away, Wayne had once again gone to see her in the hospital, the same one at which all of our family had gathered back in March of 1989.

Wayne said that of all the circumstances surrounding Mom's declining health, the one which he found so painful was Mom's inability to verbally express herself. Her most recent stroke had taken away her voice. He tried talking with Mom but she could do little more than nod or shake her head. Even this, Wayne said, was slowly diminishing and reducing her ability to communicate to a state of near non-existence. Wayne said it hurt him deeply.

He had completed rearranging some things in her room and was preparing to leave; he turned to her and said: "Mom, I've got to go. Take care of yourself—I love you." As he turned to go, Wayne said he heard Mom speak in a clear, precise voice: "Good-bye, you precious thing."

Wayne turned, unable to believe what he had just heard; and he said he could not even speak, he was so overcome with emotion. Wayne said that had to be an incredible miracle, hearing Mother speak after so many months of her voice being silenced. *(After all Wayne had done in caring for Mom throughout her declining years, I am so thankful God saw fit that my brother, Wayne, would be blessed to hear Mom's last words.)*

Mom died on May 8, 1989; she was 84 years old. She clung to life for almost two months, much to the amazement of the same doctors who had said Mom would not even survive that weekend back in March.

I did not attend my Mother's funeral. I had a business seminar to moderate and just could not get away. Attending to our company's crucial business did not lessen the sorrow and regret I felt for having made this decision.

Over the years I have continued to regret the decision I had to make but I have realized that in life you do not get do-overs; and so I have put this behind me. I especially grieved not being there with my brothers—that part saddened me the most.

And, in the process, I want to believe Mom would have understood....

---------◊---------

For a number of years I heard Mom and several of our family members question what we might have been like, or what we might have become, had all the landholdings of Chas Elbridge Packard and William "Bill" Foster remained in the possession of these two ancestors. It is an interesting question—considering all the land deals in Chas Elbridge's safe which the devious and greedy uncle confiscated back in 1913 when this grandfather died

or the "foolishness" of great-grandfather William "Bill" Foster when he supposedly traded away hundreds of acres for a fiddle? (Interestingly enough, oil was discovered on both of these respective acreages during the early to mid-1930s!) Would these ancestors—and most of us, by way of inheritance—likewise have become very, very wealthy? And is it possible that all of this oil money would have corrupted most all whom it embraced?

Having spent all these years researching and probing into the lives of both families, I've been duly impressed by the accomplishments of the descendants from these two families. And I have wondered—upon having all this money "dropped into our laps"—would it somehow have robbed us of our drive, ambitions, and determination to succeed on our own?

I've discovered that like so many other families, our two families have produced incredible numbers of educators, college professors, accountants, physicists, doctors, lawyers, and all kinds of chemical and mechanical engineers. And a few successful entrepreneurs, as well. These are my conclusions: Firstly, there is nothing wrong with having lots of money, as long as you work hard and earn it. And secondly, if I had the power to go back in time to make any changes—I would leave everything exactly the way it happened!

I recently attended a reunion of most of my Oenaville Grade School classmates from those wonderful years of so long ago. Along with the others, I, too, had received an invitation to join in this trip down memory lane. The agenda was simple, as were the directions:

"If it has been such a long time since you have been to Oenaville, just remember that all roads in Texas lead there. Every state road map has it in big, bold letters. If you still have trouble finding it, just follow your heart." (Oenaville Voice, Scott Ewing, 1990.) Many times I've wondered why I have returned to this part of Bell County so frequently, especially now that there is so very little of what once had been.

I don't know the answer to that question. Maybe I'm looking for something that I know I will not find. Maybe I'm just walking over the same ground that so many of us had run and played on, looking for all those special friends and family members with whom I had shared so many special moments. And I remember those days. And sometimes, it is almost enough. . . .

(This concludes our family story, a story I hope you have enjoyed; and just so you know, I consider myself imminently qualified to have been the one to tell our story. You see, in all of my research about Oenaville, I came upon an interesting little tidbit. It seems that back around 1950, our little country elementary school was involved in some inter-county interscholastic competition among several other similar-sized schools. There were competitions in math and arithmetic, spelling bees, and a whole list of academic subjects. A number of us participated. Apparently, I was entered in the storytelling competition, for which I won a ribbon. . .a white ribbon. . .I only finished in third place. . . .!)

Remember what Mark Twain spoke through his "Pudd'nhead Wilson" character: "Truth is stranger than fiction, but it is because fiction is obliged to stick to possibilities; truth isn't." ("Pudd'nhead Wilson's New Calendar," The Tragedy of Pudd'nhead Wilson, Mark Twain, 1897.)

Family Photos

Capt. Charles Howard Packard Steam Boat skipper

Ex 2nd Lt William M. (Bill) Foster
(end of civil war - central Texas c. 1865)

John Bradson and Rose Alice Foster Belton, Texas 1896

Oenaville, Texas farm community Late 1800's

Robert (Age 6) and Inez (Age 4) Centreville, LA 1930

Chas. Elbridge & Mary Margaret Packard Family picture 1900
Centreville, LA

*Chas. Elbridge Packard Sr. & 3 sons
(Frank, left, Ira Bowman, Right, Harry, Front)*

*Bowman Packard (R) and best friend, Boots
(Known as Boots 'n Bo" 1926)*

Charles Bowman Packard 1941-42 Temple Texas

Our Sister Inez (Packard) Walters 1943
(Wearing her favorite gardenia flower)

Little Brothers Wayne (L) and I.B.jr (R) Pump station 1949

*Packard Brothers Wayne (L) IB jr (c) Chas Bowman)holding King)-
Pump Station 1949*

Lt. Charles A. Walters Army Air Corps Pilot 1943

Football Game Oenaville Grade School 1947-48

Acknowledgements

I wish to thank my Texas researcher, Mrs. Nina Fuller of Belton, Texas for her considerable and extensive gathering of reference data regarding our Foster ancestors; Mrs. Shirley Breaux of Franklin, Louisiana for her many kindnesses and help with background about our Packard ancestors; and a very special thanks and gratitude to Mr. Ralph Cowgill of Middletown, Kentucky and Mr. Alan Packard of Olathe, Kansas for the treasure trove of information they provided on the Fosters and the Packards, respectively. (Ralph Cowgill is married to a descendant of Randolph Foster, a younger brother of our John Foster, Jr.) These gentlemen—distant cousins, I might add—graciously shared deep background on family origins and history of the Fosters and Packards— all the way back into the 16th and 17th Centuries!

And only love of family can begin my expression of gratitude to all the aunts, uncles, and family generations past whose remarkable memories have made this story possible and complete.

To Mary Elizabeth Holden, my high school English teacher, who often urged me to be a writer. . .how disappointed she would have been, had she lived to find that this would be my only literary effort.

And lastly, though far from least, my deepest thanks and gratitude to a Temple High School classmate, Diana Lambright Cannon, for her considerable "ramrodding" of this story. An accomplished and retired English and business teacher on the order of Mary Elizabeth Holden, Diana has shaped, organized, and generally molded the words of my story into her more perfect and easily more readable version—for which I am grateful.

REFERENCES

Historical References

Around & About Oenaville, Freddie Lee Whitlow & Mae Greenway.

Colonial America, Oscar Theodore Barck, Jr., 1968.

Colonial South Carolina: A History, Robert M. Weir, KTO Press, 1983.

Daily Life in Colonial New England, Claudia D. Johnson, Greenwood Press, 2002.

Elizabethan England, William W. Lace, Lucent Books, 2006.

Gone to Texas, A History of The Lone Star State, Randolph B. Campbell, Oxford University Press, Inc., 2003.

In Colonial New England, Deborah Kent, Benchmark Books, 2000.

Louisiana, Off the Beaten Path, Gay Martin, 2003.

Oenaville, Vicki Ewing Montgomery, Oenaville Community Association.

Oenaville Voice, Scott Ewing, 1990.

"Texas Land Grants," Texas General Land Office Brochure, Archives and Records Division, 1994.

The New Handbook of Texas, Vol. 4, The Quarterly of Texas State Historical Association.

The Tragedy of Pudd'nhead Wilson, "Pudd'nhead Wilson's New Calendar," Mark Twain, 1897.

Family References

Descendants of John Foster, Sr., Ralph Cowgill, Middletown, Kentucky, 1999.

John Foster (1757-1837) and Randolph Foster (1790-1878), Gordon Leigh Briscoe, The Foster Family Association, Richmond, Texas 77469, 2003.

The Packard Family Genealogies, Alan Packard, Olathe, Kansas.

ABOUT THE AUTHOR

Having spent half of his 70 years compiling family history and genealogical data, the author has wrapped up this compelling collection of family tales and legends in his book, The Crepe Myrtle.

Born and raised in the small Central Texas town of Temple, the author has chronicled the lives and adventures of his Packard and Foster ancestors in the interesting and entertaining blending of actual American history, with that of his own families'.

Spanning more than 450 years, The Crepe Myrtle is a saga which has its beginning in 1500's Elizabethan England, and concludes in 1900's Central Texas.

Charles Packard closes his book with true-life family stories – notable of his older sister and her World War II pilot husband, Col. Chas A. Walters, Sr., as well as humorous sketches about an older brother, Dr. Robert G. Packard. Dr. Packard, who taught physics at Baylor University for half a century, also served in WW II, first as an Army Signal Corps specialist in the Pacific, and later in occupied Japan as a Japanese interpreter.

Despite encouragement from a much admired Temple High School English/Lit teacher, who urged the author to take up writing as a career, The Crepe Myrtle is Packard's first and only literary effort.

This book is dedicated in her memory………

CPSIA information can be obtained at www.ICGtesting.com
Printed in the USA
BVOW05*1716120215

387413BV00004B/36/P